# DOCTOR WHO

## VANISHING POINT

STEPHEN COLE

*For Josie - and all the adventures still to come*

Published by BBC Worldwide Ltd,
Woodlands, 80 Wood Lane
London W12 0TT

First published 2001


Original series broadcast on the BBC



ISBN 0 563 53829 5


Printed and bound in Great Britain by Mackays of Chatham
Cover printed by Belmont Press Ltd, Northampton

# Acknowledgements

I would like to thank Peter Anghelides, who bought me a copy of Matt Ridley's *Genome* (Fourth Estate, ISBN 1 857 02835 X) for my birthday; a book that proved both hugely informative and entertaining, and very useful in helping formulate some of the more overtly genetically informative explanations in this book. Peter also nudged me to question my synopsis and arrive at better answers. I am grateful to him.

Sincere thanks also go to Vicki Vrint and Sue Cowley, who were generous with their time and gave helpful comments on the prose; to Justin Richards and Mike Tucker for friendship and Vanishing Pints in Liverpool, and to Paul Magrs and Jeremy Hoad, together with Jo and co. I'd also like to mention David and Penny Isard, whose holiday cottage in Trenale, Cornwall was a fantastic hideaway in which to write the first 20,000 words.

Extra-special thanks are due to Jill Boothroyd, for putting up with so much, for so long.

*Why is light given to a man whose way is hid,*
*And whom God hath hedged in?*
*– Job, 3:23*

# Chapter One

The sea stirred and shifted like a living thing under the thunder. Its dark mass rose and fell, battering at the crags and cliffs of the little cove with increasing force, spitting salt spray into the charged air to spite the night, the gathering storm.

Etty cursed and crouched, one hand feeling the scrubby ground before her, the other wielding her lantern like a lucky charm against the night that had fallen so quickly. The flame danced madly inside the glass, as if believing that by moving about it could cheat extinction as the gale began to grow. The landscape was a host of shadows ranged around her, a focus for the sea's rage and nothing more.

She hunted more urgently for the last few clumps of rhineweed she needed to fill her basket. Storm or not, she had bellies to fill.

A sudden gust of wind whipped her shawl up and over her head, blinding her, and the sky cackled with more thunder. The lantern slipped from her grasp, and she heard its glass crack dully. The flame inside died as it broke free of its cage, leaving only the grey ghosting of the full moon to light her path. The foaming sea hissed at her, warning her away. Etty dropped the useless lamp into her basket and shivered as the first rain started to fall. Her simple dress, threadbare, grey and forlorn under the shawl, was soaked in seconds. It was time to go back.

Smoky clouds blew across the moon's laughing face. The wind fell for a moment, and she heard the noise.

At first Etty thought she'd imagined it; she could hear only the frustrations of the holy ocean taken out as always on the uncomprehending manlands. But there it came to her again. It was a regular, pounding sound. Footfalls on rock, many of them, a heavy, marching rhythm. People coming. Coming closer.

Lightning abruptly lit up the landscape, freezing the windswept scene for one bleached-bright moment. It showed Etty nothing. The sound was coming from the stone path, just over the rise, her way back to the farmhouse. But no one came here; no strangers had cause to come here, to the very edge of the manlands. She'd been to the City often enough, of course, but no stranger had bothered her here for years.

*Coming closer.*

She should run, some instinct told her, hide. She looked about. There was no shelter here, no cover. The rain was coming down harder. Her body felt so heavy, as heavy as the footfalls, but her insides felt light as butterflies, buffeted about as if the growing gale was inside her.

The footsteps stopped. Whoever was coming must be on the scrubby grass now, approaching the rise.

The basket slipped from her fingers as a shadowy shape came into view. It was man-shaped, tall and broad. The other shapes split away from that one, carefully walking down towards her.

'Who are you?' Etty took a step back, clutching on more tightly to her shawl as the men formed a semicircle in front of her. 'What do you want?'

No one spoke. The shapes stood still as statues. She could hear only the sea's ragged breathing and the wind.

'You don't scare me, you know,' Etty snapped, pulling herself up to her full height, sticking out her chin. Rainwater had plastered her long fringe to her forehead and she brushed it from her eyes.

No one moved. The men were poised before her unnaturally, like walking scarecrows suddenly rooted back into the earth.

Etty took a deep breath. 'You'll let me pass, please. I've got to be getting back –'

'You are Ettianne Grace,' said the figure in the middle, his voice low and flat, surprisingly quiet for such a large man.

It took Etty a few moments to register his words. No one had called her by her family name in such a long time. She had so little family left. Her heart sank like a stone in the sea. These people knew her. They had come here for *her*.

'What if I am?' she challenged.

'You are going to come with us,' the man said, his voice light and singsong, like a child repeating a phrase it had learned by rote, any meaning bled from it. It reminded Etty of Braga, back home. She imagined him staring worriedly out of the window into the storm, waiting for his mother to return and start the stew.

'What is this?' Etty said, pulling the shawl more tightly around her. 'What do you want with me?'

The moonlight sputtered under scudding clouds as the man in the middle took a step closer. He had a bald head and jug ears. His features were lost in the darkness.

'*You* are going to *come* with *us*,' came the slow, stilted voice again. The bald man jumped forward and giggled. 'Awake or sleeping.'

The other men started to chuckle, too. They followed their leader and took a step closer towards her.

Etty fell back, eyes wild, an animal hemmed in by these hunting men. The sea, confined by the rock of the cove, roared behind her in sympathy. The noise, like her blood thundering in her ears, reminded her she was as trapped here as were the pounding waves, however hard she might struggle.

She moaned fearfully as the men closed in on her, faster now.

'Excuse me,' another man's voice called out. 'We're looking for someone with knowledge of the area. Could you lend us a hand?'

This new voice reminded Etty of a child too, but this time of a breathless boy in a playground, bounding about with precocious refinement, wanting to play with everyone at once and uncertain where to begin.

The men froze at the sound of the stranger, and turned. Through a gap in their ranks, in a flash of obliging lightning, Etty caught an impression of the man who had spoken: a quizzical smile on thin lips, dark locks of hair wild about the angular face like the storm, eyes wide open and curious, heedless of the driving rain. There was someone beside him, a lot shorter, clutching a dark coat miserably about herself - unlike her companion, clearly wishing she was anywhere but here.

'You're people, I see,' the newcomer said strangely. 'Humans? How dull. I've seen so many people lately. You don't have any really good monsters around here, I suppose, do you?'

Etty wanted to scream for this man's help, never mind the nonsense he was spouting. But, as in an old nightmare, no sound would come from her throat. She tried to catch the man's eye. She wasn't even sure he could see her.

'Our friend's fallen and may have hurt himself,' the newcomer went on, rocking on his heels and looking brightly at each man in turn, as if this were all an exciting game. 'We need help to find him.'

The men said nothing. Etty imagined they were staring at the newcomer as hard as she was.

'Flashlights? Ropes? Local knowledge?' the newcomer continued hopefully.

'He was mucking around on the cliff tops back there,' the girl beside him added, indicating behind them, her voice sterner, impatient and confident, an adult's voice. 'How far could he have fallen?' Her voice fell lower. 'And how many limbs might the stupid show-off have broken in this gravity?'

The newcomer looked at her and started hopping briskly from one foot to the other. 'I keep telling you, Anji, you're imagining the gravity thing, it's Earth normal - well, give or take a...' He trailed off, shivered suddenly as if noticing the storm for the first time, and turned back to the men. 'Could you take a moment to come with us and help us look?'

'Please,' added the girl - Anji? She sounded suddenly heartfelt.

At last, Etty managed a croaking cry, and the strange newcomer dropped to a crouch to look through the men's legs at her, cowering on all fours in the wet grass.

He frowned at her, then smiled warmly. 'You can come too if you like.'

Suddenly the bald man lashed out, kicking the newcomer in the head. He fell backwards and out of Etty's sight with a surprised cry.

'Doctor!' Anji shouted, adding something lower in shocked protest and rushing, presumably, to where he had fallen.

The bald man stalked towards the girl.

'All you had to say was "no",' she complained bitterly from the darkness. Then she gasped, a sound almost lost as the whipped-up waves hurled themselves furiously against the rocks below them. And suddenly the bald man was staggering backwards, almost crashing into Etty, clutching his groin.

The other five men started to advance on the fallen doctor and his friend. 'Oh, that's fair odds, isn't it?' said Anji, her voice pitching higher with fear.

Etty scrambled up. No one was looking at her now, she could run, she could get... She stopped herself guiltily before she could end the sentence with 'away' instead of 'help'.

And then the bald man's hand closed around her ankle. Etty struggled to free herself, overbalanced, fell heavily on something slick and slimy against her skin. She cried out instinctively, then realised it must be the rhineweed. Her hands flailed out for the basket and her fingertips brushed at the wicker, scrabbling for a grip. Her leg was cramping up. Finally she lifted the basket and brought it down as hard as she could on the bald man's face. He grunted but his grip didn't slacken.

'Leave us alone!' Anji shouted, distraught. 'Just leave us alone!'

Etty could hear scuffling, people slipping on the wet grass, blows landing. The bald man got on to all fours and yanked on her leg as if seeking to drag her along by it.

'Why me?' she shrieked, smashing the basket down on him again, but it was hopeless, too light. 'Why?' But, deep down, she thought she probably knew. Punishment. Punishment from the Creator, who wanted never to know her for what she had done. Etty felt hot tears mixing with the rainwater. This man was going to drag her away somewhere, and then he and the others would –

Suddenly the newcomer was standing over her. There was a cut to the side of his left eye where he'd been kicked. Now he trod deliberately on the man's wrist, the toe of his battered shoe smearing mud over Etty's leg while the heel dug itself in. The bald man's hand spasmed open at last and Etty snatched her leg free, scrambling away from him.

The doctor crouched over the bald man and placed a hand against his throat. 'Go back to wherever you came from. You understand? Whatever you were meant to do here, you've failed.'

It was the bald man's turn to scramble away now. Etty tried to make out the expression on his heavy-set face. He just looked confused.

'Go!' the doctor shouted.

The other men staggered over to join their leader, and, without another word, they trooped away. The moon hid its face again, and only when Etty heard the sound of heavy boots thumping on the rocky path again did she release the breath she'd been holding, along with a low moan of relief.

'Are you all right?' the man said, his quiet voice carrying clearly through the storm.

'You're a doctor?' Etty said, suspiciously.

'I'm *the* Doctor.' He emphasised the difference as gently as he put an arm round the girl.

Etty stared at the two of them, hugging her legs for comfort so her knees were up under her chin. 'And you're Anji?'

'That's right,' Anji said. Her smile was bright like the moonlight. 'We won't hurt you.'

'You can fight,' Etty observed.

Anji shrugged. 'Self-defence classes. I should've brought my rape alarm.'

'We were lucky,' the Doctor said thoughtfully, rubbing the back of his neck. 'They could've killed us, but their hearts weren't really in it. I don't think they'd been told to expect any trouble - certainly they weren't banking on *our* being here.'

'And they didn't know what to do?' Anji said sceptically.

'No, I don't think they really did.' The Doctor seemed to notice that Etty was still sitting miserably in the mire. 'Please,' he said, stretching out his hand to her. 'Won't you get up? Perhaps there's somewhere a little more sheltered we can go to?'

Etty took his hand, and let him pull her up. But his grip was sticky. She looked at her hand and it was dark red.

Anji had noticed it, too. 'Doctor? You're bleeding...'

The Doctor slapped his clean hand against the back of his neck, and that came away smeared nearly black, too. He patted the back of his head gingerly. 'Ah!' He smiled, even as he winced, pleased to have solved the mystery. 'Head wound. Feels nasty. Must've picked it up in the -'

Abruptly his eyes closed, his legs buckled beneath him and he collapsed to the wet ground.

'Doctor?' Anji crouched beside him, then looked up anxiously at Etty. 'Help me with him!'

Etty stood and stared. She'd met these people barely five minutes ago, and already her entire world felt as if it had been upended, like the basket of rhineweed at her feet. She started to shake.

Anji looked at her sternly. 'You can go into shock later, OK? But right now, I need you. Is there a hospital near here?'

Etty shook her head dumbly.

'We need somewhere warm, and light. We're going to have to carry him to wherever you live.'

'Carry him?' Etty whispered, terrified at the thought of bringing such strangeness back home with her.

'And quickly. We need to see how bad this cut is.'

Anji was clearly distraught herself, forcing herself to cope.

Etty could relate to that, at least.

Leaving the basket on its side where it was, she took the Doctor's feet as Anji slipped her arms under his shoulders, and lifted.

# Chapter Two

*You'll slip and fall.*

*No, I won't.*

*You* will, *you idiot. Stop showing off.*

*Oh, Anji, I never knew you cared.*

*Fitz, for the last time –*

The last time Fitz had had an exchange like that he'd been eight years old and walking with his old mum in some grotty seaside town. He'd been balancing on a dry-stone wall, pretending it was a tightrope. But Mum had been right, of course. He'd fallen off, twisted his ankle, and started crying.

At least by falling this far Anji couldn't yell at him that he'd spoiled the day for everyone. But regardless of that, Fitz reflected with a shiver, she'd been right: it could well have been a warning for the last time. He'd assumed the cliff edge to be more stable than it actually turned out to be. And the Doctor, he'd been laughing at Fitz's daredevil antics, and that had egged him on – Fitz had always been a sucker for an appreciative audience. For most things, actually, thinking about it. But luck had been on his side for a change, and stopped him crossing over to the other. He'd been able to break his fall, to grab hold of some of these slimy plants on his way down. If he wasn't such a toned, lithe – well, perhaps just a little scrawny – specimen they'd never have held his weight.

Even so... How embarrassing.

His left ankle was broken as a result; there was no doubt about it. Well, it was badly sprained, anyway. It was definitely more than just a twist. Definitely. Fitz gently massaged it, and winced. He couldn't believe how dark it had got so quickly. He'd heard what might have been the Doctor and Anji crashing about looking for him, but the wind had carried his voice away every time he'd called to them to say he was down here, caught between the devil and the deep blue sea. Well, between the deep blue sea and a big shelf of rock, anyway.

Fitz was feeling particularly unsettled because the sea was

moving in some pretty peculiar ways down here. It was doubtless a trick of the fading light, but it seemed to be flowing up and over the weird black spires of rock protruding from the waves, as if the entire ocean was just some sort of ornamental water feature in a planetary garden. It wasn't... natural. He was almost glad when night fell completely and he could barely see.

The roaring of the sea made Fitz feel terribly lonely, and it was getting cold out here, now, too. He imagined this was how famous explorers felt, far from home, struggling for survival out in the elements. Except famous explorers brought their coats with them. Fitz's coat had needed a good few repairs lately, and worry over further wear and tear had made him leave it in the TARDIS.

'Base Control,' he muttered into a pretend walkie-talkie to distract himself. 'Kreiner here. Over.' He changed his voice to a muffled squawk, and play-acted he was clutching a headset. 'This is Base Control, reading you, Kreiner. What's your position? Over.'

Fitz smiled wryly, despite himself. 'Right over. Over the edge. Over.'

Birds called plaintively in the distance as if protesting at his little joke. Fitz tried to stand. 'It's agony to move, Control, but I reckon I've got to head inland. Storm's coming, I think. Got to find shelter. I'm finished otherwise. Over.'

He impersonated a little burst of static. 'Roger that, Kreiner. I'm sending my best people out to you. Anji and the Doctor. Be with you in no time. Over.'

Fitz mimed throwing the walkie-talkie into the ever-shifting bulk of the ocean. 'With the Doctor, it's never over,' he muttered, and limped away.

The going wasn't too bad. The land wasn't too overgrown, nor the gradient too steep, as he worked his way around the mountain, taking the journey slowly. 'I've a nose for adventure and I was born to follow it,' he declaimed dryly. Fitz almost dared to hope he'd find his own way back to the cliff top, that maybe he'd find the Doctor and Anji making their own way down to meet him. They could just get straight back in the TARDIS and leave. The Doctor had proved his flashiness as a pilot by steering them through white holes and strange matter and Christ-knew-what-else to get to this place - wherever it was. So now he could just go ahead and prove how adept *he* was at getting them to the nearest pleasure planet to get over the experience.

Having become used to leaning his right hand against the cliff edge, Fitz gasped as he nearly fell straight into an opening in the wall. Regaining his balance, he peered inside. It was a passage of some kind, leading into the cliff side, and he breathed a sigh of relief. Fitz contemplated informing Base Control of this new development, but it had suddenly started raining, and he decided he couldn't be arsed. Instead, he just pushed his tall, gangly body through the gap.

It was a relief to be out of the wild weather, but this cave was pitch-black. It smelled funny, too. Like a toilet. Nice one, Adventure-nose. Local kids, perhaps, caught short. But they couldn't surely have come here for a pee the same way he had. So that suggested there was a safer way out. Pleased with his logic, Fitz walked gingerly across the cavern.

Suddenly he cried out in surprise. Two huge, bright, yellow eyes had just snapped open, shining at him like car headlights, blinding him, bathing him in a death ray that was... Fitz paused. As his eyes adjusted slightly, he realised they probably *were* car headlights. And now he could hear a metal door sliding open.

'Where are the others?' a voice asked softly from the darkness behind the headlights.

'Others?' Fitz asked weakly. 'I've not seen anyone.'

'What's your number?'

'That's a little forward isn't it? We've not even been introduced.' Fitz swallowed hard. 'So... My name is Fitz. Fitz Kreiner. Professional adventurer. And wrestler. Who are you?'

'You're not one of the others, are you?' The voice sounded let down, like a child being denied a trip to the zoo. Then an enormous figure lumbered in front of one of the headlights, blotting it out. The silhouette was rippling with yards of either muscle or blubber. 'I don't know what I should do, now.'

'Smile and wave me on my way?' Fitz suggested hopefully, pointing to the direction he'd been heading in. 'This is the way out, isn't it?'

'I'm here to guard the transport, that's all,' the big man said. 'To not let anyone see.'

'I haven't seen anything,' Fitz said hastily.

'Now I suppose I'll have to kill you.'

Fitz was keen to point out there was something of a leap in the big man's logic there, but the speed with which the giant moved for him left Fitz with no time to utter a single word. Fitz had seen a great move on a TV action show once where the hero turned his attacker's momentum against him. You had to fall back, press your foot against his belly and sending him sailing over your head. Fitz tried it but in his panic forgot he'd twisted his ankle. He yelled in pain as he took the big man's weight for a few seconds, then again as the giant collapsed on top of him, and as podgy fingers reached for his throat.

'There's no need for this,' Fitz gasped, pulling at the man's wrists. 'Get off me, let's talk, please!'

It was no good. Fitz's head felt like a balloon, swelling with the pressure. He was going to burst, and prayed he wouldn't be conscious when that happened. His vision was already blurring, the bright glare of the headlights turning blood-red.

'Listen!' Fitz choked, and suddenly remembered the other great move he'd seen on that show. With the last of his strength he slapped down both palms hard against the guy's ears.

It worked. The man shouted out and let go. But Fitz still couldn't breathe; without his hands on Fitz's neck for support the guy was smothering him all the harder with his bulk. Bucking and writhing, light-headed and fighting for breath, Fitz finally heaved him off as hard as he could.

There was a loud cracking sound, and the man fell silent.

Fitz got up and hobbled to the far side of the cave, tears of relief stinging his eyes as he took huge whooping gasps of the cold, rank air. The man wasn't moving. Perhaps he was unconscious. 'What the hell is wrong with you?' he shouted at the man's body, reproachfully. 'Just stay there, right? I told you, I'm a professional adventurer. I'll have you.'

The man still said nothing, still didn't move. He was unconscious or...

Groaning, Fitz limped over to the crumpled heap of the man's corpulent body. He prodded it gingerly with a finger. Nothing. The man's head was lolling at a mad angle. He must've landed headfirst on the rock, and his neck snapped under the dead weight of his body.

Fitz started shivering. He got closer. Yes, dead weight was definitely right.

'Nose for adventure,' he muttered, bitterly, wiping it. 'Never takes it long to find something that really stinks.'

# Chapter Three

'Is it much further?' Anji yelled into the wind.

Etty shook her head again. Her pale face looked tired and drawn in the moonlight, and wore a slightly pained expression with what Anji suspected was familiar ease. It had to be a tough life out here at the best of times, without fighting lunatics and carrying strangers halfway across these moors. The odd thing was that her face almost seemed to suit looking a little haggard; it didn't affect the fact she was quite a handsome woman. Perhaps she'd been born worn out and never quite recovered. It made it hard to guess her age, but Anji reckoned Etty could only be in her mid-thirties.

For her part, Anji reckoned she must look quite a state herself. Her arms ached from carrying the Doctor, and her fingers were numb with cold. And the rain! She'd never known anything like it. It wasn't like raindrops falling; the air seemed saturated with water. It was like walking through an endless procession of particularly vindictive garden sprinklers.

She thought again of Fitz. He hadn't been wearing a coat, the muppet; he must be soaked through by now. Where the hell was he? She forced herself back off the topic when the image of him lying sprawled at the bottom of a cliff, or bobbing face down in the dark ocean, kept coming to mind.

At last what had to be Etty's farmhouse came into view ahead of them. Anji almost wept with relief to see the warm glow at so many of the windows, beckoning them on. As they got closer, Anji realised the farmhouse, which seemed pretty large, was shaped like one of those funny loaves - a cob? - with a smaller one on top. There were a number of outhouses and barns about, too, by the look of things. Anji wondered if Etty kept animals, and, if so, what they would look like. The Doctor, after more than a century of nothing but humans for company, had become hell-bent on meeting as many googly-eyed monsters as possible. Anji wasn't so keen.

A little boy of about seven or eight, dark-haired and as serious-looking as Etty, opened the door and peered out fearfully. 'Mother?'

Etty let go of the Doctor's legs and dashed across to him, sweeping him up into her arms. 'Braga,' she said, kissing him.

'Mother, what's happening?' the boy said. 'I was scared.'

'So was I,' Etty whispered. 'But the Creator doesn't have me yet, my precious.'

'I'm sorry,' said Anji, uncomfortable to be intruding, 'but please can we get the Doctor inside?'

'Who are you?' Braga marvelled, looking over his mother's shoulder.

Anji smiled. 'Friends.'

'Visitors,' said Etty more sharply, putting the boy down. 'Run a hot bath, Braga. Go on, now. And boil some water for me. I'll make us all a hot drink.'

Braga nodded solemnly, and ran to obey.

Anji and Etty carried the Doctor inside, and laid him on a couch. The farmhouse was all whitewashed walls and slate floors, quite austerely furnished. A flat viewscreen was built incongruously into one wall in the living room, and a futuristic-looking control panel was built in beneath it.

The sight of it made Anji feel suddenly uneasy. Etty was right - she *was* a visitor. Etty and Braga weren't human as she was. This was an alien planet, for God's sake. She looked down anxiously at the Doctor. His complexion was pale and waxy, his lips almost purple. What if he was out cold for days, or never recovered? What if she couldn't find Fitz?

First things first, she told herself, and started rubbing the Doctor's hand briskly, trying to get some warmth into her own at the same time. Etty watched her with hooded eyes. Those eyes spoke of a hard life, too, grey like stone, haunted and cold, and yet there was something more to them, some depth that wasn't quite human. Almost as if there were shoals of tiny creatures darting about deep in her eyes' cold saltwater.

'Shouldn't you call the police?' Anji asked, suppressing a shiver.

'No police,' Etty snapped. 'I shan't have them poking about round here, turning the place upside down.'

'But surely they should -'

'No police,' she said again, brusquely, and that was clearly the end of the matter. 'Now, we'd better get him undressed and into that bath.'

Anji sighed. Under any other circumstances, she reflected sadly, that might be fun.

The only light in the bathroom had come from a single candle. It had helped Anji not to peek as she and Etty manhandled the Doctor into the tin tub.

Now the Doctor was curled up in Braga's little bed while the boy slept in his mother's room. Etty had been away doing something or other - she didn't seem keen to explain what - and now she and Anji were sitting awkwardly together down in the living room. Etty had made a hot, bitter drink for them all. Anji thanked her host like a good house guest but secretly decided Etty was a *long* way from being human if this was her idea of a good cup of tea.

'I thought I was going to die out there on the moor,' said Etty, her voice distant.

'Me too,' Anji admitted.

'To die not knowing... Never knowing what my place here has been for.' A tear rolled slowly down Etty's cheek. 'I've always made out I never cared if the Creator took me for evermore or didn't, but -' She faltered. 'Out there, the thought of dying *alone*... Of my life ending up on a Diviner's desk, of it all coming out.'

'A who's desk?'

Etty ignored her. 'What would they tell Braga? What reasons would they give for my going?'

Uh-oh, thought Anji. We've got one here. 'Etty, you're *not* dead. It's all OK now.'

'A punishment from the Creator, maybe,' Etty said softly. 'Or the old standard. If anything at all.'

Etty trailed off and just stared into space.

'Punishment? For what?' asked Anji, puzzled. She got no answer. 'Isn't God supposed to forgive all our sins?'

'Only the ones He can see,' Etty said softly.

'To be honest,' Anji said, 'I'm not sure I even believe a god exists.

Where I come from, I was raised to believe in lots of them, and they're great stories, but...'

Etty turned sharply to stare at her.

Anji could almost feel the temperature dropping in the room.

'Who *are* you?' Etty demanded.

'A visitor. A friend.'

'That's Braga's answer, not mine.'

Anji felt flustered. 'We're from a long way away, that's all. I promise you we'll be out of your way soon.' It was clearly time to change the subject, so she racked her brain for some small talk. 'You have a lovely place here,' she managed lamely.

Etty shrugged, arms folded defensively across her chest. Her whole manner had changed. 'It suits us.'

'It seems very large just for the two of you? Is there -'

'We live here alone,' Etty said quickly, sharply.

Sore point, Anji reflected. Don't ask about Braga's dad. Always assuming females aren't self-fertilising round here.

'Well,' said Anji with forced brightness, 'I'll finish this, then I must go out and look for my other friend.'

Etty was still staring at her.

'Do you have a torch or something?'

'No.'

'Is there anyone nearby who might be able to help?'

'You want me to go back out to help you look,' Etty said.

Anji smiled with relief. 'To be honest, I'd love you to.'

Etty nodded. 'To where your friends are waiting for me?'

'What?'

'It's all been a trick, hasn't it?'

'What are you talking about?'

Etty wouldn't look at her, staring into the fire, speaking with the detached calm of someone trying to take dreadful news as best they can. 'I've got two of you in the house, now. I've let you in.'

Anji's eyes flashed with anger. 'We could've been killed trying to help you.'

Etty shook her head, a triumphant I'm-too-clever-for-you gesture, her eyes fixing spitefully on Anji's. 'It's part of your trick, to get inside here.'

'Look, I know you're scared -'

'Part of your trick to get what you want -'

'- but you're not thinking straight -'

'- to get me like you got Treena and Ansac and -'

'For the last time,' Anji snapped, 'it's not a trick!'

'She's right, it's no trick,' a soft voice insisted. '*This* is a trick.'

Anji and Etty turned together to find the Doctor leaning uncertainly in the doorway, a grey blanket wrapped about his body like a toga, holding a small towel. With a few deft movements, he tugged it, twisted it and looped it into a fairly impressive rag doll.

He threw it over to Etty. 'Not a very good trick, maybe,' he admitted, as Anji jumped up to help support him. 'But then, I'm not feeling quite on form.'

'Why didn't you stay in bed?' Anji chided gently.

'Because Fitz is still missing.' The Doctor was looking straight at Etty, whose eyes were brimming with tears as she stared down at the towel doll in her lap. 'And because something terrible happened to Treena, and to Ansac. And the threat of that something still scares the wits out of Etty here.' He shuffled unsteadily closer, then sat down beside her. 'And because I want to help. If I can.'

Etty burst into tears and buried her face in the Doctor's towel, sobbing out the tension and the fear. The Doctor patted her shoulder and muttered soothing noises. 'When you're ready, why don't you tell us all about it?'

Anji shook her head in quiet amazement. Even concussed, the Doctor could refresh certain parts other aliens couldn't reach. Anji sighed and took advantage of the distraction to pour her drink on to the fire. It crackled and spat, a reaction she sympathised with.

Over the next half-hour it became clear that the Doctor could barely reach the front door, let alone clamber over mountainsides in a storm. It would be dawn in a few hours; at first light, he reckoned he'd have stored enough energy to lead a proper search for Fitz. And, in the meantime, Etty would tell them her story.

Anji listened and, as the nightmare events tumbled out of Etty's chattering lips, she was glad it would soon be dawn. As if her fear might fade a little with the unquiet night.

# Chapter Four

*The day before*

Nathaniel Dark sat down heavily in the travel shelter, gathering his heavy Diviner's robes about him. They were a curse in summer, a blessing in winter. On grey, nondescript days like this they were nothing very much, just the clothes he had to wear. One more ritual he'd lost heart in. Like trudging down here, the same old avenue, ready to travel to the same old stifling, overcrowded office to roast under high-watt rays and go blind over papers and reports, tiny workplace windows barely letting in a hint of daylight.

He'd arrived too late this morning. The travelbus was too full of people. Dark didn't want to have to stand crammed in with the crowd of commuters. He wasn't exactly desperate to get to his workplace, to begin the day's investigations into the lives of the dead. He would wait for the next one.

The doors of the travelbus hissed shut.

'Wait!'

Dark looked up in mild surprise at the sound of the girl's voice. She was racing towards the bus, weighed down with bags. She knocked on the bus window but it was already pulling away, and her knocking swiftly became a gesture that suggested she didn't appreciate the driver's timing.

'Thank you so much,' she shouted after the bus as it hovered off down the road.

'It was full anyway,' Dark said, hoping to make her feel better.

'Terrific.' The girl flopped down beside him. 'If I'm late one more time, my boss fires me. I'm already having to work nights to make ends meet as it is...' She jumped up again, full of nervous energy. He'd not seen her on the bus before: a pretty blonde, probably ten years younger than he was, neatly dressed in a pale-blue suit. Dark was almost midway into his thirties now, yet the stab of jealousy he felt to see her energy, her insouciance, was a child's reaction.

Her green eyes narrowed when she actually took in his black robes of office.

'A holy man,' she said, watching him like a hawk.

'How do you do?' Dark mumbled.

'So, Mr Diviner, what significance will you give my missing that bus when it's *me* who's taken without the Creator's blessing?'

Dark looked away, fudging a placating smile, hoping she'd leave the attack there. She didn't.

'Don't tell me, I think I already know.' The girl made an exaggerated show of thinking. 'You'd weigh up my life, turn it inside out and end up deciding that I died to remind us all that *while we may know our God we may never understand Him.* Right?'

She'd missed her bus, she was late, her boss would be unhappy. She was frustrated and taking it out on him. He shouldn't react. 'Sometimes there is insufficient evidence to –'

'That's what your lot said about my brother,' the girl snapped. 'He was killed in the second bombing, when the civil building went up. Him and a hundred others.'

Her voice was getting louder. Dark couldn't handle this right now. 'Please, Miss…?'

'Too much effort to trawl through the business of that lot, was it? Fell back on the old favourite?'

'No,' Dark snapped, rounding on the girl. 'No, we did not. We went through the files on all of them, on every single one of them. We are sworn to do that, we *exist* to do that, and we continue to do so.' He calmed down a little, shocked at himself for his outburst. 'Sometimes we just can't find the reason for death.'

'If I'd been born a Diviner, I'd ask the Creator myself,' the girl said in a low, angry voice. Dark glanced around nervously, but the avenue was empty – there was no one about to hear her blasphemy. Nor to notice his failure to chastise her for it.

'Got nothing to say, holy man?'

Dark couldn't meet her gaze. If he was honest with himself, right now he agreed with her.

And it was tearing him apart. Drawing blanks day after day. Sitting in the prayer halls with the bereaved, watching their faces crumple as he ground out the old judgement on their loved ones. A life lived without the Creator's blessing to crown it was a pauper's life, everyone knew it.

There just seemed no reason to His decisions any more.

Dark was sick of thinking. Clouds milled lazily about in the washed-out sky. Their towering shapes, swollen and dark with rain, absorbed him for a while.

As the minutes passed, the girl calmed down a little. 'Look, about that just now... I'm sorry. OK?'

'OK.' Dark forced a polite smile. 'I do understand, you know.'

The girl stiffened, and Dark cursed himself silently. It had been the wrong thing to say. Of course he didn't understand, not really. He'd never had anyone close taken from him by a sudden death; and Diviners weren't allowed to be close, not to anyone outside family. Nothing must be allowed to cloud their impartial judgements. But what would his own fate be? If he was killed tomorrow, what meaning would be derived from his passing?

*...so that while we may know our God, we may never understand Him.*

'I want to understand,' Dark muttered.

The hum of heavy electric motors approaching made them both look up.

'Our bus,' the girl announced. 'Might as well go in and get sacked in person.'

'I hope it doesn't come to that.'

'Not sure if I do or not. I'm not cut out for filing. Where's the excitement in that? My name's Lanna, by the way.'

Dark was about to introduce himself when the ground started shaking. Birds clattered from the spindly trees lining the avenue and a noise like thunder and breaking glass rolled through the air. A huge cloud of dark smoke was drifting up from behind the high, domed roofs of the cluster of houses opposite.

'Bomb!' the driver of the travelbus shouted at them, eyes wide with shock. 'Another bomb, must be!'

Dark stared uncomprehendingly at the dark charcoal smudging in the grey sky.

'That could've been us!' shouted the driver.

'Looks like another busy day for you,' he heard Lanna mutter softly beside him. 'Another day closer to Vanishing Point.'

Dark didn't get into work for hours.

'Where've you been?' Cleric Rammes snapped. 'You look a state, a disgrace to your office. Things have gone mad here.'

This whole thing is mad! Dark wanted to scream at his boss. 'The bomb damage blocked my way in,' he said shakily. 'I've been helping the police clear the site, look after the injured.'

Rammes looked closely at him, noticing now the dust and the dirt and the blood on Dark's robes. 'Did any of them feel the Creator's blessing before it happened?'

'I don't think so,' Dark said, his lip curling as he fought to keep himself calm. 'There were some survivors. I asked them, but they were shouting and screaming...'

'Praise the Creator's Design, Nathaniel,' Rammes said pointedly.

Dark looked at the floor. 'The Creator be praised.'

Rammes considered. 'Must've been quite an ordeal for you, Nathaniel.'

'Yes, it was.'

'Well, I'm sorry, I can't let you go.' Rammes waved his hands round the bustling offices. 'You're needed here.'

'I understand, Cleric Rammes.'

*I want to understand.*

Rammes nodded then, let him pass, let him get to his desk - or the approximate area, anyway; it was so covered in files and loose leaves of paper it was hard to pinpoint it exactly. Dark felt drained as he slumped in his wooden chair. If he and Lanna had caught that crowded bus after all, they would be dead now. It had been pulling up outside the town hall when the admin wing had blown apart, bombarding the general area with huge slabs of falling masonry. Dark had stared at the shattered vehicle for so long, at twisted metal and children's coats and fragments of things still on fire.

*Praise the Creator's Design.*

He wondered what the Holiest would find to say about this. To explain away another truckload of people dead before their time. To explain why the killer responsible was still at large.

*Sometimes we just can't find the reason for death.*

Dark glanced about him, at other wan faces scrutinising faded photographs, computer displays, credit transactions, diaries. Dark had honestly felt all the answers were written there once, that it was possible to determine the path the Creator had laid out for the individual to follow from close study of the life as it was led. But Lanna was right, since the terror campaign, since the explosions –

*While we may know our God we may never understand Him.*

Dark balled his fists into his eyes. Lanna was right. It wasn't good enough.

'You're to drop this one, all right?' Dark looked up. Rammes was bawling out Stilson, now, one of the clerks drafted in from the coastal Mission to help with the extra workload. 'I don't care how much work you've put in, the Holiest have instructed it be left alone.'

'The woman calls every day, Cleric Rammes,' Stilson said stiffly. 'Her family's file keeps growing larger and we've got no answers for her. Nothing.'

'The Holiest will give her answers,' Rammes shouted, stopping all office chatter dead. He threw the heavy file in a waste basket. '*They* will answer her in time. *They* are aware of the situation.'

Dark's eyes locked with Stilson's own. Go on, Dark pleaded silently, tell him. Tell him that *we're* the ones who're really aware of the situation. That the Creator's failing us all and the Holiest don't have a clue about what to do next. That people in the street are calling us fakes, charlatans, telling us that it's Vanishing Point, that it's *us* keeping everyone else in the dark.

That the structure of our world is blowing apart.

But Stilson said nothing, of course. He looked down at his desk and simply reached mechanically for the next file on his pile. Rammes strode off, satisfied.

Long hours went past before Dark summoned enough courage to remove the file from Stilson's waste basket, and hours more before he dared take it to a cubicle in the evidence room to study it in private.

There was a tape in the Grace family's file.

Dark had seen so much death today he thought he might've become hardened to it. But somehow, watching the grainy, security-camera footage play out silently on the little monitor, he found himself more shocked than he'd been at the sights he'd faced up to today.

He didn't want to have to watch it again; but, then, there was much he didn't want to face up to.

You had to start somewhere.

'Play,' he said quietly.

*The camera is positioned to the right of the bank's entrance as you walk in, looking down from the ceiling. The resolution is poor; the screen seems to be buzzing with flies. Oblivious, people go about their business, coming into camera shot, picking up reflected doubles in the glass partition to the left of them, before each couple vanishes from view again.*

Dark shook his head wearily. Bank robbing. Such an old-fashioned form of crime, and all the more brutal for it.

*A woman, tall and animated, is at the teller's desk, and a man, his back to the camera, is waiting a little way behind her. Four more men bustle in to the branch, dark hoods covering their faces.*

Dark checked the file. The woman was Treena Sherat; there were photos of her here. She had been a statuesque woman, handsome, and with a world-weary quality about her face and in her slightly hooded eyes that made Dark smile. The man was... There was no suggestion as to who the man was. Dark studied several entries in the file.

It seemed that was one of the big problems with this case. None of the robbers, nor the man inside, could be identified.

*One of the masked men is waving his gun about, banging a fist down on the counter top. He must be shouting, and we can imagine it's a suitably florid mix of demands and threats. Treena Sherat is standing rigidly beside the robbers. It's impossible to make out the expression on her face. The man whose shoulder we're looking over might be a mannequin: he's stock-still. But perhaps he has said something, because now the robber who has made all the threats turns to the man, while his gang oversee the bundling of the money into holdalls. Something is being said. The conversation is unexpectedly long. Then the masked robber raises the gun. It points towards the man.*

*Treena Sherat grabs hold of the gun, wrestles with the robber. She is trying to stop the man from being shot, trying to take the gun away. The man stands still, reaching out a hand. There is a flash from the gun and smoke. The man falls backwards, he has been hit. Treena Sherat lets go of the gun, jumps away to the periphery of our vision, places her hands over her face.*

*In utter silence, the image still swarming with flies, the gunman walks up to Treena Sherat and shoots her in the chest.*

'Stop,' Dark said, but too hoarsely for the microphone to pick him up.

*The killer notices the camera. He raises the gun and fires.*

*The screen becomes a snowstorm.*

Dark cleared his throat. '*Stop.*'

A reason for Treena's death had already been declared. Dark knew without bothering to look which words he'd find stencilled here.

The Old Favourite, Lanna had called that judgement.

He read on. The robbers, the murderers, had never been found. There weren't even any suspects apprehended and questioned. The robbery might just as well have been undertaken by invisible men. By ghosts.

Dark shook his head, trying to take all this in, and yet there was more in the file. Treena's baby daughter had vanished, several months before her mother's own death. The baby had never been found, despite, apparently, quite exhaustive investigations. And one of her cousins had been found dead in mysterious circumstances, his left hand mutilated... No wonder Treena's sister was shouting so loudly for explanations, for answers. And no wonder the Holiest were pretending not to hear her at all. Ettianne Grace...

Dark ejected the tape. He stared at the file, at neatly-typed papers and transcripts, excuses and photographs, while outside the night gathered.

The night was cold, and the bulletins all said a storm was moving in on the City from over the godlands.

There was a girl in a tight top and short skirt waiting at his stop for the travelbus, standing under the street light. He recognised her. She'd changed her clothes. He had the strange feeling that perhaps she had been waiting for him.

'Hello, Lanna,' Dark said politely, confident she wouldn't notice the heavy file bulging beneath his robes.

'Holy Man,' she greeted him, without much surprise. Her face was pale, made paler by the crimson lipstick she was wearing and the thick black eyeliner disguising the red beneath.

'You've been working late,' he observed.

'I told you. I have to work nights.'

He remembered, and nodded politely. 'I'm glad you didn't lose your job.'

'Who cares? We might've died today.' She was eyeing him more tenderly than she had on their first encounter. 'If we'd just been a few minutes earlier. If we'd been on time.'

Dark nodded, but said nothing.

Lanna took a step closer to him. 'Both of us, together. We would've been dead, just like that.'

He studied her. She was making a link between them. But Diviners can never get involved. They can only watch. Lanna would know that.

The image of Treena came back into his mind.

*It's impossible to make out the expression on her face.*

'What does your sense of destiny make of that, then?' Lanna said. She was watching him intently.

*Something is being said.*

'What are you going to do now?'

Dark considered the black sky, the first few drops of rain. 'You know, I think I'm going to walk back home today.'

Lanna frowned. 'You'll get soaked.'

'I expect I shall.' It didn't seem to matter. It was time to do things differently.

*I want to understand.*

'You sure you don't want company?' Lanna said. 'You holy types can't be alone all the time, can you?'

Dark smiled awkwardly and set off into the night. 'I'll see you again soon, I'm sure,' he called.

'At the travel shelter tomorrow?'

Dark patted the file inside his robes as the rain fell down a little harder. 'No,' he called back, smiling faintly. 'Not tomorrow.'

# Chapter Five

The storm had blown itself out. Anji watched the first glimmers of the alien sun rising, and shivered. The horror story of murders, mutilations and missing children Etty had just told them was more than enough to put the creeps into her, but the stuff she'd mentioned so casually about this Creator...

Etty had to be crazy. Delusional. How *could* God exist for sure? The whole point about Him was that you believed even though you had no proof of His existence, no matter how hard your faith was tested. You had faith. God wasn't God if you knew His address, for Christ's sake. How *could* it be true?

Delusional. Crazy.

She came away from the window in case she saw a big ethereal eye looking back at her.

The Doctor glanced at her, could see she was bothered, and nodded reassuringly, his 'later, later' nod.

'Were you close to Treena?' he asked Etty.

'Used to be,' Etty said. 'We had a... a falling out. We never really got over it. And then, when I had to move all the way out here...' She broke off for a few moments. 'Her husband, Derran, he didn't like to travel too far beyond the City, and I was so busy...' She broke off, awkwardly. 'There's never the time, is there?'

'To say all the things we need to? Never,' the Doctor agreed fervently. 'What about Derran? Can't he help your campaign to get to the bottom of things?'

'No,' said Etty sharply, focusing back on him again. 'We lost touch. Haven't seen him since we buried Treena, a year ago.' She looked away, softened her voice, though clearly not in an attempt to garner more sympathy. 'There's only me.'

'Only you and *me*,' said the Doctor brightly. 'And Anji here.'

Anji's smile was as watery as the first light.

'And Fitz, too, when we find him.'

'You believe me, then?' Etty was still suspicious.

'An open mind is a blessing in our line of work.'

'Which is what, exactly?'

'Oh, having adventures, helping people out, saving worlds, that kind of thing. Any one of those thugs from last night could be your sister's murderer.'

Etty looked at him. 'I... I thought you might have been the man they said Treena was trying to save.'

'If the Diviners are telling you the truth, he vanished into thin air,' the Doctor reminded her gently. 'He didn't appear from out of it.'

Etty wasn't having that old flannel. 'I saw you when you were in the bath,' she said, and it was the first time Anji had seen her smile even faintly. 'There isn't a mark on you.'

'Hmm.' The Doctor jumped to his feet. He had suddenly gained colour in his cheeks and looked much better for it. 'Which reminds me, I should get dressed. We *must* find Fitz...'

Anji nodded enthusiastically. Etty had only grudgingly accepted they had lost Fitz on the fringes of the 'water mountains' - which were, typically, the biggest no-go area on the entire planet. It was sacrilege and certain death to trespass there, and the Doctor's excuse that they hadn't noticed the KEEP OUT signs hadn't gone down a storm. The Creator was said to live there - said to, because no one who had gone looking had ever come back again.

But that was only people native to this world, right? The Creator wouldn't be interested in an outdated loser from a speck of a planet sixty squillion light years away. Would he?

'Come on, Anji,' said the Doctor. 'Oh, and Etty...'

She looked at him expectantly.

'Lock the door behind us.'

Fitz had made painfully slow progress across the dark moor. Painfully being the right word. Since his work-out with Fatso he could barely walk. But lingering in a cave with a corpse, waiting for those mysterious 'others' would surely have ended up hurting a lot more. And at least he had a coat now - the big man had left a huge blue fleecy effort in the passenger seat of the van with no wheels (there was a mystery he couldn't be bothered to waste effort sussing out right now). And it had stopped raining, too, so maybe the whole world wasn't out to get him after all.

Suddenly he caught sight of something up ahead. A torch or something, bobbing in the blackness.

'Doctor! Anji!' Fitz shouted, wanting to cry with relief.

There was no reply. The torch bobbed closer, and several shadowy shapes with it.

'Doctor?'

They'd found help, of course. They'd found some local strong men to help haul him back up the side of the cliff.

Course they had. No other explanation.

No...

Fitz turned on his good heel and beat a stumbling path in a direction he hoped would take him well out of their way. It was still very dark. They wouldn't have seen him yet.

'That's Seven's coat, isn't it?' a voice called, singsong and guileless.

'Yes,' came another. Oh, Jesus, thought Fitz. Oh, sweet, sweet Jesus, I'm for it now.

The torch bobbed after him, dragging the shadow-men in its wake.

'Hello, Seven!' called the first voice. 'Where are you going?'

Nowhere fast, thought Fitz bitterly, as his ankle humiliated him completely, giving way and sending him crashing to the floor.

The torch drew nearer, and with it, thundering footsteps. They'd kill him.

Suddenly he was in the spotlight. The torch beam burned into his eyes, travelled up and down his body. He screwed up his eyes and waited for his kicking to start.

'Hello, Seven,' the man holding the torch said again. 'Why are you running from us?'

What were these guys on?

'Is it a game?' said someone else, a someone Fitz imagined was probably bigger and nastier than his light voice would suggest.

'Er, yeah,' said Fitz, disbelievingly. 'A game.' I thought I'd change my entire appearance and body shape while I was at it, you weirdos.

'Well, get up. The mission went wrong.'

'Oh. Did it?'

'Now I don't know what to do. We're going to have to go back.'

'Back to the cave?' Fitz thought of Fatso lying there, dead in the corner. 'Must we?'

'Of course we must. Then back to Hox in the City.'

The torch beam was taken out of his face, and Fitz blinked rapidly. Strong hands gripped his clearly quite magical coat and hauled him upright.

'Careful!' Fitz said, wincing. 'I've hurt my foot. Let's take it nice and slow, eh?'

'We'll help you,' said someone else, and a muscular arm slid round Fitz's shoulder.

This was like being mugged by a gang of kids' TV presenters. How could they think he was this Seven character? But, as the dawn dabbed its first smudges on to the sky, Fitz could see they were all wearing some pretty way-out gear. Did clothes really maketh the man on this planet?

Whatever, he couldn't let them take him to the City, to meet whoever had sent them on this mission. Chances were, whoever had sent them on this 'mission' would be a little harder to convince. If only he could make a break for it...

But the strong arms held him upright and brought him nearer and nearer to the stinking cave.

'Tell you what, lads,' Fitz said. 'I'll wait here.'

'Wait for what?' said the torch-carrier, who was apparently their leader, a big bald guy with ears like a Mini's mudguards and a long, fawn-coloured coat.

'Wait for you. To get back, I mean.' Fitz thought quickly. 'I mean, if the mission's failed, we'll be coming back, right?'

'You're talking funny, Seven,' Jug Ears said dismissively, yanking open the door to the vehicle inside. 'Get in.'

The others started to troop silently into the back, and Jug Ears took the driver's seat. But why? This heap wasn't going anywhere, it had no wheels for God's –

Jug Ears started the van and it rose steadily upwards what felt like a foot or so from the floor.

Uh-huh, Fitz thought. A hovervan. Very space-age. He smiled winningly at the fashion victims inside. 'Well, have a nice trip.'

'Three-One, put Seven inside.' Jug Ears wasn't smiling now. He looked like he'd been inside plenty of times himself.

'Yes, Two.'

Suddenly Fitz found himself being hefted like a sack of spuds into the passenger seat. Three-One slammed the door shut after him and then took his own place in the back of the van.

The headlights switched on but thankfully Fitz had dragged the real Seven far enough into the cave not to show. He noticed that someone had stuck strips of coloured paper beside all the controls on the dash, next to the steering wheel. When they were operated in a set sequence, the hovervan pulled jerkily away.

'You *have* passed your test, right?' asked Fitz, to a resounding silence.

A few moments later he found himself staring out of the window as the murky landscape sped silently by.

He didn't exactly feel like he was riding on air.

'Do you buy all that stuff about the Creator, Doctor?' Anji asked.

The Doctor didn't answer for a while, apparently absorbed in the view as they walked towards the clifftops. The water mountains had looked impressive at dusk the night before, but in the bright yellow light of the new morning they were truly breathtaking. Huge black spires of ragged rock, masses of them clustered together over the churning ocean, linked by thin ridges of land. They stretched out into the sea like giant railings: no entry.

She repeated the question; Anji had soon cottoned on to the Doctor's ways of stalling for time. 'Well, do you?'

'Etty certainly does,' he eventually said.

'I'm not asking Etty.' As with anything that spooked her, Anji wanted to rubbish Etty's mad ideas, laugh at them. Make them more manageable. So, when there was a further silence, she persisted. 'I mean, is it likely some supreme being is sitting up on high on His mountain, reaching down and *throwing switches* in the heads of his people, graciously letting them know the true meaning of their lives?'

'Depends on your definition of "supreme being".'

'Tell me Doctor, was God an astronaut?' Anji asked, mock-earnestly. Then she shut up. Dave, her boyfriend, had often enthused about that sort of lunatic fantasy. She could picture the 1970s paperbacks lining his cluttered shelves. And now Dave was dead, directly as a result of becoming involved with aliens. And what had that meant? All Anji had been able to imagine was some cosmic neon sign somewhere in the heavens flashing IRONY down at her.

She glanced over at the gleaming spires of the water mountains and suddenly felt like crying.

'I think the process of throwing switches was being described figuratively,' the Doctor said disarmingly. 'Do you think she made up the mission of Diviners, too? Why should she?'

'How should I know,' Anji muttered, folding her arms tightly across her chest. 'But it can't possibly be true. Life happens, it's just random stuff, there *is* no meaning. Seeing meanings when there's nothing there... It's a child's idea, a dreamer's.'

The Doctor looked at her. 'Then why does it frighten you so much?'

'It doesn't.' Anji said unconvincingly. 'Because it's not really God. It can't be. What would God be doing here of all places?'

The Doctor smiled. 'Instead of watching over somewhere really important like Earth, you mean.'

Anji shot him a glance. 'Sometimes you're *so* infuriating.'

He laughed happily. 'And you're so parochial! To get the most out of travelling in the TARDIS...'

'Now you sound like Fitz. Pack it in.'

'Shh.' The Doctor silenced her with a single stony glance. His whole manner had changed in a moment: he was suddenly tense. 'Listen.'

Anji did as she was told, but she could hear only the rustling of the long grasses in the wind. The world lay silent in the early morning. No, wait, he was right. There was something, something like a mosquito whine, far away... getting closer.

'Doctor?'

'There.' The Doctor pointed directly into the sunlight. 'Now, who could that be?'

Anji squinted to see. A small dark shape was approaching, moving fast. For an awful moment she thought it was some charging animal, but now she could see it was a vehicle of some kind, skimming the surface of the moors.

'Those men from last night?' She turned to the Doctor, fear making her insides twist.

The Doctor nodded. 'Perhaps. Perhaps we should try asking them again what they wanted with Etty.'

'We've got to hide!' Anji said, tugging his sleeve.

'Too late.'

Anji's stomach sank right down to her muddy shoes. The vehicle had changed its course subtly. Now it was coming straight for them.

Fitz's heart leapt when he recognised the two figures standing by the cliff edge.

'Pull over, please!' he said urgently.

'Why?' Two asked, looking at him quizzically.

'Because... Well, because...' Oh Jeez. 'Well, because, you see that man? I really like his coat. Look, it's velvet, I think.'

Two narrowed his eyes. 'Yes, you're right. It's the man from last night. The man who hurt me. Tricked me into going away.'

The hovervan started to speed up, heading straight for the Doctor and Anji. They were running, but it was hopeless.

They wouldn't stand a chance.

'Stop it!' Fitz shouted. 'Stop it, you bloody idiot.'

'He hurt my wrist,' Two explained calmly.

Fitz tried to wrestle the steering wheel away from Two. The hovervan lurched and rocked, careering crazily over the grassland. Two looked murderously at him, thrust out a massive hand and grabbed Fitz's still-bruised throat.

'He couldn't have hurt your stupid wrist that badly,' Fitz gasped, still gripping the wheel. He yanked and tugged on it with all his strength, but, even so, it wasn't enough to shift it.

His eyes were rooted to the view through the windscreen. They were so close now; time seemed to slow down. Anji had fallen to her knees and was scrambling back up, slipping on the wet grass.

The Doctor turned to help her, crouched down beside her, looked up defiantly as the speeding vehicle bore down on them.

# Chapter Six

'Anji, when I say jump...'

The whine of the approaching vehicle drowned out her panting for breath, cut through the pounding of her heart. She nodded, tensed her legs, readied herself...

'*Now!*' the Doctor shouted.

Anji hesitated for a split-second - '"Now"? Not "Jump"?' - and her false start cost her momentum. While the Doctor had leapt well clear Anji knew she hadn't. She shrieked as the flying car dipped to crush her legs, threw herself into a sideways roll, over and over.

At the last possible moment the vehicle swung away. Her eyes widened as she caught a speeding glimpse of who must be responsible. But now Anji couldn't stop her momentum.

'No! Anji!'

She had a spin-cycle view of the world for a couple of seconds, then the ground fell away. She clutched at the slick, spongy grass but couldn't stop herself going over the cliff edge, feet first.

A flash of movement to her right. The Doctor. Anji grabbed for him just as she fell over the edge with a shout of terror.

For a sickening second Anji was in free fall, and taking the Doctor down with her.

Then the fall stopped short. Part of her wanted to close her eyes but she knew her life depended on assimilating the situation, on reacting to it, on getting the hell out of it. She caught crazy glimpses of churning water, of sharp rocks and shrieking gulls, of pale sky and crumbling rock. When she realised what her predicament was she wished she'd just left her eyes closed and pretended it wasn't happening.

Her arms were wrapped tightly round the Doctor's waist, her legs kicking against thin air. The two of them were hanging from the cliff face with what was easily a two-hundred-metre drop beneath them.

Anji took a very deep, shaky breath. 'I know it's pointless to bring this up at this precise moment, but you did say you were going to say, "Jump".'

'Didn't I, then?'

'No, Doctor.'

'I didn't say "look before you leap", either. Pity.'

'What are we going to do?'

'Hang around for a while?'

'That isn't funny. That could never be funny.'

The Doctor lifted his legs, bringing them under her shoulders and hooking his feet round her waist so she felt a little more secure.

'Thank you.'

'I've got quite a good handhold here on a clump of plants,' the Doctor reported. 'Good strong roots... Luckily, you're not too heavy. The soil's more like a thick clay, it's holding –' He broke off and suddenly changed the subject. 'Did you see who was sitting next to the driver?'

'Fitz.' Anji shuddered as she remembered the vehicle about to crush her. 'He saved my life, you stopped me killing myself.' She looked down and wished she hadn't. 'Or postponed the event, anyway. I'm doing well for myself, aren't I?'

'It's Fitz I'm worried about,' the Doctor announced candidly. 'How has he fallen in with that rabble?' A loud sigh sailed down to Anji. 'He's always been so easily led, that boy.'

'Stop this thing,' Fitz croaked. How did the brakes work on a car with no wheels? Who gave a damn? 'Let me out, please.'

Two slackened his grip on Fitz's throat. 'That was bad of you, Seven, to do that.'

'Bad of *me*?' Fitz shouted at him, still in shock, rubbing his sore neck. 'You killed them! They went over the edge.' Fitz felt heavy hands clamp down on his shoulders, holding him in place. 'Look, I'm not even Seven, you idiots! Can't you see? I look nothing like him, I just... I just pinched his coat, that's all!'

'If you're questioning what's right, Seven, you'll need a double dose of the Wiper.'

Wiper? Fitz frowned as a bizarre image came into his head. 'What, the windscreen wiper you mean?'

Two shook his big, bald head and smiled.

Fitz doubted it was the sort of smile he used to woo the ladies.

'Is there *no* way you can pull us up?' Anji said, for a fourth or fifth futile time, the strain sounding in her voice now despite - or more likely because of - the Doctor's best efforts to distract her from their predicament with idle chitchat. He'd covered everything from the weather to the endless gravitic anomalies in this area of space that made reaching planets such as this one a dangerous but irresistible challenge for a seasoned traveller, cooped up on one world for so long.

'No, really, there isn't,' he answered patiently. 'But don't worry. Everyone knows all the best mountainsides have hermits halfway up them. He's bound to have spotted us by now and called for the fire brigade.'

'How are your arms doing? Hanging on in up there?'

'I'll let you know when I can feel them again,' he answered brightly. 'You know, it really is an interesting view from up here.'

Anji groaned. Her own arms were cramping up from clutching on to the Doctor's waist so tightly. 'You know, my dad used to tell me that if I had nothing worth saying -'

She broke off at the sound of something like a pebble hitting the cliff face to her right, sending a tiny cascade of mud trickling down towards the sea.

'What was that?'

'Sounded like something falling, over... *There!* Yes!' Something had excited him. 'Anji, over there! I can make out what might be a tiny ledge, below us to our right.'

Anji looked. 'Can't see it from here.'

'Yes, yes you can.'

She squinted. There was a small slab of rock jutting out, that even if she could reach she'd barely be able to balance on with one foot - but he couldn't mean *that*, surely?

He did of course.

'I can't jump on to that!' Anji protested.

'If you don't, you'll die,' snapped the Doctor, no longer pussyfooting about now a plan had presented itself.

'But we don't know if it leads anywhere!'

'And we won't ever know if we stay here until I can't hold on any longer. Now come on, I'll swing you there. Get ready.'

'Ohhh, God,' Anji muttered as the Doctor raised his legs and she lurched away from the cliff face and back again. He was trying to build momentum for her.

'It's so tiny!' she yelled. 'What if it can't take my weight?'

'Try to land toe first, as lightly and precisely as you can.' The Doctor was speaking through gritted teeth, swinging her out again. 'Did you ever do ballet?'

'Yes!'

'Good.'

'I was rubbish!'

'On the count of three, jump.'

Anji bumped back again against the cliff face. 'Hang on!' The world went dizzy around her; the overhang she was aiming for seemed miles away. 'Are you going to say "Three!" or "Jump!"?'

'One...'

'Well? Am I going on "Three!" or -'

'Two...'

Swinging out again. 'Doctor!'

'*Go!*'

Anji dropped through the air without a second thought. The sea far below roared up at her as if in anticipation, but she shut it out, shut everything out. There was only the rock and her flight towards it, that tiny slab of rock...

She landed neatly on her left foot and scrabbled madly at the cliff face for a handhold to support her. 'Ohgodohgodohgodohgod...'

She steadied herself, pressed her face hard against the sharp scree and thick silty mud, shook with hysterical laughter. Turning to her left she could see that a wider ledge led on from this one, separated by an unpleasantly large gap. But first things first...

'Well done!' the Doctor yelled, still hanging precariously from his clump of weeds, beaming at her broadly. 'Does it lead anywhere?'

She nodded. 'And by the way, who *ever* says "One, two, go!"?'

'Right-o!' So saying, the Doctor launched himself through the air towards her and her tiny stepping stone.

With a squeal of disbelief, Anji turned and jumped for the other ledge, with no time to process quite how nasty the fall would be should she miss. She made it, wobbling wildly in a sudden gust of wind, and regained her balance just as she heard the Doctor crash down on to the little lip of rock behind her.

She turned to find him poised there, triumphant like an Olympic athlete, smiling, his eyes as wild and green as the sea.

'You maniac,' Anji said simply, shaking her head, astounded.

The Doctor shrugged. 'I couldn't hold on any longer.'

He held her disapproving look and soon Anji found that she was smiling, too.

Then something seemed to catch the Doctor's eye. 'Well, well. That wasn't a stone that attracted our attention to this place...' He bent over recklessly, heedless of the fatal drop below them, and reached for something hanging from the very edge of the slab he stood on.

It was a shiny pendant on a delicate chain - a necklace of some kind.

'How did that get here?' Anji said, puzzled, taking it from him to have a look herself.

The Doctor surveyed the sky. 'A helpful magpie? I don't know. Come on, let's see where this little ledge leads us. After you.'

The sun was a good deal higher in the sky by the time the two of them had scrambled and clambered along a precarious path back up to the moorlands, and the Doctor's daft theory actually seemed their best bet for an explanation. There was no sign that anyone had been here, no sign of anyone around at all.

Nathaniel Dark felt a tingle of anticipation as the crude farmhouse dwelling came into sight. He slowed down his vehicle, approaching at a crawl. It had been a long drive, but he'd enjoyed it; it was a pleasing change from his travelbus ride in to work each day, which Diviners were encouraged to take to remind the people of their reassuring presence, the tireless instruments of the Creator. Even so, he still hadn't worked out what exactly he was planning to do here, or even what he would say upon arrival. Diviners saw the bereaved in the prayer halls; they didn't make house calls. That was established tradition. His visit here, while not technically forbidden, was still highly irregular. And the last thing he wanted was to scare Ettianne Grace any more than she must be already.

He parked carefully outside, in plain view, so she wouldn't think he was approaching her in secret. Well, he was, of course: no one knew he was here. It was a strange feeling. He had left no word for Cleric Rammes, nor any of his colleagues. What would they be thinking now? What would the Creator do to him for taking this path, for wanting to understand?

He got out of the car and smoothed down his robes. He'd not wanted to wear them today, or ever again, but hoped they would help her to trust him.

Suddenly the door to the farmhouse was pushed open and a woman walked briskly outside. The resemblance to Treena Sherat was remarkable. This woman looked just a little older, but her hair was wavy and fine and parted in the middle. Her face was squarer, and a life out here in the elements had weathered her skin, but she had the same piercing eyes...

He glanced down. She was holding a rifle and it was pointed straight at him.

*the gunman walks up to Treena Grace and shoots her in the chest*

'Ettianne Grace?' Dark murmured.

'Who are you?' the woman said, jabbing the rifle towards him. 'I'll use this. I'll not be tricked.'

'I don't want to trick you,' Dark said quickly. He told her his name, and threw his symbol of office on the ground in front of her. She picked it up warily, keeping him covered, and inspected the helical piece of silver.

'Why have you come here?' she asked him, lowering the rifle a little. 'To fob me off with more excuses?'

'No.' Dark realised he'd been holding his entire body so taut and tense it almost hurt now to relax it. 'I want to talk to you about your sister, and her child, and your family. To see if there's anything not in the file...'

'Why?'

'I'm afraid I can't really say.'

Ettianne raised the rifle. 'Or won't say?'

Dark almost smiled. 'I mean, I'm not sure I really know the answer to that one myself. All I know is that I agree with you. I think my superiors *are* fobbing you off and I believe...' He looked into her eyes, saw the frustration and fear there, and saw his own eyes looking back at him after so many wasted days and sleepless nights. 'I don't know what I believe any longer. I don't even know if I can help. I just... I need to learn more.'

The woman sniffed, apparently unimpressed. 'I seem to be meeting a lot of people wanting to help just at the moment.' She lowered the rifle, and looked over his shoulder.

Dark turned to find two strangely dressed people standing right behind him, though he'd heard no one approach. One was a girl, her skin darker and her eyes a deeper brown than anyone he'd ever seen before. Beside her was a man who Dark felt instinctively belonged to the wild places, a man who would test life - and, quite likely, the patience of others - to its limits. His hair was almost twice as long as Dark's own and his eyes were easily three times as bright. The grin hanging beneath his long, straight nose was just a little crooked, and lent a sort of edge to him; just standing next to the man made Dark feel reckless and dangerous, it was a heady feeling.

The girl looked over at Ettianne. 'Friend or foe, Etty?'

'He's a Diviner, come to visit,' Ettianne said, clearly not committing herself.

'So you're a Diviner.' The girl smiled at Dark in friendly greeting, and looked with apparent admiration at his robes. 'Nice outfit. Friar chic, I like it.' She suddenly tried to peer down his neckline. 'Hey, you haven't lost a pendant near any cliff tops recently, have you?'

'A Diviner may not adorn his body with items of jewellery.' Dark found himself automatically quoting the Book of Holy Statutes without thinking, and despised himself for doing so. 'That is,' he added swiftly, 'no.'

'Long shot,' she confessed to her friend. 'How about you, Etty? Throw out any old jewellery this morning?'

Ettianne looked at her oddly, a look Dark suspected this pair were on the receiving end of more often than not. A little overwhelmed by the way everything was happening at once, he allowed his hand to be seized and shaken by the grinning man. 'I'm the Doctor and this is Anji, so nice to meet you, Mr...?'

'Dark.'

'In name but not in outlook, I'm sure. There's a good deal I'd like to talk to you about, Mr Dark, on the nature of things here on your...' The Doctor never finished his sentence, but instead pushed Dark gently aside so he could take in his vehicle more clearly. 'What a lovely motor! How long did it take you to get here from the City?'

Dark struggled to recollect, and missed his chance to get a word in edgeways.

'Never mind. I'm sure we can shave a few minutes off that, eh?' He opened the door, paused, then closed it again and turned to the girl, Anji. 'I don't know the way to the City,' he said forlornly. 'Mr Dark, would it be possible to get a ride back with you?'

Dark raised his eyebrows. 'I've only just arrived to talk with her!'

'But she's got a gun,' the Doctor hissed in a pantomime whisper. 'Best not outstay your welcome.'

'You didn't find your friend?' Ettianne asked, unperturbed. She clearly was more used to the caprices of this odd couple.

The Doctor shook his head, suddenly serious. 'He found us. In a way. I think he was being taken somewhere against his will.'

'How do you know he's heading for the City?' asked Ettianne.

'I don't, but it seems as good a place as any to start looking, and as quickly as possible.' The Doctor paused, pushed his hands into the pockets of his black velvet coat. 'He was being taken away by the same people who attacked you last night.'

Dark had been struggling to keep up with the situation, but caught this last part clearly enough. 'You were attacked?' he asked incredulously. 'But why, who... ?'

'If you'd gone for where, when and how,' Anji chipped in dryly, 'we could give you a longer answer.'

'Perhaps we should all pool some information,' suggested the Doctor. 'As quickly as we can.'

Ettianne turned and went inside the farmhouse, and the others followed.

# Chapter Seven

Fitz was shaken awake to find that the hovervan had arrived... somewhere.

He was surprised - and slightly embarrassed - that he could have fallen asleep in such a perilous situation. But the journey had been so long, and the hovervan so warm, and it had been such a long night... Just a shame this bunch seemed reluctant to be cowed by his supreme nonchalance in the face of danger. Might've made them wonder what he knew that they didn't. Then again, with this lot of gorillas, they'd have lost count after the third thing and gone back to grooming each other for nits.

'Out,' Two instructed.

Fitz's ankle seemed a little better - until he tried to put his weight on it, stepping out of the hovervan. Held securely by that fine specimen of Neanderthal man Three-One - his moniker perhaps a reflection on his IQ points, making him top of the class round here - Fitz looked about him.

No more open spaces: they were parked in a grimy, built-up area, but with none of the clean lines and angles of any inner city Fitz had seen; not even the tall wharves and slum tenements of old London Town, so dignified in their decay. These buildings were more like giant mouldering mushrooms - great spherical sections sat like upturned cups on top of fat stalks, all lined with windows and crisscrossed with brickwork. The irregular look to the architecture, which a posh city chick like Anji would probably call 'pleasingly organic' or something, just left him feeling unsettled.

He didn't have long to take it in, anyway. Seconds later, he was being bundled inside the dowdiest high-rise of the lot. From the outside it reminded Fitz of a half-baked baguette, and nothing inside convinced him that the architect responsible wasn't one loaf short of a baker's dozen. He was bundled, limping as fast as he could, along a grotty-looking corridor that stank of cabbage and dustbins, into a service lift.

'Where is this place?' he asked, but as usual no one bothered to answer.

The lift rattled alarmingly as it cranked them up past countless floors, and Fitz was relieved to be on solid ground again when they pushed him out and on to a corridor which, while no less grotty, at least didn't smell quite so bad. He was marched past several battered and faded doors, and his suspicion that he was inside some kind of hard-luck lodging house was confirmed when he was bundled into a sparsely furnished room and locked inside.

Seven's digs, he supposed. There was a narrow bed that could barely have supported Fatso's bulk, a grimy toilet and not a lot else. No pictures on the wall. No telly. No books. No dog-eared porn. Nothing. Seven clearly took little interest in the world.

Fitz shuddered. How many times had Seven been through the Wiper?

When a token twist on the doorknob yielded a predictable result, Fitz twitched aside a grubby net curtain to stare out of the tiny window. Tiny flies jumped and danced against the cracked glass. Next door, a baby was crying for attention. The pale sun sat cheerlessly in the sky above the lumpy urban horizon. Seven's room seemed almost level with it.

No way out. And his only friends were probably dashed to pieces on rocks or else drowned in an alien sea.

Fab. But he wouldn't start dwelling on that.

He sniffed, wiped his eyes. Sat on the bed and waited for the others to come for him.

Nathaniel Dark wished he hadn't come. His visit here had been foolish, childish. He hadn't expected anyone else to be here, least of all anyone so strange, so subversive, as the Doctor. The man had another way of looking at everything, *everything*. Dark's life's work had always been to explore and express the Creator's judgement; how could he be expected now to question it? He would be branded a heretic. He should be back in his office, he should get out of here now and just –

'You're not comfortable, are you, Mr Dark?'

Dark jumped, and saw the Doctor staring at him intently, a smile that might've been a touch sardonic on his face. 'I...'

'Sitting on that stool, I mean,' the Doctor added, producing a cushion from behind his back and offering it.

Dark attempted a smile back at him, but it lacked conviction. His actions so often did these days.

'What do you make of the situation, Mr Dark?' Anji asked, perhaps to include him in the conversation, as he'd said so little since his dropping by unannounced.

'Please, call me Nathaniel.' He paused. 'I'm not really sure. I don't understand why your family should be targeted in any way... It's like the buildings in the City. The ones they're blowing up. No reason to it. No pattern. Just chaos.'

'They?' the Doctor asked.

'It's happened four times, now. No one knows who's responsible.'

Etty looked coldly at Dark. 'All part of the Creator's Design.'

'But keeping to the real issue at hand,' Anji said hurriedly, 'it can't be your money anyone's after, right, Etty?'

She snorted. 'I have little enough of that.'

Dark cleared his throat. 'May I ask, Miss Grace –'

'My name is Etty.'

'Your life may be in danger, Etty. You're certain you don't want the police involved?'

Etty glared at him coldly. 'Did the police find my nephew? Or Treena's murderer? Or the man she saved? Or the psychopath who ripped the fingers from Ansac's hand?'

'Who else could be in danger?' the Doctor broke in, tentatively. 'Even if we don't know what these people want, we can at least warn anyone else in the family who might be at risk, hmm? Treena's husband for instance.'

Dark started checking back over his file, looking for the name.

'Derran,' Etty said, a little more calmly. 'Derran Sherat. I told you, we lost touch.' She grew tight-lipped. 'Wouldn't know how to reach him now.'

'But he knows how to reach *you*, I suppose,' the Doctor said casually, looking out of the window to where Etty's child was playing outside.

Dark glanced at Etty, who nodded slowly.

'The fact that he hasn't presumably means he's all right,' Anji pointed out.

The Doctor grinned suddenly. 'Presumably.'

'If he's moved, I can find his new address back at the mission,' Dark said.

'If you're going to find him...' Etty paused, got up and walked over to an old wooden bureau. 'Be careful. Don't scare him. Since Treena's death, he's been... different.'

The Doctor looked puzzled. 'I thought you hadn't seen him?'

'He wrote to me, after the funeral. Strange letter.' She sniffed, suddenly derisive, masking her concern. 'Full of nonsense.'

'May we see?' the Doctor asked, but Dark could already see she'd crossed to the bureau to fetch it for them from between the pages of some heavily bound volume. He took the piece of paper from her. It had clearly been screwed up and then uncrumpled again.

Etty looked haunted, disturbed, drew her black shawl about her more closely. 'He said he wanted us to live together,' she said quietly, and closed her eyes. 'Said he wanted to take my hand and walk right into heaven.'

The Doctor snatched the letter from Dark and studied it himself. 'Do you have a recent photograph, too?'

'One from a few years back. Somewhere here.' Etty rummaged in the bureau and handed a small picture to the Doctor without even glancing at it.

'May I, Doctor?' Dark held out his hand for the photograph. It showed a man with dark hair, quite aristocratic-looking. 'I think I should talk to Derran Sherat as soon as possible.'

'You're absolutely right, we should,' the Doctor said, jumping to his feet.

'We?' echoed Dark.

'I wouldn't dream of letting you go alone.'

'And neither would I,' Anji added.

'Yes, yes, you would,' said the Doctor. Anji's face fell in disappointment but he gripped her by the shoulders and stooped to look into her eyes. In a low voice he said, 'Etty needs you.'

'She does not!' Dark saw Anji glance over at Etty, still standing lost in thought by the bureau. 'Etty needs a counsellor, and she may well need an armed bodyguard... She does *not* need me! *You* do, to help you find Fitz.' Her voice lowered still further. 'Which, if I could remind you, is the real reason you're going to the City at all!'

'Goodness, it hadn't occurred to me that Nathaniel's resources could help us to find Fitz, too! Good thinking!' the Doctor said hurriedly, turning to flash a quick smile at Dark. 'Anji, please. Etty knows more than she's saying, and it could be important. Try to win her trust.'

'Are you kidding? I've got more chance of winning the lottery.'

'And be careful.' He straightened up, turned to go. '*Someone* threw that pendant, remember?'

He marched out of the door, without another word. Dark stared after him. He hadn't followed all of that conversation, but it was clear Etty wasn't the only one with explaining to do.

Anji sat down again in her chair and sighed. 'I'll wait with you, then, Etty, if that's OK.'

The woman seemed to come back to them. 'Of course. I could do with some help today. I'm behind. All this talking...'

Dark went over to Etty, cleared his throat. 'It was nice to meet you, Miss Grace.'

'Was it?' Etty sniffed. 'Well, it'll have been nice to have met you when your lot come back to me with something to say apart from excuses.'

Dark nodded. 'Yes... Yes, of course.' He smiled nervously, nodded farewell to Anji, and followed the Doctor from the farmhouse.

The man looked down at a photograph of himself. Dark hair, neatly combed and parted on the left. A slightly awkward smile, as if his face didn't care to bend in that particular direction. Grey eyes sunken beneath heavy brows. He'd probably been handsome, once. The picture was only a few years old, but he felt no kinship with the man staring back at him.

Derran Sherat was nothing any more.

A fly buzzed and landed on the picture, many-jointed legs testing the glossy surface. It moved slowly, as if cautiously exploring the photograph's likeness. He swiped down his hand and crushed the insect against the paper face. Then he discarded the picture on the floor.

There were many, many more in the old shoebox. So many memories and disappointments.

He clicked on his table lamp, the light through the tiny window too dull to do anything but sleep by. While he was leaning forward, he clicked off the radio and its news update on the Town Hall explosion. The authorities were no nearer to finding the terrorists responsible, and no one was claiming responsibility. The death toll was still fifty-seven, as it had been yesterday. It wasn't really news at all.

He imagined the grubby millions in this city were busy twitching and jumping, wondering what would go up in smoke next. But he was just digging through the old photographs again, reminding himself of what life had been about before it had ground to a halt in these filthy lodgings. He looked sourly at the basket of sunfruit beside him, bright and bristling with goodness and vitality, took one of the fat yellow fingers, and peeled it. His mouth worked mechanically, swallowing down the sweet white flesh inside without pleasure.

The next face on his pile of photographs was a woman's. Her hair was wavy, quite long as it hung over her thin face. Her eyes seemed bright, and she was laughing. It seemed to him now she was the most beautiful person alive in the world. And, in the next picture, there was Derran Sherat, standing next to her, trying to smile. And next to him was his wife. Dear Treena.

Derran Sherat had died when she had.

His life was coming undone, and memories printed on scraps of card couldn't hold him together. Nothing could any longer.

The door to his room was abruptly flung open. He looked up in surprise to see the large, bald man filling the doorway. The man's quarters were downstairs. He had known the man's name once, he was sure, but couldn't recall it now.

'How dare you burst in like this?'

The bald man ignored him, pointed at the photograph.

'Ettianne Grace,' the bald man said.

Then he took a step closer.

# Chapter Eight

They were coming.

Fitz jumped off the bed at the sound of the footsteps. He looked around him, pointlessly, just in case he'd missed anything lying around he could use as a weapon. They had him and they knew it. He could tell by the leisurely pace with which they were coming for him. He wasn't going to be marched off to his doom: he would be limping and they would be sauntering.

At the last second, it occurred to him to take off Seven's coat, and shove it under the bed.

The door opened, and Three-One and another heavy walked in.

'How dare you barge in unannounced!' Fitz shouted in his best Lord Snooty voice. 'You've got the wrong room!'

Three-One frowned, and tapped on the outside of the door. 'Blue corridor, red door,' he said. 'That's where we put you.'

'You did not!' Fitz retorted.

But Three-One's mate had seen a suspect sleeve sticking out from under the bed. 'Put your coat on, Seven. You know the rules.'

Fitz crumpled. 'I don't, you know, fellas. I really don't.'

Coat in place, they took him away without another word, one on each arm.

'Slow down, I'm wounded!' Fitz protested. Needless to say, they took no notice.

The corridors were empty. There was no one to see him go: no friendly neighbour he could tip the wink; no caretaker wondering what all these oddly-clothed men were doing tramping about on his nice clean floors... They probably owned the building. It was their HQ, maybe - but headquarters for what?

Back into the service lift, rattling and juddering down floor after floor... Then bundled out and hauled along another stinking corridor and into another airless room and -

This room was full of people; Fitz counted a dozen. They didn't look like they were prisoners; then he realised he recognised four of them from the hovervan. Everyone was wearing the *de rigeur* comedy coat. They looked like some bizarre vaudeville troupe on their uppers.

Fitz went over to a pale-looking skinny blonde who was wearing a long shiny plastic mac, keen for a distraction. He smiled at her. 'Just thought I'd check you're wearing that kinky coat 'cause you have to and not through, er, personal preference?'

She looked at him without interest, then turned away. 'I wear it because I'm Thirteen.'

''Course you are, love,' Fitz muttered. 'Give me a ring in ten years' time.'

The door opened again, and a short, red-faced man came through. With his brown whistle and wiry grey hair standing up off his head, he looked like a cigar someone had forgotten to stub out. The crowd rippled as everyone in the room took a step back to avoid him. Behind Stumpy came Two, forcing a terrified woman - she looked a bit like Joan Simms, the plain-but-kind-looking sort - into the room before him. She was done up in a dodgy fur coat and an armlock. Fitz wanted to shout at Two to let her go, but everyone else was silent. It occurred to him that Stumpy might not be as stupid as the rest - maybe he was Number One. Maybe he'd realise Fitz was an impostor. Was that good or bad? Fitz slunk to the back of the room, and agonised in silence as events went on without him.

Starting with the locking of the door.

'Let me go!' Joanie shouted. Good for you, girl, thought Fitz.

'Keep a tight hold, Two,' Stumpy said, his voice rich and mellifluous, clearly a compensation for his half-pint appearance.

'Yes, Hox.'

'Yes, *Mr* Hox,' Stumpy corrected him, as he unlocked a cupboard built into the wall. Not One, then. He qualified for a name, not a number.

Inside was a quite horrible-looking machine, which Mr Hox dragged out into the room. The Wiper, presumably. It was built around an ordinary chair. A bronze helmet shaped a bit like a barber's hairdryer hung down from a framework thick with wires. There were two metal clamps attached to the armrests. No guesses what *they* were for. Fitz glanced about the faces of his fellow wipees, but no one seemed too concerned. Only Joan Simms.

'Why am I wearing this ridiculous garb?' she said, squirming in Two's grip.

Garb? thought Fitz.

'Once the Wiper has scoured certain portions of your brain,' Hox said breezily, 'you'll find you'll see the world more as a set of details, impressions and associations. And instructions, of course.' He smiled apologetically. 'Certain things we imprint so very deeply, there really isn't a lot of room for much else.'

'But why? Why are you doing this to me?'

Hox smiled, but spoke with the air of a busy doctor shouting 'Next, please!' when you've still got stuff to show him. 'Because you've no family, you'll not be missed. Except by the Creator, of course. And, after you've gone through the Wiper, He will have lost you for ever.'

'No!' Joanie struggled harder. 'You can't do this.'

'We can, I assure you.'

'You're mad.'

'And you are Eleven-Six,' Hox said, patting the seat of the chair. 'From now on.'

Two forced her down into it, covering her mouth with an enormous hand to stop her screaming. Fitz looked around the faces of his fellows once more but most of them weren't even looking, just waiting. Waiting for their turn.

'I'm afraid I must leave the honours to you, Two,' Hox said, as Two finished strapping the woman in. 'I must be getting back to Mr Cauchemar - he's bad today. And the screams always put my teeth terribly on edge.' He handed a pile of what looked a bit like shiny gambling chips to Two. 'You know how to operate the machine: it's red, green and blue. There's a disc for each Number, clearly marked, all right?'

Two nodded happily.

'Put yourself through it when you've done everyone else.' Hox said, bustling over to the door. 'Oh, and Two, *this* time with the Grace woman, you will not fail in your objective. Whatever obstacles you encounter. Understand me? You *must* not.'

Hox unlocked the door and slipped out of the room. Two scrutinised the discs carefully, then placed one into a slot in the helmet. He pushed it down over Joan Simms's head, and her calls and shouts gained a tinny resonance, almost robotic. That didn't make them any less heart-rending when Two flicked three switches and the helmet began to hum and vibrate, and the woman's screams became louder than ever. Her whole body went rigid and shook; he suddenly had some inkling of what his old mum's electroconvulsion therapy must've been like.

A couple of horrible minutes later, Two lifted up the helmet. The woman was silent now. There was bruising round her eyes. She opened them and blinked, slowly, mouth hanging open. She looked like a punch-drunk goldfish. Two released the clamps and she got up without saying a word.

Fitz took her hand, tried to make eye contact. 'You OK?' he hissed. She simply nodded, but her vacant expression made more noise. She'd been lobotomised or something.

Then Two held up his next gambling chip and waved it at Fitz. 'Your turn, Seven,' he said.

'Uh-uh,' Fitz said.

A second later, Three-One and friend were at his side to escort him in style. 'No!' Fitz shouted. 'You don't want to do this!'

'Sit down.' Two shook his head like a disappointed father on a school parents' evening. 'We've got *instructions*.'

The helmet slid down over his head. It smelled like your hands do when you've been handed a load of coppers in your change. His wrists were clamped down. This was like sitting in an electric chair, except he knew he'd wind up leaving Death Row for the secure ward in a hospital somewhere.

'Please!' he shouted to the blank-faced crowd. 'Help me! This will be one of you next! Help me!'

Then the power and the pain started up. Fitz carried on screaming.

# Chapter Nine

As the sun began to go down, Anji realised with a mixture of guilt and relief that she'd never really done a proper day's work in her life. She hadn't even seen a farm before, let alone worked on one, and it wasn't something she found herself regretting now. How did Etty manage this place, with so much land, by herself? Anji's admiration for the woman, surviving out here and bringing up a kid all by herself, had certainly upped a notch.

Mind you, counting against the woman was the way she'd had Anji cleaning out the animal pens today, doing all the stinking, sweaty jobs that didn't require much skill. She was grateful at least for the overalls Etty had lent her, also for the way the animals here seemed quite similar to those back home. So at least she wasn't freaked out there; except by the cows. The cows were a lot larger. Actually, they were massive. Anji sighed at the lack of profundity of her insights into the workings of the universe: *What I Learned in Outer Space* by Anji Kapoor - impressive pause - They have bigger cows.

Oh, and I nearly forgot: God exists out here, too, and He lives on a jumble of mountains where water goes the wrong way.

She realised she found both facts equally hard to take in. 'And I thought Boston was a culture shock,' she muttered, leaning on her broom handle and sighing. I'll never get used to this kind of life. Especially if it involves mandatory periods of employment as intergalactic farmhand. Take me home, Doctor. You promised.

Except, of course, he was off investigating with the slightly dishy Friar, getting up to God knew what. Whoops, God probably did know round here.

Could she get used to the Doctor's maniac way of living?

Well, home for now was Etty's farmhouse, and so, tutting over the blisters she'd picked up on her palms, she headed back there.

There suddenly came a loud clang from somewhere, like a gate slamming shut. Anji followed the noise. Soon she came across a closed gate, sure enough, but there was no one around - only a horse, eating grass on the far side of the field. But in the mud by the gate there were footprints. Footprints that didn't match. One foot was big and wide, the other small, wedge-shaped.

Suddenly feeling a little colder, Anji hurried back to the farmhouse. The smell of baking filled the kitchen. Etty was inside, hair in disarray, rinsing her hands in the sink.

'Where's Braga?' Anji said.

'I'm here!' the little boy shouted, jumping out from behind his mother.

Anji grinned at him, but the expression slipped a little as she looked back up at Etty. 'I think I heard someone out the back. Slamming a gate.'

'Lay the table for supper, Braga,' Etty said quickly. 'Then log back on to school and finish your homework.' When he started to complain, she flicked water from her wet hands at him. He squealed with laughter and ran away.

'Gate, you say? Must've blown shut in the wind,' Etty said, drying her hands.

'Who would've left it open? The horse could've got out.'

'I don't know. Braga maybe. I'm sure it was nothing.'

'Shouldn't you ask him? There were tracks, too. Odd-looking tracks.'

'I told you, it's nothing.' Etty threw down her towel on the kitchen table. 'Are you trying to scare me deliberately? Do you not think I've been through enough just lately?'

Odd, thought Anji. Playing the sympathy card was well out of character; Etty was trying to keep her from pursuing this. The Doctor was right, there was something Etty was holding back.

Anji shrugged and smiled in apology. 'You're right, I'm sorry.'

Etty grunted acknowledgement, and turned to the range, removing a large steaming lump that smelled quite meaty but looked more like clay. 'Thanks for your help today,' she said without much feeling. 'Come and eat with us.'

'Great,' Anji said, matching her enthusiasm. 'I've really worked up an appetite.' She paused, uncertain, gesturing to the grey lump. 'That's not beef, is it? From one of the cows, I mean?'

Etty shook her head, though probably more in bafflement at her ignorance than to actually enlighten her, and carried the joint through to the dining room.

Anji was about to follow her when she heard a noise from outside. She crossed quickly to the window, peering out into the twilight.

But again there was nothing to see.

'Not much to go on,' commented the Doctor, turning from the screen. Dark saw over his shoulder that the image had become static, buzzing with a billion flies. 'It's a shame we only have the testimony of that one camera to go on. A new angle would give us a fresh perspective...' He smiled. 'Or is that just tautological?'

'Eject,' Dark said, and winced at how loud the mechanism seemed in the quiet of the data centre. The Diviners' Mission was more or less empty of people at this time of night, and Dark had clearance to be here in the usual way of things; but, even so, he wasn't ready for a run-in with anyone he knew about his absence today. He jumped at every unfamiliar noise the heating made, or given off by the electrics.

The Doctor seemed amused; he knew perfectly well what was bothering Dark. 'Still no excuse prepared for your truancy?'

Dark glared at him, thrusting the videotape into his pocket. 'I should've told them something, said I was ill.'

'You didn't want to lie. That's commendable.'

'So instead I should give roundabout answers to each straightforward question I'm asked, as you do?' On the long journey back from Etty's, Dark had been trying to probe the Doctor for information, but the Doctor seemed to have got far more out of the conversation.

The Doctor met his gaze. 'I could give you answers, Nathaniel, but I don't know if you'd believe them. From what I gather, you live in a strict society that is ruled by absolutes.'

Dark turned and keyed in a search program for Derran Sherat's address. It should take only a few minutes. 'From what you gather? You sound like you dropped in on us from out of the sky.'

'Tell me, can you log a search pattern for the type of vehicle I saw?'

Dark raised an eyebrow. 'For your friend, the one you say was kidnapped? The "real reason" you came with me?'

The Doctor smiled tightly. 'Fitz could be in danger. And the people who have him now threatened Etty, too. So you'd be helping both her and me. Do you find that straightforward enough?'

'I have a feeling there is little that is straightforward about you, Doctor.'

'Thank you,' the Doctor said. Then he sat down in a swivel chair, and spun through a 360-degree turn. 'Although I feel there's something *you* find straightforward that I'm missing. From talking with you and with Etty, it seems to me it's more than just faith that makes you believe in the Creator.'

'We have evidence of His existence every day.'

'You've seen Him?'

'Well, no,' Dark began, 'but -'

'Have others?'

'Doctor, what are you -'

'I'm not attacking you, merely interested.'

'But...' Dark was baffled. 'But you can't *not know* about the Creator's manifestation!'

'Of course I can't.' The Doctor smiled disarmingly. 'But pretend I'm a simpleton. Or a child. Why shouldn't I believe that, when we die, that's the end of things?'

'Because it isn't,' Dark said, indulging him. 'No death can ever be without meaning. The Creator is with us, with all of us, and with His blessing, when it is our time, the purpose of our lives is made clear to us in blissful understanding.'

'You're quoting a textbook again, aren't you, Nathaniel?' the Doctor scolded lightly. 'Use your own words. Speak plainly. I'm only a child, remember?'

Dark considered. 'When death can be foreseen, from natural causes, old age, long illnesses... the Creator imparts His message. What that person's life has been for, all the things that person has made possible for others.'

'Give me an example.'

Dark remembered his own mother's death, the bliss on her face as she reeled off the random moments of her life that now, it transpired, held such importance. The pain, the emptiness and the misery he felt, trying to acknowledge the compassion of the Creator, allowing her to live with Him in bliss instead of in pain in her home. Still trying, months later…

Still trying.

'The meaning of His message may be great or small,' Dark said eventually. 'Just as the meaning of a life may be great or small. To raise children, who will go on to do great things. To found businesses that will advance our world. To have been lost all one's life, only to recover Good and Truth at the end of one's days. Life is a journey -'

'And the Creator decides where you get off,' the Doctor observed. 'It's lucky His judgement is trusted, if He can switch off lives like table lamps.'

'Not so. He grants everlasting life,' Dark said.

'Ah,' said the Doctor.

'Giving death true meaning. Until eventually, all life meets all death, at the Vanishing Point.'

'Hmm?'

'When everyone goes to heaven.'

'The end of the world?' wondered the Doctor.

'When the last soul has been saved.'

The Doctor nodded thoughtfully. 'Why do Creators always have to plan ahead for the absolute destruction of their flock's achievements? I wonder.' He clapped his hands together. 'Anyway, you were saying, *saved*, of course… provided their life has the proper meaning. So there's no room for conjecture?'

Dark looked at him curiously. 'The Creator knows what we cannot. Of casual meetings that inspired others. Of what those others have gone on to achieve.'

'I see,' the Doctor said. 'A sweetener for those about to die. Like presenting a mint along with the bill at the end of a fine meal.'

'The Creator's words are imparted with a sense of profound bliss, like no earthly pleasure. The Creator has named that person in His Design, and so they shall be with Him for evermore.'

'That's the textbook speaking again.'

'It's - it's the only way I can explain it, even to a child.' Dark scowled, suddenly mistrustful. 'You mock me, Doctor, but I do not understand why.'

'There's no possibility that these enlightened people could've been mistaken?' the Doctor said gently. 'I mean, have you checked?'

'There is no mistake,' Dark said flatly. 'His word is too widespread, and the facts plainly tally. We are all responsible for each other, and our destinies are forged together.' Dark gestured at the room they stood in. 'This building, the work that I and my colleagues have undertaken all our lives, is testament to that.'

'Yes, so I gather,' the Doctor said. 'All those unfortunates killed in accidents, or by misadventure, or at the hands of others, die without the Creator throwing that switch inside them to release His meaning, mm? So you Diviners do it for Him, for the sake of those left behind.'

'We are His instruments,' Dark said passionately. 'The mark left behind on society by each individual, their interactions with others, all this information is necessary to extract meaning from life.'

'The soul is held in limbo until you give the yea or nay?'

'Of course.'

'It's fascinating, you know,' said the Doctor, spinning round again in his chair, 'to find a religious system that has more need for private detectives than it does for preachers.'

'Doctor, I don't understand you,' Dark said. 'The way you speak, it's as if... as if you *really* don't know these things. The way the world works.'

'Tell me,' the Doctor said, switching the subject as he so often did. 'You must've measured the effect on people who've experienced this effect. Found out what actually communicates the Creator's message.'

'The Creator communicates it!' Dark said exasperatedly, snorting. 'You really *are* a simpleton.'

The Doctor didn't react. 'I mean, what effect does his word have on the brain?' Dark stared at him blankly. 'You know, what part of the brain is stimulated, which chemical transmitters respond... This feeling of bliss you mention, is it produced through endorphins or...' The Doctor trailed off. 'You don't know what I'm talking about, do you? Surely you must have some basic knowledge of the way the mind works, of how the brain operates on a genetic –'

Dark shouted out in alarm, involuntarily.

The Doctor stared at him. 'What did I say?'

'You... That word...'

'What, "gen–"'

Dark hushed him, frantically, feeling his entire body starting to sweat. 'Doctor, please. Even speaking that word is a category-G offence, the greatest crime you can commit.'

The Doctor looked indignant. 'But you *know* the word.' He suddenly turned as if to reinspect the Diviners' crest above the door, a double-helix design picked out in silver, then swung back to Dark, his eyes searching. 'Do you know what it means?'

'I do not need to. Its connotations are unholy.' Dark took a deep breath before stating flatly: 'The word is forbidden.'

'Piffle!' the Doctor exclaimed mysteriously. 'Forbidden by whom?'

'By the Holiest. It is in the Sacred Doctrine of –'

'Your bosses, you mean. Those closest to the Creator.' The Doctor smiled unexpectedly. 'His right-hand men.'

'Yes. More than a hundred years ago, the Holiest discovered that this grotesque science was being dabbled in.'

'And?' the Doctor's eyes were wide and pale. 'An inquisitive mind brings down the wrath of God, does it?'

'The instruments were confiscated. Knowledge has limits.'

'Imposed from on high?'

'It is not enough for us to be clever. We must be wise.'

'But some feel they are wiser than others. The Holiest, for example.'

'The Holiest are not beyond reproach.' Dark was feeling more and more uncomfortable. 'It's rumoured that one of the Holiest simply disappeared when –'

'Rumoured? Hearsay isn't clever *or* wise. You deal in absolutes, remember?'

Dark had had enough of this, of answering questions that were self-evident to anyone in the world apart from, it would seem, this strange, difficult man. 'Suppose you tell me where you're from, Doctor.'

Instantly the Doctor appeared shifty again. 'I'm a traveller. I'm from many places.'

'*I* am not a child, Doctor,' Dark said, losing his patience. 'Don't give me a child's answer.'

The Doctor stood up petulantly. 'That's as straightforward as I can be in answering that question. I don't *know* where I'm from.'

Dark gestured to the console. 'Well then, perhaps you'd like me to run a search for you?'

The Doctor turned away.

Dark suddenly felt himself trembling. 'Doctor, I know that this database will find me all the details I need on Derran Sherat. His age, his location, life history, it'll all be there. But you...' Dark felt a shiver run through him. 'I have the strangest feeling... I don't think I'll find you here. Or your friends.' He looked pleadingly at the Doctor. 'How can that be?'

The Doctor bounded up to him. 'Why do you *need* me to be in there? I'm standing right in front of you, aren't I?' He looked at Dark again, that same unnerving stare. 'Poor Nathaniel! Even when you're given absolutes, you can't believe in them.'

Dark stiffened. 'What do you mean?'

'Your Creator. You believe He exists.'

'Because He *does* exist.'

The Doctor shrugged. 'But you no longer believe *in* Him, do you? In His Design. Isn't that so?'

'That's... No, you're...' Dark felt he could begin a hundred sentences, but finish none of them.

'That's been true for a long time, now,' the Doctor went on, nodding to himself. 'The scale of the bombings, the senseless deaths, they've just made things worse, haven't they?'

'Yesterday,' Dark breathed. 'When I saw the extent of the damage from one of those things... Not damage to buildings, to property, but to the *people*, the terrified people all around me...' He stiffened. He had to grind out the words. 'The fault is in me. I haven't searched hard enough for His meaning in these events.'

'Oh, come on, Nathaniel,' the Doctor thundered, thrusting his face into Dark's own, so close Dark could barely focus on his bright-blue eyes. 'Finding a meaning is easy. It's understanding it that's the hard part. Discovering how that meaning relates to *you*.'

Dark opened his mouth but couldn't say another word.

The Doctor passed him a handkerchief. 'You see,' he said softly, 'nothing is ever straightforward, nor should it be. Faith can never be untested, or unearned. The Creator's presence may be an established fact, but not what He's *doing*. That's what requires your belief.'

Dark wiped his eyes and nose, remembering Lanna's words at the travel shelter, the moment things had first crystallised. *If I'd been born a Diviner, I'd ask the Creator myself.*

Suddenly, a high-pitched buzzing started up from the console behind him, like an angry fly trapped in a glass.

'What is it?' the Doctor asked worriedly.

'I'm not sure,' Dark said, impatiently blinking away tears, willing the screen into focus. 'Nothing like this has ever happened before...'

The machine's whining soon stopped. A glaring yellow error box appeared, into which a message started typing itself.

'Entry excised,' the Doctor read. 'Excised?'

'The file on Sherat, it's been... it's been *deleted*.' Dark stared bewildered at the screen. 'But that can't be... I made no mistake with the search components, I've done a thousand of these.'

'I'm sure,' the Doctor said thoughtfully.

Dark hit several buttons on the console but knew it was no good. 'This is impossible.'

'Apparently not,' the Doctor said briskly. 'Absolutes, Nathaniel, remember? We have to believe in them, but we still need to understand the reasons behind them. So, who would have the power to eviscerate your records? To delete people from your population database?'

'No one,' Dark said, staring at the screen in outrage.

'Not even the Holiest?' the Doctor asked lightly.

'Well, in theory, perhaps...' Dark stared at him. 'What are you saying?'

'Well, they clearly forbid some things... why not others?' He stroked his lip thoughtfully. 'And while you Diviners may do the legwork, it's the Holiest who have final responsibility for interpreting the Creator's Design, correct? Leaving you to report it back to the populus...'

Dark stared at the sickly-yellow box on the screen and felt his whole life tilting crazily. He was suddenly questioning every fundamental he'd ever known. He wished he'd never gone to Etty's, never met the Doctor, never seen Treena's file.

Never questioned anything.

'The system has crashed,' said Dark flatly. 'It'll take a few hours to restart it.'

'Well,' the Doctor announced, yawning, 'we're not going to find out anything more here tonight.'

'We should go to the police before someone gets hurt, whatever Etty says,' Dark said, starting to reinitialise the system. 'Let them worry about all this.'

'And just walk away?' the Doctor murmured. 'No... You know, I don't think you were meant to discover that excised record. I don't think anyone was. Like it or not, you're involved, Nathaniel.'

'Me? But I've done nothing!' Dark protested.

'For far too long,' the Doctor agreed. 'But that's changing now, isn't it? I don't think our answers lie with the police. Not just yet, anyway.'

Dark shook his head wearily. 'You seem to have all the answers yourself, Doctor.'

'Not quite,' the Doctor confessed, suddenly forlorn. 'And right now I'd settle simply for knowing Fitz is all right, wherever he is.'

'In the morning, perhaps I can run a check on the system for a man fitting the description you gave me of the driver that tried to run you down.'

The Doctor cocked his head. 'Does that mean you're going back to work tomorrow?'

'Later today, you mean,' Dark said, noticing the clock on the wall: just a few hours until dawn. He took a deep breath and looked meaningfully at the Doctor. 'Well... If we're to have our answers, there's work to be done, isn't there?'

The Doctor smiled, nodded.

'You... don't have anywhere to stay here, do you?'

'No.'

'Then you can come with me.' Dark crossed to the door of the data centre and checked that the corridor was clear. 'I have to say, though, I've no idea what I'm going to tell Cleric Rammes about where I was yesterday.'

'Don't worry about that, Nathaniel.' Dark could hear the smile spreading through the soft voice behind him. 'I think I can get you a Doctor's note.'

# Chapter Ten

Anji woke up and found it was light, the grey unfamiliar light of a new day creeping in through someone else's window. She was reminded of student parties, of waking up on a floor or a sofa and spending minutes at a time remembering how you ended up there. Except the truth of course was very different. The headache she had now was from lying awake most of the night after an evening of stilted conversation, and the taste in the back of her mouth wasn't cheap cider and other people's cigarette smoke: it was some alien meat she didn't even know the name of. Again and again as the hours crawled by, between flinching from every unfamiliar sound, Anji had longed for a toothbrush and a blob of Colgate. For a change of clothes. For anything familiar, comfortable.

Something started banging at the front door.

Anji's heart leapt higher than she did off the sofa. She slipped on her jacket and shoes, crossed the living room, disorientated, and tried to remember which way would lead to the door.

'Doctor?' she called. It had to be him. Who else would come knocking?

She walked over to the living-room window. From there she could see down the driveway, and she expected to see Dark's car parked outside.

There was no sign of it. But there were three figures walking towards the farmhouse, shadows detaching themselves from the gloomy autumnal dawn. One of them was holding something with both hands.

It looked like some kind of shotgun.

'Etty!' yelled Anji.

'I know,' Etty said, rushing over to join her by the window. Anji stared at her in surprise - the woman had dressed, shirt and skirt thrown on hastily, and even had shoes on.

'Expecting company?'

'No.' Etty looked out of the window and crossed her arms tightly across her chest. 'There're three of them.'

Anji nodded. 'At least. I heard knocking.'

'That wasn't them.'

'Then...?'

'Not now,' Etty said.

Anji's stomach twisted tight. 'Fine. Well, even if there is just the three of them, there's only two of us. And they've got a gun.'

'So have we.' Etty nodded casually to the rifle she'd used to threaten Dark when he arrived yesterday, resting in the corner, but her darting eyes betrayed her own fear.

Anji looked worriedly at her. 'You'd use that?'

'To protect...' Etty faltered. 'To protect my child, of course I would.'

'They haven't come here for Braga,' Anji hissed. 'They've come for you! Now, quickly, how many doors are there?'

'Front and back.'

'Let's get them locked,' Anji said, and Etty nodded. 'Then we'll have to set up some kind of barricade.'

They worked swiftly to block off the back door, slamming anything they could find up against the whitewashed wood. Then Anji ran after Etty to the hallway, her leather soles slapping on the cold slate floor.

'That cabinet,' she said. 'Come on, help me with it.'

'It won't stop them for long,' Etty pointed out.

'It's a start. Come *on*.'

They started pushing. Braga's voice floated down from upstairs. 'Mum? What is it, what's wrong?'

'Nothing!' Etty's voice rose above the protesting shrieks of the heavy wood as it dragged over the slate. 'Stay upstairs. Don't come down for anything, understand?'

'But what *is* it?' His voice was lazy, whining. He was chiding his mother for not giving a straight answer. He knew nothing. Lucky thing. Anji wished desperately as she looked round for the next piece of the barricade that there was someone else here to look after her, to lie to her, to pretend everything was OK. But no, everything was down to her, and if she made a mistake she was dead.

She could hear the cold drag of their footsteps coming closer. It was her imagination, had to be. They couldn't be so near so soon.

'The bureau in the living room?' Anji suggested, desperately.

Etty nodded, and they ran to fetch it.

Dark led the Doctor through the cold, quiet streets to the travel shelter. It was overcast, and looked like rain again, but the Doctor had been quite keen to take the travelbus: he wanted to see more of the City in daylight. In fact, his enthusiasm was indecent for this time of the morning. Dark felt more as if he'd had a long blink than any amount of sleep. For all he knew, the Doctor hadn't even closed his eyes.

As he walked he felt the weight of the security tape tapping against his leg. The Doctor was keen to scrutinise the footage of Treena's death for anything they might've missed. Dark felt he was already too intimate with each silent frame of the thing. He could picture the look on Treena's face as the gun was swung round to bear on her, her mouth opening wide as...

He shook his head to try to clear it, and took in a now familiar figure waiting at the travel shelter, in a smart, dark suit. Behind her make-up, Dark decided she looked as tired as he was.

'Good morning, Lanna.'

She nodded in greeting. 'Where were you yesterday, Holy Man?'

Dark swallowed. 'I was...'

'He was in meetings,' the Doctor said quickly.

Lanna looked at the Doctor, her green eyes wide and catlike. 'With you, was he?'

'With me, yes.'

Now Lanna looked at Dark again, eyes closing a little. 'All night?'

'We were up till terribly late, yes,' the Doctor said brightly. 'I didn't get a wink of sleep, you know.'

'You're a dark horse, Holy Man, aren't you?' Lanna smiled, and nodded at the Doctor. 'I know what you mean. I had one or two... *meetings* myself last night.'

Dark suddenly understood what Lanna must be. An awkward silence ensued. The travelbus, naturally, did not break it by arriving on time.

'I'm looking for somebody, Lanna,' he announced suddenly.

'You should've said,' she replied, unblinking.

'A man,' the Doctor elaborated. 'A handsome man, quite swarthy...'

Lanna looked at him in bemusement. Dark wondered what she must be thinking. He fumbled in his robes for the photograph of Derran Sherat - then saw the Doctor handing the picture to Lanna himself.

She studied the picture, suddenly serious. 'What do you want him for?'

'We just need to ask him some questions,' said the Doctor.

'I don't know him... but he fits the description of...'

'Yes?' the Doctor urged her, wide-eyed.

She looked mistrustfully at the Doctor. 'Are you with the police?'

The Doctor shook his head. 'No. They once very kindly lent me one of their boxes, but no.'

'We have to find him, Lanna,' Dark said earnestly.

Lanna tapped the picture against her chin. She looked worried now. 'Some of the girls should still be about. I'd like them to see this. They might be able to help.'

'All right,' the Doctor agreed.

'Thank you, Lanna,' said Dark.

'Wait here. I shouldn't be long.' She smiled at Dark briefly, then turned and jogged away.

'Bit of a long shot, I suppose,' Dark muttered. 'But you never know -'

'Is this the only city?' the Doctor asked abruptly.

'Of course not.' Dark resigned himself to another round of questioning while they waited. 'It's only the largest.'

'Hence its imaginative name.'

'It needs no name. It is the first and oldest city still standing.'

'There are ruins of others, then?' The Doctor was throwing his head about from side to side, taking in each spindly tree, each house in the avenue.

'Yes.'

'Where? Have you seen them?'

'No.'

'How old is the City?'

Dark found he was growing less unsettled handing out answers that should be common knowledge. 'It was founded hundreds of years ago, to the Creator's Design.'

'Ah. And how about the world?'

'What do you mean?'

The Doctor was still staring around in fascination at the ordinary street. 'When did the Creator found that?'

'This planet has existed for billions of years. The Creator has existed for all time.'

'So why did He choose *your* water mountains?'

'Because we are the only people.'

The Doctor stopped short. 'The only people in the universe?' Dark shrugged. 'How sweet,' the Doctor said, but he would not be drawn on what he meant, and Dark was feeling too tired to pry further.

It was some time before Lanna returned, cheeks flushed red not just with running, it seemed, but with excitement.

'Well?' asked the Doctor anxiously.

Lanna looked again at the photograph as if sizing up its subject in a new light. 'I thought it might be him - and the girls are pretty much definite.'

'Who?' The Doctor was practically begging her for the answer.

'He's a freak,' gushed Lanna, 'if it's who we think it is. Last winter, he came up to one of my friends, Marie. She agreed to go back to his place and then...'

Dark shifted uncomfortably. Perhaps Lanna noticed, because she trailed off for a moment, became more solemn.

'You should be careful if you're going after him. Marie'd not seen him before, but thought he seemed nice. Quiet, you know, polite. Professional. But back at his... he was weird. When she wouldn't do as he said, he got angry... violent.'

'He hurt her?' asked Dark.

Lanna offered the picture to him. 'Went for her with a knife. Surgeon's knife, she said. Her hand needed fifteen stitches...'

Dark shuddered and stuffed the photo into his pocket. 'Did you report this?'

'Marie didn't think the police would be overly sympathetic.' Lanna shrugged. 'We warned our own.'

'Assuming this is our man, where did he take your friend?' demanded the Doctor.

'I don't know the number. But it was a big apartment block, on Badi Street…'

Dark nodded. 'I think I know that road. It's a fair walk from here.'

'Then what are we waiting for?' the Doctor said, slapping Dark on the shoulder. 'You're ill again. Mystery bug. But don't worry, I'm sure you'll be coming into work later.'

'What's going on here, Holy Man?' Lanna asked. 'What are you supposed to be divining here with… *him*.' She gestured to the Doctor, now jogging on the spot, eager to be off.

'I… I'm afraid I can't really say.'

Lanna pursed her thin lips. 'Why aren't I surprised at that?'

Dark looked nervously about him to check they were still alone. 'All I *can* really say to you is… well, thank you.'

'No need. If you find him, give him a lump from me.'

'Not just for this…' Dark sighed. 'When we first met, talking to you - it made things clearer for me. Helped me see things differently.'

'Now I've met your *friend*,' Lanna said, looking at Dark with a trace of disappointment, 'I'm seeing things slightly differently myself.'

Dark wasn't sure what to say. He felt he wanted to explain - not just his relationship to the Doctor, but everything he was feeling. How many men did she have taking her in order to confide things, the things they couldn't tell their wives and families? 'I'm sure we'll bump into each other again soon.'

'Come *on*, Nathaniel!' the Doctor called. He'd already wandered some way down the avenue.

'That's our destiny, is it?' Lanna asked satirically. 'Well, you'd know about that, Holy Man…'

Dark held her eye for a few seconds more. 'It's this way, Doctor,' he called, then hurried off in the opposite direction up the avenue. The Doctor caught him up and then overtook him as they headed for West Side, the oldest, dirtiest part of the City.

* * *

When the first strike sounded against the front door, Anji thought her heart would crack her ribs with its pounding. She stared transfixed by the way the door seemed to pulsate, jumping on its hinges with each hefty swing of fists or gun stock.

'Maybe we should try to sneak out the back way,' she muttered.

Before Etty could speak, the pounding started up behind them too, from the door in the kitchen. She shook her head nervously, tightened her grip on the gun, her blue eyes fidgeting in her face.

Anji jumped as the front door smashed open, coming up hard against the mahogany cabinet. Etty charged forward, grabbed the table they had used to shore up the door and pulled it back, toppling it on to its side.

Anji stared at her, frantically. 'What are you doing?'

'A shield,' Etty said. They might come in firing.' She uncocked the rifle, checking for the umpteenth time that it was loaded.

'Oh, Jesus,' Anji muttered to herself as the cabinet creaked noisily across the floor. There was a horrid inevitability to the scene, as if this was a reconstruction. She could hear Nick Ross's voice in her head: *The armed intruders broke open the door in moments, and shot both the owner of the farmhouse and her attractive companion dead...*

But only after a struggle, Anji decided. They wouldn't make it easy.

Nick Ross wasn't having it: *...shot dead after a short and pointless struggle...*

No, thought Anji, switching off his image in her head.

*Don't have nightmares -*

She crouched behind a table. The door leapt forward again. There was a splintering crack from the kitchen; the door must be starting to give way.

'Mum!' Braga called down from upstairs, concerned now. 'What's -'

'Keep away!' Etty screamed, staring at the front door starting to flap on its hinges. 'Don't you dare move, you hear me? Stay in your room!' Anji saw that the woman's knuckles were white around the trigger of the rifle.

Then the banging stopped.

'Ettianne Grace?' a voice asked slowly from behind the half-open door.

'Get off my property!' Etty shouted.

'We have come for you,' another voice said.

There was a blast of thunder from behind them.

'The door,' breathed Anji. The one with the gun must be shooting the lock off the back door.

'Stay away or I'll kill you!' Etty yelled. 'I've got a gun.'

'We have, too,' the lazy voice said. 'If you shoot at us we'll kill everyone here.'

'They know I'm with you,' Anji whispered. 'And Braga.'

'We've had instructions this time. We'll kill everyone.'

Etty said nothing, just stared down at the rifle in her hands as if, suddenly, she mistrusted it. The front door slammed open into the cabinet once again as the attack on the entrance was resumed, harder than ever.

'A window?' Anji whispered. 'Get Braga. We could maybe slip out through a window -'

'Too late,' croaked Etty.

Anji gasped as a man's face, red and thickset, appeared in the crack in the doorway. He was putting his shoulder to the battered wood, heaving with all his might.

And behind him was another man. Anji stared in horror from behind the table, as her heart seemed to stop beating altogether. He had a long, expressionless face topped with brown hair tugged down into a straggly fringe. A few days' stubble growth flecked his pale skin. His grey eyes were staring out, like those of a zombie. Unknowing, unfeeling. Just here to take Ettianne Grace, or to kill whoever else he could find.

'Fitz,' Anji whispered, as the crashing from the kitchen told her that the back door had finally given way.

# Chapter Eleven

Heavy footsteps came clomping up behind them. Etty raised her gun, ready to fire.

'No, don't,' Anji said, panicked, her head swinging between the man and Fitz still fighting their way through the front door and whoever was coming through from the kitchen.

Fitz had a gun, a heavy-looking revolver of some kind. He was aiming it at Anji.

'Fitz, no!' she screamed.

Etty turned to her sharply, maybe at the mention of Fitz, maybe just to see what she was screaming at.

And a big, bald man in a huge, fawn-coloured coat came rushing towards them from behind, wielding his shotgun like a club. His face was screwed up in anger.

Etty didn't have time to get the rifle up before the man knocked it out of her hands with the barrel of his own weapon, metal ringing on metal. Etty cried out. The intruder reached down and grabbed her by the hair.

'Get off her!' Anji spat, grabbing hold of his leg, trying to overbalance him.

'You're Ettianne Grace,' the man told Etty dully as he yanked her up, her hair thick in his clenched fist. Anji recognised his voice: he was definitely the leader of the men who had attacked Etty out on the moorland, who had taken Fitz, who had tried to run her -

'Down, Anji!'

Anji was so surprised at Fitz's words she actually turned and looked up at him. He was still pointing the gun - but not at her, at the intruder. She ducked down, heard the revolver fire, and a shout from the big man. He released Etty, staggered back, a red stain rapidly spreading over his shoulder and down his arm.

'Jesus! I hit him!' Fitz said, eyes wide and boggling.

The man beside him in the doorway seemed less impressed. He turned on Fitz, his face twisted in anger and incomprehension. Fitz tried to bring the gun to bear on him but with a growl the man swatted it aside.

Anji tore her eyes away. Even with blood pouring down his arm, the intruder behind them was coming back for another go, moving towards Etty. Anji scrambled up and grabbed hold of his wounded arm, trying to twist it back behind him. He grunted with pain, but he was strong, reaching out murderously for her neck with his free hand.

But Etty barely noticed. She had raised her gun again and this time she was going to use it.

'Not Fitz!' Anji shouted, as fat fingers closed on her throat.

Etty fired. Anji jumped at the loudness of the shot. Smoke and the stink of cordite blew across the room, but Anji couldn't see what was happening. The man who held her brought his face up close to hers. He had beautiful eyes, Anji found herself thinking. It was ridiculous but true, they were sea-green, piercing, sad-looking eyes.

'You don't want to do this,' she gasped, hopefully. 'Please...'

There came another loud crack beside her, like a cricket bat whumping a ball for six. Anji was suddenly free, and she collapsed choking to the floor. The intruder had fallen back heavily against the wall. Now he lay silent and still, apparently unconscious, a bloody gash opened in the side of his bald head, a red stream trickling over his rubbery ear. Etty lowered the rifle, which she now was holding by its barrel, taking huge ragged whoops of breath.

Fitz and the other man had seemingly disappeared in that puff of smoke. 'Where did they go?' Anji asked.

'I don't think I hit either of them,' Etty said. 'Just the wall over their heads.'

'Fitz saved us,' Anji said reproachfully, going over to the door. 'That man will kill him even if you didn't.'

'They're maniacs, all of them,' Etty said, tears welling up in her eyes.

'We have to find out what they really want.'

'They want *me*.'

'Yeah, but why?' Anji crossed to the battered door and picked up Fitz's gun. It was still warm from his grip, and holding it made her feel a fraction more secure. 'I'm going to look for Fitz – he might need help.' She pointed at their attacker, slumped bloodily in the corner. 'You watch him.'

'No need,' Etty said quietly. 'I think I killed him.'

Anji looked at her, dumbfounded. She couldn't think of anything to say, and was guiltily grateful when Braga suddenly appeared, terrified and cautious, at the top of the stairs. She signalled to Etty that he was with them.

'Get back to your room!' Etty shouted at him. 'I told you to stay there, didn't I? I told you!'

Anji took Braga's first wailing cry as her signal to get going and start her manhunt.

'Anji, wait,' Etty called.

'I can't,' Anji snapped, and pushed through the front door. In the cold grey light, everything seemed unnaturally still and peaceful, the odd architecture of the buildings making them seem more like sculptures or statues in a garden of rest.

Gun raised, Anji set off unsteadily to search.

Fitz pelted down the muddy track as fast as he could with his limp. He was surrounded now by the weird collection of outhouses and farm buildings. Three-One was right behind him. Suddenly he felt a hard tug, realised Seven's long coat-tails had been streaming out behind him, and that now Three-One had a fist full of them.

Fitz tried to squirm out of the coat, but Three-One had caught up with him, had a hand on his shoulder. Fitz slipped in the mud on his bad leg and fell hard on his back. Three-One tumbled with him, and Fitz was barely able to roll out of the way to avoid being crushed. He scrambled up, yanked off his coat and, as Three-One got up, threw it over the man's head. His mum had always told him never to kick a man when he's down, but Fitz decided it was eminently safer to do so while the man in question was blind on the ground than back standing up. His foot connected - his bad foot, of course - with something hard, and Fitz shouted louder than Three-One did.

'Hope that hurt you more than it hurt me,' Fitz muttered. 'But I doubt it.'

He shambled off towards what looked like it might be a barn, and threw himself over the low wooden gate, landing in a pile of wet straw. It stank. This whole planet stank. He'd had nothing but aggro ever since he'd got here. Panting for breath, Fitz lay listening for any sound of his attacker approaching, and said a belated prayer of thanks that Anji at least had clearly bounced back from falling off that cliff. But where was the Doctor? Fitz sighed with frustration. He knew nothing about the situation here. For now, all he could do was hope that Anji was OK, and that she could deal with Two better than he'd been able to.

For a second he was back under that smelly, claustrophobic helmet, his breathing amplified in his ears, the current smashing through him. But he hadn't ended up lobotomised like the others. Maybe because he was an Earthling, better by design. Or maybe it was because he'd had his head rewired and mucked about with so many times before - alien leeches, virtual reality generators, even the TARDIS had had a go - and his brain's workings had been left a little eccentric as a result. Whatever, he'd been able to fake the zombie effect, no problem, and when Two had said they were going back to kidnap this Ettianne woman Fitz had realised he was going to be chauffeured right back to where they'd left the TARDIS. He was even given a gun to defend himself with. Nice one. All he had to do was bide his time ready to escape.

Well, he hadn't done that quite yet. He could hear footsteps, and heavy cloth being thrown on the floor. He'd have to go back for that coat, Fitz thought: it was lovely and warm. Always assuming he'd ever have the chance to feel the cold again after this. He held himself still, not daring to move. Only when the footsteps seemed to wander off a little way did he start crawling softly through the straw to the other side of the barn.

He hobbled out, carefully, couldn't see anyone as he looked around. To his right, a concrete path led back down towards the farmhouse, so he edged his way along to see what lay to his left. Not much - just another, larger barn, with a few old-looking farm vehicles, and the wreck of an old car. Most of these vehicles actually had wheels to roll on, showing their age and a good deal of rust. Must be why the hovercars still had steering wheels, he supposed. For familiarity's sake. Thank you, Sherlock Kreiner.

His next deduction was that this must be the perimeter of the farm buildings; ahead of him there were only fields and grasslands stretching out, flatter than a pancake. An expanse of grey cloud was hogging the sky, beating the tiny turquoise strip of sea back to the horizon. His breath was steaming in the chilly air. It reminded him that he could murder a cigarette right now. And murder reminded him of his predicament. Should he head back to the farmhouse, check on Anji? Three-One might have picked up the gun he'd dropped...

The decision was taken for him when he heard more footsteps, ringing out slowly on the concrete around the corner. 'Oh, God,' he muttered, and started limping towards the barn. When he reached it and opened the rickety wooden doors, he found they gave on to another set of double doors, stronger, more secure.

Doors with no handles.

He stared, nonplussed, tried to close the doors he'd just opened behind him and swore quietly when he found he couldn't: there wasn't room, he'd squash himself.

The footsteps were getting closer. They were joined by others, moving faster.

'Hello?' Fitz whispered, knocking on the inner doors, self-conscious at the thought that he was probably asking cows and chickens for a helping hand. What the hell! He was desperate enough to try anything.

'Come on,' he muttered, breaking out into a cold and clammy sweat, banging on the door now, hammering as hard as he had on the farmhouse. 'Please... *please*...'

The rush of footsteps got still louder. Whoever they were, Fitz realised helplessly, they were almost on top of him.

'Don't go in there!' came a woman's voice, strained, shouting.

Fitz stopped pushing at the doors, confused for a moment. Then they opened inward and light spilled out over him.

Fitz took a step back.

'Anji!' It was that Ettianne's voice. 'You mustn't look!'

Fitz *was* looking. This wasn't just a barn: it was a room. A large room. And there were people were hidden inside. Crouching. Lying down. One was even sitting on a swing.

Except they weren't people. They were freaks.

Staring at him in wonder. Hunchbacks and stringbeans and spastics and *freaks*.

One by one they started to shriek.

# Chapter Twelve

Dark had never had much cause to visit West Side. He'd passed through it before a few times; there was an ancillary records centre on its outskirts where dead case files were archived, which was how he'd heard of Badi Street at all. It was a street leading off from the main thoroughfare that he'd used before as reference point. And, of course, a number of the families he'd counselled hailed from there, but generally it had impacted on his life very little.

He wasn't sorry. This was a miserable place, neglected. The buildings were tall, but stooped like old men, and damp clung to the mouldering stonework in oily stains. Faces, ghostly and pale, rose up in windows from time to time as they passed by. Shabby, run-down people walked by and stared. Dark couldn't blame them: they stood out sorely, he in his Diviner's robes and the Doctor in his eccentric finery; they didn't belong here. It made Dark feel uneasy, but the Doctor was predictably bluff and cheery, striding along the pitted and patchy pavement.

'Is it much further?' asked the Doctor, and not for the first time.

'We're getting close,' Dark answered patiently. 'I think we can cut through here.' He indicated an alleyway, narrow and intimidating. Floating from tiny windows came the noise of radio chatter and crying babies. Fire escapes sent rusting ladders spiralling down to the street, and high up, lines of laundry hung in rucked-up rows between the two buildings.

The Doctor changed course without another word and hurried down it. At the far end, he swung back to Dark, who was following more cautiously, and pointed at something out of view, grinning and almost hopping up and down with excitement. He looked like a child at the zoo seeing a funny animal for the first time.

'That's the one!' he whispered. The volume of the babies and radios seemed to be rising incrementally as if each were responding to the other, but the Doctor's voice still carried. Dark hurried to join him.

The Doctor was pointing at a vehicle parked halfway down the deserted street.

'That's what almost ran you over?' Dark checked.

'Precisely.'

'There's no identification plates...'

'I don't imagine traffic offences bother them unduly.'

'I meant, how can you be sure?'

'Just take it from me.' He frowned. 'Like *they* took Fitz. And perhaps they're here now to take Derran Sherat. We must see, come on.'

The two men ran down to the van. It was empty, parked outside a towering tenement.

'This place would seem to fit that young lady's description,' the Doctor said.

'Should we go looking for them?' Dark wondered dubiously. 'There must be scores of rooms in there.'

'We wait for them to come out,' said the Doctor. 'Avoid a confrontation unless we -'

An enormous explosion blasted out glass and fire from a window on the far right-hand side of the third floor. Dark and the Doctor threw themselves to the ground.

'On the other hand...' muttered the Doctor. He jumped to his feet and sprinted through the swing doors into the building.

'Should I call the medics?' Dark shouted after him. 'The police?'

Thick smoke was billowing from the window now, blowing back down the way they had come, left towards the alleyway. Surely the noise of the explosion would've drowned out even the loudest of the screaming brats and newscasters. Someone would be getting help.

And, right now, the Doctor could probably use his.

Dark raced into the burning building after the Doctor.

The freaks in the barn, apparently tired of screaming, now started running about - those that could, anyway. They charged through the room, dithering, moaning, trying to hide.

Unable to believe his eyes, Fitz staggered backwards and cannoned into someone. But it wasn't Three-One. It was Anji, and she shouted in surprise.

'What the...?'

'Don't worry, Anji,' Fitz said with forced confidence. 'I won't let them hurt you.'

'Don't be ridiculous, Fitz, look at them.' Anji nudged Fitz aside as she looked on in fascination at the bizarre scene. 'They're terrified. They're not going to hurt anyone.'

So much for the grand reunion, thought Fitz sulkily. But then she squeezed his hand, firmly, and shot him a quick smile, which helped.

'It's all right,' Ettianne shouted, pushing past them both, trying to settle everyone down. 'Stop running about, come on now.'

All the others, the monstrosities Fitz had glimpsed, had gone into hiding. He looked about the place for signs of them, but not too closely. This was clearly some kind of dorm, converted from the barn. Single beds, all neatly made, lined the walls. There were tables and chairs and books and games, and pictures pinned up around the brightly painted walls. There was even a swing and a rocking horse. But there was something pathetic about the place. Something that spoke of fear and secrets and making do. It was the sort of place Anne Frank's lot might've had if the family hiding them had lived in the sticks instead of the centre of town.

A little man with a bent, frightened face peeped out from behind a table, and Ettianne went over to soothe him. 'Don't be scared. They're friends, good people.' She glared at Fitz. 'Aren't you?'

Fitz nodded dumbly. Then he clutched hold of Anji in surprise as a streak of red slipped down to the floor in front of them from somewhere up in the rafters. It was a girl, tall and willowy in a simple crimson dress. One of her legs was twice the size of the other, and this she used to take the brunt of her fall. She straightened up, and Fitz found himself looking up at her; she must be topping six-six. Long auburn hair that reached right down to her waist had fallen over her face, and now she wiped it away Fitz was relieved to see she looked quite normal. Her eyes were a pale blue, one a little lower than the other, and her nose was a long ridge. Her thin lips twitched into a self-conscious smile at her abrupt entrance.

She looked at Anji. 'Your skin,' she said, grinning wildly. 'It's so lovely and brown - brown and smooth like a berry.' She looked about twenty but she spoke wonderingly like a child. 'How did you get to be so brown?' She reached out long fingers to touch Anji's face.

'Stop that, Vettul,' Etty told her.

'But she's so lovely, Etty,' Vettul said, still staring in awe, 'and so brown...'

Anji, now she'd recovered herself a little, was smiling back at this weirdo.

'Well, thank you,' Anji said, uncertainly.

'What's up?' said Fitz bluntly. 'Never met anyone with dark -?'

'I've never met anyone,' Vettul interrupted, with a broad smile. 'No one from outside.'

Fitz and Anji traded puzzled looks. When Fitz looked back again, he found Vettul's milky blue eyes fixed on him now. 'You are very beautiful,' she said solemnly.

'You must be joking,' Anji snorted. She just smiled as Fitz stood there speechless, blushing crimson.

'Vettul, stop that,' Etty instructed like a dog trainer getting cross with a puppy. 'Come here.'

'No, wait,' Anji said. 'Was it you that warned us this morning, banging on the door?'

Vettul nodded shyly. Fitz looked over at Etty, who was distracted trying to disengage herself from the little man, while Anji stuck a hand into her pocket, rummaging for something. She finally pulled out a necklace. What was she planning to do, bargain with the natives?

'This is yours, right?'

Vettul squealed with delight and took the necklace, nodding.

Anji looked down at Vettul's dodgy pins. 'And I guess it must be you that left the tracks I saw...'

'I followed you out to the cliffs,' she said, with a guilty glance at Etty. 'I liked watching you. You and the other man.'

'The Doctor?' queried Fitz. 'Is he OK? When you both went over the cliffs -'

'Vettul saved our lives,' Anji said, her smile growing wider. 'Drew our attention to a way back up. But we never saw you...'

'The Creator won't share His world with us,' Vettul said, 'but He has to share this land with us.' She smiled slyly at a small, wizened woman hiding in the corner. 'Myra and I know it better than anyone. And *I* know how to hide.'

'Vettul,' Etty said, quite distraught now, 'you know you are never to go outside, never, not unless I say it is safe.'

'You never say it is safe!' Vettul spat at her. 'You never let us do anything except sweep out the animal pens.'

'That's *enough*, Vettul.'

The strange girl turned back to Fitz and Anji, pouting. This was clearly an old argument between the two of them. Suddenly Vettul pulled a face, imitating Etty's scowl, and giggled when Fitz started to smile.

'Etty, what's going on here?' Anji asked. 'Who are these people?'

The woman looked sadly at the little man gazing up adoringly at her. 'They're no one,' she said quietly. 'Nothing.'

'That's no kind of an answer,' said Anji.

'There's no time for anything else,' Etty said. 'You may have found your friend, but that other madman is still on the loose.' She looked at Fitz. 'Where did he go?'

'I don't know.'

'How did you get here?'

'A big van. Parked down the end of your track.' Fitz said, a little overcome by all this. He'd been expecting a hero's welcome, not a surprise freak show and some Nazi housewife's interrogation. 'I think he was heading for it when I saw him last.'

'Or for the farmhouse,' Anji said.

Etty and Anji gave each other looks that seemed to speak of some unutterable realisation.

'Braga,' Etty whispered, and pushed past them and out of the place without another word.

Fitz blew through his lips, shaking his head. And to think he'd thought he was escaping the madhouse. He gave a polite smile to Vettul, who had started staring at him again, and turned to Anji. 'We've got some catching up to do,' he said.

'Starting with her,' Anji said, and ran off after Etty.

Fitz was left just standing there, feeling suddenly more conspicuous than he had when wearing Seven's coat. Strange faces were beginning to peek out from behind furniture to size him up.

'Better get after them,' he mumbled weakly to Vettul, and scarpered as fast as he could. The girl's eyes may've been watery and weak, but Fitz swore he could feel them watching him all the limping way back to the farmhouse.

# Chapter Thirteen

'Stop them, Nathaniel!'

Dark had staggered up the final flight of stairs leading to the third floor and was rounding the corner when the Doctor's voice carried to him, as if borne on the thick white smoke that was pouring down the corridor.

He peered panic-stricken into the fog. 'Doctor? Where are you?'

There was no reply, just what sounded like a door slamming, and raised voices. And footsteps, racing for him.

Suddenly Dark found himself knocked aside, and what little breath he had left was slammed from him as he impacted with the wall. Caught by surprise, he could only watch as three or four figures raced past him, half-carrying, half-dragging something between them. With an effort, he dragged himself back up and moved to the window in the stairwell. A few seconds later he saw the figures, three men and a woman, race over to the van. Each was dressed colourfully, except for the man they were carrying. Dark couldn't see his face but his build was slight, his hair was black. He was lifted carefully into the back of the van by the woman and by a short man with wild grey hair, dressed in a dark-brown suit.

'Sorry, Doctor,' muttered Dark. Once he'd forced the window open on its stiff hinges to let out some of the fumes, he staggered back down the corridor, searching for the right room. There was so much smoke, it was difficult to see where it was coming from, and his eyes were streaming. A young woman, skinny and fair and bewildered, brushed past him, clutching a baby, the pair of them coughing and spluttering.

'Hurry along out of here,' he called. 'The police will be here soon. Is there anyone else here who might need help?'

The woman shrugged and vanished into the swirling smoke. Dark stared after her. Then a door swung open and the Doctor's face popped out in front of him, eyes wide and clear.

Dark jumped. 'Doctor,' he said, slumping back against the wall in relief. 'Doctor, they were taking someone away!'

'I know. I know.' The Doctor nodded furiously. 'Did you see who it was?'

'He had black hair. It could've been Sherat.'

'He was certainly too short to have been Fitz,' the Doctor murmured sadly. Suddenly he lashed out at the door frame with his foot in temper. 'I'm not going to wait another hundred years before I see that boy again.'

Not sure, and not wanting to be sure, whether the Doctor was exaggerating or not, Dark moved the subject on. 'You didn't recognise any of the others?'

'I don't know. There were too many of them, couldn't stop them...' He glanced back inside the room at something out of Dark's view. 'And I had to put out the machinery that was on fire.'

'Machinery?' Dark coughed, the back of his throat dried up by the fumes. 'What caused the explosion?'

'You won't like it,' the Doctor said, shaking his head now with equal ferocity. 'In fact, I'd better find you somewhere to sit down.'

'What are you talking about?' Dark said trying to push past him into the room, where the air looked a little clearer.

The Doctor tutted scornfully. 'Someone's been using the G-word again.'

Dark stared, feeling himself flush. 'What?'

'Genetics.'

Dark recoiled. 'You're... you're sure?'

'Quickly, come on,' the Doctor said. 'We can't have much time before the emergency services arrive and impound everything.'

He vanished back inside the room, and Dark followed. The place was a mess, the walls blackened, the windows shattered, what little furniture there was badly scorched. To his right, a door opened on to a dingy toilet and bathroom, but his attention was taken by the still-smoking mass of electrical parts standing on a table in the middle of the room. The Doctor stood poring over it, and Dark looked over his shoulder. This machinery hadn't been manufactured in the processing plants: it had been man-made. Even the sight of it made him feel slightly nauseous. To be looking upon forbidden artefacts...

'What is all this?' whispered Dark. 'What's it for?'

The Doctor pulled a face as he considered, poking about in the blackened innards of the machine that must've caused the explosion. 'It's for manipulating genes...'

'Genes?'

'... and fairly advanced, too, for a lash-up.' He turned to Dark and smiled. 'Whoever made it has done rather well for himself considering he's been operating in a realm of science that doesn't officially exist. It's a shame you have no facilities for DNA fingerprinting, because -' he tapped something that looked like an electrode with some kind of deposit on its tip - 'a little piece of him shall always be here.'

Dark shook his head glumly. 'I don't understand this at all, Doctor.'

'Then it's lucky I do,' the Doctor said firmly, starting to dismantle the equipment. 'You know, some of these cannibalised parts *have* been manufactured...'

'That can't be,' Dark said flatly.

'It must be, because it is. Empirical evidence, remember? Perhaps the Holiest weren't as successful in quashing that little scientific rebellion as they thought.' He clicked his tongue. 'Now, while I get busy with this, you look around here for clues.'

'What sort of clues?'

'Use your initiative, man,' the Doctor said irritably. 'Anything that might suggest Sherat was here, or anything to say where they were going.'

'Why would Sherat have a room full of that... that...'

'This isn't his room,' the Doctor said without looking up. 'I don't think anyone actually lives here, do you? No covers on the bed, no home comforts, no expression of individuality... Only a half-hundredweight of forbidden equipment. No, this room -' the Doctor sniffed the smoky air theatrically, and lowered his voice to a hoarse whisper - 'has the air of a lair. A hide-out. A place with a purpose.'

Dark gingerly peered inside a cupboard. It was empty, and he let out a shaky breath. 'But Lanna said Sherat took her friend here. Took her to... you know...'

The Doctor nodded. 'Which suggests he's involved, doesn't it? But how? Do the Holiest know? Is that why they excised him from the records?'

'We don't know that they did,' Dark objected.

'True,' the Doctor said, still dismantling components with a worrying confidence, dropping sections of circuit boards into his pockets. 'Anyone with the power to construct genetic manipulation devices like these could probably hack into your mainframe on a coffee break.'

Dark sighed, barely understanding a word but getting the gist clear enough. He poked inside another cupboard. A fly buzzed around his face, and he brushed it away. Police sirens would surely come screaming along outside soon, and he half-wished they would come now. To take things out of his hands. He still wasn't in this too deeply, he could explain...

He realised yet again he had no explanation for anything around here.

There was a big pile of blankets on the floor inside the cupboard. Dark lifted them up.

And staggered backwards with a shout.

'What is it?' the Doctor asked mildly.

Dark pointed.

There was an ancient-looking skeleton under the blankets, twisted into a bony pile, wreathed in the artificial stink of the smoke. Flies hopped from bone to dusty bone. A wide band of gold still hung from a shiny white finger. The finger next to it was missing.

'The skull's been split open,' observed the Doctor. 'I wonder who he was.'

'This can't be happening, Doctor,' said Dark, staring fearfully down at the stack of bones.

'It *is* happening, Nathaniel,' murmured the Doctor reasonably.

'But that ring. The design.'

The Doctor looked more closely. 'The double helix?'

'The rumours were true,' Dark whispered, a tear squeezing itself out of one eye and trickling down his cheek. 'It's the Holiest, Doctor. The Holiest who disappeared.'

'Well, well.' The Doctor crouched down, waved the flies away. He gently took the dusty skeletal hand and studied the ring.

'Please, Doctor, don't touch it,' Dark hissed.

'The ring or the bone?'

'Either.'

'Why?'

'You must have respect.'

'We owe respect to the living,' the Doctor proclaimed, fiddling with the ring. 'To the dead we owe only the truth. Who said that? I wonder.'

Dark laid a nervous hand on the Doctor's shoulder. 'He was one of the Holiest.'

'He's been dead for a long, long time.'

'His special powers will linger long after his death.'

'Special powers?' The Doctor snorted. 'What are your Holiest, *Homo superior*?'

'You mustn't mock, Doctor.'

The ring wouldn't come free. Suddenly the entire finger bone cracked off, and the ring fell into the Doctor's palm.

Dark gasped.

'Well, one of his fingers is missing already,' the Doctor reminded him as he dropped both finger and ring easily in a pocket already stuffed with electronics. 'Interesting.'

Dark was appalled and was about to say so when the sound of sirens finally did come, a dreadful wailing like an angry monster come looking for trouble.

'We mustn't be found here,' the Doctor said. 'Too much to explain.'

'Far too much,' Dark muttered, still staring, desolate, down at the bones.

'Particularly to a people for whom genetics has some kind of religious significance and yet -'

Dark flinched, he couldn't help himself. 'Doctor, please don't use that word.'

'So! Genetics! Genetics, genetics genetics!' The Doctor scrawled the word out in the air with a finger. 'Gennnn-ett-ICKS! A man has been murdered, Nathaniel -' he nudged the bones of the Holiest with a scruffy shoe – 'and you're offended by semantics?'

Dark shut his eyes, panic rising as quickly as the Doctor's voice, as quickly as the sirens were approaching. 'We must go, Doctor.'

'Wait a minute,' the Doctor said, standing stock-still. It was as if something monumental had just occurred to him. 'Of course. I see it now, this whole business about category-G offences... Category G, *cat G*, don't you see? It's an acronym, notation for the four DNA bases, cytosine, adenine, thymine and guanine... Almost like a joke. A joke no one on this world could ever understand. So why...?'

Dark tried again, ignoring the Doctor's gibberish. '*Please*, we have to get out of here!'

'Yes,' the Doctor agreed suddenly. 'I've got everything I need, I think, to perform some experiments of my own. Come on.' He strode out of the room – then came striding back in again, shutting the door behind him. There was a key in the lock and he turned it. 'Too late!' he hissed.

The doorknob rattled as someone tried it from the other side of the door. 'This is the police,' a gruff voice called. 'Open up.'

Dark swallowed hard.

'The bathroom window,' the Doctor said, crossing over to it. He wrapped his hand in a filthy towel and used it to clear the frame of the shards of broken glass still fixed there.

'But we're three floors up!' Dark exclaimed.

'Does it matter?' the Doctor enquired breezily as a heavy thumping started up behind the door. 'Seems we're for the high jump whatever we do.' Then he smiled, slyly. 'There's a drainpipe just to the right here.'

'The Creator be praised,' Dark said wryly.

'Hitch up your skirts and do what I do,' said the Doctor. He was already swinging himself out through the window feet first, gripping the rusting drainpipe with both ankles and using that support to grasp hold of it with his hands. Then he slid effortlessly down to the deserted side street below.

'Now,' the Doctor called up. 'I want you to do follow me down, on the count of...' He started counting his fingers as if racking his brains for a suitable figure, and failing. 'Oh, never mind. Just get down here!'

Dark stared dumbly down at the Doctor below him. The police were concerned with the front of the building for now, where the damage was most obvious, but they'd soon work out the only possible escape route for anyone hiding inside. The pounding was getting louder from the other room, the exhortations to open up more aggressive. He glanced back, shuddered at thought of the body of the Holiest buried back under the blankets.

Dark struggled to copy the Doctor's fluid movements, to keep his head clear, to concentrate. The pipe was cold as he gripped it with both hands, the brackets that held it to the wall rusted and weak. As he shinned his way slowly down, the pipe creaked ominously.

'Faster, man!'

Dark craned his neck and saw the Doctor looking nervously down the alleyway. Dark knew that he *was* being too slow, too -

The drainpipe creaked more loudly and without warning started to pull away from the wall. Dark was so horrified he couldn't even cry out. The world whistled about him as he fell.

The section of pipe clattered heavily to the ground, but Dark found his fall halted by the Doctor's arms.

'Splendid effort, Nathaniel,' the Doctor praised him, spinning him round. 'I'd have done the same myself if I'd been following me down. With the pipe broken, they can't come through the window after us!'

Then Dark was plonked down on his feet and the Doctor was turning on his heels and running, away from the scene of the crime.

'Hold it there!' a voice called from the window above. 'You, hold it!'

Suddenly Dark was running, frantically, after the Doctor. No, this wasn't just running. This was being on the run.

The Doctor's long brown hair was streaming behind him. The pockets of his long coat, filled to bursting, bounced and snapped around his legs like enthusiastic puppies as he ran. As Dark drew alongside him, the Doctor threw back his head and laughed with the exhilaration of his flight. A madman. Quite, quite mad.

Only when they were a long, long way away, lost in the silent streets that stretched round here for miles, did Dark realise that, against all odds and his better judgement, he was actually smiling, too.

# Chapter Fourteen

'What now?' Dark asked once he'd got some semblance of breath back in his body. Every muscle seemed to ache. He never knew he had so many of them.

A light rain was falling, but there was no one about to be hurried by it into shop doorways or under the cover of the trees. So much of the City seemed deserted. He and the Doctor had sought sanctuary in a dowdy café in a miserable, wide-open street, empty save for the proprietor and a feeble-looking old man with eyes as watery as the cold broth barely touched in the bowl before him. The place smelled of disinfectant spray, which couldn't be much more pleasant a stink than that it was meant to mask. But the café was bright, and warm, and offered somewhere safe to sit down and think. Dark had ordered them hot drinks. The Doctor had slugged his back in an overenthusiastic gulp, then gasped and hissed and had to cajole the owner into giving him some ice cubes for his scorched throat.

'We need somewhere we can go, a safe place to work and study,' the Doctor said, before crunching down noisily on his second ice cube.

'There's a prayer hall near here,' Dark mused. 'But it's not a large one. And it'll be hard to find anywhere private: there'll be a performance on this afternoon.'

'Performance?'

Dark nodded. 'Twice weekly, after the public proclamations, the halls open their amphitheatres for a celebration of great and famous lives divined...'

The Doctor seemed interested. 'With actors? Musicians?'

Dark nodded. 'Of course.'

'How lovely. I do so enjoy a little vaudeville.' The Doctor finished crunching his ice cube. 'But perhaps not today. What about going back to the Diviners' Mission?'

'Just a little suspicious, wouldn't you say, Doctor?' Dark gestured to his robes. 'The police will have seen me, dressed like this... They could link me to the body of the Holiest.'

The Doctor fished the golden ring from his pocket. 'With this missing, they shouldn't necessarily know immediately, and with no DNA testing they'll have to go by dental records, if indeed he's ever been declared officially missing.' He smiled wanly. 'I don't think that's a problem for now. But it makes you think...'

'I'm sick of thinking,' Dark muttered.

'Leaving the ring on the finger of that poor bag of bones - the only instantly identifiable mark.'

'It's the most callous, sacrilegious -'

'Yes, yes,' the Doctor said, waving a hand impatiently. 'Most of all, it's supremely arrogant. That wasn't clumsiness, or an oversight. Whoever murdered your Holiest has been carting the bones around with him for a long, long time. Why leave them now to be discovered?' When Dark didn't attempt to answer, the Doctor continued anyway. 'I think it's a message, a warning to anyone who might come looking, if ever he had to abandon the place. Whoever's done this isn't afraid of being caught and punished.'

'To kill one of the Holiest... to bundle up his bones in a cupboard...' Dark stared at the Doctor, slowly nodding his head. 'They can't be afraid of anything.'

'And that's what really frightens me,' the Doctor admitted with a sad smile. 'People with nothing to fear usually have nothing to lose. They tend to make the deadliest of enemies.'

Dark felt a shiver shave his spine. 'Doctor... what if this is it?'

'What?'

'Vanishing Point.'

'Where all life meets all death?'

Dark nodded, looking out at the white sky through the café window, recent events bulking up in his mind. 'With all that's happened, the things we're finding, this could be the start of it.'

'It could,' the Doctor concurred. 'Or it could be just the start of another working day. Until we know differently, let's treat it that way, shall we?' He snapped his fingers and grinned suddenly, an eat-you-all-up grin. 'Starting with one of those currant buns.'

A few minutes later, Dark watched stoically as his strange friend devoured the second part of his breakfast.

'We need access to your Diviners' data bank,' the Doctor

mumbled with his mouth full, crumbs flying from his lips. 'That description-matching program you said you had -we must use it to try to trace that vehicle, or the people you saw.'

Dark nodded. 'Perhaps... perhaps if we go to the ancillary record centre I can call in to the Mission from there? That won't seem quite so suspicious - and at least I'll have a reason for being in the area if it's made public that a Diviner was spotted running from -' Dark suddenly felt too sick to finish his sentence. He was starting to think like a criminal as well as act like one.

'Good idea,' the Doctor said vaguely, and started to munch on a third ice cube from the small pile melting on the table in front of him. 'Like I say, I shall need a place to work.'

'It's not used very often. I may be able to secure us an office,' Dark said, considering. 'Doctor?'

'Mmm?' crunched the Doctor, doodling a shape in the little pool of ice-water on the table.

'What do you think that machinery back there was being used for?'

'I think someone's sick,' the Doctor said. 'Very, very sick. They're using that technology to try to heal themselves.' He pulled a piece of circuitry from his pocket and tapped his finger on a small raised design on its edge. 'What's this?'

'Just the metalworker's seal.'

'You recognise it?'

Dark looked at him strangely. 'Of course. All electronic components are marked to show they've been checked.'

'Definitely local, then,' the Doctor mused.

'But how could anyone ever learn to understand -' he lowered his voice - '*genetics*, let alone build it?'

'Perhaps they read an instruction manual. As I said, some of those parts have been factory made and assembled specifically for the dissection and splicing of genes.' The Doctor nudged Dark under the table and lowered his voice, glancing round to check they weren't being overheard. 'You understand that? Somewhere on this planet genetic equipment is being designed and produced quite legitimately, and our mysterious murderer got to hear about it and stole some of it. How did he know where to go?'

Dark shrugged.

'Wait a minute,' said the Doctor. 'If the Holiest have slapped a ban on genetic testing, how do they enforce it?'

'All things are known to the Creator. Anyone persisting in such unethical research would never know His paradise.'

'Perhaps that's not enough of a deterrent for some people.' The Doctor finished his doodle and gestured to it. 'Do you know what that is?'

Dark smiled, puzzled. 'It's the Diviner's seal, our mark.'

'It's a double helix, a simple representation of a strand of DNA.' The Doctor started speaking slowly in a monotone, like he chanting a litany. 'DNA stands for deoxyribonucleic acid, tiny chains of sugars and phosphates linked by bonds of hydrogen. They're the chief constituent of the *genes* that are located on the *chromosomes* that make up the *cells* of organisms all over the universe-'

'We're made of cells, of course we are,' Dark said. 'But as for the rest... what are you talking about, Doctor?'

The Doctor smiled, and his voice came back to normal. 'It's the stuff of life, Nathaniel. Endless streams of it coursing through your body. Now, do you think it's just coincidence that the double helix has become the mark of your religion? That the very concept of genetics is forbidden by a statute named in honour of the DNA bases?'

Dark said nothing, he just stared down at the watery symbol on the table as it became less defined, blobbing back into just a puddle.

'The nomenclature is doubly interesting, actually,' the Doctor enthused. 'Ever heard of the planet Earth?'

Dark looked at him blankly.

The Doctor shrugged. 'I need to do some tests,' he said, changing the subject. 'How close is this Diviners' depot of yours?'

'It's some way, I'm afraid. We've been running in the wrong direction.'

'Half the police in this city were after us,' the Doctor said, seeming to take personal offence at this. 'I'd say it was the right direction at the time.'

'At the time, true enough.' Dark half-smiled. 'I've been expressing the same sentiment in the last couple of days about my entire life.' He finished his drink and stood up. 'So, shall we try another direction?'

The Doctor smiled. 'Lead on.'

Anji could hear Etty screaming for Braga even before she entered the farmhouse, and she slowed her pace, heart sinking. This was going to be horrible.

She pushed her way in through the ruined front door, shuddered to see the bald man's body still lying sprawled there on the floor. He looked strangely peaceful, even with the livid gash scarring his skin. The image haunted Anji as she laid down the heavy revolver on the bureau, grateful to be rid of it. It confronted her again as she came back to the hallway and waited for Etty to come down.

She could hear the woman sobbing in an upstairs room. It was a heart-rending sound, and Anji wanted to go to her, comfort her somehow, but doubted Etty would welcome her efforts. Grief was a private thing, right? No one had been able to console her much over Dave. Not really.

She realised she was assuming little Braga was dead already. Lost in her own thoughts, she jumped when Fitz burst in through the door.

It was bad timing. Hearing the door slam, Etty came rushing down the stairs, wet eyes, rubbed red-raw, wide and hopeful. Finding Fitz standing there in place of her son, with a gormless smile on his face, made those eyes narrow with venom.

'He's gone,' she ground out. 'He's been taken by your sick friend.'

Fitz glanced nervously at Anji. 'That was no friend of mine, lady, believe me.'

'He's gone!' Etty screamed. Anji went awkwardly over to comfort her, but Etty brushed her embrace away with a savage swing of her arms and stood in the corner, hands over her face. 'He's gone,' she said more softly, her whole body shaking.

'You're sure?' Anji said softly. 'You checked outside?'

'I shouted for him, and he didn't answer. And he's definitely not in the house. And he wouldn't have gone out.'

'Are you sure? He could be playing, he didn't stay upstairs -'

'He's *gone*.'

Anji could hear herself saying the words just a few days ago, telling herself the same was true about Dave in the TARDIS mirror. The words not sounding real. Sounding stupid in her mouth.

'I'll go and see if the van's still there,' Fitz offered.

'Good idea, Fitz,' Anji said. 'Be careful.'

He limped across the hall and picked up the revolver. She wished she could go with him. She'd *told* the Doctor she couldn't help Etty...

Etty turned, a low wail starting up in the back of her throat, and put out her arms to be held by Anji. Anji felt herself well up and hugged Etty, as tightly as she could.

Fitz hobbled along the track to where they'd left the van, full of foreboding. There was nowhere to hide here: it was all wide, open spaces. He should've said he was an agoraphobic: he could've stayed in the farmhouse then, done the comforting for Etty himself. 'A stiff drink and an upper lip to match, my dear,' he'd have said, 'that's what's needed here.'

He knew it was no joking matter. To have something like this happen to your kid - that had to be the worst thing that could happen. Fitz remembered that when he was growing up, if he came home with a black eye or a split lip from the big kids picking on him his mum would fret and fuss no matter what she was going through with all her illnesses and her treatments. She'd be off up the road swearing at the headmaster. All her focus, all her fight went into looking out for him. Not that he'd appreciated it much at the time. In fact, it usually led to his getting another good hiding for being a grass. He'd actually ask them to hit him where the marks wouldn't show. Big act of mercy they'd shown him there, going for stomach and ribs.

Anger gave him resolve. OK, so he wasn't in the playground now and Three-One was a bit bigger than your average schoolyard bruiser, but the principle was the same. And Fitz wasn't taking another kicking, not from anyone.

The drowsy hum of electric engines started up. Fitz saw the hovervan coming towards him from the grasslands off the track. He wasn't wearing Seven's coat, so hopefully Three-One wouldn't recognise him. He could be anyone.

'Hold it, Three-One,' Fitz bawled in his best US marshal accent, pulling out his revolver. 'Get out of the car and assume the position.'

The hovervan continued its smooth glide towards him. What should he do? He couldn't shoot a tyre, for obvious reasons... Go for the windscreen? He couldn't discern if Etty's boy was sitting up front. What if he hit the kid? That would be just his luck.

'I said, hold it!' Fitz shouted again. Taking a deep breath, he stood directly in the path of the van, his gun clearly visible and pointing straight at Three-One's face. Would he fire? Could he?

The van slowed, and Fitz struggled to keep his grim expression in place. He realised he hadn't actually expected to be taken seriously.

'All right,' he said, accent still fixed since he didn't trust his own voice not to wobble. 'Now just let the kid out of the van, no tricks.'

The van bobbed closer until it came to a halt just twenty feet or so from Fitz. He waited. Nothing. Three-One was just a dark shape through the windscreen, occluded by the brightness of the sky on the glass. There was a smaller shape next to him.

'I said, give me the kid.'

A quiet hum as the window wound down. Fitz tensed himself for a confrontation. He was going to pull this off. No more kickings.

A shotgun appeared through the window.

Fitz stared at it dumbly for what felt like the longest moment of his life.

He would twist aside. He would dive towards the front of the van and get out of the line of fire.

See, he was moving already.

But the gun had already gone off.

# Chapter Fifteen

Fitz felt his eyes bulge as the shot slammed into his leg. He landed hard on the ground, whimpering. He crawled clear of the van and fired his own gun in the air, a warning - he was armed, he wasn't taking another kicking.

He glanced down at his leg, where a crimson stain was ruining his corduroys. He wasn't going to be *giving* any kickings for a while, either, that was for sure. He waited for the van door to open, convinced it would come at any moment, followed by the dread footsteps of his assassin coming for the final shot.

*Please, God, no. You're up there, you've got no excuses.*

Fitz fired the gun again, winging the top of the van, closing his eyes in case it ricocheted off again and hit him somewhere else. Just push off, Fitz thought. You win, you got the kid, now just go.

Three-One must've heard his prayer anyway. The van pulled smoothly away. Fitz watched it go, wondering about firing another token shot after it, but didn't want to antagonise the big man any further. He'd shot Fitz in his bad leg. Never mind, you've got another one, his mum would've said.

All her focus, all her fight, fixed on him.

Fitz looked over to the farmhouse, an impossibly long way away. Thought of Etty inside, desolate, desperate. He'd loused up. Big surprise.

Trying not to look at his leg, trying to pretend it was wet with the dew on the spongy grass he lay on, Fitz dragged himself up and began the long painful hop back to shelter.

Anji had sat Etty down on the couch with a steaming hot cup of whatever-it-was, and now she was perched uncomfortably beside her, holding her hand. She stared longingly at the blank viewscreen on the wall, wishing the Doctor would get in touch with some good news. Or just call to say hello, to remind her that she and Fitz weren't all alone on this mad world.

It had been so good to see Fitz, to realise he was OK, but everything had happened so quickly since he'd turned up that there hadn't been a chance to really say so. Now he was gone again, and probably back in trouble. Hadn't she chased after him enough back on EarthWorld? How long should she leave it *this* time before going after him?

'What am I going to do?' Etty whispered, staring into space. 'Does the Creator really hate me so much for what I have done?'

Anji dragged her attention back from thoughts of Fitz to the claustrophobic confines of the cold room. 'You mean looking after...' She broke off, awkwardly. 'After *them*? Vettul and...'

'My poor mooncalves,' Etty said, nodding.

Anji was puzzled. 'Mooncalves?'

Etty shrugged. 'Just our names for... well, the ones that are different. The Creator has turned His back on them, and now He has turned his back on me.'

Anji couldn't think of anything to say.

'What am I going to do?' Etty repeated.

Anji knew she had to keep Etty talking. If she was talking, she wasn't thinking so hard. 'Fitz will be back soon with news,' she said. 'Tell me about the mooncalves.'

Etty nodded. 'When my mother died seven years ago I came here,' she said distantly. 'It had to be either me or Treena, but she was married and... Well, I wanted to get away from the City.'

'I loved the City,' Anji said herself, suddenly remembering with a stupid fondness her crowded trek into work each morning, each day dizzy with the rings and tunes of different phones and text-message bleeps. She still carried her mobile around with her. Useless now, of course, a relic, but a symbol of what she'd been, and the successes she'd accomplished in a familiar world.

She remembered she was supposed to be listening to Etty.

'...it's the family secret,' the older woman was saying. 'Sometimes our children are born monsters.'

'That's a bit harsh, isn't it?' Anji said. 'Like you said, they're just different.'

'There's no room for difference in the Creator's world,' Etty said. 'We're all of us born nice and symmetrical, with two eyes, arms and legs, and all of us able to tie our own shoelaces and feed ourselves and organise our lives...'

'There's no... disabled people?' Anji asked in disbelief. 'No Down's syndrome, or cystic -'

Etty looked oddly at her. 'What are you talking about?'

Anji remembered that she was supposed to be acting like a native. 'But... well, they're still people, aren't they?'

Etty looked at Anji suspiciously.

Anji pressed on regardless. 'And they must be worried about you. Should we go back and tell them about -'

'No,' Etty said swiftly. 'No, I'll explain in my own time.' She shook her head. 'They all get on so well with Braga. They're probably closer to him than they are to me.'

'Vettul seemed quite childlike in a way. How old is she?'

'Twenty-one years old. She's Ansac's girl.'

Anji nodded. This was a good subject for mining. 'She's lovely.'

Etty sniffed. 'She's the biggest monster of the lot with all she gets up to.'

'What about the others?'

'You're really not afraid, are you?'

Anji looked at her, puzzled. 'Why would I be?'

Etty took Anji's hand. 'Thank you for saying that. But there aren't many that think like you. Vettul and the others, they'd be killed if people knew about them.'

'That's why you keep them locked away here, never meeting anyone?' Anji asked gently. 'Surely you're exaggerating. Doctors must be able to help them, surely?'

'I'm not exaggerating anything,' Etty snapped, pulling her hand away. 'More than a century ago one of my ancestors took his child to a hospital to be *helped*. Her name was Annetta. She was malformed, and she couldn't learn things like other children. The first of the mooncalves. When the doctors saw Annetta they took her from my great-grandfather.' She paused. 'And then the police took *him*.'

'Took?' Anji braced herself for the explanation.

'Neither of them was ever seen again. They were both branded criminals and disposed of.'

'What do you mean, criminals, disposed -'

'They were the first and probably the only people ever found guilty of a category-G crime,' Etty said bitterly. 'And I think they were killed.'

'But that's... What do you mean, "category G"?' Anji was painfully aware that she was throwing Etty more questions than sympathy.

'The greatest crime that can ever be committed - according to the decree that followed, anyway. And carrying the harshest penalty.' Etty looked down at her lap.

'And the Creator allowed this?'

Etty sniffed. 'No reason was ever given for the deaths, no meaning implied. My family were questioned, sectioned, searched and scrutinised, but no conclusions were reached.'

Anji squeezed Etty's hand, and the next part of the story with it.

'When the next mooncalf was born, my family knew they must keep it secret. Another followed. They needed a place to hide them away from the world.'

'And so they came here, right?'

Etty nodded. 'This land has been owned by my family for generations. My great-grandmother agreed to harbour the mooncalves, even though she knew she was risking her life. After the deaths, she said she could never find peace with the Creator in life so she didn't care what would happen to her in death. She said the mooncalves could work here, those that were able, have a better quality of life, and never be seen. Not even by the Creator on his own doorstep.'

Anji didn't understand. 'But if He decides the meaning of life then...'

'When the first of the mooncalves died, no god spoke to him. My family waited for the Diviners to summon them, but none came. No one *ever* came.' Etty let a tear slide down her face. Anji watched it dangle improbably from her chin. 'And when my great-grandmother died, the Creator spoke to her. Said the land she'd tilled single-handed and the crops she'd grown so selflessly had fed many... She went to Him. She didn't want to go, even, but He took her.'

'But that's crazy,' Anji concluded. 'What about whoever looked after them next?'

'The same. Judged worthy by the Creator.'

'But if being just a bit different is the greatest crime you can -'

'I don't understand it.' Etty's voice was cold, but she was starting to work herself up again; Anji could see from that suddenly focused look in her deep-blue eyes that signalled the start of the storm. 'I only know that healthy children have got fewer with every generation. It is a curse, but one the Creator is blind to. I keep seven hopeless, helpless people in that barn. I've made myself an outcast for their sake.' Fresh tears came. 'And now my own fine, perfect little boy is gone because *I* failed him.'

'That's not true, Etty,' Anji said. 'You stopped that man from -' She bit her tongue.

'I killed him,' Etty said softly. 'So what's to stop his friend killing Braga in return?'

'They didn't come all this way just to kill anyone, I'm sure of it,' Anji said fervently. 'They had instructions, remember? They were after you.'

'Why?' Etty asked plaintively.

Anji sighed. 'I don't know.'

'*Anji!*'

Both women jumped at the shout from the hallway.

Anji felt her insides tense up. 'That's Fitz,' she said. 'Maybe he'll be able to -'

Etty cried out as Fitz staggered through the door into the living room, his trouser leg soaking with blood. All he was able to do was reach out to Anji and collapse on the floor in a dead faint.

Dark took in the Mission opposite, across the busy road. It was, in keeping with its area, a lot dowdier and less splendid than his usual office of work. The dull stone was dark with damp, and the double helix carved above its double doors held only a little more shape now than the Doctor's doodle in the water.

The Doctor strode confidently across the road, effortlessly judging the speed of the traffic and managing to reach the other side without having to alter his step. Dark followed more cautiously and then led the way inside.

It didn't take long to spin a story to the secretary on the door about office-space shortages and work overloads in order to gain access to a room with monitor, video controls and computer equipment. The Doctor immediately started to empty his pockets on to a table top, grinning with a schoolboy's glee as he started to construct something new. 'I'll just get this up and running, and then we should get a message through to Anji and Etty at the farmhouse.'

'Telling them what, that we've learned nothing definite whatsoever?'

'That we're working on it.'

Dark turned away with a shiver and left him to it. He slumped down in a chair in front of the monitor screen. He knew he would have to call in to Cleric Rammes back at the office soon, to explain his absence. But how could he even begin to explain anything?

Instead, he found himself pulling the tape of Treena's murder from his pocket and slipping it into the slot beneath the screen. Soon, the familiar grainy film was back playing to the same old audience in a different theatre. Offering no more clues.

'These things you say you're looking for, Doctor, the clues *you're* after...'

'Yes?'

*The camera is positioned to the right of the bank's entrance as you walk in, looking down from the ceiling.*

'Patterns in... DNA, you said?'

'That's it.' The Doctor sounded preoccupied. 'They're very small, so you have to know what you're looking for...'

*The resolution is poor; the screen seems to be buzzing with flies.*

'...and then be able to blow them up in size so you can see.'

*Oblivious, people go about their business, coming into camera shot, picking up reflected doubles in the glass partition to the left of them, before each couple vanishes from view again.*

Dark sat up straight in his chair. 'Forward search,' he snapped.

*Treena Sherat grabs hold of the gun wrestles with the robber. She is trying to stop the man from being shot, trying to take the gun away.*

The Doctor blithely carried on. 'Once they're found, I'm hoping the patterns will be able to –'

'Pause!' Dark shouted.

'It, or me?'

'Come here, Doctor!' Dark breathed. 'Look!'

Dark pointed to the left-hand side of the screen.

A beaming grin spread across the Doctor's face. 'Reflection.'

'A different angle you wanted, right, Doctor?' Dark said, grinning back. 'If we can isolate that visual area, clean it up, enlarge it and run the tape again with *that* as the focus...'

'Good man, Nathaniel,' the Doctor said, holding out his hand to shake. Dark reached for it but then exclaimed as the Doctor spiked the back of his hand with a pin.

'What was that for?' Dark asked in annoyance, sucking the little red bead that had risen.

The Doctor just crossed back to his table and tapped the pin on a small glass slide. 'We both have our work to do. You know, researching and developing all this equipment... must've cost our mystery criminal a fortune.' He looked up with a knowing smile. 'I don't know where he finds the money. Perhaps he robs banks.'

Dark felt a chill run down him, and set about transferring the tape of Treena's murder on to the computer drive. He spent a while fruitlessly dabbling with the software, finding out how painfully limited his computer skills were, until eventually he was forced to ask the secretary for help in searching out the relevant manuals that would explain the formulae he needed to enter. Was it his imagination, or was the secretary somewhat suspicious now of what Dark was up to? Suppose he contacted Cleric Rammes?

Dark should talk to him first. But what could he say?

The computer buzzed and ticked as it worked to clean up digitally the specified segment of the tape excerpt. It was going to take time.

Dark drummed his fingers on the desk. The Doctor sang softly to himself. He was doing something to the Holiest's fingerbone with a scalpel or something, but Dark decided he didn't want to look too closely. Other thoughts crowded in on him. Had the news of the explosion in the tenement block been reported yet? Was his description being circulated?

He punched in the access number that would connect to the

Mission, to Rammes's personal monitor. There was no point postponing things any longer.

The carrier signal wasn't taken up for some time, but, after a minute or so, Rammes's flushed face pushed into view on the monitor. But he didn't seem angry, foaming at the mouth with rage. He just looked tired, drawn, disappointed.

'Well, Dark?'

'I...' Dark sighed, unsure what to say or even how to look.

'What do you have to say for yourself?'

'I am working from the ancillary Mission today, Cleric Rammes.'

'I'm not interested in where you are calling from,' Rammes said, his tone still soft and reasonable. 'Perhaps you can tell me instead why you're not here, and why you failed to arrive at our Mission yesterday but saw fit to use its facilities all night.'

Dark kept his face carefully in front of the camera eye, so the Doctor wouldn't be visible behind him. 'It's quiet at night. It's quiet here. I couldn't face the main office, Cleric Rammes, I... I need to think.'

'Is this to do with the explosion, Dark?' Rammes asked suddenly.

Dark bit his lip. He knew about Badi Street. 'Explosion?'

'The one you were almost caught in. Yesterday.'

Relief flooded him as he looked down. 'Partly,' he said simply.

'Don't be ashamed, lad. I can understand that shock can do things to a person. Things that are out of character. But you must come to us if you have worries and doubts. You must come to us whenever you have feelings that scare you, so we can help you.' He lowered his voice. 'We've always watched over you, Nathaniel. We care about you. We'll *always* be watching over you.'

Dark swallowed hard. 'I... I just need to get certain facts straight in my –'

'You took the Grace woman's file, didn't you, Nathaniel?'

Dark's eyes snapped back up to meet Rammes's own, which seemed almost translucent on the monitor.

He knew his silence had given Rammes his answer.

'The Holiest wish to see you,' the older man said simply. 'Summons is for tomorrow, at noon, at this address.' He read out a street name and a number. 'We *can* help you, Nathaniel, help you to heal. Help you to feel whole again. Please arrive punctually tomorrow.'

Dark felt so terrified he could barely nod. The screen cut to black, the afterimage of his face ghosting on the glass. The image faded, but the spell cast remained unbroken, the fear fixed and real.

# Chapter Sixteen

Dark spun round to the Doctor, but he clearly hadn't heard a word, dancing around a strange sculpture of wires and components and muttering softly under his breath. 'Everything sorted?' he asked casually.

Dark stared at him for a few moments. Then the details of the exchange poured out in a panicked rush.

The Doctor didn't seem bothered, just thoughtful. 'Why don't they summon you right away? I wonder.'

'The Holiest sort and determine each tiny strand that binds our world.'

The Doctor blew a silver whistle that he'd produced seemingly from nowhere. 'Quoting from textbook, red card.'

How could the man be so fatuous? 'I just meant that they're immensely occupied with all the minutiae that governs our –'

'Then we must use our own twenty-four hours to match their industry.' The Doctor paused. 'Forty-eight Elmslaw Road? That sounds a somewhat prosaic address for the Holiest to set up shop.'

'The Holiest have no set workplace,' Dark said patiently. 'They move through towns and cities and countries, watching, assessing, advising.'

'I'm sure they move in suitably mysterious ways, while they're about it.' The Doctor nodded. 'So you know God's exact address but His right-hand men are of no fixed abode.'

'The whole world is their home.'

'What about the tools of their trade, whatever they may be?'

'Copies of the sacred litanies and doctrines are held in each of the Diviners' Missions for reference, if that's what you mean,' Dark said tersely. He couldn't help feeling a little frustrated that the Doctor was asking another round of simpleton questions instead of acknowledging the importance of this summons. 'Doctor, the Holiest never summon a Diviner. They consult with the Clerics, of course, but rarely in person. If they wish to see me...'

'It suggests you've rattled their cage,' said the Doctor. 'Congratulations, you're on your way to getting the answers you need.'

'But *they* will want answers from *me*,' Dark protested. 'I can't seek to interrogate the Holiest Council, it's absurd.'

'No. It isn't,' the Doctor insisted. 'The Holiest may be many things, but at the end of the day they are *people*. Flesh and blood, like you and me, with all their own fears and agenda. The only difference is that they know more than we do, and that's a balance we have to redress. And if they give you any trouble...' He threw something spindly and white from his pocket across to Dark, who caught it automatically. He shuddered as he looked down and saw what it was.

'Give them the finger,' the Doctor said with the faintest of smiles.

Hox came through the door to find Cauchemar lying half-off his single bed, being sick into a pail. The new woman, Eleven-Six, was standing stupidly beside him in the poky room, not reacting to the awful noise, or to the smell. Just standing there.

'Idiot woman, I told you to look after him,' Hox said, settling beside Cauchemar and supporting his shoulders.

'I gave him fruit,' said Eleven-Six slowly. 'When he asked for fruit.'

He looked at her critically. 'If this happens again, you are to go to him, hold him as I am doing now, and support him.' The sickness had passed, and Hox dabbed a thick streak of drool from Cauchemar's foam-flecked mouth, swatted a fly away. 'And you are to clean him like this, and help make him comfortable once more.' Hox eased Cauchemar's head back on to his pillow. 'Is that understood?'

Eleven-Six nodded vaguely, and Hox suppressed a sigh. He stroked his master's greying hair. It *would* happen again, of course. Cauchemar's condition was worsening with horrific speed. He'd seemed stable for so long, but now, just as all his plans were nearing completion...

'Ettianne,' Cauchemar muttered, his face pale and contorted with pain, dark eyes fixing his own. 'Is she here? Has she been brought to me?'

Hox shook his head. 'Something went wrong. The woman had help again.'

Cauchemar spat into the pail, his face back now in its habitual sullen set. 'She had help before,' he sneered. 'Who are these people?'

Hox shook his head. It was a poor time to be delivering bad news, but he knew Cauchemar well enough to know how angry he would be at the thought of his manservant keeping things from him. 'There's more, sir. Unit Two-Two-E-Two is dead, and apparently Unit Seven-Two-C-One resisted his conditioning.'

'Impossible.'

'The surviving unit insists that Seven acted against us, but you know what simpletons our steers are. I shall get to the bottom of things when he arrives in person, naturally. It won't be too long now.'

Cauchemar fell silent. All Hox could hear was the ticking of the ornate clock on the shelf. It was a real antique piece, and Hox had admired it and secretly coveted it for so many years. It had stood grandly in countless fine houses over the centuries. Now it squatted in these filthy lodgings, an unlikely reminder of past glories.

Cauchemar shut his eyes tight as if each tick of the clock were bruising him.

'This won't do, Hox,' he hissed. 'This really *won't* do. I must have her.'

'And you *will*, sir.'

'You understand me? I *must* have the woman beside me.'

'Sir, I –'

'Another setback,' Cauchemar moaned. 'I cannot afford delays.'

'There is some good news, sir,' Hox ventured, knowing now was the time, when despair was at its darkest, to lift his master's spirits. 'We now have Ettianne Grace's son.'

Cauchemar pushed himself up on his elbows. 'The boy?'

Hox nodded, relief flooding through him as a rare smile caught one end of Cauchemar's mouth and pulled.

'The boy,' Cauchemar went on. 'She named him Braga. She loves him, Hox.'

'Naturally, sir,' Hox concurred.

'If we have him...'

'We *do*, sir.'

'Then, she will come to us.'

Hox narrowed his eyes. 'It seems likely she will bring help with her.'

'Then we shall have to deal with that help,' Cauchemar said. 'I shall plan our next steps. And meanwhile, you must find two new subjects. I don't care for the details of what our steers have or have not done. If they leave our service, they must be replaced. Immediately.'

'Naturally, sir.'

Hox nodded, keeping the ingratiating smile firmly on his face. He dared not betray his dismay at the thought, even while Cauchemar's eyes were closed. Hox loved to plan precisely the actions he would take; to be so rushed like this...

'And Hox... I require further... technology. You must acquire it for me.'

'The matter will be attended to, as soon as it is safe to –'

'And quickly, Hox,' Cauchemar whispered hoarsely, sinking back down on the bed. 'Quickly. We must be prepared to act soon.'

'Of course.' Hox nodded, grateful the interview was over. He glanced back as he left the room, the door swinging shut on Eleven-Six as stiff and still as a mannequin, and Cauchemar as quiet as she.

Dark waited tensely in the office for the computer to finish its cleaning up and enlarging of the section of tape. It had crashed several times; it was constructed for handling simple data, so this level of restoration was clearly almost beyond it. The Doctor had taken the back off it and fiddled, and it seemed to be handling the work better now. But, bored with waiting for both that and for his own lash-up of technology to do whatever it was meant to, the Doctor had wandered off to browse through the old records. In the repository, endless files bulged with life stories and histories going back for generations, a celebration of millions of lives. All gathering dust here, in a mildewy building lost in the empty backstreets of the city.

He wondered where the story of his own nothing life would be stored following his meeting with the Holiest tomorrow.

A bright ping! from the computer brought Dark back to the present. An image began to load itself into the video frame, a succession of blue and grey lines building up into a picture.

'Doctor!' Dark called. 'In here.'

The Doctor opened the door and pushed his head inside. 'Progress?'

'Tape's almost ready to run, concentrating this time on the reflected image.'

The Doctor ignored him, peering instead at his experiment, quietly humming away to itself. 'Yes... progress indeed.' He looked up, and his face clouded as if he were grappling with something just beyond the periphery of his understanding. Then he blinked. 'How terribly interesting.'

'Doctor?' Dark enquired pointedly.

'Your records in there,' the Doctor said idly, shifting the subject. 'They're complete, right? A census of all deaths on the planet?'

'Of course they're complete.'

'I've been accessing them by year.' He drifted off, staring into space. 'Some interesting statistics are emerging, but I don't suppose you -' He suddenly pointed enthusiastically over Dark's shoulder. 'Look, the tape's almost ready to run, you should've said...'

Dark rolled his eyes and turned back to the screen. The square image was almost complete. He hit a button and it began to run, a jerky, awkward progression of frames. Another chilling variation on Treena's murder. Dark was relieved to find that, even after so many viewings, it affected him as strongly every time.

*Treena Sherat grabs hold of the gun, wrestles with the robber. She is trying to stop the man from being shot, trying to take the gun away.*

'Wait a minute,' the Doctor murmured.

Dark knew what he meant. There was something... *wrong* about the way Treena grabbed for the gun.

'I'll run that again.' The computer was clicking and buzzing furiously as it tried to comply.

'Can you loop it?'

'I think so,' Dark said, scrabbling through the manual.

'Quickly,' whispered the Doctor.

They watched it twice more. Then the Doctor brought his hand crashing down on the table.

'We've been missing something,' he said. 'The wood for the trees! Something vital.'

*The man stands still, reaching out a hand. There is a flash from the gun and smoke. The man falls backwards, he has been hit. Treena Sherat lets go of the gun –*

'Her face,' breathed Dark. 'When the gun goes off, she's not grimacing...'

'She's smiling,' the Doctor confirmed. 'Nathaniel, we've been seeing what we *expected* to see. But Treena Sherat wasn't trying to wrestle the gun away from that robber. She was trying to aim it, to bring it to bear on that man.' The Doctor jabbed furiously at the screen. 'At *him*.'

Dark edged the tape onwards, frame by frame. As the man was hit, full-on by the blast of the gun, he was thrown sideways. His face came up clear in the glass, eyes wide in terror and surprise, mouth twisted in pain.

'No.' Dark shook his head. 'Doctor, it can't be.'

'Oh, it is,' the Doctor answered. 'Absolutely it is. That's Derran Sherat.'

# Chapter Seventeen

'What are we going to do?'

'Frankly, Fitz, I don't have the faintest, foggiest bloody clue.'

Anji looked down at Fitz and forced a tired smile on to her face. She wasn't sure which had been the most traumatic - washing and dressing his injured leg, which was now lying gift-wrapped in bright white bandages, listening to his weird story of numbered nasties and brain-draining helmets, or discovering that he was wearing navy-blue pants with a large carrot on the front.

Hours must've passed, but the cool white vagueness of day still plastered the window unchanged.

'Where the hell is the Doctor?' Fitz muttered.

'He'll be in touch when he's found something out, I'm sure,' Anji said, wishing she actually was.

'I should be in a hospital, not some kid's bed in the middle of nowhere,' Fitz complained.

'And what hospital is going to take you? You don't exist here, remember?' Anji patted his hand and sat down beside him on the bed. 'It doesn't look too bad, anyway.'

'How dare you?' Fitz complained mildly. 'I blacked out from blood loss.'

'More likely from the sight of it.' She found herself unable to stop herself sneaking a masochistic glance at the carrot. 'A little goes a long way, so they say.'

The silence between them wasn't awkward, which pleased Anji. It really was good to see him. She supposed they'd come a long way since EarthWorld, and not just through time and space. It was doubtful they'd ever really have been friends if they hadn't been thrown together by chance - Fitz was from a time some forty years or so before her own, for Christ's sake - but she was starting to see there was more to him than the idiot persona he so often hid behind. And, most of all, right now it was just nice to kick back for a few moments, to feel safe with someone you knew, even if you had met them only a couple of lunatic weeks ago. To enjoy feeling that way while you could.

Anji looked around at Braga's room, at the box of toys, the computer, the drawings slapped up on the walls. Some crappy model he'd made of a bird, which doubtless meant the world to Etty, standing proudly on display. She bit her lip, not wanting to concentrate on what had happened, not wanting to start crying again.

'Etty's been gone a while,' Fitz said at length.

'Mmm. I think she went out to see to Vettul and the other mooncalves.'

'Mooncalves?' Fitz half-smiled. 'Funny. Haven't heard that word in a while.'

'I've never heard of it.'

'It was old-fashioned in my day. My mum used to call me a mooncalf. Someone who idles the days away...'

'No! You? Really?' Anji said in mock amazement. 'Quite sweet, though.'

'Problem is, it also means an idiot.' Fitz grimaced at her. 'Or a freak. Monster.'

'Oh.' Anji frowned, remembered her conversation with Etty. 'I could believe their cows were raised from mooncalves,' she reflected, 'but Vettul and the others aren't monsters.'

'Yeah, well. You can never judge by appearances, can you?'

The carrot on his undies returned to her mind unbidden. 'Hmm, guess not. Funny they should use such an "Earth" word, though, isn't it?'

'Well, maybe it's just the TARDIS's translation, and it's more tuned in to my wavelength. Scary though that thought is,' Fitz added before she could.

Anji shuddered. 'No, scary was dragging that bald guy's body down to the cellar. I kept... I was half-expecting him to come back to life...'

Fitz looked at her. 'The cellar? Out of sight, out of mind?'

'No,' said Anji.

Fitz looked embarrassed. 'No, 'course not. Sorry.'

Anji cast about for a change of subject, and remembered Fitz's earlier comment on Etty's whereabouts. 'Poor Etty. She wants to be alone. I didn't argue with her, to be honest, just told her we'd get her if anyone called. I mean, what can you say to make things better?'

Fitz shrugged. 'How about, "Could be worse, you could be shot in the leg too"?'

Anji ignored him. 'Whoever's taken Braga obviously wants to have some hold over her.'

'Maybe the plan was to take the boy all along,' Fitz supposed. 'I don't know, I didn't get the instructions the same way they did. Brain too tough, you see.'

Anji looked at him, not without affection. 'If it's had as much done to it as you say, it's probably not much more than a bag of slop by now.'

'Charming bedside manner, nurse.'

Anji screwed up her nose at him. 'Who did you say could be responsible?'

'Hox,' Fitz reminded her. 'Mr Hox or his boss, Mr Cauchemar.'

Anji sighed. 'They don't sound as friendly as Mr Howard or Mr Billy, do they?'

'What?'

'Never mind.'

There was suddenly a cacophony of banging on hollow wood, Etty rushing up the stairs. She was holding a piece of paper.

'I found this in the pocket of that man's coat,' she said urgently, pointing back down in the direction of the hall with one hand and waving the paper in Fitz's face with the other. 'What does it mean? Do you know?'

Fitz took it and read. 'Three-One-B-Four... Three-Four-B-Nine... Seven-Two-C-One...' He shook his head and passed it to Anji. 'Sorry, Etty. This is just a list of all the great unwashed and brainwashed. Their... well, just their names, I guess. Sorry.'

Suddenly there was an insistent ringing from downstairs.

'Phone?' Fitz wondered.

'The viewscreen,' Etty said, rushing out of the room.

'The Doctor,' Anji said triumphantly, flashing a huge smile at Fitz and following Etty down the stairs.

'Answer,' Etty shouted at the screen, and the ringing stopped.

The screen was still dark, black as night.

'Who is this?' Etty said shakily, clutching herself tight.

Silence.

'Who *is* this?'

Anji wondered if the thing was working properly.

Finally: 'Ettianne Grace?'

The voice was cold and crisp, slightly disdainful. Anji knew its type, had heard it chorusing from slickers in city wine bars and consultants in private hospitals. It was a voice that said, *Listen to me when I'm speaking. I know best, I know* what's *best, for you.* Booming out of the black viewscreen, it made Anji shudder.

'That's Hox!' came a shout from upstairs. 'That's his voice, the one who set all this up!'

The voice came again, drowning Fitz out. 'You are Ettianne Grace?'

'Yes.' Etty glanced at Anji, and Anji offered her a hand. It was eagerly seized. 'Yes, I'm Ettianne Grace.'

'We have your son, Ettianne. And, unless you do exactly as you're told, we are going to hurt him.'

'Please, don't,' Etty whispered.

'You have transport.'

'Yes, I have a travelcar.'

'You will come to the following location in Upper West Side at midnight tonight.' The voice went on to give an address that meant nothing to Anji but Etty nodded and muttered it over and over under her breath. 'You will arrive alone. We will be watching.'

'What will you do to me then?' Etty asked, sounding utterly broken.

'If you do not comply with these instructions we shall hurt your son. Hurt him so badly. Again and again and again...'

'No,' Etty said helplessly.

The voice kept repeating, as if it was on a loop. '...and again and again and...'

'Stop it!' Etty shouted. 'Please, I'll do whatever you tell me.'

'*...again and again and again and again...*'

'Please!'

The voice cut off.

The viewscreen was silent and dead.

Treena Sherat's distorted face was still flickering silently on the screen in the records centre.

'Her own husband?' Dark couldn't take it in.

'The man excised from your holy files, yes,' said the Doctor.

'It makes no sense... Why would she get her own husband shot?'

The Doctor shrugged.

'But Etty met Sherat at the funeral,' Dark protested. 'She's received letters, she would've known, she would've said something.'

'Yes, you'd think so, wouldn't you?' the Doctor brooded. 'I'm wondering just how much Etty really does know.'

Vettul and the others were waiting outside their home when Etty came up the track to see them.

'We knew you'd come,' Vettul explained.

Etty sniffed, refusing to be unsettled. If Vettul knew half the things she said she did then she'd already be looking after the mooncalves all by herself.

'I have to go away,' she said.

Instantly there was commotion. Douglass rushed over and clutched her as he had done in the barn, and she smoothed his silver hair to comfort him. Myra burst into tears, convulsive sobs shaking her tiny body, while Meesha and Sian pressed their heads together in their familiar mute display of misery. The only time Etty ever heard them make the slightest sound was the little guttural heaves from the backs of their throats when they cried. Murph looked about uncertainly, rocking himself in his battered old wheelchair cobbled together from bits of old farm machinery, not really understanding what was happening but sad because everyone else was.

'It's all right,' Etty assured them. 'Everything is fine.'

'It is bad to lie, Etty,' Vettul said softly, the only one apparently unmoved. 'You've always told us.'

Etty glared at her. 'Be quiet, Vettul.'

'It's Braga, isn't it?'

Etty let out a shaky breath and finally nodded.

Now Vettul looked sad, hanging her head on her long neck.

'Bad men have taken him,' Etty went on. 'And I've got to go and bring him back.'

'Why have they taken Braga?' Douglass murmured into her dress.

She rubbed the back of his head. 'I don't know, my dear.'

'How long will you be gone?' Myra squeaked.

Etty tried to smile. 'Not very long.' She paused. 'And, I want you to stay in the house while I'm away. Vettul will take care of you until I come back.'

Vettul beamed around at the others, who looked suitably astonished. Murph groaned and started to complain at the thought of Vettul being in charge, his hoarse voice straining to articulate the words. Vettul clipped him lightly round the head in reproach, and he burst into giggles.

Etty regarded them all, her other children, trying to keep herself calm, unhurried, wanting to leave them with no fears, no concerns. They mustn't be upset. It would be cutting things fine, but she could spend a little time with them now and still get to the City before midnight. There was time to settle them in.

'Come on, then, everyone,' Etty said lightly. 'Let's go to the farmhouse.'

Vettul started off at a clomping run, leading the way, but Etty called her back. The girl came up close, looking down at her serenely.

'Vettul, the man you saw, Fitz...'

'Yes?'

'He has been hurt. He's going to stay here. Anji wants to find her friend in the City. So we're going to have to leave Fitz here to get better.'

Vettul grinned.

'You're to leave him be, Vettul,' Etty said sharply. 'Stay away from him.'

'Why?'

'He's a stranger.'

'If he's hurt, I should look after him. That's what nice people do, you've always told us.'

'For goodness' sake, Vettul...' Etty struggled to keep control, gesturing to the barn. 'It's right that you look after the others, but Fitz is an outsider. There are different rules...'

'Different rules for us?' Vettul said quietly.

'Of course there are,' Etty said impatiently. 'You're different, don't you understand that after all this time? *Different*.'

Vettul took a light step back with her good leg, wide eyes dull and shallow. 'I know.' She paused. 'You've always told us.'

The girl said nothing more all the way back to the farmhouse. Etty reflected on how much easier things had been between them when Vettul had been a child. While all the others acted much the same as they always had, Vettul had changed as she'd got older. She really was different.

She was a woman, now.

Back at the farmhouse, Anji was trying to explain how the communicator worked to Douglass, who was looking at her in wonder as if she was some kind of angel. The others looked on, similarly in awe.

'Have I got this sussed, Etty?' Anji asked, breaking off her explanation, pointing to the controls.

Etty nodded curtly. She felt a twinge of ludicrous jealousy as Anji carried on, smiling and indulging their silly questions. For so many years Etty had been the only one... the only figure they would ever trust and love. And here was another *normal* person, one younger, kinder than Etty with her sharp tongue and her rules and restrictions. Anji could afford to laugh, to be soft. She didn't have to worry about raising them properly, or about their long-term welfare. No, that was Etty's task. That was what Etty did best. Worrying about other people's futures because she didn't have one of her own.

Braga had been her future.

'We must go soon,' Etty told Anji. 'Perhaps you should say goodbye to your friend. I'll take over here.'

It was an instruction rather than a suggestion. 'Sure,' Anji said a little awkwardly, and went upstairs.

Vettul came up quietly behind Etty. 'We'll miss you terribly,' she whispered. 'Can I sleep in your bed?'

'No. Meesha and Sian will share it.'

Vettul pouted, stamped her tiny, twisted foot.

'If you think you're so grown up now, miss,' Etty said, 'now's your chance to prove it to me.'

'Oh, I'll prove it to you,' Vettul said, with a sudden smile. 'I promise.'

Fitz sighed as he heard the smooth engine whine of Etty's car disappear into the distance. He wished he could do the same. He flexed his leg, and found it didn't hurt too badly. Truth be told, he had milked it just a little bit. But after his last run-in - or hobble-in, he supposed - he wasn't about to volunteer himself for any more active service for a little while. Anji lacked his experience in such matters, of course, but she'd bonded with Etty more than he had, and would be a calming influence for her on the long trip to the City. They could talk about woman things and stuff.

He sighed again. He could hear the sound of excited whispers and things shifting about downstairs. It wasn't restful. Anji had told him the mooncalves were all harmless, just big kids, really. And it wasn't as if he wasn't used to mixing with nutters, after all: he'd seen enough on visits to his mum in the hospital. And he'd been very pleased to hear that the mooncalves were under strict instructions to stay out of his hair, and generally avoid him like the plague unless there was something he really needed.

About a minute after the car had gone, Vettul was bending through the doorway to join him in Braga's room. Right.

'Hello, Fitz,' she said, enunciating his name as though it had fifteen zeds and smiling brightly.

'Er... Hi.'

'You are hurt.'

Fitz smiled bravely. 'Oh, it's nothing, really.'

'Perhaps I could give you something,' she suggested innocently.

'I've had some painkillers, thanks,' Fitz said shiftily.

Vettul nodded, watching him closely through her wonky eyes. Then there was a ringing noise from downstairs.

'Uh-oh,' Fitz muttered, swallowing hard at the thought of Hox booming out another round of threats.

'I'll get it,' Vettul said happily, and dashed from the room.

'Careful,' Fitz called. She was just a kid. Not normal. It wasn't fair for her to be terrified by a pint-sized maniac with bad hair.

Wincing, he got up and hobbled downstairs, swearing as his wound jarred on every step. He heard Vettul shout 'Answer!'.

'You're not who I was expecting,' came a very familiar voice from the living room.

Fitz quickened his stumbling pace.

'Did you want to speak to Etty?' Vettul was crouched in front of the screen, staring in wonderment at the flickering image before her, the others clustered round her.

'Yes! Yes I did! I still do. Where *is* Etty... or Anji?'

'Or Fitz!' Fitz proclaimed, wobbling towards the screen.

The Doctor didn't often look surprised, but Fitz was gratified to see his jaw fall open and his eyes swell to about twice their usual size.

'Fitz!' he shouted, distorting the speakers, and making the mooncalves squeal with laughter around the viewscreen. He leaned forward and seemed to kiss the screen and there was more laughter. Fitz laughed louder than anyone.

'Fitz, how are you, what's been happening?' the Doctor asked, almost bursting with excitement. 'How did you get there, where's Anji, and Etty? Is everything all right?'

The smile faded from Fitz's face. 'Uh...' He cleared his throat. The mooncalves turned as one to look at him, smiles wavering a little now as if they realised the party was over as suddenly as it began. The glare from the screen felt suddenly like an unwelcome spotlight.

'Fitz?' the Doctor asked again, expectantly.

'No, everything's not all right,' Fitz began with a sigh. 'It's bad news, Doctor, but at least you don't have to worry about shooting the messenger. Someone did that already.'

'Hello, boy.'

Hox watched uncertainly as Cauchemar, crouched on the edge of his bed, peered forward at the Grace woman's son. The muffled scream of the baby along the way had started up again. Hox had no fondness for children: helpless, idiot creatures, taking time and money and sleep, and giving back only love. A poor exchange. The men and women who passed through Cauchemar's machine were left little more than children, but at least you could make them do things. Speaking of which, his latest acquisitions, snatched from the rundown streets, would soon be ready to use. They would have a new Two, a new Seven.

Cauchemar spoke again, irritated by the silence of his audience. 'I greeted you, boy.'

'Where am I?' the boy asked. He was trying to be brave, but wasn't very good at it, sucking his finger and staring round nervously with wide eyes that shied away from their surroundings.

'You're in the big City now,' Cauchemar croaked. 'It's a wondrous place, full of sights and stories and struggles. It is a dark place of dreams, of adventures and madnesses. Around us in the City, good and evil tear each other apart every day.'

Braga said nothing. He was still just sucking his finger.

Cauchemar's voice was thick in his throat. 'You don't know me, do you, child?' The boy shook his head. 'No one knows me. Not even the Creator knows me.' Cauchemar placed a heavy hand on each of Braga's shoulders. 'But you should like me, Braga. I am... *good* with children. Am I not, Hox?'

Hox smiled and nodded. Cauchemar sniggered.

'I don't know you, sir,' the boy said, trying to be respectful.

'What of the Vanishing Point? Do you know of that?' Braga nodded, fearfully. 'It will be upon us soon, Braga. Very soon.'

'No,' the boy said in a small voice.

'It shall, oh yes, it shall,' Cauchemar assured him, an uneven smile creasing his face. 'And no one shall be saved. The stories are wrong, you see. *God* is wrong. Soon, this fabulous city, with its dreams and adventures and madnesses, will be aflame, and the flames will reach up to heaven, and the Creator will roast. There will be no room for life, not anywhere. *He* will vanish.'

Braga broke free of Cauchemar's grip, ran for the door. Hox barred his way, clamped hold of the boy's arm and twisted him back round to face Cauchemar.

'There's nowhere to run,' Hox said. 'Not from us. And not from what we're going to do.'

Braga squirmed and twisted to be free, so Hox threw him forward on to his face.

Cauchemar seemed to keel over himself, dropping off the edge of his bed on to his knees. Hox started forward, fearfully, but Cauchemar raised a hand to halt him, then lowered his head until it was touching the floor and level with Braga's.

'And this chaos, this beautiful end to everything... It isn't just me that will make it happen, Braga. Your mother will help. Your poor dear mother.'

'No!' Braga shouted, his voice choked with tears, as if in sympathy with the baby several walls away.

'She will, Braga,' Cauchemar explained patiently. 'She's going to come with me. She's going to help me end it for everyone. Even you. Did you know, she's coming for you now?'

Cauchemar looked up at Hox as if for official approval on this statement, and Hox nodded.

'She's passed our checkpoint. And she's brought someone with her, despite my advice to the contrary.'

Cauchemar whispered into the terrified boy's ear: 'Did you ever think your mother would kill you, Braga? I don't suppose you did.' He raised himself up and sat painfully back on the bed. 'I don't suppose just anyone can see what's coming in life. Not even the Creator can do that.' He laughed weakly, exhausted by his efforts. 'Only me.'

And me, thought Hox, dreamily. After all these years I can see through your eyes, Cauchemar, as easily as I can see through my own. All the anguish and the terror to come.

It didn't frighten him; what benefit did fear bring? Service was its own reward.

But, as the boy went on crying, Hox found himself wondering if he had ever felt afraid of anything other than Cauchemar.

His master was lying back down on the bed now. The boy had rolled over into the same repose in miniature on the floor, little hands clutched tightly over his red eyes.

# Chapter Eighteen

Sitting on a bench on a hill, almost one with the night in his black velvet coat, the Doctor looked out over the City, lost with his thoughts.

Anji leaned her head against the plastic window of the hovercar's passenger door. After an hour of driving there still wasn't much to take in beyond the twilight sky, which was smudged with autumnal crimsons and browns. It would make a fantastic shade of eyeshadow, she decided, and was surprised - and slightly guilty - that such a frivolous thought could occur to her at such a time of tension.

She felt guiltier still a few minutes later when Etty's stepping on the brakes shook her from what was becoming a promising catnap. Anji guessed she was just tired out. She felt she'd been in crisis mode ever since she'd got here, a mood as flat and unbroken as the horizon they were heading for.

The road - more a navigation tool than of practical use to a flying car - seemed to stretch out straighter than anything the Romans could've managed. The distant toadstools of tiny settlements were starting to appear more frequently, which hopefully meant they were getting closer to the City. How long till midnight now? Etty kept wanting to ask, but bit her lip.

There seemed little hope in Etty's face.

'What about Braga's dad?' Anji found herself asking instead. There, it was out. For a while now she'd been thinking about Etty and the way she'd been behaving. Here, perhaps, was one little mystery on this planet she could clear up.

Etty glanced at her, but her face was still emotionless. 'He doesn't know his father.'

'Does his father know him?'

Etty's habitual sniff made a particularly noticeable appearance. 'Knows *of* him. And that's all.'

'OK.' Anji turned her head back to the window. Fair play, this probably wasn't the best time to indulge her nosiness. 'Just clutching at straws, I suppose. Wondered if he could have anything to do with this.'

Etty shook her head.

Oh, sod it, Anji thought. 'Your sister's widower. Derran, was it?' Silence. 'He's Braga's father, isn't he?'

Etty kept her eyes on the road ahead. She nodded slowly.

Anji suddenly felt a good deal more awake. At least some things, it seemed, were universal: sexual intrigue and death, if not correctly-proportioned cows.

'Want to tell me what happened?'

Etty didn't answer, and Anji didn't push it. As the minutes counted down, a dark mass began to form on the horizon, like a low cloud. As it resolved itself further, Anji realised it must be the City, its lumpy skyline splashed with tiny lights, gradually coming into view.

'I was too young and too inexperienced to know better,' Etty announced at last, her low voice casual, drained of feeling. 'Treena was my younger sister. She met Derran when she was just eighteen and I was twenty-five.' A smile began to creep into her voice, despite herself. 'He had something about him - experience, I suppose.'

'Older man, right?' Anji nodded. 'Been there myself once or twice.'

'It was more than that, though,' Etty said. 'He was clever, distinguished, had independent means. He was a scientist... used to be a doctor. Someone you could trust. He sort of drew you to him. There was something *in* him, something that burned...'

Indigestion probably, Anji postulated, the sudden *Mills and Boon* turn upsetting her own quite delicate stomach. But then she supposed that if you'd cheated on your own sister's boyfriend you'd want to dress it up a little, make out how helpless you were to resist.

'Did you love him?'

'More than Treena, I think,' Etty said. 'But she was always the pretty one.'

Try competing with three sisters, Anji thought wryly. 'So when did it happen, before or after they were married?'

'They were married.' Etty paused. 'It started when Treena was having problems conceiving.'

'They wanted kids?'

'Yes. Very much, especially Derran. It was a real worry. Everyone in the family thought Treena's problems were a judgement on the mooncalves, but there was nothing we could say. Just had to hope. Derran used his connections, put Treena on some kind of special drugs to make her more fertile. She was sick with them for ages. Really sick.'

'So in the meantime, he came on to you?'

A pause.

'Said I reminded him of someone,' Etty said, her voice flat once more. 'Not Treena. Someone else, from his past. From a long time ago. His first and only love.' Etty scoffed quietly, but the scorn wasn't quite convincing enough.

'Good line,' Anji muttered.

'We had an affair, I got pregnant, it all came out.' Etty's voice was flatlining now. 'Treena said she'd never speak to me again.'

'And what about Derran?'

'He wouldn't leave her,' Etty said, her voice tinged with incomprehension, as if this was a difficult concept to grasp even now. 'She'd finally fallen pregnant too.'

Busy boy, Anji thought, wondering if she should've started this conversation after all.

'She miscarried again,' Etty went on, talking quite easily now, like a tour guide explaining the background to some minor exhibit. 'But my mother was ill, and my father wanted me to go, avoid a scandal, stay out of everyone's way where I could do no more harm.'

'And sent you packing off to the farm.'

'To atone for what I'd done. Deal with my decisions. Look after the mooncalves. Everyone thought Braga would be joining them. When he was born and he was perfect I did nothing but cry with relief for days.'

'But what about Derran? Sounds like he got off scot-free.'

'Treena blamed me, not him.'

'And he never came to see you again?'

Etty shook her head. 'It was like he was... content that we should be apart. Now that I had his child.'

'And you've had to bring up Braga entirely alone? Without help?'

Etty scoffed again, and this time the bitterness was entirely genuine. 'My family put all their energies into supporting Treena. It took six years but she finally had her baby. And then... then that was taken from her, too.'

'And they never found a trace of it?'

'Of her.' Etty shook her head. 'As I said, our children are cursed. The Creator will never watch over them. I...' She broke off, her voice drying in the back of her throat. 'I always knew having Braga was too good to be true.'

Anji squeezed Etty's leg. 'OK.' Come on, she told herself, say it with some feeling. 'It's *all* going to be OK.'

The last traces of fire faded from the sky as the night closed in.

*Of course, Nathaniel. Of course you must go home.*

Dark walked alone through the City, heading back to his apartment. He was cold and desperately tired. He needed to think - no, he needed *not* to think. To clear his head. To walk freely through the city, perhaps for the last time.

Now that the Doctor had found his friend, Dark wondered if he would just leave, go back to wherever he'd come from. But the Doctor had shaken his head.

*'I can't leave now,' he'd said. 'There's a mystery here.'*

The Diviners' Mission loomed overhead like a tombstone planted at the side of the street. Lights blazed in windows as the night shift sorted their way through inferences and observations, desperate to derive meaning and comfort.

*'File deleted,' Dark confirmed. 'But that can't be...'*

He thought of the Doctor, of the resolve on the man's face, superhuman in adversity. Even as they'd shaken hands at the end of this evening, he'd wished for a fraction of the man's power.

*'Here's my viewscreen number. If you need me, go to one of the arcades, use this access code.'*

*'Thanks. I'll keep working on my experiments here.'*

*'The clerk on duty...'*

*'He won't even know that I'm here. We'll meet tomorrow morning. I'll call for you.'*

A clock chimed, its mournful bell heavy with meaning. It was getting close to midnight. The realisation made him sick with fear, not just for Etty, if he was honest - even with all she must be going through - but for himself.

Tomorrow he was to appear before the Holiest Council.

'*Another day closer to Vanishing Point,*' Lanna had said when the bomb had gone off.

He wasn't surprised when he found her waiting at the travel shelter, and, from the look on her face, neither was she.

'Did you find the man you were looking for?' she asked by way of greeting.

'No, we didn't,' Dark said, shuddering at the thought of what they'd found instead.

'Suppose it just wasn't meant to be.' She pouted in exaggerated sympathy, her lips red and shiny like her skirt. Her jacket was light, and meant for summer days.

'You look like you're cold,' Dark observed.

'I *am* cold. Where's your friend, Holy Man?'

'Busy.'

'Oh,' she said. 'You're alone, then?'

Dark didn't trust his voice to say yes. He just nodded.

Lanna touched his hand, and he didn't flinch. They stood together, alone in the empty street. The fluorescents mounted in the shelter shone as coldly as the night air. Her fingers were faint warmth on his skin.

Dark's voice made a tentative return. 'I think I want to be with someone tonight,' he said, very, very quietly. 'Someone to stay with me until the morning.'

She kept hold of his fingers. 'I see.'

He looked down at the cracked pavement. 'I... I don't have much money, I'm afraid.'

She took his hand properly and they started to walk. 'It'll do,' she said.

'Fitz.'

Vettul's low voice through the door was grave as a judge's in the darkness, rousing Fitz from his uneasy sleep. 'Fitz, come quickly.'

'What is it?' he whispered.

She opened the door silently, and he wasn't sure whether she was in the room or still waiting outside it. 'I heard noises,' she said. 'From the stables.'

'That'll be horses, then.'

'No,' Vettul insisted. 'The horses are in the paddock. The stables are empty. I *heard* something.'

'Well,' Fitz said shakily. 'We'll take a look in the morning.'

'I'm going to go and see,' Vettul said.

'Don't be daft!' Fitz hissed.

No answer.

'Vettul, come back!'

Uneven footsteps trotting down the stairs.

Well, it was her lookout. What was he meant to do? He was an invalid. Even the Doctor had seen he was in a bad way, had told him to take things easy while he worked out what they should do next. But Fitz was worried, and had been ever since he'd said a reluctant goodbye to the Doctor on the viewscreen. Anji had gone with Etty to try to find the Doctor. She'd agreed she wouldn't come too close to Hox's meeting place, mindful of the threat to Braga's safety if she did. Fitz had tried to impress the importance of Etty's going alone on the Doctor, several times, but he'd shown little sign of taking notice. What if he went charging in on his white horse and got the kid killed? Would that be Fitz's fault, too, just like losing the boy in the first place?

And now, was he going to let some waif with dodgy pins go out into the night to face whatever the hell was out there?

Cursing, muttering under his breath, he changed stiffly into his newly washed clothes, which weren't yet properly dry, hobbled nervously down the stairs.

A lantern had been lit in the kitchen - a night light for Vettul, maybe - and he took it with him outside. The buttercup glow made little impression on the darkness.

Where were the bloody stables, anyway? Did she mean the building he'd crawled through to get away from...?

There was a noise up ahead, just off the track, like a door closing.

'Vettul?' he whispered, and realised she'd have to be standing on top of him to hear that. 'Vettul!' he called, shuffling forward.

Another thump sounded from the darkness, and a quiet shout of pain.

'Vettul!' Fitz shouted, breaking into a stumbling run.

A crack of light was allowed out by what had to be the stable doors. Fitz took a deep breath, grabbed hold of the cold iron handles, then flung them open.

Inside it was bright, he couldn't see. 'Nobody move!' he shouted; it sounded good, and if they actually obeyed, his eyes might have... time to... adjust...

There was only Vettul inside, kneeling on a blanket over the straw, clothed in a long white nightdress that came down over her big leg and twisted feet and spilled out over the floor like a milky puddle. Next to her, resting on two breezeblocks, was what looked like a portable gas fire, with several rows of tiny white teeth bared and burning blue and orange.

'Isn't that a fire hazard in a barn full of straw?' Fitz said, lamely.

'It is cold,' Vettul said.

'That's because you've got bugger all on,' Fitz replied. 'Come on, back to the house before you catch your death.'

'I'm staying here.'

'Why? What are you playing at?'

She said nothing, playing with her long auburn hair with bobbin fingers. She looked like a painting of someone beautiful that had gone subtly wrong somehow; as if the artist had been wearing the wrong prescription glasses or something. That said, there was definitely something to her...

'We should go back, make sure the others haven't woken up,' he suggested. 'Would you like my shirt?'

'No.' Vettul stuck out her pointed chin. 'But I would like you to take it off anyway, so I can see your skin.'

'Whoah,' Fitz said. 'Could we slow down a little here, please? What's all this about?'

Vettul paused, looked down, apparently embarrassed all of a sudden. 'It is not about anything,' she said quietly. 'How could it be about anything, or anybody? I am *nobody*. Nothing.'

Fitz let the door swing closed behind him and walked cautiously closer. 'Feeling sorry for yourself,' he diagnosed aloud. 'Well, that's OK. We all do it from time to time.'

'"We",' Vettul whispered. '"All". You speak as part of the world.'

'You're still a part of the world,' Fitz argued. 'You just haven't been discovered yet.'

'No one would wish to. I am deformed. I am ugly.'

'Are you fishing, here, by any chance?'

She laughed at him. 'Fishing?'

'For compliments, I mean,' Fitz said. 'Look, Vettul, if it helps, you're not ugly... I mean, you're...' He felt himself growing flustered. 'I mean, I'd never call you a mooncalf.'

'But I wait, all day, every day... I wait for something to happen to me,' she announced, almost slyly. She patted the blanket, an invitation for him to sit.

He weighed things up, decided his leg was killing him, and that the fire was warm, and that he would sit beside her.

'We both have bad legs,' she said.

'We're regular twins,' Fitz agreed.

'Do you love Anji?'

Now Fitz burst out laughing. 'That's a good one. Er, no. We're not together in that way. We're just friends.'

'Then are you lonely?' Vettul asked in her solemn voice.

'I used to be,' Fitz said. 'But I'm not any more. I met someone special. You saw him tonight, the Doctor.'

Vettul looked at him closely. 'I go to bed and dream of meeting someone special.'

'Well,' Fitz said, moving swiftly on. 'Anyway. The Doctor is my friend. And he makes friends very easily, so I get to meet people from all over.'

'You have travelled all over the world?'

'Oh, yeah,' Fitz said, thinking back with a face paralysed somewhere between smiling and sadness. 'And then some. I've been to some pretty far-out places.'

'I would like to travel,' Vettul said, eyes suddenly bright. 'Travel everywhere in the world, see everything I have ever read about or watched on the monitors, everything!'

'Maybe you will someday.'

'No.' Vettul shook her head as she spoke, a mannerism that reminded Fitz oddly of the Doctor. 'I will not meet people like you do, like *normal* people do.' She paused. 'I am *lonely*.'

She made it sound like a medical condition that needed spelling out to the layperson. It made Fitz want to hug her. Would that be such a bad idea? She was keen, clearly, after all...

He felt her arm slide round his waist, and awkwardly shifted himself aside. 'Er, Vettul...'

'What is it like to be normal, Fitz?' she said quietly.

'Normal?' Fitz looked back on his life, on all the things that had been done to him, and let out a short and bitter laugh. It was high melodrama, sure, but Fitz had never been shy of a bit of that.

'Normal? I wouldn't know where to start.'

As it turned out, she started it for him. Her arm snaked back round his waist, she moved closer and pressed herself against him. He found himself responding.

Alone on a bench on a hill, almost one with the night in his black velvet coat, the Doctor looked out over the City, lost with his thoughts.

It was an hour before midnight.

The City lights twinkled cosily in the dark like a billion birthday candles, speaking of security and family warmth, of love and everyday life. Things he would never know, never really miss.

But there was evil there in the City, in the shadows and quiet, and it whispered warmly to the Doctor. It wouldn't wait much longer. It promised adventure, rush and flight. The chance to be a part of real life.

The Doctor got up and started walking back towards the City, towards the lights and the darkness.

# Chapter Nineteen

'They said I should go alone.'

'I know. But I can't just leave you to it.'

'You must.' Etty looked far too calm under the yellow glare of the street lamp. Anji didn't trust this act. 'They'll hurt Braga.'

'They might hurt *you*.'

Etty smiled a fraction. 'And what could you do about that, anyway, Anji?'

Good question. The bad answer was, of course, probably nothing. Anji turned away, folded her arms, checked her watch. Ten minutes and it would be midnight here.

They'd pulled up at a building site, or a quarry or something. Huge digging machines lay abandoned by massive mounds of earth and rock. With their blades and scoops still raised high in the air on long metal necks, they looked like weird animals defiantly rearing up. Bright sodium spots in the distance spoke of the cluster of low outbuildings that were the rendezvous point. For now the two of them were huddled under the last street lamp in the deserted street by an empty building hemmed in with scaffolding.

'There has to be something we can do,' Anji muttered. 'There has to be.'

'This isn't down to "we",' Etty said. 'It's me.'

With that she turned and walked towards the outbuildings. Anji started off after her, then froze. She *could* follow, but what if she *did* get Braga killed? She balled her fists, indecisive, then turned away again and slapped her palm against the cold metal of one of the scaffolding poles. The pale metallic noise rang shrilly into the night.

A similar sound came back to her as if in answer.

Anji froze. She turned to check on Etty but she'd already been swallowed up by the thick darkness. The noise came again, a soft *ching*, someone knocking on metal.

'Who's there?' Anji whispered. Nothing moved in the stark

yellow light of the street lamp. Strange continents of rust sat in the orange sea of each pole, crisscrossing along the walkway. But no sign of anyone.

*Ching*.

The sound was coming from ahead of her.

'I'm warning you,' Anji said, 'stay back.'

*Ching*.

A footstep behind her.

*There's two of them.*

Anji shouted in frustration and alarm as she was seized round the neck and pulled backwards. Thick fingers stifled her scream. She thought her spine was going to break as she was dragged backwards, but she kept her balance, kicked out hard and connected with whoever was coming at her from in front. There was a muffled shout, but now Anji was down herself, face down in the mud, she couldn't breathe with the arm round her neck, with the dirt in her mouth and nose and -

'Get off her.'

A pause, a fraction less pressure on her neck.

'*Off* her.'

A whistling of air, a kung fu sound effect. Then the noise of something heavy trying to break through metal, and failing.

Anji saw the sprawled body of her attacker, unconscious.

'Really very stupid, aren't they?'

'Doctor!' Anji jumped up and threw her arms round him. Then, suddenly self-conscious, she managed to modify the movement into grabbing him by his lapels. 'Try to get here a bit sooner next time, could you?'

'Where's Etty?' he asked, gently pushing her away.

Anji pointed to the outbuildings. 'Doing as she's told. But where's...'

'Fitz?'

'No, there was someone else here, another one of those maniacs. I kicked him.' Anji pouted. 'I'm sure of it.'

The Doctor glanced about. 'I didn't see anyone.'

Anji bit her lip. 'Doctor, if they know Etty didn't come here alone...'

He strode off towards the outbuildings. Anji tore after him, glancing about habitually for any further attack from the dark. The Doctor suddenly paused, listening intently.

'I can't hear anything,' he whispered, 'can you?'

Obligingly, there came a noise to their right. Then a light flickered on in a window of some taller building, three or four storeys up.

Anji looked up at him. 'I hear a spider saying "Will you step into my parlour?"'

'Loud and clear.' The Doctor nodded decisively. 'Come on.'

Etty tried the door of the building hut but it was shut. This was the third she'd tried now, with no success. This had to be the place. Why didn't someone come to her? What kind of sick game was this?

She was so scared she could barely move, but she managed to walk round the building in search of another way in.

Coming full circle, she found the door was now ajar.

Her footsteps were hollow as she walked slowly inside. Every instinct told her to run but she kept on with a dread compulsion, as if in a nightmare. It was pitch-black inside. Anything could come for her here, she wouldn't stand a chance.

'Is anyone there?' she asked, her voice booming slightly in the little room, dreading an answer.

None came. Then she heard soft singing, a child's tune. Was it a recording or...?

'Braga,' she croaked, heading for the sound, deeper into the dark.

*'You brought people with you. You brought help.'*

The harsh voice seemed to be coming from somewhere close by. The singing had stopped.

*'We told you what would happen.'*

'Where's Braga?' she shouted into the dark.

*'Look in the next room.'*

She heard an electric hum and a pale-yellow shadow flickered close by as a light came on in the next room. Etty moved towards it, holding her breath, clutching her arms close to her body, tears dripping down her face.

The room was empty.

The lights went back out and there was silence again.

'Stay here, Anji,' the Doctor whispered at the doorway to the darkened building.

'What, you reckon it's any safer out here, do you?' she retorted. 'Forget it. You've got a shadow.'

'I should hope so,' the Doctor said, casting an anxious glance over his shoulder. He pulled out a torch and clicked it on.

They moved inside, shoes crunching down on stone and grit. The building was clearly unfinished: inside as outside, it was all concrete and breezeblocks.

'There are stairs through here,' said the Doctor, the selective view of the torch picking out stone steps coiling away into darkness.

'They're leading us upstairs so they can cut off our escape route down here,' Anji whispered.

'More than likely,' said the Doctor noisily, jogging off up the steps.

Following more slowly behind, Anji had time to notice the glimmer of torchlight on the fine wire stretched just across the top step.

Just before the Doctor swept into it.

She opened her mouth to shout a warning but only the boom of an explosion came forth. Everything was light and blinding and Anji was falling through air, the breath stamped from her. Then she was skidding through grit and debris.

'Doctor!' she screamed, as the world seemed to fall in around her.

The explosion shattered the windows of the cabin Etty stood in. She fell forward to her knees, a red flare slinging angry light at her.

Something close behind her cast a misshapen shadow. She rolled over, hands up and over her for protection. As the brightness faded she could see, hanging from the ceiling up by the window, a toy bear. It was Braga's.

What had to be a lock of Braga's hair was stuffed down the fabric noose, and in a daze she reached up for it. Her fingers came away sticky.

The fur of the bear was wet, matted with blood.

* * *

The Doctor woke, a loud creaking from above insinuating itself into his consciousness. His eyes snapped open. Blackness. The torch was still warm in his bruised, scratched hand, and he shone it upwards.

A supporting beam was giving way above him. In moments he could be flattened by falling masonry.

The Doctor tried to get up, and winced. His legs were pinned down, a joist had fallen and trapped them. Served them right, idiot limbs. No other part of his body would've so wilfully crashed through a tripwire. The far end of the joist had wedged itself against the wall just above the floor. It had actually helped shelter him from the pile of fallen concrete about him; otherwise his legs would be jelly in trousers right now.

'What a piece of luck,' the Doctor murmured happily.

Another ominous creak sounded from the ceiling.

'Anji,' he called. 'Anji, are you all right?'

There was silence. A trickle of concrete dust fell on his face, and he sneezed.

'Bless you.'

'Anji?'

A low moan. The creaking of the supporting beam above him nearly drowned it out.

'Anji, it's me, the Doctor. Are you all right?'

'No.'

Her voice was redolent with self-pity but not with pain. 'Where are you?'

'Under this building. Nice going with the tripwire there.'

'Anji, I'm so sorry. Do you forgive me enough to lend me a hand?'

She was suddenly serious, businesslike. 'Where are you?'

He shone the torch in the direction of her voice.

'OK, I see you.'

Anji was soon beside him. She must've been sent sprawling into the next room, which didn't seem quite so damaged.

'It's the joist there,' the Doctor said, gesturing. The loudest creak yet cackled demonically above them. 'Quick, before the roof falls in.'

'I can't shift it,' Anji said, panicking.

'You must!' the Doctor shouted, writhing his legs beneath the block of timber.

'Give me the torch. I'll try to find something to use as a crowbar.'

He passed it to her, and the light bobbed away, a giant firefly scanning the room. More dust and grit showered him in the half-light.

'I'll try this,' Anji announced, wielding a section of piping.

A sound carried distantly across to them. A shriek of pain, of distress.

'Etty,' the Doctor whispered. 'Come on, Anji.'

The ceiling cracked and groaned.

Anji heaved up on the pipe jammed in under the joist. 'It's not budging.'

'It will,' the Doctor said calmly. 'It will. Try again.'

'Oh, Doctor...'

'Again. Come *on*, Anji.'

Etty's wailing went on. A slab of concrete pounded into the floor beside the Doctor's head.

'Doctor -'

'I'm all right, Anji, try again. One - two -'

'*Three!*' Anji bawled.

And the joist shifted just enough for the Doctor to pull free.

In a second he was beside her, helping her up and out of the room, and in another second the ceiling was smashing down behind them.

They ran headlong through the shaking building, eyes fixed on the faint glow of the sodium lights outside. But as they reached the doorway, more masonry crashed down beside them. Anji was knocked sideways and cracked her head on the door frame. The Doctor lifted her up and swung her over his shoulder, sprinting forward as the entire building came crashing down behind them.

The din was incredible, the ground shook, but the Doctor barely noticed as he fell to his knees and held his friend close to him.

'Anji!' the Doctor whispered urgently. 'Anji, wake up.'

She ignored him. From behind her ear came a trickle of blood, berry dark in the torchlight.

He laid her carefully down on the muddy ground and shrugged off his black coat to use as a blanket.

'I'll be back soon,' the Doctor promised, and ran off to find Etty. Her wailing cry was like a siren, warning the world away from here.

Etty clutched the wet, sticky bear to her breast and slumped to the ground outside the building, her voice given out, her throat stinging and strained. She wanted to cry, but such a simple expression seemed beyond her. She just stared down at the note in her hands.

A shadow lurched forward at the periphery of her vision. A dark shape detaching itself from the night, coming towards her.

'Give me my son,' Etty hissed. 'Give him to me.'

'I can't,' the familiar voice said. 'Not yet.'

The Doctor came closer. He was in his shirtsleeves, looking powdery and pale in the sickly light of the lamp.

'This is your fault,' she said softly. 'I was meant to come alone. It's the end of everything, now.'

She passed him the note, saw his eyes scan over it.

TOMORROW WE DO THINGS PROPERLY. GO TO CORNER OF BADI AND DOWNS. WAIT MIDNIGHT TOMORROW. ALONE.

I WILL SHOW YOU VANISHING POINT.

WEAR THIS.

'This?' the Doctor queried.

Etty showed him a white plastic bag into which had been stuffed a sea-green shawl. 'So they can recognise me.'

'Not quite a white carnation or a bunch of flowers under the clock at the station, is it?' the Doctor murmured as he folded the note and put it into his trouser pocket. 'I'm so sorry, Etty.'

She eyed him coldly. 'For risking my son's life?'

'No.' The Doctor squatted down beside her. 'Because there are things I must tell you. About your sister. About...'

He trailed off as twin lights pooled briefly across Etty's face, looking at her curiously as if it were some kind of trick she'd performed herself.

'Headlights,' Etty said dully. 'Someone's coming.'

'Police?' muttered the Doctor. 'Of course, the explosion... We must get back to Anji.'

Etty felt herself stir a little at the girl's name. 'Is she all right?'

'We were both caught in the blast. She's hurt.' The Doctor stood up. 'The police mustn't find us here. There's too much to do. Come on.'

He headed off towards the huge mound of rubble that marked the fallen building, still dwarfing the surrounding structures, and Etty found herself following.

'Where is she?' Etty asked quietly.

'Just round here,' the Doctor said as they turned the corner of one of the outbuildings.

There was movement here, lights flashing. A police car was hovering, and there were uniformed people setting up lights and cordons.

Barely breaking step the Doctor dragged her down to her knees into cover. She almost cried out in surprise, but he held his finger to her lips. Then he used it to point ahead of them.

Much closer to them than all the other activity, two cowled figures stood over what looked to be a bundle of dark fabric on the ground.

'Anji?' Etty whispered.

The Doctor nodded. 'But who are those two? They're not police, or Diviners.'

Suddenly a powerful torch beam cut through the two figures. 'There's no one about here,' said a gruff male voice. 'No one hurt. Just her.'

The cowled figures said nothing. A medic crouched down next to Anji, administered some kind of medicine. The Doctor looked on worriedly.

'I'm going to take her in for questioning,' the gruff voice said, more thoughtfully. 'A suspect with shoulder-length hair and black velvet coat was seen at the crime scene on Badi Street, along with... well, with the one dressed as a –'

'Badi,' Etty whispered fearfully, thinking of the note. 'That's where I've got to –'

But the Doctor shushed her angrily.

One of the cowled figures was nodding.

'Take a patrol, Sergeant,' the gruff voice continued. 'Fan out over this whole area. See if we can find accomplices.'

'Oh, Anji...'

Etty could see the Doctor was torn between rushing over and taking on the entire police force to rescue his friend, and slipping away before it was too late. To see policemen checking round seemed suddenly so wonderfully normal, reassuring symbols of the world she remembered from her city days. Perhaps she *could* go to them for help, tell them everything. They would listen, they would take responsibility from her, there would be no more decisions to agonise over, no more...

What if Braga's kidnappers were watching her now, from the shadows?

*Midnight tomorrow.*

The Doctor was oblivious to her racing thoughts. He was staring ahead, staring at the cowled figures.

'The girl will come with us,' one of them said, in a voice that was reedy with age. 'She must answer *our* questions. Bring her to our transport.'

Without another word, Anji was lifted by two medics on to a trolley and wheeled away. The two cowled figures followed ponderously after her. A passing policeman's torch caught on something, a coruscation of gold light on a pale hand protruding from a dark sleeve.

A ring of some kind.

'The Holiest,' the Doctor breathed. 'Of course. They sort and determine each tiny strand that binds your world...' His voice hardened. 'Then what? They slip them round your neck?'

Etty looked down at the sodden bear clutched in her hand, the trailing noose.

When she looked up, the Doctor was already some way off, heading back towards the outbuildings, slipping into the shadows with a disquieting ease.

# Chapter Twenty

The viewscreen was chiming its alert as Fitz limped back to the farmhouse. He hurried inside, chilly fingers fumbling with his shirt buttons, and found Murph staring up at the blank screen, expectantly, saying 'Hello?' over and over. Hadn't quite got the hang of it.

'Answer,' snapped Fitz. Etty's face fizzed into view. She looked tired and tense, shifting about.

'Well?' Fitz asked breathlessly. 'What's happened?'

'Where's Vettul?' Etty demanded by way of greeting. 'Why didn't she answer?'

'She's...' Fitz was caught hopelessly off guard. 'Never mind her, what's happening? What about Braga?'

'He wasn't there.' Etty swallowed, sniffed. 'Things... happened.'

'Things?'

'Murph shouldn't be hearing this. Where's Vettul, Fitz?' she repeated.

'She...' Again, Fitz dried up, distracted by Murph gurgling with glee by his side. Murph tugged at Fitz's trousers, which weren't properly done up and almost ended up round his ankles. 'I think Murph would like a word.'

Etty smiled and said hello as patiently as she could. 'You should be asleep, Murph. Why isn't Vettul looking after you?'

'Vettul not here,' Murph said in his usual sheepish voice, looking coyly away.

'I don't know where she can be!' Fitz said pensively. 'Why don't you tell me what's –'

'She been outside with you,' Murph said helpfully.

'You *should* be asleep, Murph.' Fitz sighed. 'You little sod.' He felt his toes curling. 'Something came up, Etty. That is to say...' *Change subject.* 'Etty, you look awful...' *Nice going.* 'That is, I mean...'

'Fetch Vettul and make her put Murph to bed,' Etty said, her eyes staring hard. 'Then we can talk.'

'I'm here,' Vettul said casually.

Fitz hadn't heard her sweep into the living room. He couldn't quite meet her eye as he passed on Etty's request.

Vettul looked at the screen and nodded lightly, flicking her amazing auburn hair like a reject from some hairspray commercial. And Etty was looking at Fitz now the way a few girls' mothers had looked at him in the early hours of a Sunday morning when they'd never laid eyes on him before. He blushed as Vettul wheeled the protesting Murph away.

'It's not what you think, Etty,' he lied.

'Listen to me,' Etty said, her top lip curling down. 'Anji's been hurt, taken away to somewhere, to heaven knows where -'

'What?'

'The Doctor was nearly killed -'

'What do you mean, nearly killed? Is he OK? Where's Anji now?'

'Braga may have been hurt... and... And we've spent over an hour stumbling through the dark trying to get away from that wretched meeting place. I've learned such terrible things... and all the time, back there in my home, you... You and...' Etty looked away, unable to carry on.

Fitz felt himself losing his rag. 'Look, never mind me and Vettul. Would you please tell me what you're talking about? If my friends are in trouble - Where's the Doctor?'

'He's all right. He's trying to call the Diviner, Nathaniel. And he wants you down here.'

Fitz felt his heart sink. 'There? But how can I? I mean, my leg, and there's no car, and...'

She sniffed. 'He says he needs you.'

'He does?'

'You'll have to take one of the farm vehicles,' Etty said. 'Vettul will have to show you.'

Fitz gulped. 'But that journey will take me for ever in some old tractor.'

'You can be here by early morning if you hurry.'

'I'll get lost.'

'You've made the journey twice already. Now, get me Vettul. She has to understand which vehicle to take out. She's driven it before but I need to check she can show you the controls...'

'I'm sure she can.' Fitz spoke before he could stop himself. 'She's not stupid, you know. You make her sound like a little kid.'

'You listen to me,' Etty tilted her head to one side, her voice suddenly hushed like the headmistress from hell, disgusted with a wayward pupil. 'Vettul is still a child. She has a child's experience, a child's view of the world.'

'Because you won't let her have any other.'

'I don't believe this,' Etty spat. 'I look after her for most of her life, and you've spent how long - an hour? Two? Doing... doing whatever with her, and yet you know her better than I do, is that it?'

'I just take people as I find them,' Fitz retorted hotly, 'and if you hadn't hidden Vettul away all her life then maybe other people might have the chance to find her, too -'

'Oh, I know what you found.' Etty was livid now. 'Where did you look first, under her shirt? Where did you poke about next, eh? You found what *you* were looking for, you -'

'How dare you?'

It was a whisper colder than the wind outside, and it seemed somehow to fill the room. Vettul was back, just behind him. The way she seemed to just appear was uncanny.

Etty had shut right up, was practically panting for breath. Fitz found he was trembling from the confrontation. Weirdly, he felt that he and Etty were now the guilty couple.

'Vettul, there you are,' he said weakly. 'I've been trying to explain to her that you're not a child any -'

'You've been trying to excuse yourself, Fitz,' Vettul said sadly. 'Nothing else.'

There were big tears in her wide, uneven eyes, and her pointy narrow nose was running.

'I'll get the bale loader ready, Etty,' she announced. 'I know where the fuel is.' And she swayed from the room, thump-*thump*ing on her twisted legs.

Fitz glanced over at the screen. But Etty was gone. The pale, scratched face of the Doctor was glaring back at him.

'I think that's quite enough wasted time. Get here, Fitz, as fast as you can.'

'Is Anji all –'

'As fast as you can,' the Doctor repeated.

There was a dangerous look in his eye. Great. Now Dad was mad at him as well as Mum.

'All right. Where do I go once I'm there?'

'Meet me at the City Hospital. What time do you make it?'

'My watch is still set to Earth time, where it's coming up for...' Fitz rubbed his tired eyes. 'Four o'clock in the afternoon. That can't be right, can it?'

'Pretending it is, you should be able to get there by half past eight. Follow the signs from the main thoroughfare.'

'I'll do my best.'

Abruptly, the Doctor's face softened and he smiled. 'I know you will, Fitz.'

The screen went dead. Fitz stood alone for a few minutes in the darkened room, reflecting on the exchange with Etty, on all the clever comments he could've, *should've*, made if only he'd been thinking faster.

He shouldn't have said anything at all, of course.

Fitz went to find Vettul, to say he was sorry, and to learn how to drive a space tractor.

Etty didn't react as the Doctor placed a hand on each of her shoulders and steered her away through the polished stone of the arcade. Through the arches and colonnades she could see cars speeding by, normal people going to normal places. Late-night cafés and bars were humouring the last of their customers and the streets were littered with embracing couples and people heading for home, the looming prospect of the working day starting to sober them up.

'You shouldn't have shouted like that,' the Doctor chided gently. 'It isn't a good idea for two fugitives who've just displayed dazzling guile in escaping from the clutches of the police.' He gave her a faint smile. 'But then, I know you've been through a lot.'

Etty shrugged. The escape in itself had been harrowing enough, scrambling through mud, over fences, the little bloody sponge of the bear squeezing against her thigh in the pocket of her trousers.

Their backs against walls, or flat on their faces in mud hiding from patrols, the Doctor had kept up a steady stream of whispered conversation. He'd asked her about the people he'd seen with Fitz through the viewscreen, and so, for the second time that night, she'd told the story of the mooncalves. The Doctor had seemed particularly excited about the way the diagnoses had first been made at the City Hospital.

They'd made it from the building site into some near-derelict neighbourhood; the Doctor had stolen a car and they'd circled back round into the heart of the city. Then he told her what he'd discovered about Treena, and about Derran. It was too much to take in. None of the Doctor's explanations made sense, they weren't real answers, all they did was prompt more questions. Her head felt clouded with them.

So when she'd found out about Fitz and Vettul... here was something she could vent her spleen on, something that let her bring all her incisive force to bear. But she knew the Doctor was right - they couldn't afford to draw any more attention to themselves.

Shouting had made her feel no better, in any case.

'If it's any consolation at all, I understand something of what you're going through,' the Doctor said.

'You've had your child kidnapped by a madman, have you?' Etty snapped.

'Oh, yes,' the Doctor said quietly. He stared off vacantly into space, the memory clearly tugging at him. 'And I got her out, too.'

'Safe?'

'And superb.' He grinned. 'We'll get Braga back to you, Etty. We will.'

She stiffened. 'You don't know that.'

'We *will*. You must never give up hope.'

He was quite solemn and sad. Etty found herself softening a little. She felt she could trust him.

'Could you reach Nathaniel?' she asked.

'No,' the Doctor said. 'He wasn't answering. I need his help to get people organised. I hope he's all right.'

'The Holiest want him. Of course he's not all right.'

'Well, he won't be alone at any rate,' said the Doctor. 'I'm going to tag along and submit myself for inspection too.'

Etty stared at him in shock. 'But *you* weren't summoned.'

'Neither was Anji but they seem keen enough to inspect her. I think they might've taken her to the hospital.'

'Why? Because of what happened to Annetta and my great-grandfather?'

'Yes.' The Doctor's eyes were like blue pins fixing her in place. 'I think there'll be equipment there which will confirm that the Holiest have free access to the very technology they've forbidden. And Derran must've stolen the parts in that lodging house from somewhere.'

'Derran?' Etty whispered. 'Or the person he's working for?'

The Doctor smiled, the kind of smile she'd given Braga a hundred times when she wanted to protect him from some painful truth. 'Or the person he's working for.' Then the expression dropped, the smile became almost crafty. 'Or the person he's employing. Or his accomplice.' A pause, as he studied her. 'You thought he was special, didn't you?'

How transparent was she?

'He *is* special, Etty, if you care for the word. He survived a shotgun wound at close range. His would-be executioner was the woman who should've loved him the most. His file at the Diviners' Mission, every possible detail of his life and times, has been impossibly eradicated. He's a *very* special man - and a sick one. Sick in a number of ways.'

Etty took a deep breath. 'You think he took Braga.'

'Yes, I think he's our man. Or the person he's working for. Or the person he's employing. Or his accomplice.'

This time the Doctor wasn't smiling at all.

Cauchemar munched on yet another sunfruit while the radio played. He got through countless numbers of the sugar-sweet things each day. Rich in potassium, in healing proteins easily absorbed by the body, even one as racked and hopeless as his own.

***...another explosion has been reported in the Soma district of the City, at a building site where facilities for a new educational***

*initiative were under construction; police report no casualties but extensive damage to a...*

'The Holiest report no casualties,' Cauchemar muttered, his mouth sticky and full. He turned the radio off, and the constant background rumble of traffic far below filtered back into the room, together with the intermittent buzz of an idiot fly's attempts to break through glass to reach the smoggy space beyond it. The only other sound was the squelching of sweet flesh on his teeth and tongue, and of the baby crying down the hall.

It was nonsense, of course, this desperate shovelling down of fruit. There was allegedly some random psychological benefit, the feeling of helping his pitiful immune system to cope with his body's dissolution, but its effect would be so small as to be unmeasurable. Meaningless. As a scientist he didn't care to subscribe to such unquantifiable data.

It was a point of personal frustration to him every day that he couldn't bring himself to stop eating the sunfruits, even now he was actively planning for his death.

He coughed miserably, looking out from his small window over the city by night, and wondered where Ettianne would be, what she would be doing now, how she would pass the time until tomorrow midnight. The woman would be his again.

There was a respectful knock at the door.

'Come, Hox,' Cauchemar said.

His old manservant came through obediently, immaculate as ever; not just his three-piece suit and shiny shoes, but the idiotic expression he always wore to perfection, the suggestion being that he was always slightly preoccupied with trying to anticipate your next requirement before you had even thought of it yourself. Cauchemar had been amused by the presumption for the first couple of decades. Now the end was close enough to breathe over him, distractions like Hox made his air no sweeter.

'You're feeling better, sir?'

'Report,' Cauchemar told Hox flatly.

'We scared her as you suggested,' Hox said, putting down a digital recorder. 'She'll come alone tomorrow, I'm sure of it.'

Cauchemar nodded. 'And her... help?'

'There were two people with her, a man and a girl. The man escaped the blast with superficial injuries, and accompanied Ettianne from the area.'

'Escaped? What is he, a superman?' Cauchemar's thoughts lingered enviously on the fit, healthy form of this faceless man, until Hox went on.

'The girl was injured. She has been taken by the Holiest. She's... it seems she's due for cat-G experimentation.'

'There's something different about this person?' Cauchemar frowned, coughed again. 'How can that be? Who *are* these people helping Ettianne?'

Hox shook his head, his storm of wild hair rattling above him. 'I don't know, sir. We have found no information on them, no files in the Mission registry.'

Cauchemar ground his teeth. 'How can that be? Only I have the ability to eliminate the data files.'

Hox looked shifty. 'It's left us with an... issue, sir. Certain... equipment has been requisitioned for her examination. We've been unable to gain access to the parts needed for your own treatment.'

Cauchemar stood up, bunched his fists. 'What?'

Hox cowered back. 'The raid was planned for tonight, but there's been so much activity, interest, that we –'

'None of that matters, Hox,' Cauchemar spat, grabbing the old man by his scraggy throat and slamming him against the wall. 'You will get me those parts, or I will...' He coughed. 'I will...' Cauchemar felt his legs buckling under him. Suddenly Hox was his crutch, helping him back to the bed.

'... I will shout at you, Hox, and then I will collapse, it seems,' Cauchemar said bitterly.

Hox said nothing. He looked embarrassed.

'I am asking you to give me time enough. To keep me alive just a few hours longer.'

Hox nodded. He was suddenly back to acting his old unperturbed self, looking down worriedly at him. 'I *have* found replacements for the recruits we lost, sir. Programming can begin any time.'

'This takes priority, Hox,' Cauchemar whispered urgently, clutching the man's leg with feeble fingers. 'I *will* live to confront the Creator once again.'

Hox nodded reassuringly. 'We shall obtain the equipment you need. I guarantee it.'

'And once you have it,' Cauchemar snarled, 'you shall make that stinking place of healing our next target.'

Hox tried to take this in his stride. 'Sir?'

'The last random horror,' Cauchemar went on, 'before our final, concerted assault.' He peeled another fruit cheerlessly and pushed it into his mouth. 'Do you fear me, Hox?'

Hox took a damp flannel and gently padded it at Cauchemar's forehead. 'Naturally I do, sir.'

Cauchemar closed his eyes, thick mouthfuls of the tangy fruit slithering down his throat, and the spiralling buzz of the trapped fly seemed to tug him out into unconsciousness. He dreamed of the child in the next room, of playing with him, all the stupid games fathers played with their sons. He had fathered so many through the long years, invisible children, building up numbers... Searching all the time, looking into so many faces. Drifting away, becoming someone new, drifting back, dreaming always of catching that spark of recognition deep inside. *Her* presence, given back to him.

The fever was back on him, and with it the conviction that Ettianne Grace was the vessel within which Jasmine had finally surfaced. It was Ettianne, in carrying his child, in caring for it, who had dragged *her* out of sleep, of hiding. He had made mistakes before but it *had* to be Ettianne. Jasmine lived; her spirit was as invincible, as indefatigable as his own.

Ettianne's image swam before him now, mingling with Jasmine's, filling the room even as the dull ache filled his body, as the baby's wailing cry drifted back into his hearing.

Soon Jasmine would retreat back beneath, obedient to him always. And he would sink with her, and the world would sink with them.

# Chapter Twenty-one

Dark woke to find the sun hadn't yet risen. He greeted the news with mixed feelings; a stay of execution, or prolonging the inevitable?

Lanna's body had felt like a furnace through the night. He'd talked for hours, told her everything, and she'd listened and held him so close he thought he might melt, and finally he'd slept.

Her face was angular, all hard lines. He saw how thin her lips were without make-up, and yet they had felt so full when she'd brushed them against his. She never kissed, she said. She never normally kissed.

It had felt good, and right, being with someone in the darkness, for a while. But eventually their shared warmth had become uncomfortable, the night together a labour. The sheets clung wetly to him whenever he shifted. She didn't seem to be suffering. But, then, she was better practised at sharing beds than he was. Predictably, he found himself resenting her.

If he'd given her no money, would she have still listened? Or talked of her brother? The one who was lost in the explosion, who died so that while we may know our Creator we may never understand Him? Dark wished he could have the night again, and have her as a friend, a proper lover, not a service.

He wondered what she was lying there wishing for. She'd tossed and turned in her sleep and edged him over to the side of the bed, closer to the red numerals of his bedside clock. Monotonous pranksters, he watched them wink cheekily and become new numbers over and over. He spent so long staring at the clock that in the end the numbers reduced to abstract patterns, so much easier to deal with...

They hardened to crystal clarity when the banging on the door came. An hour had passed. He was cold.

Lanna had gone.

Dark jumped up in bed as the knocking came again, louder, more persistent. He imagined the cowled forms of the Holiest clustered outside his front door - they knew about him and Lanna, one more crime against him, and they'd taken her...

No. She'd just gone. He supposed that was what she did. Passed difficult hours with people she didn't know, then left them to it. She had to keep detached, just as he did, she'd said so, she'd told him.

He'd known that all along, hadn't he? He just hadn't really believed it.

'Nathaniel, you must be in, *please*.'

'Doctor,' Dark breathed in relief. He scrambled into a nightrobe and rushed into the hall to the front door. He supposed that in a way it was good that Lanna had left: he wouldn't have to face awkward explanations. Was there *anything* in life that could be simply explained?

'Nathaniel,' beamed the Doctor.

Dark stared at his visitors from the night in vague alarm. 'Doctor, I... what's been happening? How -'

'In a moment. May we come in? You'll remember Etty, I'm sure.'

Etty nodded to him forlornly. She'd been crying. She looked in a state, but somehow more beautiful for it. He had a strange compulsion to reach out to her, to hold her. It was good that Lanna wasn't here, he told himself, and felt strangely guilty for doing so.

'Sorry to come by unannounced. I hope we're not intruding.' The Doctor pushed past him into the little apartment, and Etty tagged along with him. 'I tried to call you as you suggested, but couldn't get through.'

'I'd turned the viewscreen off. I was... lying down. I'm sorry.' Nathaniel smiled awkwardly. 'Please, now, you must tell me everything.'

'Oh, I shall. There's lots to do before your appointment at noon.' The Doctor swept in to Dark's little apartment. 'I need you both.' He steepled his fingers. 'It's time to put plans into practise.'

Lanna was slumped miserably in the travel shelter. She wished now she'd said something to Nathaniel before leaving. But what was there to say?

She couldn't afford attachments. Not in any sense. Lanna told herself she would never see him again. Perhaps no one would ever see him again after noon today.

A noise made her look up. A smart car was buzzing lazily along the deserted avenue. Lanna couldn't see the driver through the tinted windows, but the car slowed down as it approached her. She straightened her clothes automatically, checked her watch. Time for one more, she told herself, and forced a smile in the direction of the car window.

The rear door opened with a quiet click.

Lanna nodded to herself, took a deep breath and sauntered over. Ignoring the tired nag of her face muscles anchoring the seductive grin to her face, she pulled the door fully open and slid on to the smooth leather of the back seat.

Then she saw what was beside her, and she screamed.

It was too late to get back out. The door slammed shut and the car pulled lazily away, leaving the street once again dark and deserted and silent.

Fitz switched off the juddering motor, and the din of the big green bailer's engine cut out into silence. He found his body was still shaking, even now the vibration had stopped, and his head was throbbing. Perhaps the space tractor would've been preferable after all. The hovervan had been like riding air - this farm truck was like driving a tank. He'd been sitting on a rattling plastic seat that had turned his buttocks into shrapnel for half the night, driving down weird roads and with no real idea where he was going, shivering from the cold night air under old Seven's coat. Still, he'd found his way. Now he just had to find the Doctor.

The City Hospital was a collection of concrete domes, nestling among the high-rises and towering toadstools of the architecture. There was only one car park and there didn't seem to be anything to pay, which was a relief. Now all he had to do was -

'Have you been waiting long?'

Fitz jumped up in his seat and whacked his head on the roof of the driver's cabin. 'Doctor!'

'You dozed off, didn't you?' the Doctor said reproachfully. 'Still, you made good time.'

'Good time? Well, I didn't *have* one,' Fitz said sourly. He grabbed the Doctor's hand through the window and shook it. 'Good to see you, Doctor.'

The Doctor grinned. 'And you, too.'

'I am happy to see you, too, Doctor. Since you have brought Etty's car but not Etty.'

The Doctor turned at the sound of the high voice, at an awkward landing from the back of the truck.

There she was, pale as a ghost in her long white smock, looking about herself and smiling, shaking. No longer in a world of her own.

The Doctor looked enquiringly at Fitz.

Fitz gave a sickly smile. 'Doctor, meet Vettul.'

'I have done, through a screen, remember?'

'She, er, forced herself on me.'

The Doctor raised an eyebrow.

'As a passenger, I mean,' Fitz added hastily. 'She wants to see the world.'

'Even if the world doesn't want to see her.' The Doctor nodded sympathetically. 'You really shouldn't have come here, Vettul. Etty will be worried. Who's looking after your friends?'

'Myra is. She is a little cry-baby sometimes but she is caring. And Fitz told me you would understand.'

Vettul was still staring round her in wonder. Jeez, if she felt this way about a car park...

The Doctor sighed. 'I meant in particular, you shouldn't have come here, to the hospital. It's the most dangerous place in the world, Vettul.'

'It is?' asked Fitz nervously.

'For people who aren't alike, yes.'

'For freaks like me, you mean,' Vettul said sourly.

'No,' the Doctor said. 'I'm afraid in the eyes of this world, we're all freaks. I think Anji's in there now and I think she's in danger. There are things we need to do, so come on.'

Fitz got out of the truck. Vettul strode up to the Doctor. She was tall enough to look down even at him.

'I am coming as well.'

The Doctor shook his head. 'It will be dangerous.'

Vettul looked at him. 'I do not want to die without knowing I have lived.'

'I don't want to die full stop,' Fitz chipped in, 'if that's of any interest to anyone.'

'Be sure to mention it to anyone you meet in a strange coat,' the Doctor said, turning his back on them both and heading for the main building. 'Now, come on.'

'Where is this Holiest doctrine of yours kept?' Etty wondered as Dark drove her along the gloomy avenues into the city.

'My superior will have a copy somewhere in his office,' Dark said, 'I'm sure of it.'

'How will finding some nonsense of the Creator's help any of us?' Etty grumbled.

'We have to have faith, Etty,' Dark said, keeping his eyes firmly on the road ahead. No, he was peering at the travel shelter ahead, studying it intently.

She didn't know why, there was no one waiting there.

They pulled up outside the Diviners' Mission. She studied Dark, sitting there trying to make out he wasn't scared, for both their sakes. None of this came easily to him, she was sure. And yet here he was, helping the Doctor, wanting to help her.

He smiled nervously at her and she found herself smiling back.

'Shall we?' he said, and she nodded.

Fitz looked down at Vettul lying still on the hospital gurney, swaddled in white sheets, an oxygen mask over her face. She was just an ordinary patient, he told himself, as if the occasional doctors and nurses walking by, haggard and uninterested, could overhear his thoughts. He tried to affect a swagger in his step. Yes, this was just an ordinary patient (on a trolley that hadn't really been found discarded outside an operating theatre) being wheeled through these funny low corridors by two ordinary if very good-looking doctors (who hadn't really stolen their clothes from a changing room) who were on their way to a ward to do the rounds, or something. They certainly weren't looking for a girl born on another planet or forbidden equipment of any kind, oh, no. Not them.

God, he could use a new leg and a kip - Whoops! He found himself catching himself every time he took God's name in vain. Just in case the Creator was somehow listening, and didn't like it. Brrr.

The Doctor read a name on the door of an office that looked promisingly empty and called it out, as you would to a colleague you knew well and felt comfortable with. He really was a pro, Fitz decided. There was no reply, so the Doctor opened the door and looked inside.

'There's a terminal,' he whispered triumphantly. 'I'm going to see if I can get a plan up and running.'

'What, a *new* plan?' Fitz said, panicking. 'We've barely decided on the old one, what are we -'

'A floor plan,' the Doctor explained. 'Stay here.'

Fitz did so, feeling foolish.

'I want to get up,' Vettul murmured.

'Not *yet*.' Fitz pretended to examine her eyes. It wasn't a hardship, he decided. 'If we can get into the data store, you can get up then, all right?'

A few moments later, the Doctor emerged holding a printout. He studied it intently for a few moments.

'Data store is on the second floor,' he said, showing the plan to Vettul, who studied it eagerly. 'Can you lead Fitz there? He's rubbish with maps.'

'I am not!' Fitz protested loudly. A passing medic looked at him oddly. The Doctor glared at him, and Vettul tittered through her oxygen mask. He could see how thrilled she was to be given something to do.

'Anyway,' Fitz went on. 'Any sign of where Anji might be?'

'There are a few possibilities. I'd better get started.' The Doctor crossed the corridor and bumped clumsily into a passing doctor, before apologising profusely.

'Nicely done,' Fitz said, deadpan.

'Thank you,' the Doctor said, opening his hand to reveal he'd just palmed a pager. He studied it briefly. 'Now you can contact me from any of these internal phones when you find something. Number's 176. Off you go. And be careful. I can feel...' He shivered. 'Evil. It's closing in, all the time. So close now.'

With that, he wandered off into the trickles of hospital traffic.

Fitz sighed and looked at Vettul. She wasn't smiling any more.

# Chapter Twenty-two

Cleric Rammes heard the commotion in the main office all the way from his office. Puzzled and annoyed, he slammed down the file he was studying and was soon striding down the corridor to see what was happening.

'I will not leave here until I get some satisfactory answers,' a woman was shouting, her eyes warning off any Diviner who tried to get too close. Rammes recognised her at once.

The excited noise and chatter of the rest of the office died away as his workers saw him.

'This kind of disturbance is entirely forbidden here, Miss Grace,' he said.

She spun round and looked at him. Her eyes were fierce and bright. 'So, you know me, then.'

'The outstanding elements of your case are under consideration.'

'Listen to you.' The woman was furious. 'I've never come to you with a case, with elements. I've come to you about *people*, people I loved who are dead or missing with no explanation. That's what I have asked you to *consider*, time and time again.'

Rammes narrowed his eyes. 'You well know, Miss Grace, that the Creator's Design –'

'Is never to be questioned? I should imagine that suits Him well.'

There were outraged mutterings from the office.

'The Creator is with you, inside you. To question Him you must question yourself. Ask yourself what you think you are doing here.'

She smiled at him strangely, in a way that was almost disquieting. 'I know *exactly* what I am doing here.'

'Your case is to be reviewed by the Holiest at an hour to be ordained,' Rammes said firmly. 'Go to the prayer halls. There are many who must suffer ignorance for now, while always trusting in the Creator.'

'We may feel Him inside us,' the woman said, her voice loud but trembling, 'but we see only *you*, Cleric Rammes. And if the Creator chooses to speak only through you... I cannot trust in Him any more.'

Silence blanketed the office as Etty began to walk up to Cleric Rammes.

'You are upset,' Rammes said. 'It is only natural.'

'And you are all hiding something,' the woman said. 'I suppose that is only natural, too.'

She pushed past him, her shadow, thick and dark on the wall, fleeting past as she walked quickly away.

'Stilson,' Rammes ordered, 'make sure she gets out of here, then find out how she got in.'

Everyone in the office was staring at him, disquieted.

'Get back to your work,' he barked.

He walked heavily back down the corridor, not allowing himself to dwell on the conversation. He pitied the Grace woman. She was inviting the worst form of judgement on herself. She would never reach the Creator. Never.

Rammes sat back down in his chair and looked surlily down at the file he'd been reading. The sallow face of Nathaniel Dark looked guilelessly back at him from an old photograph. Rammes had read the file again and again, looking for clues that would point to the whys and wherefores of Dark's spiritual dissolution. There had to be something...

The face staring up at him from the file was almost too guileless. It was a mask. It knew something he didn't and was laughing at him.

Rammes felt suddenly uncomfortable, kept looking round. Everything seemed still in place, yet he somehow expected to see someone else in the room.

'Do you have it?' Etty asked Dark, away from all the fuss, back inside the car.

Dark nodded, trembling, and pulled out a simple black wallet from the pocket of his robes. Inside was a computer disk. He held it as if it was going to explode at any moment.

'The Holiest Doctrine?' she asked dubiously. She wasn't sure what she'd been expecting but this seemed monumentally unimpressive.

'I think it must be,' Dark said. He smiled weakly at her. 'We got it. And hopefully the Doctor can get something *out* of it.'

He held out his hand. They smiled and shook on it. It felt good to think they might have achieved something.

Nathaniel suddenly seemed distant.

'You're thinking about midday again, aren't you?' she said.

'Quite a couple, aren't we?' Dark observed. 'Nemesis at noon, nemesis at midnight.'

Etty realised he hadn't let go of her hand. He saw her looking and self-consciously released it.

'That was quite a distraction you provided, anyway,' Dark added, forcing a smile.

'Is there anything else that needs stealing?' Etty asked. 'Because I could very happily go back in there and shout at your lot again.'

'We'd better get on with learning what's on this disk,' Dark said, 'at the records centre.' He smiled at her as he started up the car. 'Although I think it's probably best if you vent your spleen on the receptionist there *after* we've got a printout.'

'It should be the next room on the left,' Vettul mumbled through her mask.

'My left or yours?' Fitz wondered, his arms aching as well as his leg now, from pushing her along.

She flicked out a long finger and pointed in the direction she meant instead. There was no one about. Funny that. Who would go filing at six in the morning? He gratefully brought the trolley to a halt and peeped in through the door.

The room was lined with tall cabinets and, on a central table, stood six computer terminals.

Vettul was suddenly beside him. He could tell from the way her breath ruffled his hair.

'Any good with computers?' he whispered to her.

'I've used Braga's lots and lots. I should be able to run a simple search pattern.'

'That's a relief.'

They went inside and shut the door. 'You don't have to keep doing it, you know.'

'What?'

'Giving me things to do because you want me to feel good about myself.'

Fitz almost laughed. 'It's tempting to let you think that, but I actually asked because I'm rubbish with the things. All a bit after my time. So how about you stop second-guessing me and get busy, eh?'

She looked at him, amused, and set to work.

'What am I looking for once I'm in the system?'

He pulled out the piece of paper the Doctor had given him, carrying the date of Treena's death, and passed it to her. 'Try to find out the names of everyone admitted to Casualty on this date. Preferably someone treated for gunshot wounds who isn't this Treena woman.' He studied the filing system. 'Because I've got to find her in here.'

While Fitz started deciphering the way things were filed on this planet, Vettul stabbed uncertainly at the buttons on the computer console. She was trying to disguise her lack of confidence by pretending to be deep in concentration. Fitz had done that himself often enough. He remembered how he'd felt on his first few trips in the TARDIS, seeing the bigger picture for the first time. He'd almost gone to pieces. Vettul was handling this better than he ever could've. Then he thought back to the way she'd stared out Etty. This kid had something to prove.

'There's nothing,' Vettul said. 'No record of anyone with any kind of wounding except Treena Sherat.'

'Bugger. Still, at least it's information of a sort,' Fitz said. 'I can't suss this system at all.'

'There are some numbers next to her name.' Vettul looked at Fitz. 'Perhaps it's a reference to the files?'

'Vettul, you're becoming a show-off,' Fitz said. 'Go on, hit me with the numbers.'

She did, and the cross-referencing made sense this time. He soon found the file.

'Go and keep a lookout,' Fitz said, remembering belatedly that they could be discovered and shopped at any time. Vettul hopped over to obey while Fitz looked at the file.

There were some gruesome photos of Treena's corpse inside, from the mortuary. Fitz felt a bit queasy, was grateful they were only in black and white. He flicked swiftly through the file and found a whole section full of gibberish, of endless three-letter words made up of Ts and As and Cs and...

Didn't those letters have some kind of meaning?

Treena Sherat's file had been stamped, CAT G. Fitz puzzled over the definition for a while, then something struck him. He turned back to the gory photos. There was something wrong. The devil was in the detail. He checked the scrawled notes beside the pictures.

A day after her death, Treena had the index finger of her right hand removed. Why the hell would that be?

Fitz shuddered. Whoever had done it had never been found.

The Doctor was fast running out of patience, and, he suspected, time with it. The areas he'd noted as looking hopeful for harbouring strange secrets had so far proved laughably mundane. A gaming room, a new wing under construction, a storeroom...

He was practically running through the domed transfer corridors now, and hopping up and down with impatience inside the many lifts that sank or rose petulantly from floor to floor. People were looking at him strangely. Well, just let them try to stop him.

The penultimate place on his memorised map was labelled SCANNER STORE. It didn't sound particularly suspicious, but he couldn't afford to leave any stone unturned.

Finally he reached it. With a cursory glance to make sure there was nobody watching him, he tried the door.

Locked. Entry dependent on tapping the right code into a keypad set into the door. Promising.

Just then, the Doctor heard bleeps from the other side of the door. Now, that *was* promising. He just had time to dash round the corner before a furtive-looking medic peered through the door to check the coast was clear. He closed the door and tapped a four-digit code into the keypad.

The Doctor waited for him to go, then sneaked back and input the same code. Nothing happened. He tried it again, just as fruitlessly.

'Excuse me,' the Doctor yelled, chasing after the medic who was by now some way down the corridor. 'I wonder, have you seen a young woman lying around in the scanner storage room?'

The medic swung round, a look of horror on his face. Very promising.

'I'm so sorry, I didn't mean to startle you,' the Doctor went on as he skidded to a halt in front of him. 'Tell you what, just tell me the entry code to that room and I'll be on my way.'

'Entry code?' The medic looked flustered, and started glancing warily about him. The corridor was empty. 'I don't know what you mean.'

'You do,' the Doctor insisted, 'the code you must use to gain access to that room you just left.'

'Out of the question,' the medic said quickly. 'I can't possibly tell you.'

The Doctor considered this, forlornly. 'Oh.' Then he brightened. As the medic turned to go on his way, the Doctor grabbed him round the neck and twisted his arm behind his back.

'Tell you what,' he whispered in the man's ear. 'If you *do* tell me, I shan't break your arms and legs. How does that sound?' He steered the medic back the way they had come, back to the locked door. 'Actually, that sounds dreadful, doesn't it?' he continued. 'Imagine the sort of dangerous, desperate man that would even suggest such a thing. I should do what he says if I were you.'

The medic paused in front of the keypad, arm outstretched. 'But it's forbidden,' he squeaked. 'Category G.'

'What do you do in there? What have you done to my friend?'

'I don't understand. I just do as instructed.'

'Good. So open the door.'

'You're dead if you go through there, dead.'

'Then why are you hesitating?' the Doctor enquired. 'Just let me in quickly and have a good gloat at my expense later in the morgue.'

The medic pressed in the code. The door hissed open.

'Thank you,' the Doctor said gratefully, slackening his grip on the man's other arm. 'Oh, and just in case I do somehow survive, I promise I'll tell the authorities you struggled against me really hard.'

With that, he whumped the man's head against the door, and bundled him inside.

The door gave on to a darkened walkway. Checking the medic was unconscious, the Doctor walked cautiously towards the door at the walkway's end. The whole atmosphere of this place was different from that of the rest of the hospital, charged somehow with a weird energy. With mounting excitement, the Doctor flung open the inner door.

Then he stopped dead.

He'd found Anji. Or part of her, anyway. He could see only her face and her left arm. Her eyes were tightly shut. The smooth skin was stuck with the hooks and barbs of electrodes and hypodermics. The rest of her was hidden beneath a mess of micromesh sheeting, wires and scanners. Flickering monitors buzzed and flashed all around her, coding the same four bases into a billion tiny codons in a billion combinations. Coloured pens scratched records of unknown activity on to moving graphs, describing whole mountain ranges of zigzags.

An illuminated display flashed idiotically: *Category G, Category G, Category G.*

# Chapter Twenty-three

'Anji,' the Doctor whispered, taking in the mad technology around her, assimilating its function, wondering if he could shut it all down and take it all out without hurting her. 'Anji, are you awake?'

Her eyes snapped open. 'Doctor?' She looked at him as if she couldn't believe he was there. 'Are you real, or is this a dream?'

The Doctor considered. 'Do you mean, are we all the constructs of someone else's imagination and that any moment now our existence might end when that person wakes? Or do you mean you're not sure if I'm some kind of hallucination brought about –'

'You're real,' Anji said weakly. 'So no chance of my not aching so much when I wake up, huh?'

'Where does it hurt?'

'Everywhere.'

The Doctor studied the monitor displays. 'They're mapping your genome, and somewhat crudely.'

'What?'

'Cataloguing your DNA, sequencing your genes. Finding out how you tick.'

'Why?'

The Doctor whistled softly through his teeth. 'It's terribly interesting.'

'That's no reason,' Anji protested.

'I was simply making an observation. Your body is so quaint, Anji, depends on such laborious chemical procedures…'

'Thanks. You should tell that line to Fitz. Really gets a girl going.'

'The Holiest are doing this to you because they have no trace of you on file. On this world, everyone is accountable.'

'Accountable to the Creator?' Anji said.

'The Creator is the organising principle, and the people here are rather like your genes, plodding along, going about their business in a fairly mundane manner…' He started fiddling with the controls.

'Doctor?' Anji sounded uneasy. 'Why aren't you getting me out of this?'

'Bear with me,' the Doctor said, studying the information flashing up on screen. 'I've been wanting to run a few tests on you myself, and since we're here... Just a small poke into chromosome 13...'

'Doctor?' This time she sounded irritated.

'Hmm. I thought as much.'

'Care to share?' Anji enquired satirically, squirming now in her chain-mail harness.

The Doctor smiled. 'You know, only three per cent of human DNA consists of actual genes, the recipes for useful proteins that enable your body to function. The rest is all junk.'

'Ninety-seven per cent of my genetic make-up is junk?'

'Mmm. Junk DNA is the popular expression. Your body is choked with genetic gibberish. Pseudogenes, retrotransposons, LINE-1s...'

Anji seemed quite mollified by this revelation. 'But how come there's so much of it? I'd have thought that with evolution, natural selection or whatever...'

'The genome is a book that has written itself. It's the *product* of evolution,' the Doctor said. 'Humans are still a very remarkable genetic outcome. My personal favourites.'

'Gee, thanks,' Anji muttered. 'Well, as I wasn't born here I guess it stands to reason my genome or whatever is different.'

'I've done some DNA testing of my own,' the Doctor told her. 'In Nathaniel Dark's genetic make-up, human-comparable junk DNA accounts for one per cent. Just one.'

'That's just showing off.'

'It's as though someone has very diligently gone through and edited out all the rubbish, all the genetic relics and reverse transcriptase and -'

'You what?'

'Look at it this way: if the human genome is a book, then the genome of this race is more like the back of a cereal packet.'

Anji considered. 'Could it be just some kind of Diviner's perk? Like being a saint or something?'

The Doctor gave her a doubtful look, just short of withering. 'If I can get my hands on the Holiest Doctrine I hope to confirm it isn't.'

'But who could *do* that?'

The Doctor didn't answer. He began following a coil of wire away from the CPU that must be running the scan. 'The Holiest lack even that one per cent. Nothing happens inside their bodies without due reason.'

'And they're the ones closest to the Creator? Well then, that figures, doesn't it? The Holiest and the Diviners... Cleanliness is next to godliness, after all.' She winced. 'Doctor, please, this stuff really is uncomfortable.'

The Doctor followed the wire to a terminal and studied it thoughtfully. 'You haven't asked me what the one per cent of junk DNA left behind is for.'

Anji didn't reply for a few moments. 'It's their godswitch, isn't it?'

'Their what?' the Doctor said, taken aback.

'The thingie that lets them know the meaning of their life. When it's their time to depart, or whatever. It's encoded into there, right?'

The Doctor yanked out the wire from the junction box. 'Very good,' he conceded. 'It must also contain some kind of strange genetic entity that can actually *encode* experience for the Creator's reference, when keeping track.'

'But then it's not junk DNA, is it?' Anji said, clearly finding herself on a roll. 'It's got a purpose.'

'I said human-comparable,' the Doctor muttered.

Anji went very quiet.

The Doctor started working rapidly now, disconnecting leads and wires and gradually revealing Anji's body beneath. 'The godswitch, if you like, is located on chromosome 13 in Nathaniel. You have twenty-three types of chromosome, just as he does, and you have similar base patterns in exactly the same place.'

'I've got a godswitch?' Anji whispered. '*Humanity* has a godswitch?'

'Either the raw potential for one, or the relic of one long ago discarded.'

'No. You're making it up.'

'Keep still.' He began to remove the electrodes. 'The theological implications needn't be so staggering,' he explained. 'It could just be that the Creator, whoever or whatever He may be, just adapted the junk-DNA sequence, mutated it to fit His own requirements.'

'But it suggests that the people on this planet could be related to humanity, surely? Where are we, Doctor? *When* are we?'

'I don't know. Hold on, this might hurt...' She squealed as he removed the needle; it clearly did. 'The same natural phenomena that help keep this planet isolated from any alien visitors pretty much scrambled the TARDIS's navigational systems.'

'Isolated... Everyone's accountable,' Anji remembered. 'And the Creator works through everyone who has this stretch of DNA. Etty said that, when the first mooncalves died, no one came looking.'

'The mooncalves are genetically different from the norm. It wouldn't surprise me to find they have no godswitch.'

'How would that be?'

'You said yourself that everyone's accountable here.' The Doctor drew closer. 'But supposing, long ago, an alien arrived here. Got through against the odds, with a good deal of skill -'

'- and luck -'

'- just as we did.'

He disconnected the last of the equipment, and pulled back the micromesh blanket covering Anji. She moved her arms gingerly to straighten her simple hospital smock. Then she squeezed the Doctor's arm in gratitude. He bent down and kissed her forehead.

'Without that "strange genetic entity" of yours,' Anji reasoned, 'he'd be an invisible man.'

'But the DNA sample he left behind on his genetics equipment,' the Doctor said softly, 'is very garish indeed.'

There was a noise from the walkway behind the door, a furtive scuffling.

Anji glanced up at him nervously. 'I don't suppose that's some helpful porter come to give me my clothes back?'

The Doctor pressed a finger to her lips and crept over to the door. It was flung open in his face, sending him flying backwards. Anji yelled in alarm.

A small, skinny man in a bright-red coat with a black holdall was standing in the doorway, and beside him was a slightly shorter, far plumper man in a brown suit with wild grey hair.

The plump man looked first at the machine, then at the Doctor in mild surprise. 'I do hope you've not damaged that machinery.'

'Are you from maintenance, then?' the Doctor said from the floor. 'Only there's a hot-drink dispenser outside and it's run out of continental blend. Perhaps you could nip out and fix that first.'

'Doctor, I know his voice!' Anji breathed. 'You're Hox. The one who took Braga, who threatened us...'

'And you are the two people who've been helping Ettianne Grace.' Hox tutted, patronisingly. 'You've put us to a good deal of bother.'

'That's comforting to know.' The Doctor got up warily, rubbing his head. 'How did you get in here?'

'Hacking into the security overrides is no great difficulty to my master.'

'I thought you had the air of a butler about you. That below-stairs countenance, it's very quaint.' The Doctor pointed to a glossy black communicator clipped to his waist. 'Makes a noise like a bell, does it?' Then he smiled warmly at the man in the red coat. 'And you are...?'

'This is Seven Two-C-One,' Hox said pleasantly.

'Tell me, did you ever have a real name instead of a serial code? Who were you?'

Hox shook his head. 'He can't remember very much. Not since we did things to his brain.'

'They wipe their minds, Doctor,' Anji called, distraught, 'make them into homicidal maniacs.'

'We prime them with our own instructions,' Hox said imperiously. 'All the skills they need.'

'Not just hackers, then,' the Doctor said. 'You're butchers, too.'

Hox and Seven advanced slowly, unsettlingly.

The Doctor held his ground. 'If you can prime people with your own instructions, why come here yourself? For something only you can identify? Yes, of course. You've come for equipment to repair your master's machinery, correct?'

Hox's pleasant smile stayed in place but he said nothing.

'Your master being Derran Sherat?'

Anji reacted, but Hox didn't, still calm, still smiling. 'That is only one of many names he has taken,' he said.

'Which explains the hacking ability, and how your master was able to excise his Sherat file from the Diviners' record - along with a good many others, I'm sure.'

'You presume to know my master?'

Hox and Seven were still advancing.

'He's very sick, I know that.' The Doctor glanced over at Anji. 'His body's falling apart from the inside,' he explained to her casually, before turning back to Hox. 'He's lived for a very long time; his body's awash with telomerase.'

'Your words are meaningless to me.'

'Beep! Category G!' the Doctor piped up. 'I'm so sorry. It's a chemical substance enabling longevity of the cells... But your master's cells are badly mutated. How long has he been hunting for a cure?'

'My master *seeks* no cure,' Hox said, growing graver. 'He simply craves enough time to bring about... resolution. *Retribution*.'

'I'll stop him, you know.' The Doctor crossed his arms. 'Whatever he's up to, whatever he's planning, I swear I'll stop him.'

Hox seemed unimpressed.

'What does he want with Ettianne Grace? Well?'

Hox moved with unexpected speed. There was something in his hand; he was bringing it to bear. Suddenly the Doctor was falling backwards, shouting in pain, the air a thick gas around him and his eyes burning.

A fist smashed into his stomach and he doubled up, choking. He caught snatches of the confused scene through his watering eyes. Anji was shouting. She'd thrown herself at Hox, but he was stronger than he looked, and he threw her aside. She fell heavily against the wall.

The Doctor scrambled over to try to help her but was kicked hard in the ribs. He banged his head on the bed frame, right on the spot where he'd banged his head before. The world exploded in bright-red dots of agony. He tried to get back up but it was no good: he was too groggy. Hox and Seven weren't affected by the gas: they must've been given immunity, child's play for their master...

Something was beeping. *He* was beeping. The pager, where was it...?

Still reeling, the Doctor felt himself hauled to his feet and marched through to the next room, a storing area of some kind. A door in the wall loomed up before him marked KEEP OUT. No such luck - it opened and he and Anji were bundled inside.

Fitz was back pushing Vettul on the trolley. How long could their luck hold? He was getting increasingly funny glances from other doctors now, who must've noticed him pass by this way and that several times before. The excitement was wearing off for Vettul, too. As the hospital was becoming busier, she was starting to recoil from the sight of so many people all around her, overwhelmed. Swamped in the white blankets, her big eyes were constantly darting back and forth as if everyone who came close was a threat. So much for the big world outside. Be careful what you wish for, Fitz thought glumly.

Right now, he wished the Doctor would answer his borrowed pager. He'd tried calling a few times with no response, and was experiencing a familiar sinking feeling.

He wheeled Vettul into a new block, one that looked brighter and posher than much of the hospital.

'You might as well try it again,' Vettul whispered.

Fitz parked his trolley and crossed to the wall-mounted phone and dialled.

There was a very faint beeping from somewhere. Odd, he thought, and hung up. The beeping stopped.

Looking around to check no one was standing nearby, he dialled again.

The beeping was back. It was coming from the wall he was leaning against. But there were no doors round here.

The door must be round the other side, in the next corridor.

'What's happening?' hissed Vettul as Fitz jolted her back into movement.

'Progress,' Fitz whispered back. 'I think.'

He pushed her along, trying to count the number of doors they were passing so he could count them back the other side and work out how far along the beeping had been coming from. At last a left turn came, and another left turn from there. Now they were doubling back on themselves and so soon they should come to...

There were masses of doors set into the wall. Fitz tried counting along but soon got hopelessly confused.

'Which one can it be?' he muttered.

'Try calling again,' Vettul suggested.

Fitz disconsolately pushed her over to the nearest phone, which was opposite a door marked SCANNER STORE. Just as he picked up the receiver, he heard four sharp beeps and then saw the door swing open. A groggy looking man with a bump on his forehead staggered out.

'Promising,' Fitz muttered. He swiftly dialled. 'Hear anything?'

Vettul nodded. 'Very muffled. Coming from inside there.'

Fitz left the phone off the hook. Flexing his tired muscles, he pushed the trolley over to the man leaning in the doorway. 'You all right, mate?' he called as he approached.

'I was attacked,' the medic said.

'Aw, that's a shame,' Fitz sympathised. He didn't slow down. With an outraged squeak the medic tumbled back through the door as the trolley thwacked into him. Fitz then used the trolley to wedge the door open, shoving it through awkwardly over the medic's body to get out of sight as quickly as possible.

'You hurt him!' Vettul said, tearfully as she shut the door after them.

'You can't make an omelette without...' He trailed off. She really *was* upset. He started to feel guilty. 'Oh, come on,' Fitz said. He could now hear the beeping Vettul had picked up on outside. 'Isn't it obvious to you he's caught the Doctor and locked him up in there?'

Vettul shook her head miserably, getting up from the trolley and checking the medic's crumpled body. 'I think he will be all right,' she said, staring at him and stroking his face.

'Course he will,' Fitz said as he strode along the walkway.

He opened the door at the end cautiously. The beeping of the pager got slightly louder again. There was a funny smell in the air, chemicals and onions. He coughed, and felt his eyes stinging. The room looked a mess. There was a huge machine by the single bed, and by the looks of things it had been gutted. There were parts and components littered over the floor. This had been done by someone who knew what they were doing. The Doctor?

Something light came down on his shoulder and he jumped – but it was only Vettul's hand.

'The beeping's coming from in there,' she said, and crossed to the door. Fitz had to run to overtake her.

'I'd better go first,' he said. Bracing himself, he pushed open the door.

The room was empty, but the beeping was coming from what looked to be some kind of chemical store cupboard. Fitz warily turned the lock and opened the door.

'Yes!' Fitz shouted, and turned triumphantly to Vettul, whose grin was wider and whiter than the Cheshire cat's. 'We're putting the band back together!'

There they were. The Doctor and Anji, gagged and bound but still alive.

'Ladies first,' Fitz said as he crouched down beside Anji. She was squirming, trying to speak, desperate to say something. Probably to praise him to high heaven for coming to her rescue... He yanked off the strip of gaffer tape covering Anji's mouth.

'Turn that sodding bleeper off for God's sake,' she snapped the second she was able. 'It's driving me mental.'

Fitz grimaced and started searching the Doctor's pockets. 'Who did this to you? The medic outside, right?'

'No.'

'Oh.' Vettul shot a glance at him.

'Hox and some tame zombie in a red coat.'

'Bit of a way from Butlin's, isn't he?' Fitz stopped the pager from bleeping. 'Don't think I know one with a red coat.'

'I think he was the new Seven Thingy-Thingy.'

'You mean I'm replaceable?' He tore the strip of tape from the Doctor's mouth, too. 'How gutting.'

The Doctor didn't look very pleased to see him either. 'Fitz, that door said KEEP OUT,' he said accusingly. 'Can't you read?'

Fitz grinned. '"Dyslexics of the world, untie!"' he said, and got to work on the rope binding the Doctor's hands. 'Vettul, get Anji out of that lot.'

'Quickly, Vettul,' Anji added.

'Yes, if you wouldn't mind,' the Doctor explained. 'We're sitting on a bomb.'

Fitz's grin faded. 'What?'

Anji squirmed impatiently. 'This hospital. It's their next target. Nathaniel told us there had been a load of bombs going off in the city.'

'But a hospital?' Fitz was appalled. 'Sick bastards.'

'Hox and that poor unfortunate haven't been gone long, but the second they're clear they'll activate,' the Doctor said. 'Please hurry.'

Vettul's long fingers were more adept at loosening knots than Fitz's, and soon Anji was helping the Doctor get free. Vettul offered to go looking for Anji's clothes. Fitz offered to help Anji into them - then shut up quickly at the look he got.

'They must be stepping up their terror campaign,' the Doctor muttered to himself, before gasping with delight as his hands came free, and rubbing them to restore circulation. 'If only I knew what they wanted...'

He crouched down and pulled out a black sports bag from behind a box, while Anji moved aside some jars of chemicals to reveal a small black box: some kind of timing mechanism, Fitz supposed. Or perhaps it was the detonator.

'Get out of here, you two,' the Doctor instructed. Fitz nearly bumped into Vettul, who had crept back in brandishing Anji's clothes in triumph.

'Can you defuse it?' Anji asked tensely, getting changed again under her smock.

'It's pretty crude, actually,' the Doctor observed. 'Simply take out this wire and the pulse will -'

Just as he yanked the cable the black box blew itself apart, shattering glass and igniting chemicals. Fitz threw himself at Anji and Vettul, clearing them from the doorway as the broken glass came flying.

'Doctor!' he yelled back at the room.

The Doctor crawled out on his hands and knees, his face blackened with soot. 'See? Crude. What kind of booby trap was that meant to be?'

'One good enough to start a chemical fire,' Anji hissed as an alarm started piping at high volume above them. Sprinklers came on, and soon they were all wet through.

'Wait.' The Doctor scrambled back inside the store, and reappeared a moment later with the holdall. He waved it triumphantly at them.

'Are you mad?' Fitz shouted over the alarm, terrified. 'That's a bomb! Don't wave it about!'

'Well, Seven carried it here without any problems,' the Doctor said casually. 'I'm sure it's perfectly safe without the detonator.' Then he started shaking the bag vigorously. 'See?'

Fitz whimpered.

There was another, louder explosion from the chemical store. The flames were so fierce now that the sprinklers were as much use as tackling a bonfire on November the Fifth with a watering can.

'We have to get out of here,' the Doctor said, gratefully accepting his velvet coat back from Anji. 'We must stop Hox getting away.'

'He can lead us to Braga,' Anji said breathlessly, pulling on the last of her clothes.

'If you're in the market for good reasons for leaving, how about roasting to death?' Fitz pointed out. 'Not to mention what these doctors will do if they find Vettul.' She was clinging on to Fitz now, terrified.

The biggest explosion yet burst out from the storeroom. The ceiling blackened and sagged.

'Out of here!' the Doctor shouted. 'Now!'

Fitz helped Vettul to her funny feet. She looked at him miserably.

'I want to go home,' she whispered.

'Would you settle for the hospital car park?' he said, bundling her through the door ahead of him. 'It's a start, isn't it?'

Anji crouched over the medic, who was still lying flat out by the door. The dark smoke that had chased them from the room was starting to linger in the walkway around them. Vettul, the tallest there, stooped to keep her head out of the worst of it along the ceiling.

The Doctor was banging on the door; it wouldn't open. Fitz hadn't thought of that: there must be some kind of deadlock mechanism, and if you didn't know the code you couldn't get back out.

The Doctor crouched down over the medic. 'The code, man, what's the code?'

The air was thickening with smoke and fumes. Fitz felt the world turning hazy about him. Another explosion from the scanner room threw him to his knees. Vettul fell forward on all fours, hacking coughs ripping out of her. Anji was hammering on the door.

'The code!' Fitz heard the Doctor shout once more, as his consciousness began to doggy-paddle away into the darkness. 'We have to get out of here! What is it? What *is* it?'

# Chapter Twenty-four

Anji fell backwards as the door opened and was nearly trampled by a gang of fully suited firefighters as they piled into the walkway pointing nozzles and hoses in all directions.

'Man down!' shouted the Doctor, hauling up the medic and helping one of the firemen take him outside, away from the fumes. Of course, Anji thought, these weren't medical staff; they wouldn't necessarily know she was this world's Most Wanted. And, in all the smoke and confusion, surely they wouldn't dwell on Vettul's appearance. Vettul was trying to drag Fitz out of the way. One of the firemen was helping her.

Anji made some frantic hand signals. Come on, girl, cover your legs. Vettul noticed and did so.

A few moments later they were all outside. The Doctor was impatiently brushing aside some nurses trying to check he was all right, keeping the black holdall out of their reach.

'Clear the area,' the fire chief was shouting at a small, curious crowd gathering. More doctors by the looks of them. The alarms were still blaring; didn't these people know their fire drills?

'That woman,' the doctor in front said, pointing at her. 'And her accomplices...'

Whoops. This one and his little helpers knew exactly who they were.

'Stop them!' ordered the doctor. 'They mustn't escape!'

'Out of here!' yelled Anji.

Fitz, propped up on his elbows on the floor beside Vettul, looked at her as if she was asking him to swim the channel. He was haggard and pale and clearly not up to running anywhere.

The fire chief lunged for her, and Anji kicked him in the groin. As he doubled up, the Doctor dashed behind him and shoved the man into the crowd of doctors, scattering them. One of the nurses stepped forward, fancying his chances. In response, the Doctor assumed a ludicrous kung fu pose and squawked like a parakeet.

Miraculously, the nurse backed swiftly down, opting instead to help up his bosses.

'Come on!' the Doctor shouted. 'Anji, catch.' He threw the bomb-in-a-bag to her.

She clutched it to her chest, trembling, and slipped it very carefully over her shoulder. While she did so, Vettul helped Fitz up, and now the Doctor swept him almost romantically into his arms and led the way through the smoky corridor.

'There's an emergency exit this way,' the Doctor informed them; presumably he'd just casually memorised the floor plan while finding his way to her.

Sure enough they found an exit round the corner. The Doctor kicked the double doors open, triggering another alarm to add to the general cacophony. He grinned for a moment at Anji, seemingly particularly pleased by this. Then they were running out into the grey daylight across concrete, a loading bay of some kind. Soon they were in a car park. It had been raining; the ground was cratered with puddles. If Anji hadn't already been soaked through from the sprinklers she might've taken some solace in at least missing a downpour. Typical.

'Keep your eyes open for Hox,' the Doctor yelled, Fitz clutching on round his neck like a damsel in distress. 'Or the man in the red coat.'

'There are men with blue coats over there,' Vettul said, pointing.

Half a dozen security guards were running towards them, heavy feet crashing across the wet concrete. 'Great,' said Anji.

'At least they're not carrying guns,' the Doctor said.

'Peachy,' muttered Fitz, lying limp in the Doctor's arms. 'They can just bludgeon us to death with their truncheons.'

Anji looked at the Doctor. 'What do we do?'

'What do you think?' the Doctor said. 'Run!'

Anji was still sore and bruised from her experiences in the scanning machine. Her clothes were chafing on the track marks all down her arms, and she shuddered. 'Where did you park the car?' she puffed.

'This isn't the right car park,' the Doctor realised.

'What can we do?' Vettul moaned tearfully. She was tiring, fierce red patches burning both cheeks, soaked through and shivering in the cold air. And while she was light on her bare, gnarled feet, it must hurt like hell to be running so much and over concrete. 'Etty's car could be miles away.'

'She's right,' the Doctor said grimly. 'We'll have to take another.' He hefted Fitz in his arms. 'Fitz, hold your legs straight. Which is the bad one?'

Fitz pointed, but the Doctor was rushing him feet first towards the window of the nearest car like a battering ram. Fitz howled as his steel toecap smashed through the driver's window.

'Ah,' said the Doctor guiltily. 'That one.'

Anji reached through the broken glass and unlocked the door. The guards were yelling at them to stop - yeah, right. Everyone piled inside, Anji keeping the holdall steady at all times, and the Doctor yanked some wires down from beneath the steering wheel.

'Come on,' Fitz urged crossly. The guards were close now.

At last the car lurched into life, lifting crazily off the ground. The security guards scattered as the Doctor revved the engine and shot towards them. Anji could see one of the guards talking into what looked like a walkie-talkie.

'They're calling for reinforcements,' said Anji. 'Or radioing ahead to close the main entrance, or something.'

'Don't worry' the Doctor said, grinning wildly and gesturing with his head. 'They won't stop *that*!'

A huge hovering white vehicle, clearly an ambulance, was driving urgently ahead of them, its yellow lights flashing on and off as its siren shrieked.

'Not more alarms,' said Vettul, screwing up her eyes.

'And more guards!' Anji pointed out. Ten or more of the blue-suited figures were rushing towards them, and these ones *were* armed.

'Down,' Fitz snapped to Vettul, throwing himself on top of her. A bullet smashed through the window by Anji, and powdered glass stung through the air.

The Doctor sped at sickening speed round the corner and practically into the back of the ambulance. 'Hold on!' he shouted as they were buffeted in the ambulance's slipstream. There was another gunshot, and another.

'It's going to stop, it's going to block our way,' Anji moaned. 'I bet you, the ambulance is going to –'

It didn't stop. Suddenly they had cleared the hospital gates and were tearing off down the road, and the whoops of joy in the jolting car, Anji's included, were louder in her ears than any of the alarms had been.

# Chapter Twenty-five

'But what does it mean, Doctor?' Dark asked as the Doctor finished scrutinising the printout.

Anji watched as the Doctor put down the wad of paper and crossed to the window of the office. He angled his face to receive some of the watery sun now breaking through the cloudy sky, and put Etty, seated beside him, into shadow. 'It means I was right,' he said thoughtfully.

As ever, Anji thought wryly. He'd even managed to find his way to this Diviners' records place without taking a wrong turning. They'd parked the stolen car and fled through grubby alleyways on foot to reach here. The Doctor had recognised Dark's car outside and swiftly broken in so that Vettul could be kept out of sight. Then he'd picked up a stray hair from her dirty white dress - all he needed to run 'a couple of tests'. He'd stretched the long blonde strand between his fingers, and Anji was suddenly put in mind of the time she'd plucked the first white hair from Dave's head, promising to let him have it back when he started going bald as well as grey. Taking it for granted they'd be growing old together. Her heavy sigh had almost blown the hair from the Doctor's hand, and he'd scowled at her. Experiment first, she guessed, sentiment later.

Fitz had agreed to stay and babysit the bomb with her. Something was going on between those two, Anji was sure. She'd furtively asked Fitz, but he'd just winked and managed a cheeky grin: 'My old mum always used to say that if you see someone without a smile, you should give them one.'

Corny old rat.

The receptionist on the door had peered oddly at her (Anji just hoped her face wasn't up on 'WANTED' posters or something) but recognised the Doctor from his being there yesterday and summoned Nathaniel. He and Etty had been busy decrypting a disk that apparently carried the Holiest Doctrine.

When Etty had seen Anji walk in she'd simply got up and thrown her arms about her. Anji's arms were still bruised and hurting from the examination she'd undergone, but she'd hugged the older woman back just as fiercely.

While they were waiting for the final printout of the disk's contents, the Doctor ran his tests. He hadn't yet told Etty that Vettul was outside, and Anji hadn't felt quite able just to launch it into conversation herself. And, whatever he'd learned, he clearly wasn't going to share it with her in here. She'd waited in tense silence for the printer to finish chuntering and buzzing over whole reams of the form-fed paper.

'Recognise this?' the Doctor asked Anji now, passing it to her. It was all letters, the gibberish code of genetic bases again.

She didn't recognise it, of course, but for him to be asking her at all she had a fair idea what it must mean. 'It's the code for the godswitch, isn't it?'

Dark and Etty both looked at her oddly, but the Doctor nodded. 'What's the time?' he asked.

'An hour until noon,' Dark said, ashen-faced.

'We don't want to be late,' the Doctor said, patting him absently on the back. 'Come on, I'll drive us there. It'll be a bit of a squeeze for all six of us, but -'

'Six?' Etty queried. 'I thought it was just your friend Fitz outside waiting for us?'

'Ah... Surprise!' the Doctor said, with a hopeful smile.

Anji winced.

Hox watched as Cauchemar concentrated, feverishly assembling the pieces of machinery into some mysterious structure that might make him well again, if only for a short time. Cauchemar's hands kept slipping as if they were cold and numb, though it was overpoweringly hot in his room. His breathing was ragged; it seemed to chafe his throat.

Did he know of Hox's failure? Hox knew he should say something but...

'The hospital still stands,' Cauchemar snapped suddenly, without looking up.

There it was, then.

'It does, sir,' Hox conceded. 'There was a fire, and some damage to –'

'Some minor damage and no lives lost.' Cauchemar spat in Hox's face, and Hox tried to keep his expression neutral as the slime slid down his cheek. 'You can explain your failure, naturally.'

'It can only have been the Doctor, sir,' Hox said, beginning to babble. 'There was nothing wrong with the bomb, and he was tied up, on top of it, there was no way he could've freed himself –'

Cauchemar's voice was low, reasonable. 'Of course he freed himself. The news reports are full of the escape from the hospital. There was a chase, but he and his accomplices evaded capture. A mystery man...' He scoffed. 'You know they're blaming him for the bombings, don't you? *Him*. Circulating descriptions, putting on a real manhunt... for *him*.'

'A useful distraction, sir,' Hox ventured.

'This hour is mine!' thundered Cauchemar, half-rising. 'Not his! Mine!' He quietened again, fell back in his seat. 'I will not have it taken from me, Hox. I will see the Doctor dead before I am. I will kill him, Hox, like I killed in the old days.' He pushed away the tools and sunfruit on his table and reached for his stubby old blunt knife. 'All the old touches,' he muttered, turning it sulkily in his awkward hands.

Hox nodded enthusiastically. 'But first we must make you well enough for the ordeal still to –'

Cauchemar interrupted him, slapping his palm down hard on the table. When he lifted it the corpse of a fat fly was crushed against his yellowing fingers.

'They smell the sickness,' Cauchemar said, eyeing the fly's crispy black body almost with fondness. 'They come to the corruption. They cannot help but be attracted. It is the same with this Doctor, I am sure.'

'He knows you are unwell. He means to stop you.'

'He means nothing.' Cauchemar wiped his hands. 'He is an insect before me. When I am stronger, I shall crush *him*.'

Hox nodded enthusiastically. 'I *did* get you all the parts you need?'

'You brought me enough,' said Cauchemar grudgingly. 'The machine won't be as comprehensive as that at Badi Street, but then it doesn't need to be.' He chuckled mirthlessly. 'I am beyond all cure. But I can patch myself up, eh, Hox? If we dig deep enough I'm sure we can find a vein in me somewhere. Isn't that right?'

'Of course, sir,' Hox said nervously. 'To save you unnecessary travel I shall fetch the healing apparatus to your rooms.'

'Do so,' Cauchemar nodded. There was a long pause. 'Is there time before tomorrow to have this Doctor found and brought to me?'

'I'll instruct a watch to be taken,' Hox said.

'You will hunt for him yourself.'

Hox paused awkwardly. 'You have not forgotten, sir, that Ettianne Grace is to be collected at midnight and taken to you...?'

'I think of little else,' Cauchemar croaked. 'But she will come alone - you can send our steers to take her. I know her. Know what she would do for the boy. And now *she* knows who is responsible for holding him...' He breathed in sharply, either in pain or in painful remembrance. 'We have been alone together before. She shall come to me alone again, one last time.'

Hox went then to fetch the healing apparatus. Cauchemar stared in a rapture into space, his memories spinning around him just as the flies did.

Outside the records centre, it was obvious Etty was speechless with rage to find Vettul waiting in the car with Fitz.

'Would you keep it that way, please?' the Doctor asked. 'I'm sure Nathaniel would appreciate some quiet and calm to compose himself. Right, Nathaniel?'

Dark was staring at Vettul. 'Who is this? She... she's...'

'She's what?' Fitz said heavily, challenging him.

'She's...' Dark shook his head, wearily, holding up his hands in apology. 'Nothing.'

'That's right,' Vettul said quietly.

'That is *not* right,' Fitz said. 'I'm Fitz, by the way,' he said warily, but shook Dark's hand anyway.

They all arranged themselves in the car. Etty planted herself firmly between Fitz and Vettul and Dark insisted Anji have the front seat, next to the Doctor in the driver's seat. He squeezed himself in next to Fitz.

'How could you be so stupid, Vettul, coming here?' Etty hissed. 'Who's looking after the others?'

'Myra is,' Vettul pouted. She was obviously over the moon to be reunited with Etty but wasn't being given the space to show it.

'Myra? But -'

'She is perfectly capable of doing so.'

'You're the most irresponsible, reckless -'

'Look, Etty, Vettul's here now,' Anji pointed out calmly. 'And she helped to save the Doctor and me. If she hadn't been here we'd both be dead by now.'

Etty was clearly not about to be mollified, but when Vettul told her forlornly what had happened to Treena, about the way she had lost her finger and been classified category G, she slumped back into a shocked silence.

'It's all right,' Vettul whispered as she reached cautiously for Etty's fingers. 'Just for now, I can look after you.'

Anji was glad to see Etty take the hand without another word.

'Where am I going, Nathaniel?' the Doctor asked softly, starting up the car.

Dark gave him directions. The atmosphere in the car was thicker than the fume-filled air back at the burning hospital as the Doctor drove away.

'What did Vettul's DNA tell you?' Anji whispered to him.

The Doctor kept his voice equally low. 'That she's an outcast from the Creator's heaven.'

'No godswitch?'

'No. Which suggests to me that one of Etty's familial ancestors was never part of the Creator's programme. An outsider. Not pointing any fingers...'

'The man who ended up as Derran Sherat.' Anji puzzled over the implications. 'So now we know for sure that the godswitch is specially designed for everyone who lives on this planet, right?'

'That's right.'

'The Holiest's means of controlling the population.'

'Controlling?' The Doctor glanced at her. 'I'm not sure about that. This Creator exists, I'm sure, and is certainly an organising force of some kind.'

'Oh, yeah? What, so God's just a computer or something?' Anji snorted. 'What a cop-out! That's like a bad *Star Trek* episode.' The mere mention of the show made her think of Dave again, which didn't help things.

'I'm not saying anything of the kind,' the Doctor said softly.

'These people are being manipulated by some machine...'

'No.'

'Well, then, some little old man hiding behind a curtain pretending to be a wizard –'

'It's far more complex than –'

'Oh, so my tiny Earthling mind can't comprehend such things.'

'You're getting upset, Anji.'

Anji grimaced, glanced quickly over her shoulder to see if everyone was listening, but no one seemed that bothered, lost in their own thoughts.

'I'm not getting upset,' she said, more softly.

'You are.' The Doctor stared hard at her at the next junction, as if looking inside her. 'Thanks to our conversation, your genes are being stimulated, switched on and off, even as we speak. Your brain is signalling your pituitary gland to tell your adrenal cortex to make a hormone called cortisol. It's making you more responsive, giving you more energy, but it's also interfering with the way your white blood cells fight infection.' He smiled, infuriatingly. 'You should take care. If the mood is sustained, you'll come down with a cold or something.'

The Doctor checked a direction with Dark and turned left.

Anji took a few deep breaths. 'What's your point?'

'Simply that you're using hundreds of genes simply to make the cortisol, to distribute it, and to react to it,' the Doctor said. 'It's travelling round your body in a path so convoluted it makes our journeys in the TARDIS seem straightforward. But what's in control of this process? What set up the order for your proteins and the receptors and the hormones and whatever else to interact in such a way, and what sets it off?'

'My brain did,' Anji said. 'Because you're messing with it.'

'But surely it's an unconscious reaction to release the cortisol, isn't it? An involuntary one? Why would your brain find it desirable to lower your resistance to disease whenever you feel worried or under attack?'

Anji considered. 'Then it's the genes themselves.'

'It's a genetic process, certainly, but genes wouldn't know how to set the process off. Genes have never *caused* stress, have they?'

'All right, then, maybe it's because the body, brain, whatever, gets confused, it can't help itself.' Anji frowned. 'God knows it's easy enough to get confused when you're around.'

The Doctor grinned. 'So it's my fault, then? External stimulus is in control of the chemical process?'

'Well... no, but... Everything's mixed together, isn't it?'

'Exactly,' the Doctor said, clicking his fingers. 'Interaction. Your brain runs your body. Your body runs your genes. Your genes run your brain, and all at the same time. And unfortunately, like the trade-off between your cortisol and your lymphocytes, not every decision taken can be good for your health long-term.'

'So you're saying that...?' Anji widened her eyes and nodded her head for help.

'I'm saying that the Creator, the organising entity if you like, is as mixed up in the process of life here on this world as everyone else. It may be omniscient, but not omnipotent. I don't think it's some centralised force, sitting back and raising or lowering a thumb like some lazy Roman emperor deciding who lives or dies for its sport. Whatever its nature, the Creator is an actual part of the people, and they a part of it.'

'That's a bit mystical, isn't it?'

'It may seem that way,' the Doctor said defensively. 'But ultimately it must've happened through advances in genetic science. This world is essentially a decentralised system, engineered and refined to such an extreme stage of development it *appears* mystical.'

Anji groaned with tired frustration. 'But *why*?'

'I don't know,' the Doctor admitted. 'Although...' He looked suddenly concerned, glanced cautiously in the rear-view mirror, causing Anji to glance behind her to see what had caught his eye. Obviously, he'd wanted to check on Dark. It was more as if a waxy effigy of the Diviner had been squeezed into the car beside Fitz, looking miserable and sick to his stomach with nerves.

'Over at the records centre,' the Doctor said more quietly, 'Nathaniel showed me some files. All the deaths, and all the reasons, transcribed and recorded there year after year, decade after decade, century after century for posterity. And yet...'

'What is it, Doctor?'

The Doctor was clearly troubled, but shook his head and forced a smile. 'I don't know. Perhaps this is just the way things turned out. The system simply evolved that way.'

Anji rolled her eyes. 'There's nothing simple about this set-up.'

'Then let's take another example. You wouldn't call the investment market you worked in when you were on Earth "a bit mystical", would you? And there's no one person solely in charge, is there?'

Anji saw where he was going with this at last. 'But there *are* influencers...'

'Yes. A mass of individuals and organisations participating in an efficiently designed interconnected system.'

'And everything one person does affects another, right?'

The Doctor nodded benignly, proud of his pupil. 'No matter how minutely.'

Anji considered the analogy and shuddered. 'Talk about the futures market!'

The Doctor shrugged apologetically. 'I'll admit it's a cold comparison.'

'So our invisible man, Derran Sherat, is like a rogue trader in the system?' Anji felt she was grasping this now. 'Someone who doesn't care if he crashes this marketplace as long as he comes out of it OK?'

The Doctor nodded slowly. 'He'll risk the destruction of this whole society to get what he wants.'

'And was it him who took Treena's finger?'

'If her body was pronounced a cat-G, it's likely, yes. He must have taken it for a particular purpose.'

'But why? What *does* he want?'

The Doctor didn't answer. Instead, he braked gently and pulled up alongside a typical dwelling in a typical avenue in this alien suburbia. It seemed entirely deserted.

'Forty-eight Elmslaw Road,' the Doctor announced.

Dark, looking straight ahead, didn't answer. He showed no sign of having heard at all.

The Doctor turned to him and cleared his throat. 'We've arrived,' he said.

'Doesn't look like much, considering who's paying the rent,' Fitz said.

Dark got stiffly out of the car. Anji felt for him. He looked lost as he surveyed the house, his black robes baggy and folded about him as if he was a child in swaddling clothes.

Fitz was right, she decided. Number 48, complete with curtains, glossy-white front door and a neatly kept garden, was a house just like all the others in the street. Perhaps its humble nature was the point. But still there was something sinister about it. Anji felt gooseflesh rise on her spiked arms, and rubbed them gently.

'Everyone stay here,' the Doctor said, climbing out of the car. 'Nathaniel and I will go in alone.'

'Oh, all right,' Fitz said swiftly. Clearly the fumes had cleared from his head and he was back to his old self.

'Of course we must stay here,' Etty said, squeezing Vettul's hand. 'If those people realise Vettul's nature, they'll destroy her.'

'I won't let that happen,' the Doctor promised.

'I want to come,' Anji made herself say.

The Doctor saw through her and smiled sadly. 'No, you don't. But thank you for saying so.'

Anji's eyes misted over. 'What if you don't come out again?'

'We will,' the Doctor said.

'Of course you will,' Fitz said, glaring at Anji presumably for even voicing the thought.

The Doctor nodded, but then paused, stooped in the car doorway. 'Good luck, everyone.'

He closed the car door, and led Dark gently by the arm to the front door. It opened, but although Anji strained to see she couldn't detect anyone standing in the doorway.

Dark and the Doctor stepped inside, and the door closed behind them.

* * *

The hallway smelled old, Dark decided, musty, of great-grandparents who didn't get out any more.

Didn't get out, or couldn't get out?

The door swung softly shut behind them. Dark tried it, but it refused to budge. He let out a shaky breath. Ahead was a flight of stairs leading up to whatever was kept in the upstairs rooms, but the Doctor patted his shoulder and coaxed him on into the living room.

It was gloomy - the curtains must be closed. Dark took a step inside, keeping his eyes on the drably coloured carpet. He looked around selectively. The walls were bare, but there were one or two ornaments on the bricked-up fireplace. There were two armchairs, and a table upon which a mug of steaming hot liquid stood, with a small plate of fresh sandwiches. And there was a couch.

Dark's heart leapt.

Lanna was sitting on the couch.

'What are you doing here?' the Doctor said softly, striding into the room, checking it was empty.

Dark stared at her. Her make-up was smeared, and her eyes looked red again. She'd been crying.

'Lanna?' he asked.

'They made me come,' she said. 'They saw me leaving yours... They *knew* me...'

'They?'

Lanna looked down. 'Who do you think?'

The Doctor was looking at her suspiciously. 'The Holiest?'

'They asked me things.'

'About me?' Dark asked her.

'Partly.' Lanna looked at the Doctor. 'More about him.'

'And you told them?' the Doctor enquired.

Lanna nodded, looked away. 'All I know.' She looked guiltily at Dark. 'All you told me last night. All of it.'

Dark looked at the Doctor and flushed.

'Well, I see they gave you a delicious cup of tea and laid on a spread for your trouble.' The Doctor's voice grew a little harder. 'It's a little like when you go to give blood, isn't it? Which seems strangely appropriate.'

'Please be seated, Doctor.'

Both he and Dark spun round at the sound of the low, old voice.

They found three cowled figures suddenly in the room, their faces lost in shadow, their very presence exuding menace.

The figures walked slowly forward, towards them.

# Chapter Twenty-six

The apparition in the middle spoke again. 'Return our Doctrine to us, Nathaniel Dark.'

Dark stared at them in mute horror.

'The disk you stole from your superior this morning.'

Dark looked terrified at the Doctor, and pulled the disk from his pocket. The Holiest pointed at the table, so he placed it down there.

'I... I'm sorry.'

'You will be seated also, Nathaniel Dark.'

Dark almost staggered backwards to the couch, absolutely terrified.

The Doctor remained standing. 'What a kind invitation. Very cosy, if a little unexpected. I mean, God's envoys, the Holiest of Holies, buttering bread and making the tea?'

'I made these,' Lanna said softly.

'Does the Creator pay well for a char?' the Doctor demanded of the three figures, unintimidated. 'What does he do, sift through the experiential tracts imprinted in the thirteenth chromosome and derive a mean average wage?'

The Holiest said nothing. The one in the middle took a step closer to the Doctor, and Dark squirmed on the couch. Lanna held his arm, looking as scared herself.

'I'm so sorry, Holy Man,' she whispered as the other two cowled figures moved silently round to sit in the chairs facing them. Tears were welling up in her eyes. 'I meant to say goodbye...'

Dark was barely listening as Lanna babbled quietly on.

'They made me come here. *Made* me...'

'Be silent, Lanna Seft.' The Holiest halted in front of the Doctor. 'You assume, Doctor, that by understanding science, you can understand all?'

'Well, it's a good place to start.' The Doctor gestured at Lanna. 'What is this woman really doing here?'

'What are *you* doing here, Doctor?' the hunched shape countered. 'We have no knowledge of you.'

'What would you like to know? Weight? Height? Inside leg measurement?' The Doctor jutted out his chin, defiantly. 'I exist outside of your Creator's Design.'

The cowled figure didn't speak for some time. 'We know that now. When we became aware of the activities of Nathaniel Dark, we studied him. There was...'

'...a blindness.' The second of the Holiest completed the sentence, now seated in the chair on the left. His deeper voice was similarly thick with age. 'A corrosion of experience.'

'We could not see,' said the third, a woman's voice, throaty and withered.

'The girl told us of you. Of all she had learned of the boy. We knew you would accompany Nathaniel Dark.'

'For the first time... we have an outsider.'

'Not for the first time,' the Doctor corrected her. 'I suspect there has been an outsider at work here on your world for hundreds of years.'

The first of the Holiest shook his cowled head and pointed at the Doctor. 'You misunderstand us.' The gold ring on his outstretched finger caught the sunlight as he took another, menacing step closer. 'We *have* an outsider.'

It's him they want, Dark realised. Not me. Not Lanna. They don't care about us, it's him they're after, someone they learned of *through* us. All the questions... all the ignorance... It seemed so obvious now, as if the Holiest recognising the Doctor for what he was had in some way enabled Dark to see him properly for the first time. A man who didn't belong. A thing from outside the world.

'You have removed your friend from the hospital,' the second of the Holiest said. 'She too does not belong.'

'You're not listening to me,' the Doctor said, swatting down the hand of the first Holiest. 'There's an evil loose in your society's structure here. One man, with an agenda of his own, invisible to your Creator.'

'A cancer eating at our Lord's perceptions,' the woman agreed, nodding. 'A blind spot, growing, spreading.'

'It's like I said,' Lanna said, looking at Dark. 'The Creator doesn't know what happened to my brother. You've been giving out lies, excuses.'

'No,' Dark protested, unable to believe what she, and what the Holiest themselves, were saying. 'The Creator sees all. How can one man challenge him?'

The first Holiest turned to him. 'A child can tear through a cobweb with one finger,' he said, 'ignorant to its creator's needs or goals.'

'Vanishing Point,' Lanna murmured, curled like a child now on the couch beside him. 'This is the Vanishing Point.'

'Is she right?' the Doctor challenged.

The first seemed to shrink a little now before the Doctor's gaze, and shook his head. 'This is not the promised time. Our future is being stolen from us.'

'You've foreseen the future?' The Doctor sat on the couch beside Lanna, picked up a sandwich and shoved it into his mouth. 'Well, I've examined your records, at the dead-case centre. Extrapolating from the growing trend I can see the future myself.'

'Again, you feel you understand -'

'Again, nothing,' the Doctor corrected her. 'I'm not relying on science but on simple demographics. And you're right, I don't understand - but I wish to.'

'You are a newcomer to our world,' said the second, still seated in the chair.

'I'm a traveller. I'm no threat to you.'

'You are unalike. You are category G. Your very existence destabilises the Design, weakens all the Creator has achieved, *is* to achieve.'

'Stop speaking in riddles,' shouted the Doctor, banging his fist down on the table. 'You're wasting time. I can *help*. You accept that an evil is at work here - people are being murdered, taken before their time, or else butchered, compelled to commit crimes against their will.' His voice fell practically to a whisper; he looked at them imploringly. 'I *fight* evil. I can be the eyes and ears your Creator is being denied, but I must have *answers*.'

The Holiest remained silent.

'Over the last hundred years on this world,' the Doctor went on urgently, 'while the number of annual deaths has remained more or less constant, the birth rate has fallen. Fallen dramatically. If the trend continues, a few centuries from now there will be no one left. Why? Can this "invisible man" be responsible? Is he trying to bring that about, or –' He broke off, and Dark saw a dawning comprehension spread over the Doctor's face. He seemed suddenly half-fearful, half-excited. 'Or is it all a part of your Creator's Design? Is *that* Vanishing Point?'

Again there was a silence as heavy as the dark robes that shrouded the old bones of the Holiest.

'I'm asking you for the knowledge,' the Doctor said, reaching into his pocket. 'This man we're both seeking simply took it. And you know how he learned.'

To Dark's horror he threw down the finger bone and the gold ring from the skeleton they'd found in the lodging house.

Then the woman spoke to Dark. He suddenly caught the image of her old pointed face, wizened beneath her black shroud, revealed to him in his mind.

'Leave us,' she said.

Dark blinked. 'Leave?'

'Wait outside. With Ettianne Grace. With...' Her voice died off, hung in the air like dust. When she spoke again it was brittle with bitterness. 'Leave us.'

He felt Lanna clutch at his arm, and stared dumbfounded at the Doctor.

The Doctor nodded, reassuringly.

Dark opened his mouth to speak, to say he wouldn't go, that he'd stay and see this through.

But the two Holiest rose from their chairs, joined their fellow in standing over Dark and Lanna. Dark shrank away, imagining the looks on their hideous old faces, his resolve suddenly broken. He rose himself unsteadily, and Lanna followed him. They walked to the door, clinging to each other for support.

'What...?' Dark's voice caught. He swallowed, cleared his throat. The Doctor was looking up calmly at the three Holiest as they edged nearer to him, surrounding him, drawing closer. Dark tried again to speak. 'What are you going to do... to him?'

The door to the living room swung closed in Dark's face, snatching the sight away. Lanna broke free of him, opened the front door and ran from the house, sprinting away, soon out of sight. Dark stumbled out on to the little pathway leading to the pavement, and the outer door swung closed behind him too.

He stared at it dumbly and suddenly Anji was beside him.

'What happened?' She asked him, grabbing him and spinning him round. 'Who was that girl? Where's the Doctor? Well?'

'I...' Dark's head felt thick with black flies, crawling and buzzing all over his thoughts. 'He's still in there, he...'

Anji's eyes were wide. 'Is he all right?'

'I... I don't know.'

Anji ran to the front door. 'Doctor?' she called, and started knocking, banging her fist into the woodwork. 'Doctor!'

'No,' Dark said, aghast. 'No, you mustn't. We must leave them.'

'Leave them?' Fitz had come to join Anji in the front garden. 'You've lost it, chum.' He joined Anji in her assault on the door.

Dark stared around wildly, feeling naked, utterly exposed, shocked down to his spirit. Suddenly Etty was beside him, leading him back to the car, sitting beside him on the back seat. The thin girl was seated next to her, looking at him coldly, dispassionately. She was different. Another outsider. He wanted to run from her, to follow Lanna away from all this down the street.

Etty was soothing him, talking to him as if he was a child, telling him it was all right.

But, like an adult, he knew it couldn't be.

'It's no good!' Anji shouted.

Fitz yelped with pain as his shoulder once again failed to make any impression on the front door. 'What do we do?'

'Break a window,' Anji said, dragging him over to the nearest. The thick lining of curtains hid their view of what lay inside.

'Anji, we're making a real spectacle of ourselves,' Fitz said as he hobbled after her, glancing about them. 'Every net curtain in this street must be twitching. They'll have the police on to us and then what will we do?'

'We can't just leave him in there!' Anji protested.

'I know, I know, but -'

Suddenly the front door opened.

The Doctor peeped outside. He looked dazed and pale.

'Doctor!' Anji exclaimed in relief.

'Not today, thank you,' the Doctor said vaguely. 'No hawkers, no peddlers...'

'Doctor?' Fitz looked at him uncertainly, took his arm and helped him down from the front step.

'They let you go?' Anji said, joining Fitz, taking the Doctor's other arm.

The front door clicked quietly closed behind them, but still the noise made Anji jump a mile. She led the unprotesting Doctor back to the car as quickly as they could, and Fitz got in ready to drive.

As they pulled away from the house, the whole of Elmslaw Road was silent and deserted in the glare of the wintry sunlight.

# Chapter Twenty-seven

Cauchemar writhed and shook as the healing apparatus throbbed noisily with power. His arms were outstretched, lashed to the steel framework with thick coiled wires that looked like serpents devouring his flesh.

As Hox watched over his master, he saw that the thousand holes perforating Cauchemar's body from countless other procedures were weeping a clear, sticky fluid, pooling at his feet on the floor. It cascaded over the lumpy mess of his stomach. When Treena had fired the gun and the flesh been shattered by the shot, it had been Hox who supplied the raw material for grafting. He scratched absently at his own gut, where the tissue had been scraped clear and squashed into pats. It had never taken well on Cauchemar's body. That was Hox's fault, for being a willing but incompatible donor. Each time he oversaw Cauchemar's healing, each time he saw the black burned crust hanging beneath his master's chest, he was reminded of his own weakness.

'Enough,' Cauchemar shouted suddenly, roaring with pain. 'Enough, I can't... can't...'

Hox rushed across to deactivate the machine. It rattled and shook as the energy died down, and then there was only Cauchemar's short, agonised sobs sounding in the dingy room.

'Life is sore, Hox,' Cauchemar muttered weakly. 'Only death can salve the pain of existence. To take all life from this world... it is noble, it is compassionate.'

'You are most merciful, sir,' Hox agreed, undoing the straps that held Cauchemar in place, uncoiling sticky wires.

'I know it myself... and so shall Jasmine, with me. Together for all time.'

One of Cauchemar's arms slapped down to his side and stuck there, glued by pus. Hox tried discreetly to move it free, since Cauchemar wasn't yet strong enough, trembling with pain.

'You must bathe my body, Hox,' Cauchemar whispered, 'just as these healing energies have bathed my cells. Then you must make me smell sweet and dress me in the best clothes. I shall be a fine man again, a fine man.' Hox helped him stumble away from the apparatus. 'Prepare me, Hox, for our caller tonight, and for our long journey hence to the Creator.'

Fitz was grateful to be in someone's house again, back in the warm, in a comfy seat, keeping the world outside at a distance, if only for a short while. Dark didn't have a bad pad. The poor sod was resting in his room after his ordeal. The Doctor reckoned shock was playing its part, but also that such proximity to the Holiest could've caused all manner of weird reactions on a genetic level.

Whatever.

Etty and Vettul had decamped to the kitchen. They seemed to have grown closer since their reunion. They were sitting together now, sharing their worries over Braga, talking, maybe saying all the stuff that should've been said a long time ago. Fitz smiled faintly to himself. Perhaps he could sympathise with Dark after all. That girl definitely caused him weird reactions in *his* jeans.

In the living room, the Doctor seemed to have distanced himself a little from Anji and Fitz. While she was sitting next to him on the couch, arms folded round her knees, the Doctor was sat hunched over the dining table under the glare of an angle-poise lamp, tinkering with some new contraption, all wires and transistors, some of which he'd nicked from the hospital doctor's pager. The green shawl that Etty was supposed to be wearing to the rendezvous at midnight was laid out as a tablecloth, the tiny circuits and components spread over it making it glitter like a sunlit sea.

The Doctor had not been in the mood for questions, but, now the three of them were alone together, Anji was clearly trying her luck again.

'I don't understand why they let you go, just like that,' Anji said.

'You sound disappointed,' the Doctor murmured.

'They killed Etty's great-grandfather and that defenceless child,' Anji pointed out, glancing warily at the door in case they were being overheard. 'So why not you?'

'They're desperate. They know now what they're up against, and recognise that the situation is almost critical. Killing me would do them no good. I don't think the police will be after us any more, either. They'd only hamper the situation.'

Anji didn't seem impressed with the Holiest's sudden benevolence. 'What, and they thought they were acting for the best back then with Annetta, did they?'

'I suppose so,' the Doctor said. 'They were making up their own rules. I don't suppose there was anything in the manual to deal with deviation from the norm... Nothing in "Troubleshooting" on what to do if someone discovers genetic techniques for themselves.'

'Manual?' Fitz asked.

'For the Creator's Design,' the Doctor muttered, scowling as two pieces of wire failed to hold together.

'They thought they were destroying the root of the problem back then, is that it?' Anji said.

'I imagine so,' the Doctor said. 'When confronted with evidence of the impossible, a blind spot in the Creator's vision, I suppose they panicked. They developed the tools to try to track the situation - but the blind spot continued to grow. Dissolution increased.'

'But did you find out the *why* in any of this?' Fitz asked patiently.

'Not explicitly. But what I did learn, tying it in to theories of my own...'

Fitz gritted his teeth. 'Well?'

'Just as Nathaniel's been saying, the ends to all this, to the Creator's Design, is reaching the Vanishing Point. Or it's supposed to be.'

'What, it all ends in apocalypse?' asked Anji.

'No. No, it's not an apocalypse,' the Doctor breathed. 'Not in that sense.' He looked up at them both and put down his tools for a moment. 'I've not been seeing the whole picture. You see, these people haven't just had their genetic make-up edited, all the junk trimmed down by some higher power. They're *transgenic*.'

'Come again,' Fitz prompted.

'They contain genetic material artificially transferred from another species.' The Doctor looked at Anji. 'Just as in your time human scientists transferred toad genes into rats, or grew an ear on the back of a mouse, so these people have been...'

Anji stared at him in horror. 'Experimented on?'

'They have been *prepared*,' the Doctor said.

Dark was roused from his uneasy sleep by the soft, insistent bleeping of his bedroom's viewscreen. He felt hot and shaky, so tired. His mind was buzzing round in circles; through all the confusion he felt he could only cling dizzily to the fact that he had faced up to the Holiest and he was still alive.

He should be thankful, give thanks to the Creator that it was not his time.

'Leave me alone,' he whispered, rubbing his eyes, but the signal took no notice.

Then he sat up abruptly, guessing who it must be. 'Answer,' he said wearily, and slumped back down on his side.

'Lanna?'

Her face filled the big screen, staring out at him, a chink of light through the drawn curtains cutting her in two. Her face was a mess of running make-up. 'I can't sleep,' she said.

'It's the middle of the day,' said Dark. 'Maybe when it's night -'

'I don't want the night to come,' said Lanna.

'Are you afraid?' Dark whispered.

'Yes.' Lanna nodded. 'I just ran, and ran, and ran.'

'It's my fault, isn't it?'

'Yes.' Lanna looked away. 'They were watching you... and then us. Last night... all of it.'

'The Creator watches over us all,' Dark said automatically. Then he laughed hollowly. 'Or those He can.'

'I always thought He'd have better things to do with His time than watch over me,' said Lanna.

There was a long pause. Dark was aware of the outside world only from the reflection of light on the screen and the muffled voices in the next-door room. He and Lanna just looked at each other.

'You won't see me again, will you?' said Dark, in the end.

'No.' She smiled, sadly. 'I'm going to start again. Start everything again.'

Dark nodded, though he didn't smile.

'What about you?' she asked.

He paused, rubbed his eyes again, sank his head back into his pillow. 'I can't go back.'

'No?'

'Not ever.'

Lanna nodded.

'So I'm going to help Etty, help the Doctor. Finish this.' He shrugged. 'Whatever it takes.'

She nodded again. They watched each other in silence, quite dispassionately, for what seemed like an age, until Dark closed his eyes, remembering the warmth of her beside him, touching her in the darkened room.

When he opened his eyes, she'd gone, and the viewscreen was blank.

Seeing how shocked Anji and Fitz were looking, the Doctor forced an awkward smile. 'Transgenesis needn't necessarily be anything to worry about. I might be of mixed heritage myself. So is Etty.'

'And so is Vettul,' Anji pointed out, miming a large leg.

Fitz frowned. 'But you said these people were... "prepared"?'

'I think so.' The Doctor nodded. 'A deliberate and intentional cultivation by a race that were able to reduce every essence of their selves to proteins and chemicals. A people that could synthesise not just the flesh, and the blood and the bone and the sinew - not just the vessel - but the actual *spirit*.'

Fitz stared at the Doctor in confusion. 'What?'

'From the things the Holiest said...' He looked grimly at Anji. 'I believe that they discovered a gene for the soul.'

Anji put her hand to her mouth. 'And transferred their souls into genetically engineered people, to act as carriers? Why?'

'I'm not sure,' the Doctor confessed. 'An experiment? The ultimate in playing god?'

'You think the Creator belongs to this race?' Fitz said.

'No, it's more than that I'm sure. The Creator could even be a by-product, a consequence, or some kind of monitoring device. I don't know.' The Doctor's face was clouded with gloom. 'You see, the population on this planet is shrinking, growing smaller with each passing year. What if the people here, the carriers for the personality gene, exist only as a testing ground for the soul?'

'Talk about the selfish gene,' said Anji, thunderstruck. 'Driving the body, the individual as its vehicle...'

'So a judgement can be made on how the life has been lived,' the Doctor said. 'If you go to the Creator, you leave the cycle. If not, if the Diviners or the Holiest find the soul wanting, or if you die prematurely...'

'Then the cycle begins again, reborn...' Anji breathed.

'The Creator must be able to reorganise and translocate the gene into new carriers at the embryonic stage,' the Doctor said. 'A new body but the same soul parasitising the cells, in ignorance of how many times it's been through the loop...'

'...looking for salvation,' Anji concluded, her voice dying away. 'But why?' The Doctor opened his mouth sadly to respond but Anji waved him away. 'I know, I know. You *don't* know.'

Fitz struggled to keep up. 'You're saying that - for whatever reason - the body's like a vehicle, used by this personality gene for its driving test. And that if you run the lights and bash it up you fail, they won't pass you, and you have to go back in a new car and take it all over again?'

The Doctor nodded. 'If you like, Fitz,' he said quietly.

Pleased with his metaphor, Fitz attempted to extend it. 'And this mysterious bad guy old Hoxie works for has been nicking parts to make his own invisible cars that can't pass their MOT because the testers can't see them,' he said triumphantly.

'And if Sherat had never got involved here,' Anji said, 'then eventually the population would dwindle to nothing. Everyone going to heaven.'

'All life meets all death at the time of passing,' the Doctor said. 'The world empty, the carriers, the people no longer needed... Vanishing Point.'

'But it hasn't worked out that way,' Anji said. 'Sherat or whatever his name is has tainted the gene pool. There are people walking about carrying no one and nothing but their own baggage.'

'They were never part of the Design,' the Doctor said. 'Think of the countless reactions and interactions each person has to and with everyone else... Like genes themselves in the body of society, sending out signals, beginning processes that may affect all sorts of random parts of the whole.'

'Like the cortisol my body's churning out right now,' Anji said bitterly.

'Imagine your body can't process cortisol,' the Doctor said. 'It can't interpret the signals, can't assimilate the right responses... It starts to break down.'

Fitz looked between the two of them. 'This world is breaking down, and when it finally happens, the people will break down with it?'

The explosions, the deaths, whatever Sherat is planning, it's all calculated to increase the damage, widen and darken the blind spot, destabilise the system until...'

'That Book of Revelations gets opened up good and proper,' said Fitz.

# Chapter Twenty-eight

Three-One stared steadily at the street corner, lit by its sickly yellow lamp. He could see boarded-up windows, thick soot helping brickwork seep into shadows. The drizzle on the windscreen made it seem as if the scene was melting, a misshapen mess washing away in front of his eyes. Then the wiper blades would swish up and down and everything seemed normal again. It was like watching the end of the world come around every minute or so, with nothing else to see. The drowsy swooshing from the air vents was stopping the windscreen clouding over with the cold steam breathing from the boys in the back.

He had to keep watching, it was very important.

Then, as the wipers swept up and back down, she was there. Huddled miserably against the wall, carrying a white carrier bag, sheltering from the rain under her green shawl. She was alone, waiting there. She had to be his target. She had to be Ettianne Grace.

'Green shawl,' Seven observed, echoing Three-One's thoughts.

'Get her inside.' Three-One watched as the dark shapes of the men crowded in on the target. She shrank helplessly before them, clutching her bag to her chest, and gave no struggle as they lifted her off her feet and took her away. Soon the van was rocking as they pushed her inside. She was cowering under the shawl, like a child pulling bedclothes over her head hiding from terrors in the night. *I can't see you so you can't see me.*

Three-One smiled and started up the engine, flicked on the headlights. The wipers swept up and the street corner resolved itself once more. He pulled away and left it to melt.

'They've gone,' Fitz announced, shivering with cold at the end of the dark street as the sound of the van's engines faded into the night, wrapping Seven's navy-blue fleece more tightly round him.

Anji nodded. 'I just hope the Doctor's right.' She looked down at the lash-up of electronics in her hands. A small light was steadily pulsing under a dark-green wafer of plastic. The display was divided into a weblike grid of yellow lines, cribbed from Dark's map of the city. Now they could see where the van was going, follow it - and save the day, of course. Provided this thing worked, anyway.

'Back to the car?' Fitz suggested, shaking back wet hair from his forehead.

Anji nodded, and they hurried back to the faces crowding the windscreen.

'Well?' Dark said expectantly.

'Ettianne Grace has left the building,' Fitz announced. 'Start her up, and let's follow that van.'

'I still think I should've gone,' Etty said, holding on tight to Vettul's hand.

'The Doctor's right,' Anji said. 'This maniac wants you for something, Etty. The Doctor's thingummy will lead us straight to where they're holding Braga - and the Doctor can learn what it is these people want you for, maybe bargain with them, reason with them...'

Dark was already pulling away, following the Doctor's signal. Anji's stomach was churning with nerves and uneasy excitement.

But the car was just two streets along when the pulsing light on the display screen flickered and went out.

The journey had taken some time, but now the Doctor was pushed out of the van and led up some steps into the building under the shawl's dark canopy, strong arms and hands crisscrossed around him, guiding him along a passage, into a lift. They travelled up a couple of floors.

As the lift lurched to a halt, the Doctor felt the tickle of a loose wire slipping down his chest, and froze.

How long had the transmitter been disconnected? He started to fumble under his shirt, hunting for wire and connector while still trying to keep the shawl in place and hold on to his carrier bag. His fingers fumbled with tiny pieces of plastic, catching against hairs, and then he let them slip from his grip as he was shoved along again, almost lifted off his feet by his escorts. The corridor seemed silent and deserted, until behind one door there came the sound of wailing, shrieking and crying. But it sounded like a baby, not a child of Braga's age. A baby in terrible pain. It disquieted him.

A door creaked open, and he was shoved inside. It was unpleasantly warm, and smelled funny, like a room where someone's been sleeping that hasn't been opened for days. He let the bag fall to the floor between his feet and struggled again with the wires under the shawl. The smell reminded him of the first hospital he'd been to on Earth. He'd been found wandering, raving, locked up for five days in a Victorian ward packed with consumptives, as bristly doctors and stern nurses tried to work out what was wrong with him, what to do with him. The strong cloying scents they'd splashed around to hide the stench of disease reminded him of this place.

Footsteps behind him heralded new arrivals. He could hear laboured breath, and the smell of illness and decay grew stronger. Ragged breathing clotted into a kind of strangled roar of anger.

'This isn't her!'

The shawl was torn away from him. The Doctor's eyes soon reacted to the dim light in the room. He recognised the dour Hox, still squeezed into his brown suit and carrying his own rain cloud about over his head, and the tall, stiff figure beside him was familiar, too - from the buzzing snowstorm of the augmented security footage, from Etty's dog-eared photograph. He was staring into the twisted face of the man who had been Derran Sherat. The black hair, flecked with silver, was still neatly combed and parted, and his charcoal suit was well pressed and immaculate. His whole attire, the Doctor decided, was the kind of self-conscious tailoring of an invalid wheeled out to attend a funeral, determined to put on a good show. But the waxy pallor of the skin, the glassy sheen in the eyes - this man seemed more like the funeral's focus, a corpse dressed and made up for visitors to view in a chapel of rest.

The Doctor grinned into the man's snarling face. 'Have I really changed so much, Derran?' he asked, fluttering his eyelashes.

Sherat walked up to him and cuffed the Doctor hard round the face.

The Doctor kept his mocking smile in place. 'Now, is that any way to treat a lady?'

'Your men may be fools, Hox,' Sherat said thickly, 'but it seems they have upstaged you. Your task was to find this man so I could amuse myself before Ettianne Grace was brought to me.'

'We could not locate him, sir -' Hox began.

'Because you already held him, you imbecile,' Sherat spat, 'while Ettianne remains lost to me.'

'You mustn't excite yourself, sir,' Hox fussed.

'No, you mustn't,' the Doctor agreed cheerily. 'Your henchmen may be thick, but you're not looking too clever yourself.' His smile faded. 'Where's Braga?'

Sherat came closer and grabbed hold of the Doctor. The Doctor could feel the man's grip crushing the transmitter wires into his shoulder. Would he realise, or...

'I shall have the boy killed for this deceit.'

'And how will you lure Etty here then?'

Sherat sneered. 'With the congealing tatters of your corpse.'

'Not much of a draw really, is it?' The Doctor shook his head. 'No, I shall bring Etty to you, once we've talked, and once you've told me what you really want with her. Sending notes is such a schoolyard way of communicating, don't you think? And you're no spring chicken, are you?'

The Doctor straightened, carefully smoothed himself down, taking the opportunity to check the connections under his shirt were back in place, and peered at Sherat. Even now his anger had subsided a little, he wore the look of a man who has been caught in torrential rain with no protection, someone who's soaked through and resigned to it.

'Yes,' Sherat muttered. 'You shall bring her to me.'

'How long has it been, then?' the Doctor asked, ignoring him. 'Five hundred years? A thousand? How long have you been among these people?'

'No one may question me.'

'If I'm to help you, I need to know the facts.'

'Help me?' Sherat scoffed.

'You're suffering from advanced dystrophic cellular degeneration.'

Sherat was taken aback. 'You know of my condition?'

'You left some tissue samples behind on your equipment on Badi Street. You're going to end up a fleshy sack of dissolved DNA, a useless soup of unbound protein chains.'

Sherat looked like he was about to start crying. Abruptly he turned and stalked from the room without another word. The Doctor smiled a little awkwardly at the ring of hostile faces surrounding him. One of them had a black eye. 'Didn't we meet at the building site?' wondered the Doctor.

The man said nothing.

Next door, the baby was still crying.

'What are we going to do?' Fitz muttered anxiously as Dark took another turning at random. There was no sign of the van. 'What the hell are we going to do?'

'What can we do?' Etty said miserably. 'It's not worked. We've lost him, and I'll never find Braga.'

Anji turned to her on the back seat. 'Don't think like that,' she said.

Vettul nodded. 'The Doctor will realise his machine is not working and put it right...'

'The Doctor's probably dead!' Etty snapped. 'They've seen straight through his trick and killed him!'

'No,' said Fitz. 'No, they can't have. They can't.'

He and Anji shared a haunted look. If there was one thing they'd learned travelling in time and space it was that there was no such word as 'can't'.

'We'll just have to keep driving around until the signal comes back,' Anji said. 'It's as simple as that.'

Etty sat with clenched fists, working her nails into her palms in frustration, while Nathaniel silently drove them along the darkened, lonely streets.

Ten minutes or so later, Sherat came back wearily into the room.

'Big-night nerves?' the Doctor enquired. 'Bound to play havoc with your system, especially exhibiting that degree of cellular mutation.'

Sherat looked at him almost knowingly, an expression the Doctor couldn't quite place. He peeled a bright-yellow fruit, ate it in two or three half-hearted bites, then turned to the others in the room. 'Hox, arrange our units to their required destinations. You can manage that, I trust? Then report back to me here.'

Hox nodded quickly, and ushered most of the assembled heavies out of the room. Only the two large men standing either side of the door remained.

'Arrange your units?' the Doctor queried.

'My loyal servants.' Sherat pressed the discarded skin of the fruit into the massive hand of the man on the left, who accepted it without complaint.

'Your lobotomised victims.'

'Cretins they may be, but each and every one has their part to play. And now the time has come for their final sacrifice.' Sherat held up a blotchy palm. 'By dawn I will hold the City in my hand. And then I will squeeze.'

'For reasons of hygiene, I hope you'll wear a glove.'

Sherat drew nearer. 'I see it in you,' he said, studying him closely. 'For all your prattle... at last... you are someone who can understand the long loneliness.'

The Doctor met his wild eyes for some time, and finally sighed, nodded. 'Yes. Yes, I think I can.'

'How long have you lived?'

'I don't know,' the Doctor admitted. 'There's so much I can't remember.'

'I remember *everything*.'

There was a pause. Sherat was looking imploringly at the Doctor, as if he was desperate to share a secret but afraid of his confidences being betrayed - or of putting them into words.

'What caused your cellular collapse?' whispered the Doctor.

'My own researches.' Sherat seemed pained to admit it.

'Exacerbated by the journey here? White holes, dark quasars, strange radiators... Travelling so close to such phenomena in a conventional spaceship -'

'All this is the result of that long, long journey,' Sherat snapped. '*Everything*.'

'Why did you take it?'

'I was a prisoner, I had no choice.'

'Who are you?' the Doctor asked. 'You've noticed I'm not Etty, so I can't keep thinking of you as Derran Sherat.'

The man stalked over to the window, looking out over the bruised darkness of the sky over the City. 'My name is Cauchemar. I was incarcerated on a colony arkship bound for a prison world on the edge of the New Earth frontier.'

'You're a criminal?'

'A scientist,' Cauchemar said, wistfully. 'A genius.'

'In genetics?'

Cauchemar nodded. 'I achieved so much - but to go on achieving I had to live. I had to live for ever.'

'Impossible.'

'Impossible?' Cauchemar shook his head. 'My cells are immortal.'

'Oh yes, your telomeres are barely frayed at the edges, your cells can divide *ad infinitum*. But somewhere on the way to infinity the mutation started, didn't it?'

'What I saw as research, experimentation on human subjects, those small-minded fools in the colony saw as murder.' Cauchemar smiled cruelly. 'When they tried to stop me, I was forced to show them what that word really meant.'

'That's the trouble with scientists like you,' the Doctor murmured. 'So very literal. And did you take your victims' fingers as trophies even then?'

Cauchemar turned away. 'You seek to judge me, but, like the Creator, you know nothing.'

'So tell me. You know you want to.'

Again, there was that nervous, almost hopeful look in Cauchemar's dark eyes. 'There was a power surge in the main drive. The ship collided with a meteor. It was badly damaged, half the crew was lost. Prisoners - the clever ones, anyway - had to take the crew's place just to keep the ship functional.' He seemed lost as he stared out over the sleeping city. 'I met *her* then. Jasmine. The woman who was to change my life and shape my death.'

'One of your warders? Oh dear. I suppose you fell in love, or something messy like that.' The Doctor grimaced. 'You're not going to go into slushy details, are you?'

Cauchemar stayed by the window. 'What do you know of love, Doctor?'

'Enough to know its power. Its dangers.'

'She could never love me. Not knowing all she did, the things that I had done. She was...'

'I'll take it as read she meant a great deal to you,' the Doctor said quickly. 'So, broken-hearted, eventually you strayed into this region of space?'

'Or the ship was *steered* here,' Cauchemar said bitterly. 'Yes, the ship was irradiated. Crew and prisoners alike began to die. Then we were... visited.'

'Visited? How nice! Did you get out the best china?' The Doctor wondered if his transmitter was working, how long it would take for the others to arrive, and what might happen then. At least he didn't have to worry about keeping Cauchemar talking. Given the chance to share his lonely secrets, to talk openly with someone he thought could actually comprehend them, Cauchemar was almost babbling out his explanations, his earlier animosity gone. Now he was just a lonely old man, reaching out to another.

'Creatures of energy - the best brains of a race that claimed to have transcended the body and achieved a nonphysical state of bliss, so that they were at one with the fabric of the universe. They had guided us to this miserable region of space, to our deaths, because they had use for our bodies.'

The Doctor felt a twinge of excitement as his suspicions were confirmed. 'As transgenic carriers for alien souls...'

'Not as carriers - as prison cells. Walking, talking primitive incarceration for this race's undesirables, all those deemed unworthy of that blissful, unbounded state.' Cauchemar's eyes narrowed. 'You know of the genetic tract through which the personality is expressed, monitored...'

The Doctor nodded. 'Located on chromosome 13.'

'These creatures shared their knowledge with me so I could help genetically prepare the dying crew into vessels, alter them so that the cosmic phenomena could no longer harm them. They needed my genius, they had foreseen my arrival in that sector of space...'

'Or it may just have been coincidence,' the Doctor said airily. 'Whatever, the crew submitted willingly to this treatment?'

'Most of them. They knew they were dying. Here was a way of living on. Nothing was really taken away from them.'

'Save for the knowledge of their own pasts, of the experiences that made them who they were,' the Doctor said, his voice rising a little. 'Can't you see? To lose that... is to lose so much.'

'And can you not comprehend, Doctor, the pain, the torture, of dragging yourself and the dead past through each meaningless day, living with only memories?' The Doctor said nothing. 'You are fortunate. And these people became true pioneers of science.' Cauchemar paused, smiled crookedly. 'I termed them cat Gs.'

'Very droll. I think the term has been slightly lost on them.'

Cauchemar shrugged. 'It was a new beginning, a new life. And the soul essence doesn't dominate the personality: it's more symbiotic. Part of the punishment of these undesirables was to be subsumed by human desires and feelings, so that rehabilitation would be all the harder.' His lips twitched in a smile. 'Humans are so notoriously bad at telling right from wrong. Quite a test. And at the end, the human part would taste that paradise, too.'

'So this place was prepared,' the Doctor said softly. 'And these people sent to live and breed in a new colony, cut off from the rest of the universe... A more primitive way of life, a society where genetics was unheard of, given a structure so that the secret of the colony could never be discovered, and the programme never threatened.' The Doctor looked at Cauchemar with a new, guarded respect. 'You helped create a truly transgenic race. Watched over by the Diviners and the Holiest, and governed by the Creator - judge, jury and jailer.'

'The Creator,' Cauchemar sneered. 'That's simply an energy emission expressed through a gestalt genetic code.'

'There's nothing simple about an intelligence functioning in parameters such as -'

'It's nothing, don't you see that?' Cauchemar shouted and stamped his foot like a cross child. '*I* am the true Creator. *Me*.'

# Chapter Twenty-nine

Hox opened the door to the reprogramming room and nodded with satisfaction. His troops were lined up against the wall in front of the big map of the city, the image burned first and foremost into their brains. He surveyed them, rubbing his hands together, every inch the brisk professional going about his business.

To his left sat the wiper. Hox spent a few seconds buffing up the helmet, his own bent reflection looking back up at him from the bronze. It didn't seem real that he'd never use it again. No more hunting for victims by night, masterminding their capture, directing the men. He wouldn't miss the screams and the shouts once they were bundled into the machine and mutilated, but he would miss the sense of achievement. Cauchemar was a leader, he cared only about results, but Hox was a wily master of the precise detail. Preparation was all, and after all this time, the plan was ready to set into operation. He had wiped the mind of the last required carrier only this morning, and they would be deployed at last, tonight.

What would there be for him then? It was good that the world was ending.

Hox drew himself up to his full height. 'The time has come. Those bound for the outer zones will leave imminently with their cases.' He held up a small grey box with a carry handle by way of illustration. 'Now, you will step forward upon hearing your name,' Hox announced imperiously, enjoying the long-planned-for moment. He never tired of the novelty of having people serve him without question. 'One Four-D-Seven?'

A grey-haired man in a fawn raincoat that was too big for him stepped brightly forward. He was one of the first usable subjects the wiper had given them, and he still held a lopsided grin on his face that Hox had never been able to shift. Hox pressed the case into his hands. One's smile grew broader as he accepted the gift.

Hox went on down the line, staring wistfully at the different faces, the way they displayed the many manners in which the machine could change you. Some happy, some sad, some just confused and quiet. A whole crowd of people who weren't quite there, milling about in their ill-fitting coats, ready to lay down the lives they'd lost touch with just at Hox's say-so.

Hox had no one to keep in touch with, of course. He hadn't done for years. Cauchemar had seen off the old life, of course, and Hox was the happier and richer for it. He was certain of this.

It didn't take long to finish the parade, to clarify instructions and dispatch fourteen people to their allotted places. Hox watched them file out of the room, dabbing his wet eyes with a handkerchief. Now, aside from Cauchemar and himself, only six servants remained: the two that were guarding his master, and the four left here in the room.

Their work was not yet done.

Hox yelled at those left in the room to line up against the wall and wait. He lingered to see them do so without question, then turned smartly on his heel and left the room.

The Doctor looked into Cauchemar's eyes, saw the pain there, the sickness.

How long have you been mad? he wondered.

'So, this world was seeded with carriers and the rehabilitative programme put into action,' the Doctor said, keen to learn more. 'If you live a good and worthwhile life, then your inherited soul will get to heaven. And if not, it comes around again for another go. A bit like getting parole, I suppose. How long your sentence is depends on how well-behaved you are. But what about you, your own sentence?'

'The experiments I'd carried out on my own body made me unsuitable stock for a carrier,' Cauchemar said bitterly. 'My cells, as you have seen, are... mutated. I continued my self-experimentation, but it was useless. I was told I would be granted the arkship and my freedom - but they would not let me share it with Jasmine, now she was cured.'

'Did Jasmine have a say in the matter?' the Doctor asked lightly.

'No,' Cauchemar insisted. It was obviously what he believed to be true. 'They took her from me, set the ship adrift, abandoned me to a living death, alone. I drifted for years, alone... until eventually I was able to repair an escape pod and reach this world.'

'You knew the damage that would cause,' the Doctor observed coldly.

Cauchemar nodded. 'So? What did I owe them?'

'Your freedom,' the Doctor pointed out quietly.

'What good was freedom, abandoned alone in space?' Cauchemar spat on the floor. 'I wanted to *live*.'

'And you hunted down Jasmine, I suppose.'

'She had no memory of me, of course. And this time, she submitted to my will. Became mine. Loved me.'

'You must've been a very happy serpent in Eden.'

Cauchemar turned away again. 'The cellular mutation had been accelerated by the strange radiators. I constructed my own equipment to heal myself.'

'But you botched it, didn't you?' the Doctor said, almost jogging as he followed Cauchemar across the room.

'The equipment was primitive,' Cauchemar argued. 'My body too far damaged, I needed to arrest the cellular collapse.'

'For which you needed donor cells - you took them from Jasmine, I suppose?'

Cauchemar rounded on him. 'Yes,' he shouted, his voice cracking.

The Doctor stared at him. 'And it all went wrong, didn't it?'

'The procedure... damaged her.' A tear trickled down to the end of Cauchemar's nose and plopped on to the floor.

'And no one on the planet had the first idea of how they could help her, did they?' the Doctor said more quietly.

'I abducted one of the Holiest, tried to force him to help me,' Cauchemar said, his voice hollow and flat. 'The Holiest were genetic constructs of the Creator, shaped from the flesh of the dead. *They* understood what was happening, they had knowledge of genetics, they could have helped me save her.'

'I imagine from his eventual reappearance in your cupboard,' the Doctor said coolly, 'that he chose not to.'

Cauchemar nodded. 'So where else could I go?'

The Doctor's eyes widened. 'The Creator?'

'My last hope. I took her, frail and sick, to the water mountains - the repository of the controlling intelligence. I had to make Him see... that since I had made all this possible, He *had* to help me...'

'But you'd not been prepared, He couldn't see you, could he?' the Doctor said.

'And anyone he *can* see who approaches his lair is killed.' Cauchemar stared into space. 'Some kind of defence mechanism. Oh, it is a beautiful death, Doctor. I tasted some of it there, in a great cave high above the sea... Simple proximity to Jasmine was enough. Through my mind, through the channels I had opened with my experiments, I could feel the echoes of her life coming undone as the DNA of the experiential tract unravelled. Every moment of physical being felt in a single moment... Imagine it: to know yourself completely and nonjudgementally, vanishing in a blur of perfect innocence.'

'But you still had your *own* life to lead.'

'I was alone again,' Cauchemar said softly. 'This time without hope. All I could do was look for the reincarnation of what was left of her, to go on searching, dreaming of the time when I could know her again and return to the Creator, this time on my terms.'

The Doctor put his hand to his mouth. 'You think you've found her in Etty?'

'I thought I had her in Treena. I was wrong.'

'Because she tried to kill you?'

'She learned certain truths.'

'Truths? What do you know about the truth?' the Doctor sneered. 'And what's to say you're not wrong again?'

'I have seen her, there in Etty's eyes -'

'Nonsense!' the Doctor shouted. 'You're fooling yourself because you know you're dying, because you know time's running out.'

'Time is running out for the Creator. But I will live to see my work complete.'

'You've spent all your life here destroying what you helped to create, the only legacy those poor people could ever bequeath to the universe,' the Doctor said, disgusted. 'The invisible man playing his tricks, anything that will eat away at the Creator's vision. Starting up families, businesses, reaching out to as many people as possible. Betraying them, murdering them, inflicting misery, robbing and stealing and all in the name of what - petty revenge?'

'Where will I go to when I die?' screamed Cauchemar.

The Doctor took a step back, despite himself. There was a deathly silence.

'There is nowhere for me to go,' Cauchemar said more quietly. 'No paradise waiting for *me*. But I shall know the next best thing.' He marched over to the door. 'Hox!' he shouted. 'Hox, I need you here.'

'You're mad,' the Doctor said sadly.

'I have spiked this god like a stuck pig,' Cauchemar hissed. 'I have weakened him to the point of final dissolution. When it comes I shall ensure I am lost in that perfect moment of knowledge, of innocence that Jasmine knew all those centuries ago - and join her in death.'

'But you can't,' the Doctor said, wringing his hands in frustration. 'The Creator can't see you, won't acknowledge you.'

'As I have said, proximity alone is enough.'

'That's what you have planned for Etty? That's why you need her?'

'*Jasmine*,' Cauchemar corrected. 'I shall have her hand in mine when the time comes.'

'When you walk into paradise?' the Doctor mocked, recalling Cauchemar's letter to Etty. 'Ettianne Grace will never go with you, never. And having someone beside you wasn't enough for you to feel the full effect of the defence mechanism before. Why should it be any different now the Creator is weaker?'

Cauchemar was suddenly dead calm again. 'This time there will be far more than just some*one* beside me.'

Hox came into the room. 'I have dispatched our -'

'Never mind that,' Cauchemar said. 'Fetch it.'

Hox gestured along the corridor, apparently confused for a moment. 'The boy, Braga?'

Cauchemar shook his head. 'From the nutrients tank,' he said, and Hox disappeared in the opposite direction. Towards where the Doctor had heard the screaming, the wailing.

'I have not been as idle as perhaps you imply, Doctor,' Cauchemar said. 'I have continued my researches, searched for a cure for my own malaise as fervently as I have searched for Jasmine.'

'I'm sure,' sneered the Doctor.

'And when I knew there was no cure for me, that I could not live for ever, I had to be certain my final demise would be... fitting. So I got to work on a most unique project. It's been quite a collaboration, but I think I can say it's always been my baby.'

The crying got louder, closer.

Then Hox brought it in, his face impassive. A pink lump, glistening like a large joint of basted meat, writhed and squirmed in his arms.

The Doctor stared in horror. It was an infant, no more than a year old, naked and screaming. And covering its little form, growing and wriggling out of every inch of puckered flesh, were fingers and even whole palms. Its skin seemed crawling with digits, twitching and convulsing, even as he watched.

Waving at him.

'Treena's baby,' the Doctor whispered, clutching his hand to his chest. The action reminded him of the wires there... how much longer before help arrived? 'You're mad.'

'I told you it doesn't matter if Etty comes with me or not,' Cauchemar stated, grinning wildly. 'I shall take her hand and walk into heaven.'

'It's back!' Anji yelled in excitement, making everyone jump and hit their heads on the car's low roof.

Dark stamped on the brakes. 'The signal?'

'We have flashing lights!'

Etty grabbed the device from Anji. 'Where is he? Let me see.'

'Careful, careful!' Anji said. 'If you break it...'

Etty looked at the screen as if expecting to see an address flashing in big bright letters, but her face soon fell. 'You know the City,' she said, passing the thing to Dark. 'Find him.'

'Please,' Vettul said simply.

Dark looked at their tired, drawn faces, and nodded. 'Fitz,' he said, 'check these vectors on the map.'

Fitz obediently thumbed through the dog-eared pages of the road atlas, and soon they were on their way to an address that was, typically, the other side of town.

'Here comes the cavalry,' Fitz muttered. 'Ready or not.'

'Them?' Anji wondered aloud. 'Or us?'

The Doctor found it took some time for words to come.

'What is that abomination?' he choked. 'What do you think you're doing?'

Cauchemar chuckled. 'Bringing together two dozen people in one easy-to-carry bundle.'

'And Treena discovered this?'

'One day she heard the screams. I explained some of it, thought she'd understand...' Cauchemar shrugged. 'When she didn't, I knew she could never have been my Jasmine.'

The Doctor stormed up to Cauchemar. 'You self-deluded monster,' he said, his voice cracking with fury. One of the bodyguards, dressed in a bright checked coat, slammed a massive hand into his face, knocking him back. The Doctor fell in an undignified pile on the floor.

'No wonder she tried to kill you,' he said, wiping blood from his lip with the back of his hand. 'Why were you in the bank that day? To check everything went to schedule? They were robbing the place for you, weren't they?'

Cauchemar paused for a coughing fit to pass, then patted the shoulder of one of his bodyguards. 'My steers are useful but not bright. I led them straight to the scene of the crime.'

'And Treena came, too.'

Cauchemar laughed, almost fondly. 'I should've let her go in my place, but I was concerned for her. I often wonder how long she'd planned her move. Perhaps she thought it her best chance to kill me without throwing her own life away in prison.' He smiled evilly at the Doctor. 'She couldn't comprehend that the Creator could have no knowledge of me. But soon He shall. He shall.'

The Doctor could barely bring himself to look at the screaming creature, but saw now how Cauchemar hoped to succeed. The Creator recognised people via the experiential tracts on chromosome 13. But these people would've been killed, their godswitches never thrown. Yet the flesh still lived, feeding off the blank slate of the baby. How would the Creator respond when confronted with so many different experiential tracts in one living entity?

Cauchemar answered the Doctor's unasked question as if overhearing his thoughts, even over the baby's continued wailing. 'At my signal, the final assault on this old, beleaguered city will come. And it will all go up in flames.'

'The souls held in limbo until judgement can be passed,' the Doctor realised, remembering his first discussion with Dark. 'So *many* souls - that build-up of potential energy...'

'And all in one go!' Cauchemar smacked his fist into his palm. 'Such an anomaly will force the Creator into a self-defensive frenzy - and, I calculate, a total breakdown.'

The baby's shrieking finally died down a little, as Hox rocked the pitiful creature, staring down at it without feeling.

'Calculate? Guesswork, nothing more. But you know the fine balance of this place,' the Doctor protested, getting back on his feet. 'There'll be an enormous backlash of energy into each person's experiential tract.'

'Then my own children, that Ettianne has guarded for me so well, shall inherit the earth,' Cauchemar said with a smile.

'There are hundreds of thousands of innocent lives you're condemning to death!'

Cauchemar looked him straight in the eye. 'Let them die.'

Suddenly a device started beeping in his pocket. Cauchemar pulled out a small black box, studied it and smiled. 'We can terminate this conversation now, Doctor, much as I've enjoyed it.'

'What do you mean? What is that thing?'

'Come now, Doctor, you're an intelligent man. You've been transmitting a signal to your friends, so that they can come and find you - Ettianne included, I'd imagine. She must be so dreadfully worried about the boy.'

The Doctor glared at Cauchemar sourly.

'When I realised they must be homing in on you, I decided to triangulate the carrier signal and trace *them*. With this.' He waved the little box.

'You happened to have such a device lying around?'

Cauchemar ignored him, refusing to be drawn. 'And now they're well in range. It would appear your device has finally led them here. Now all I need do is give the order, and my steers will pick off your friends before they even reach this building - and I shall take Jasmine away with me.'

'Listen to me, Cauchemar -'

'Thank you for taking my confession, Doctor.' Cauchemar drew closer to him, his sour breath on the Doctor's face. 'The Creator may never hear me, but your own attention, as a scientist, has been most... rewarding.'

'I have something else for you.' The Doctor crossed swiftly to his carrier bag, still sitting on the floor. 'Your steers should perhaps have checked this on my way in.'

He reached inside and pulled out a large grey bundle.

'Oh goodness me,' he declared dryly, 'it's a bomb.'

Hox's aloof expression slipped slightly. 'It's the one I left at the hospital.'

'More or less,' the Doctor said cheerily. 'I've attached a new detonator. I thought that much explosive must be terribly expensive, a whole bank job's worth - I assumed you'd want it all back. No?' He let the grin on his face harden to a scowl. 'Bring Braga here. Now.'

'You'd be killing yourself if you set that off.'

'To stop you and your deranged scheme, I wouldn't hesitate.'

'You'd be killing the boy,' Cauchemar said, taking a step closer. 'You risked your own life coming here. That must be partly for the boy's sake.'

'I risked my life because I wanted to meet you face to face, to help you if I could. It's not too late. I have a laboratory, technology that could save you. Transport, that could take you away from here.'

'Even if I believed it were possible, where could I go?' said Cauchemar quietly. 'I'm so tired, Doctor. So very tired.'

'I know,' the Doctor said. 'I know, I understand. You've let yourself lose hope, but please, believe me, it's never too late -'

'You fool, look at me!' Cauchemar ripped open his shirt front, displayed a stomach black with scar tissue, puckered with sores. 'I no longer wish to live, and I shall not suffer others to.'

The baby in Hox's trembling arms started crying again, its fingers and thumbs flexing in agitation as it did so.

The Doctor wondered which of the digits was Treena's, which was Ansac's. His voice rose higher. 'Please, let the boy go. Let me help you, and bring peace to that monstrosity you've created.' He brandished the bomb at them. 'Don't make me do this.'

Cauchemar looked at his box. 'While we've been talking, your friends have gained access to the building, Doctor.'

'You're bluffing.'

'Am I? Be it on your own head, as you bring this building crashing down on theirs.'

'Put down the bomb, Doctor,' Hox said, finding his tongue at last. Only the thin sheen of sweat on his high, lined forehead suggested he found the Doctor's ruse to be anything but a minor inconvenience.

The Doctor's gaze flickered between Hox and Cauchemar and the baby, and between the two men standing guard on the door. He strained to hear any sound of his friends' apparent arrival, but could catch nothing over the grizzling of the baby.

'Put down the bomb,' Cauchemar insisted, taking another step closer.

The Doctor's finger tightened on the detonator.

# Chapter Thirty

'Here,' the Doctor said. 'Catch.'

He threw the grey slab of explosives straight at Hox. Hox panicked, fumbled for it, and the gurgling baby slipped from his arms, landing next to the bomb with a wet thud on the floor.

Cauchemar screamed out with rage, and dived for the baby.

The Doctor ran forward, still holding the detonator, hoping the connecting wire was long enough to carry without ripping free.

As Cauchemar fell to his knees in front of him, the Doctor trod heavily on the man's back, using it as a springboard to launch himself at the doors.

The men stepped sideways to cover the exit. The Doctor brought up both legs and cannoned into them, smashing them back against the doors and landing nimbly on one foot. As the two heavies stood there dazed, the Doctor grabbed the door handles and pulled on them hard. Each door slammed into a broad back and knocked the men forward into Hox and the bomb.

Cauchemar had picked up the baby and was cradling it protectively. 'Stop him, you fools!'

Hox got up, moving again with surprising speed.

The Doctor looked down. When one of the heavies had fallen, he'd dropped the fruit skin Cauchemar had passed to him. Now the Doctor swept the slippery peel up and threw it into Hox's path. Hox's foot slid on it and he went flying backwards.

'Sorry to give you the slip, gentlemen,' the Doctor said politely, pulling both doors shut behind him, the wire of the detonator taut now, at full stretch. He placed the device carefully down at his feet, and called to the others over the sound of the mewling baby.

'You'll observe I can still set off the bomb from out here. Even as we speak I'm rigging the wire so it'll detonate if you try to open these doors after me,' he lied. 'And don't think about removing the detonator wire from the explosives themselves: I've included a heftier booby trap than your paltry little firecracker.'

All nonsense of course, but he needed time. Hox had indicated that Braga was being held somewhere in the opposite direction to Treena's baby...

The two were cousins, he thought, with a shudder.

He heard Cauchemar bellow with rage, the scream choking off into wrenching, painful coughs. Then he moved off cautiously down the corridor.

'Braga?' the Doctor called softly, trying the handle on the first door he came to. It was locked. 'Braga!' he whispered more urgently.

'Who is it?' came a small voice.

'The Doctor,' he whispered back. 'Remember me? I've come to save you.'

'It's dark in here,' Braga whispered miserably.

'Stand back from the door.'

The Doctor took a run up and then hurled himself at the heavy wood. His shoulder stung red-hot with the impact but the door splintered open. His momentum carried him into the thick blackness of the room.

'Are we nearly there yet?' Anji asked. Fitz could hear the tension in her voice.

'Yes,' Dark replied, swinging the car round the corner and into the next street.

'Bugger,' said Fitz quietly.

Traffic was thinning out. The streets were getting emptier and emptier as they crossed through town, people vanishing like the seconds ticking away to the moment they arrived.

What then?

'Is the signal still holding?' Vettul asked.

Anji nodded, peering over Fitz's shoulder.

'Drive faster, Nathaniel,' Etty implored him.

'No, Doctor!' Anji shouted, as the gently pulsing light suddenly winked out again. 'We've lost him!'

'It's all right,' Dark said, 'we still know his location. We'll find him.'

'But if his signal's cut out...' Anji's voice died down to a whisper. 'What do you think we'll find *of* him?'

* * *

Braga was hot and wet and snivelling, terrified out of his wits. A tuft of hair was missing and a livid cut ran down his left wrist. The Doctor swept him up into his arms and out into the corridor.

The little boy clung on to him as tightly as he could. 'I want my mum,' he sobbed. 'Where is she?'

'Close by,' muttered the Doctor, 'but hopefully not too close by.' With one hand he yanked the signalling wire out of the connector taped to his chest. Anji and Fitz must've worked out his location by now - and at least Cauchemar would no longer be able to track them.

He carried Braga back along the corridor. As they passed the double doors he'd slammed shut on Cauchemar, the detonator wire he'd fed through suddenly slithered back beneath the wood like a shiny eel.

'He didn't believe me!' the Doctor exclaimed in outrage. 'Braga, don't I have an honest face?'

The doors crashed open.

'Time we were gone,' the Doctor commented, and, still carrying the boy under his arm, ran down the corridor.

Moments later Hox was shouting after them, demanding that they stop, and heavy feet were thumping on the grimy floorboards after him.

Inside the room, Cauchemar smashed his signal recorder down on the floor. The baby wriggled against his body as it cried, all its fingers and thumbs digging into him.

'He's destroyed his tracking mechanism,' Cauchemar spat as he started to haul himself painfully to his feet.

Hox darted back inside and was dutifully at Cauchemar's side in an instant, helping him up in as dignified a fashion as possible. 'But does that matter? You said the woman was -'

'A trick, Hox,' bawled Cauchemar. 'Like the Doctor's mythical booby trap.' He held out the infant. 'Take this back to the nutrients tank.' Then he felt himself sway, clutched on tightly to Hox's arm for support.

'Are you all right, sir?'

'I am dying, you fool,' Cauchemar said quietly.

Hox was gone with the infant only a few moments. When he

hurried back in, his hands were still dripping, and he had to reluctantly wipe them on his fine brown suit.

'We have to move quickly,' Cauchemar said. 'You've sent away the units?'

'All but four of them. And your personal guards.'

'It must suffice.' Cauchemar couched and wheezed. It felt as if his insides were twisting apart in fat lumps. 'Jasmine will be coming to this place. The Doctor must not escape to warn her.'

'He has taken Braga,' Hox informed him.

Cauchemar angrily pushed Hox's supporting hand away. 'He will take nothing else from me!' he bawled, balancing uncertainly. 'You understand, Hox? Nothing else!' He fell heavily to his knees. The patellae squashed up queasily into what felt more like jelly than flesh and cartilage. He exhaled through clenched teeth.

'Sir, let me -'

'Just stop the Doctor, Hox,' Cauchemar whispered. Hox walked hastily from the room. 'Find him. *Kill* him.'

'Somewhere on this street,' Dark announced, slowly turning the corner.

The car crawled along. It felt as if a monster was sitting in Anji's stomach gnawing at her insides as the headlights picked out details of the tall, shadowy buildings running the stretch of the street.

'You're right,' said Fitz. 'That's the place, all right. The van's parked right outside.'

Dark killed the engine. The car upset the silence with clicks and clinks as heated parts cooled down.

'Maybe that's just what they want us to think,' Anji suggested. 'They watch us go in from the building the other side and -'

'So where do you suggest we start, then?' Fitz countered impatiently.

'I don't know, I'm trying to think.'

'Well we haven't got all night, love -'

'Don't start trying to patronise me -'

'Shhh,' Vettul said suddenly, cocking her head to one side. 'I think that *is* the place.'

'Thank you, Vettul,' Fitz said with a self-satisfied smile at Anji. 'At least someone -'

'I can *hear* someone coming, from inside...'

'Get ready, everyone,' Dark said, opening his door.

The others scrambled out.

Fitz glanced at them all nervously. 'Who do we think should go first? I mean, under normal circumstances...'

Vettul's watery eyes were fixed on the shadowy entrance to the building, and she was smiling.

'*He* should,' she said.

The Doctor seemed to explode out of the building, kicking the doors wide open and leaping outside.

He seemed to have far too many limbs, and Anji stared into the shadow, trying to puzzle out how that could be.

Then her delight grew greater as she realised Braga was being carried like a rag doll under one arm.

'Doctor!' she yelled, sharing a victorious look with Fitz.

'Braga!' Etty shrieked, pushing past Anji and rushing for her boy.

The Doctor put Braga gently down. The boy looked around in bemused wonder, then started to run headlong for his mother. Etty stooped and scooped him up into her arms, sobbing joyfully. Vettul ran and flung her skinny arms around them both. Anji found herself welling up too as she ran forward.

But the Doctor wasn't following Braga. He was crouching by the stone balustrade, midway down the steps leading down to the pavement, looking for all the world as if he were tying his shoes. Only now did he seem to notice them at all. 'No, Etty,' he shouted, frantically warning her away. 'Get back to the car. Nathaniel, start up the engine! Into the car, all of you!'

'Uh-oh,' Fitz said, starting back worriedly. 'Trouble.'

'Etty, you have to get away,' he shouted, as if furious she should've come here at all. 'Go on, get out of here!'

Anji didn't need hearing like Vettul's to know some very large-sounding heavies were chasing after the Doctor.

The Doctor straightened and leapt down the rest of the steps to reach Anji. He spun her about while jogging on the spot. 'I'm being chased,' he panted.

Behind him two of his pursuers pushed determinedly through

the doors. Both were holding guns.

The Doctor considered the heavy-set men, like an artist sizing up his subjects. 'Quite a race. I wonder who'll breast the tape.'

Suddenly, the man in front was shouting, flying through the air, landing winded in a crumpled heap at the bottom of the steps.

'Or *ankle* it, anyway?'

The man following couldn't stop in time, and fell over the first with an unsettling smack on to the concrete.

The Doctor ran forward and snatched up their guns, pushing both into a coat pocket. 'Come on,' he said. 'There'll be others.'

Anji looked sharply at the Doctor as he bustled her over to the car. 'Is that why you stopped signalling? So you could use the connections as a tripwire?'

He shrugged. 'Pretty much. Sherrat - or, to give him his proper name, Cauchemar - was using your tracker to track *you*.' He opened the door and bundled her inside, glancing nervously over his shoulder for signs of further pursuit. But the building was still dark and silent, save for the distant cries of a baby somewhere.

Fitz was still standing by the car. 'It's so good to see you, Doctor.'

'Where's Hox?' said the Doctor nervously, ignoring him. 'What's he planning?'

'Doctor!' Vettul shouted.

Without warning another thug had burst through the doors and was chasing towards them at frightening speed. The Doctor reached in his pocket for one of the guns, weighed it in his hand, and threw it as hard as he could at the burly man approaching.

The gun bounced off his forehead, knocking him out cold.

'Bang!' the Doctor shouted without pleasure as the man fell over backwards. Then he took a deep breath and slammed his palm down on the roof of the car. 'It's not their fault,' he muttered to himself. 'Not them we need to stop.'

Dark started the engine and the vehicle rose from the ground with a building whine.

'I don't like this,' the Doctor said, reopening the car door. 'It's as if they're not really trying. We have to get Etty away from Cauchemar, and *keep* her away.'

'Cauchemar, huh?' Fitz asked, trying again, slapping the Doctor happily on the shoulder. 'He's the scary bad guy, right?'

'Just get in the car, Fitz!' the Doctor thundered. 'Why is everyone acting as if everything is OK all of a sudden? We have to stop Cauchemar, before he destroys this city and the entire life cycle of this world!'

Fitz recoiled as if he'd just been smacked in the mouth. Then he flushed, looked down and got in the passenger side without another word.

The Doctor clambered in beside Anji, who was already squashed up next to Vettul and Etty. Etty still held Braga to her chest, rocking him back and forth, smoothing his ragged hair with her hands.

'Where am I driving, Doctor?' Dark asked nervously.

'Anywhere. Away from here. Back towards your place, perhaps.' He paused. 'Please.'

As the Doctor fidgeted and muttered beside her, Anji felt the same way she had sitting next to the bomb on their escape from the hospital. The streets went by again silently outside. The mood should've been jubilant, but Anji felt as if someone had thrown a bucket of cold water over them all.

'Sorry, Doctor,' she said softly. 'We're just pleased to see you and Braga safe, that's all.'

'*None* of us will be safe until Cauchemar is stopped,' the Doctor fretted, tapping his feet anxiously, biting his lip. Then abruptly he reached forward and slapped Fitz matily on the shoulder. 'And yes, Fitz, Cauchemar is the scary bad guy.'

Fitz affected nonchalance, but Anji could tell the simple gesture made him a lot happier.

'Whatever he calls himself,' Etty hissed, 'he's evil. Sick.'

'Very sick. But his will... it's still so powerful.' The Doctor whistled sharply through his teeth. 'Hate is all that's keeping him together. He can't afford to relax it or...' He blew a short raspberry.

'What's his story, Doctor?' Fitz asked.

They listened as the Doctor told them all, in simple, blunt detail. Dark slowed down the car, his hands shaking as he gripped the wheel. Etty cradled Braga's head protectively. He was sleeping now, blissfully unaware, and Vettul stared wide-eyed at the Doctor, her face impassive. The truth hung heavy in the air, too much of it to take in. When he'd finished, there was silence.

Look at these people, Anji thought. They're shattered by all this. Everything turned around, turned on its head.

But they didn't get the chance to dwell on it for long.

A car came screaming out in front of them from a junction and slewed to a halt, blocking their path. Fitz and Vettul both yelled while Dark instinctively braked and twisted the wheel to avoid it. Their car spun through a hundred and eighty degrees clockwise. With no wheels to grip the ground there was no friction. She clutched hold of the Doctor as the street streaked around them, waiting for the inevitable sickening hit.

When it came it was with a force that slammed the breath from her, as the Doctor's side of the car smashed at speed into the vehicle blocking their way. The noise of the impact seemed impossibly loud. Etty and Braga were flung screaming against Anji and she in turn gasped as she was thrown hard against the Doctor. His head hit the window hard enough to crack the glass.

Then the car fell like a stone to the road beneath, jarring every bone in Anji's body.

As her head jerked forward she glimpsed silver and brown at the wheel of the car in front.

'It's Hox!' she shouted. 'And three others.'

'Car won't start!' Dark yelled over the warbling noise of the ignition.

'Put it in reverse,' Fitz begged him. 'Get us out of here.'

'It won't *start*!'

Anji heard a car door open, caught a blur of movement.

'This is a nightmare,' Fitz moaned, unfastening his seatbelt, rubbing his neck for whiplash. 'Where are the rozzers when you need them?'

'Is everyone all right?' Vettul called.

Anji gently pulled the Doctor's face round to hers. A dark lattice of blood streaked his pale skin.

'He's hurt.'

'Wonderful,' Fitz muttered.

'It's still four against five,' said Anji.

'Hey, it's six if you count Braga,' Fitz said derisively. 'We're laughing.'

'They're coming!' Vettul shouted.

'Lock the doors!' Anji snapped.

'And wait in here while they bash them in, and our heads with them?' Fitz retorted. 'Not likely.'

As the first man came up running to the car, Fitz kicked open his door. It slammed into the man, knocked him backwards. But there was another behind him, and another.

'Oh, great.' Fitz said, pulling the door closed again. 'That one's Three-One, the ugly mug that shot me!'

'Doctor? Wake *up*, Doctor!' Anji tugged on his arm desperately as blows started raining down on the car roof, on the windows, and as Dark kept trying over and over to get the engine started. She closed her eyes, shouted at him as if he simply hadn't heard her. '*Doctor!*'

# Chapter Thirty-one

The Doctor didn't respond. Fresh blood trickled down from his forehead over his eyes and cheek. Anji bit her lip.

Three-One was trying to stop Fitz from closing his car door. Fitz was losing the struggle, despite straining with both arms on the handle. The other guy was round Dark's side of the car. Beating at the window with something hard.

They didn't stand a chance.

Then Anji remembered the gun in the Doctor's coat pocket. She started to rummage for it.

Vettul gave a short, sharp shriek as the side window was shattered by a rifle stock. A thick arm reached in, grabbed her hair, tugged her against the window frame. Etty gripped the arm, sank her nails into the flesh, beat at it, but it was no good. Braga cowered in the well behind Fitz's seat, squashed down beside Anji's legs.

Anji held the gun, cold and heavy in her hand. Her heart raced as she pointed it at the man reaching in. Time seemed to slow down.

'Let go of her!' she shouted.

She wanted to fire. She wanted to *make* him let go.

'Leave us alone!' Fitz yelled as he was hauled outside by his blue fleece.

Anji swung the gun round to try to cover Three-One, but it was no good: she didn't have a clear shot.

Vettul shrieked again.

Anji trained the gun on the thick hairy arm again. She felt sick. The gun weighed a ton. Her finger tightened on the trigger

A hand closed around her own, around the gun. She jumped.

The Doctor's pale face was up close to hers. The jagged lines of nearly black blood under the sickly street-lamp-yellow made his face like an image in a stained glass window. 'Don't,' he said simply. 'Trust me.'

Then the gun was twisted from both their hands.

Etty held it, pointed it through the shattered window, and fired it at point-blank range into the man's chest. The noise of the shot was deafening.

Dark swung round in alarm, trying to see who was hurt.

The battering on the roof of the car abruptly stopped.

Vettul curled herself up in a ball, hugging herself, sobbing.

'Etty –' began the Doctor.

'I'll kill all of you!' Etty shouted out of the window, wide-eyed and shaking, still clutching the gun.

Her free hand fumbled for the door handle.

'Etty, no! You must stay in the car!'

'You hear me?'

She was scrambling past Vettul, who reached out now blindly for Anji. Anji held her, shaking.

Now Etty was outside the car. 'You are going to *stop* hurting the people I love.'

The Doctor tried to open his own door but it must've been knocked out of shape in the crash: it wouldn't budge.

'Nathaniel!' shouted the Doctor. 'You're closest, stop her! Get her back inside!'

'Er, I could use a hand right now,' Fitz called from out of site.

Fitz's cry for help made the Doctor try still harder, pushing desperately at the door. Anji tried to pull away from Vettul so she could lend her weight.

'Vettul, Braga needs you,' she hissed. 'Look after him, out of sight down there behind the seat. He *needs* you.'

Vettul looked up at Anji, her tearstained white face freckled with blood spats, and nodded solemnly.

Anji looked around to find that the door had opened at last and the Doctor was gone. She scrambled out after him, as Braga and Vettul clung to each other.

And found that she needed to be helping everywhere at once.

The Doctor had some thug in a bear hug, keeping him away from Fitz.

Another big man was bearing down on Fitz, who was trapped back against the bonnet, pleading, 'Not the face, not the face.'

Dark was trying to take the gun from Etty, to get her back inside the car as ordered.

And Hox was coming up behind him with what looked like a cosh, moving with that same horrible speed he'd exhibited in the hospital.

'Look out!' she shouted at the top of her lungs.

Everyone seemed to turn to look at *her*, Nathaniel included.

And the cosh came down on the back of Dark's head. His legs buckled and he fell to the ground, out of sight behind the car.

Etty brought up the gun against Hox's head.

Just as Hox brought the cosh up under her chin.

Etty's head snapped up as the gun fired, the shot going wide into the air as she staggered backwards. Then she too fell out of sight.

Three-One looked up as the shot was fired. Fitz used the distraction to bring up his good leg and kick his attacker away.

'Deal with this one, Anji,' the Doctor ordered, throwing himself across the bonnet of the car to get to Hox.

Hox swung the cosh again but missed, knocking a huge dent into the bonnet instead of the Doctor's skull. The Doctor's momentum carried him up and into Hox's chest. The two men began to grapple.

Anji swung her attention back to the huge man. He swatted her back against the car. She fell painfully on to the pavement.

Fitz came up behind her attacker. He'd taken off his fleece and threw it over the bruiser's head. And, while the man struggled to tear it off, Three-One lunged for him, knocking him to the ground. The other man fought back furiously from under the fleece.

Fitz helped up Anji. 'Not too bright, are they?' he said. 'Think in colours. But then what do you expect from a man named after a footie score.'

'He thinks that bloke is...?'

'Me. That's *Seven's* coat. The one that made him so cross back at the farm.'

Anji looked round. 'Where's the...?'

The Doctor's struggle with Hox had taken them some way away down the street.

'Two against one,' Fitz observed, running off to help, pausing only to pick up the fallen gun. 'I like those odds better. Especially holding one of these.'

'I'll get Etty and Dark inside,' said Anji, when satisfied that Three-One and his mate were still occupied beating the crap out of each other.

A big blue bruise was coming up under Etty's chin. She'd fallen on the man she'd shot dead. A soft landing.

Anji shuddered, and strained to lift Etty's dead weight in her arms.

Suddenly a pair of headlights shone brightly round the corner and into the street. Thank God. Help. Maybe this would scare Hox and the others off. She redoubled her efforts lifting Etty, held her in both arms.

The vehicle came to a halt.

It was a van, and Anji's heart lurched when she recognised it.

A man jumped out, the one who'd tripped the Doctor's wire at the building entrance. He was pointing a gun at her.

In the passenger side was a hunched-up figure. Dark hair flecked with grey. A once handsome face, now lined and sullen. Dark eyes glimmering under heavy brows.

She knew him.

*Cauchemar is the scary bad guy.*

'You'll place the woman in here,' Cauchemar called huskily. 'Or my man will shoot you dead.'

As Fitz approached the Doctor and Hox at a fast limp he could see how desperately they were fighting, both men well aware they could not afford to lose.

But the Doctor had taken a fair few lumps already. And Hox was tougher than he'd thought, he'd give him that. Now he had the Doctor on his back, pinning his arms to the concrete with his knees, choking the life out of him.

'Get off him, short arse,' Fitz shouted as he ran. 'I've got a score to settle with you, and I'm holding a bloody big gun.'

But, before Fitz could get close enough to push him off, the Doctor had slapped both feet flat against the road and bucked his whole body, breaking Hox's hold on his throat and propelling him forward. Hox rolled over and over on the wet concrete.

Fitz skidded to a halt by the Doctor, who was tugging at his cravat, taking deep whoops of breath. He glanced about for any signs of onlookers who might help them. How could this street be so deserted? Fair enough, it was the middle of the night, but even so...

Then he saw, way down at the far end of the street, thick stripy tape cordoning off the area. He stared at it, stupidly. Was it for real, or...?

And then he saw the headlights sweep round from the other end of the road.

'See that, Hox?' Fitz shouted. 'Help. Or are you going to get them beaten up too?'

Hox looked up with a frightened scowl, then seemed to relax. He started running towards the new arrivals.

'Uh-oh,' Fitz muttered.

Suddenly the Doctor was back on his feet. 'No! Come on, Fitz, we've got to stop -'

'Doctor, look!' Fitz grabbed him and pointed. 'Anji!'

Some gorilla was pointing a gun at her head.

'Let her go!' bellowed the Doctor as he and Fitz ran closer.

'Move against me, Doctor, and she will die,' came a weedy shout from the van.

'Stop fighting,' Hox ordered his grappling goons on the floor. 'Get into the van.'

Three-One got up, a livid bruise over one eye. 'What about Four-Four?'

'Four-Four is dead,' said Hox. 'Now get inside.'

The bruisers shuffled off meek as you like into the back of the van.

'Doctor, I'm sorry!' Anji wailed. 'They were going to kill me.'

'It's all right, Anji.' The Doctor had taken in the scene and was glaring at the man huddled in the passenger seat of the van, who Fitz guessed was Cauchemar. 'He'd have killed you and taken her anyway if you hadn't done what he said.'

Cauchemar nodded. 'You'd be proud of her, Doctor: she put up quite a fight.'

The Doctor smiled faintly. 'Like me, she believes in the greater good.'

'Like you, she's got under my feet. So she *has* to be trodden on.'

'Harm her, Cauchemar, and I'll -'

'You'll die along with her, Doctor.'

Fitz held his breath as he felt the revolver being drawn stealthily from his hand by the Doctor's nimble fingers, keeping his eye on Hox as he scrambled into the driver's seat.

'How did you find us?' demanded the Doctor.

'Like the Creator,' Cauchemar said mockingly, 'I watch over all. I only paused in killing her because I wanted you here to witness it.'

The Doctor's hand twitched by his side.

Fitz suddenly felt terribly uneasy.

*The greater good.*

Was he going to try to save Anji or take a pot shot at Cauchemar? Save the day, save the world, but let their friend take a bullet to the brain?

When the gun went off, Fitz closed his eyes.

Anji cried out.

Then she was rushing towards them, while the monkey who'd been holding her recoiled back against the van, clutching his scarlet shoulder. Fitz caught her and she threw her arms about him.

'Down behind the car!' shouted the Doctor.

'Get in, you idiot!' Cauchemar roared at the injured gunman.

'Nice shooting, Doctor,' Fitz muttered, holding Anji close.

The Doctor clearly couldn't hear him over the sound of the next shots. He fired twice at the windscreen of the reversing van as it rose up from the ground and started to turn. The glass fractured, then shattered inward.

Cauchemar had covered his face with his blotchy hands.

The Doctor aimed again - but Fitz couldn't see exactly at what - and pulled the trigger.

The hammer clicked home on nothing. The gun was out of bullets.

'No!' the Doctor shouted, slinging the gun down uselessly on the floor.

'I'm so sorry, Doctor,' Anji muttered. She was trembling.

'You've nothing to be sorry about,' the Doctor said, staring after the disappearing van.

Beside them, Dark let out a low groan. The Doctor knelt down to examine him. 'A nasty bruise,' he reported, 'but he should be OK.' Then he flashed them a mirthless smile. 'Until the world ends, anyway.'

Fitz gave Anji's hand what he hoped was a comforting squeeze. A fine rain began to fall as they sat in a frightened silence, counting bruises, and blessings.

Vettul suddenly poked her head through the shattered window. 'Have they gone?'

Fitz reached out a hand to touch her face. She leaned into it.

'Yes,' he said. 'All gone.'

Anji's voice was hollow. 'And Etty, too.'

The Doctor pinched the bridge of his nose, closed his eyes. 'How did they find us to set this trap? How?'

His eyes snapped suddenly open and met Fitz's. They both knew there was only one answer.

'Braga?'

Vettul looked back at Braga, and put her hand to her mouth in fear.

The Doctor reached inside the car and lifted out the struggling boy. Fitz held him awkwardly while the Doctor raided his little pockets.

He pulled out what looked like a tiny ball of lead shot. 'Tracking device? But how...?'

Fitz kicked the side of the car savagely. 'We're worse off now than when we started.'

# Chapter Thirty-two

Etty's eyes flickered open. She moaned in pain and found that hurt her all the more. Her tongue felt bloated in her mouth, and the sharp iron tang of blood was stuck in her throat.

A slight spin in her stomach and the whine of an engine told her she was moving. It was dark all around her save for a pale-green phosphorescence coming from what looked like a fish tank. Someone large was sitting in front of it. Then the engine motors died down, her transport came to a stop.

'Get off here and proceed to your location,' came the nightmare voice, the voice of the man from the viewscreen, threatening her boy.

Hox. They had her. Where was she?

The man got up obediently and opened the van's back doors. Etty caught a glimpse of a plaza, of late-night revellers wringing the last value from the day. They seemed so happy it was comforting, and she wanted to reach out for it, to shout for help. But no words came from her bruised lips, and the doors slammed shut after the large shadow-man had clambered out.

Nothing was blocking her view of the glowing tank now. She saw a silhouette floating in its green waters, its mass peppered with tiny spikes, wriggling and crawling.

A soft-boiled eye opened to regard her.

Etty moaned with fear, looked away - then heard the voice she'd told herself she'd never hear again.

'I'm so glad you're awake, Jasmine, my dear.'

'Derran?' she croaked.

'It's been so very long, Jasmine,' he cooed to her.

'Jas- What are you -?'

'We must enjoy our time together now to the fullest, my dear. It's a long journey, and Hox here will soon be leaving us. You must tell me all about the life Ettianne has been subjecting you to since taking my child away.'

He broke off into coughing. Etty closed her eyes, grateful that it was dark, that he couldn't see her cry.

Then he sniggered. 'Then I shall explain to you, and to her, exactly how I'm going to tear that sickly, wasteful life into bloody shreds.'

'No time, no time...' The Doctor was pacing up and down outside, deep in thought.

Fitz swapped a helpless shrug with Anji as he finished manhandling Dark into the driver's seat, out of the rain.

'It's my fault,' Dark muttered. The poor sod looked utterly wretched, pale and clutching the back of his head. 'I should've stopped her. I let you all down.'

'It's my fault just as much as yours,' Anji sighed.

Abruptly the Doctor clapped his hands together, making them all jump. He peered in at them through the window, getting soaked, but neither noticing nor caring. 'Right. This is the way I see things. Quickly, now. Everyone listening?'

Vettul was sitting with Braga on her lap. Anji sat beside her, and Fitz now moved back into the passenger side. He pushed the open map book off the seat and on to the floor.

No one felt much like receiving a lesson, but paid dutiful attention.

'Firstly, Cauchemar's on his way to the water mountains with Etty for a showdown with the Creator.'

Anji looked sceptical. 'He's just going to walk up to the Creator?'

'Metaphorically speaking, yes. He's been there before. He must know where he needs to get to in order to trigger the effect. Meanwhile, his parade of brainwashed victims are on their way to destinations all over the city, presumably armed with a sackload of explosives. For maximum impact he's going to want those bombs to go off at the moment he's ready to go in.'

'How are they going to synchronise all that?' Fitz wanted to know.

The Doctor held up his lump of shot. 'I doubt Cauchemar had this made purely to slip into Braga's pocket on the off chance he escaped, nor that he cobbled up a device to triangulate a signal in order to track your coming here. No, each of his carriers must have one of these tracers, and he'll be monitoring them somehow.'

Anji looked sceptical. 'Hell of a distance for the signal to travel.'

'Yes,' agreed the Doctor, 'and your car took some time to come in range.' He clicked his fingers. 'Hox must be monitoring things locally, and will be in radio contact with Cauchemar.'

Fitz stuck out his bottom lip. 'Cauchemar signals him when the time is right, and Hox passes on the good news.'

'How can we stop them?' Vettul asked in a small voice.

'How can we hope to find them?' Dark added.

Everyone looked expectantly at the Doctor.

He didn't seem to have an answer.

'Etty killed Four-Four,' Anji pointed out. 'I know it's awful but that's one fewer to deal with.'

'There was a room full of those poor saps,' Fitz reminded her.

'And Cauchemar told me that each and every one had their part to play,' said the Doctor. 'Perhaps Hox will take Four-Four's place.'

'How about we drive round looking for people in funny coats?' Fitz suggested.

Dark shook his head. 'In a city this size?'

'I guess they'll be inside the buildings, anyway, to do the most damage. Just waiting to go off.' Fitz looked down at the map at his feet. 'All over the City.'

'Why numbers?' the Doctor muttered.

'Letters too,' Anji said. 'Hang on, I've got that list we took from the bald man...'

'Let me see.' The Doctor clicked his fingers impatiently as she pulled out the crumpled paper from her trouser pocket. His lips moved as he scanned the list. 'Three-One-B-Four... Three-Four-B-Nine... Seven-Two-C-One...'

'Wait a minute,' breathed Fitz.

Everyone looked at him expectantly.

'It's this map!' he shouted, suddenly elated. 'This crazy grid thing!'

Anji grabbed his arm in excitement. 'Grid references! The locations they've got to go to, the most important information they need to hang on to!'

'Yes!' the Doctor shouted happily.

Anji rummaged in her little bag squashed under the seat and came out with an eyeliner pencil. 'Give me the map, Fitz.'

'There's a smaller one of the whole city at a glance here somewhere.' Fitz passed it over, and while the Doctor read out the list of letters and numbers, Anji worked out the co-ordinates on the grid and plotted them with big greasy black crosses.

'From these I can work out which buildings they'll be most likely to target,' Dark said, caught up in the air of sudden optimism. Fitz smiled to himself wryly. All other problems put on hold while they dealt with something that had a hope of understanding.

'It's making a pattern,' said Vettul, as the crosses piled up over the City.

Dark peered over. 'The Diviners' mark of office.'

'Of course,' said the Doctor. 'The double helix.'

'One last two-fingers up at the Creator,' Anji breathed. 'He'll tear the City apart.'

'This is something the police can help us with,' Dark said. 'If we can make them believe us.'

Fitz looked at him. 'We'll have to.'

'The Holiest will doubtless still be watching you,' said the Doctor. 'That should help your case.'

Dark just shuddered.

'I'll leave you to organise that, then,' the Doctor announced. 'I'm going after Etty and Cauchemar.'

Fitz spoke loudest above the general protest. 'Alone?'

'Yes. You'll all be needed to help here, you can only have a few hours. Do all you can to stop those bombs going off.' He paused, looked at Anji. 'I'm relying on you.' Then he smiled over at Fitz. 'I'm relying on you all.'

He walked over to the battered car Hox had used to block them and got inside. Fitz led the others out of the car, still protesting.

'Vettul,' Anji said, taking the sleeping Braga from her weedy arms, 'you told us that you and Myra know the land around the farm.'

Vettul nodded proudly. 'No one knows it better than we do.'

The Doctor started the car engine, and it buzzed into life. Drunkenly the vehicle rose a little way from the ground. 'Are there many ways of reaching the water mountains?'

'Just one,' said Vettul.

His face fell. 'No short cuts you could tell me?'

'There is only one way there. And there are some narrow passes. It is not easy.'

'A few big drops, too,' Anji remembered with a shudder.

'It's not supposed to be easy,' said Dark. 'None may visit the Creator and live.'

Fitz frowned. 'This madman doesn't want to, that's the whole problem.'

'Contact Myra, Vettul, when you get to Nathaniel's,' the Doctor urged her. 'Ask if she can organise the others to block off one of those passes, anything at all to cause Cauchemar to waste time, to delay him. He has a head start on me... I have to stop him.'

'Hey, Doctor, our car's screwed,' Fitz reminded him. 'How about a lift to the main road, then?'

'No time,' said the Doctor, revving the engine. 'Good luck.' He paused. 'Goodbye.'

Then the car bucked and lurched off noisily down the street. Fitz watched as it snapped through the cordon tape at the end of the road and vanished round the corner.

'See ya,' he whispered softly.

'Well,' Anji declared, 'I'm buggered if I'm going to let him down again.'

'Come on,' said Dark, trying to keep their enthusiasm going, 'the main road is this way. We'd better get started.'

Their luck held as they made their way back to the busier part of town. Soon, they were huddled together on a night bus, trying to keep Vettul as hidden from view as possible. No one took much interest in them, wrapped up in their own mundanities. If you only knew what we know, thought Anji. If you only knew you could be dead in just a few hours, what would you do?

Having that sort of knowledge, that sort of responsibility, made Anji feel a bit like a god herself. It was a miserable feeling.

The bus's last stop must've been a mile away from Dark's apartment, but stealing through the darkened streets Anji guessed they were all way too wired to feel particularly tired.

As soon as they got inside, Dark called up Etty's farmhouse on the viewscreen. The no-carrier signal rang softly for some time, then the image crackled into life.

Myra, a grey, wrinkly and deliberate little woman with eyes too wide apart, smiled solemnly and said, 'Hello?'

Vettul beamed at her. 'Myra! You are well?'

'Very well,' Myra said, with a quick sideways glance.

Anji saw Murph emerge into view from behind her, gurgling a merry tune with what looked like a pair of pants on his head. One of the others, a skinny little thing, was stamping around a lot of broken plates on the floor, skidding in food, while still others were playing and singing noisily. The scene, under any other circumstances, would've been funny. As it was, Anji just bit her lip, wondering what kind of distraction or delay the mooncalves would be able to make. To save the woman who loved and cared for them – and the god that did not believe in their existence.

'Look who I have here,' Vettul said, tugging the sleepy Braga into view. Myra squealed with delight and burst into tears, and the others stopped what they were doing and crowded closer.

As Anji looked on, the viewscreen was suddenly like a window looking in on a distorted world. It was hard to believe that these poor, defenceless happy people could add to the destabilising effect on the Creator, but if Etty went on to have more kids, or even Vettul, she supposed... Well, if they were 'different', wouldn't that worsen things in the long run? It was horrible, but she could almost understand now the panic, as the Holiest realised any of this was going on without their knowledge. Cauchemar had set so much horror in motion, and yet how could the mooncalves' simple happiness as they welcomed Braga back be perceived as part of that?

Fitz seemed to be reading her thoughts, collapsed in a chair, resting his weary injured leg as he said, 'Bugger, isn't it?'

She nodded dolefully.

'Hurry, Vettul,' Dark said softly. 'We must talk to the authorities. Ask your friends to help as the Doctor told you.'

'And whatever happens,' Anji chipped in, 'don't let them be tempted to go anywhere near Etty themselves. Cauchemar will kill them as soon as look at them.'

Vettul began to tell the wide-eyed mooncalves what to do.

The Doctor drove with the accelerator pedal stamped down almost flush to the floor. The straight road stretched endlessly ahead up to the featureless horizon. It was like driving in a simulation of some kind, a generated track whose designers had neglected to put in even the barest of detail.

I'll find them soon, the Doctor told himself. I'm catching them up, all the time.

Did they know a faster route? He knew only the one that he and Dark had taken, days ago. Where were they now - already on the path to the water mountains? How close was Cauchemar to ending everything?

'I talk to myself so often,' the Doctor announced to no one in particular, 'to distract my mind from asking too many awkward questions.'

The road went on like a long yawn made of asphalt. The Doctor fixed his sights on the horizon, hoping to catch at any moment the first glimmers of the dawn reflected on the holy waters.

With Myra nervously accepting what the mooncalves had to do, Dark nudged Vettul aside and dialled in a number he'd always had stored, but had never used.

Cleric Rammes eventually answered, hunched grumpily in front of his screen at home, his wispy grey hair standing up from his head. He reacted when he realised who was calling him.

'Dark,' Rammes said. 'What is it?'

'I need your help, sir,' Dark said simply.

'At this hour?'

'By morning we'll be out of time all together.'

Rammes looked at him uncertainly, almost fearfully. 'The Holiest gave you audience.' Dark nodded. 'I have been informed that no action is to be taken against you.'

'Listen to me, *sir*, none of that matters right now,' said Dark, his voice rising a fraction. 'You must trust me. The authorities might believe it coming from you...'

Dark told Rammes all he felt it was wise to: about the bombs, how soon it could all end. About the death of a city; that was fear enough to be getting on with. By the time Dark had finished, Rammes was already reaching for pen and paper to scrawl down the grid references with a trembling hand.

'If you're right, Dark, the City will owe you a great debt. If you're wrong...'

Dark waved the platitudes away. 'Please, Cleric Rammes, there's so little time -'

Rammes would not be stopped. 'The Creator be praised for shaping your life to help others.'

'No,' Dark whispered, shaking his head. 'I will not praise the Creator.'

Rammes stared at him horrified for a moment. Then attempted to recover his composure. 'You are tired, Nathaniel, you've been through so much -'

'Too much.'

'But your Creator is constant, unchanging.'

'You're right.' Dark met Rammes's gaze, unflinching. 'His nature has not changed. But He no longer means what He used to mean to *me*. That's why I'm not coming back to you.'

'You're leaving our service?'

'I *can't* come back.'

Rammes stared at him. He seemed more alarmed at this news than at learning of the bombs.

'You are deranged,' he said.

'No.'

'Unhinged.'

'Cleric Rammes, you must act now -'

'You expect me to believe what you have told me now I am witness to your state of mind?'

'Yes,' Dark shouted. 'You must trust me, Cleric Rammes.'

Rammes stared at him, either aghast or in wonder, it was hard to tell which.

'You must have faith in *me*.'

Rammes looked down, and killed the connection. The screen faded to black.

'Will he tell them, do you think?' Fitz wondered.

'I'm sure he shall. He's a good man. He just doesn't know...' Dark turned away from them, but he couldn't hide his voice catching. 'He doesn't know all that I do.'

Anji put a hand on his shoulder. 'I think we should try to get to Four-Four-whatever-whatever ahead of the police. Right now.'

'To settle with Hox?' asked Fitz.

Anji nodded. 'If the Doctor's right and Hox has taken Four-Four's place... and if he *is* in touch with Cauchemar –'

Fitz nodded. '– we can make contact with him ourselves. Tell him the game's up.'

'And if these carriers don't get the signal from Hox, they won't blow themselves to bits,' concluded Anji.

'But we don't have a car,' Dark said.

'Can't we steal one?'

'The Doctor's trick, not mine.'

Dark looked at Anji, but the helpless look on her face told him not to.

Fitz clicked his fingers. 'Hey, you must have taxis here, don't you?'

Dark nodded with relief. He'd have slapped his own forehead if his head wasn't so sore already.

'Too much time spent in the Doctor's convoluted company,' said Anji with a smile. 'It makes you miss the obvious.'

Dark punched in a number, his friends beside him, waiting for the cab firm to pick up. It seemed ridiculous, somehow, that they were stuck at the mercy of the local taxi firm as much as they were a crazed madman who wanted the city to burn. That they would be waiting here for a while, then catching a cab over to the end of the world.

# Chapter Thirty-three

'Remove it from the tank.'

Etty looked, sickened, at the struggling baby swimming in its green goo. 'You're insane, Derran.'

'My name is Cauchemar, Jasmine,' he said, stumbling towards her, his long black cloak catching the wind and billowing out like a sheet behind him. He stroked her cheek with the stubby barrel of his gun. 'Don't you recognise me?'

Etty spat in his face.

Derran, or Cauchemar, or whoever he was, wiped away the spittle and licked his finger with a smile. 'I taste you, my love. This body holds your spirit, I see that - a poor, ageing body, wasting away unseen out in this forsaken wilderness.' He waved around at the familiar landscape of home. Etty tried to get her bearings from the spires of the water mountains. Her house couldn't be too far away, if only she could -

The gun was jammed up against her forehead. 'We will proceed on foot. I desire ceremony. You will remove the creature from the tank.'

'Why should I help you? You'll kill me if I do or if I don't.'

'Don't you wish to taste that sweetness of death only I can provide? You'd sooner feel a bullet rip through you?'

'At least it would be quick.'

Cauchemar smiled and shook his head, rubbed the gun down along her neck, stroked it against her stomach. She tried to stop herself from whimpering.

She thought of the Doctor, steering her through the careless, joyful life of the City's plaza at night.

*You must never give up hope.*

Etty reached gingerly into the tank and picked up the sticky creature inside. The tiny fingers of its hand, its own hand, tightened round her wrist. The other digits flexed and bent spasmodically. Which one was Ansac's, she wondered, or Treena's? She couldn't bring herself to look.

Fighting the urge to be sick, Etty held the fat, dripping lump to her chest and allowed Cauchemar to propel her at gunpoint towards the water mountains.

They walked for some time, the baby a bundle of dead weight, staining her dark blouse. The wind was blustery and wet as the fresh first glimmers of the new day ignited in the sky. Cauchemar's wheezing became throatier, his sporadic demands to speak to Jasmine less coherent. Their pace was getting slower too. Etty tried to slow down her step as much as she dared in the hope he might just fall down dead.

'I cannot die,' Cauchemar ground out, as if she'd spoken aloud. 'I *will* not. Not yet. But *you* can, Ettianne, any time I choose.'

'Who'll carry your sick monstrosity then?' Etty sneered. 'You can barely lift a gun.'

'Really?' He wedged it back up hard against the back of her neck. 'Just keep moving.'

They were approaching the promontory that led out to the narrow ridge of land stretching out to the first spire of the water mountains. She'd never been so near before. Etty felt a pang of fear more intense than anything Cauchemar had been able to rouse in her.

'We can't get this close, it's forbidden,' she blurted out, coming to a halt. The baby writhed in her arms as if agreeing.

'We must get closer, precisely *because* it is forbidden.' He surveyed the dull reds and browns of the headland beneath the scrubby grass. 'There is a natural passage through the rock, I remember it. But where...?'

Etty looked away out to sea, a dulled glass blanket pulled over the coastland. It stretched out to the pale sky broken only by the spears of rock rising up from it. The glistening water ran up and over the protruding spires in a helical motion. It looked so beautiful, it had always looked so beautiful, the sight was her one consolation for being marooned out here – and yet even looking upon it for too long felt dangerous. No one could cross the ridges, approach the dwelling of the Creator.

'It's *forbidden*,' Etty reiterated helplessly, as if compelled to do so.

'The way is blocked!' snarled Cauchemar. 'What pathetic attempt to delay me is this?'

He began clawing at the piled rocks, pulling down the feeble barricade. Etty looked around for any way to escape, but there was no cover here, just the wide-open manlands. He'd bring her down with a single bullet.

She noticed a strange marking in the mud at her feet, a long narrow furrow curving in towards the blocked passageway. There were traces of another track parallel to it a few feet apart.

Murph, she thought, stifling a gasp. And the others?

The Doctor must've sent the mooncalves to help, to delay Cauchemar. Was he on his way here even now? Etty felt afraid and elated at once, looking round furtively for any trace of another soul in sight. But there was nothing.

The baby pulled at her clothes with its many hands and fingers, and she looked down into its milky eyes. If she took this poor monster with her, would Cauchemar be so ready to fire?

'Help me here,' said Cauchemar gruffly. 'Put down the infant. Don't try to run.'

Etty looked over at him coldly and gently lowered the child on to the grass. It stared up at the grey sky in wonder; Etty imagined this might be the first and only time the baby had ever seen the world outside. One more creature, like herself, like the mooncalves, forced to hide away from the world thanks to the man who was finally going to finish the task he'd begun so many years ago. To take her life away. To make her die hating him, even as she loved his child. It was all such a mess and yet he was ignorant to any pain he caused other than his own.

Once he had whispered so many promises to her. This thing spitting threats wasn't him, holding her at gunpoint. She was glad in a way that his name had changed, just as his appearance had withered and altered. He was a different man.

Cauchemar peeled a sunfruit and ate it morosely while staring at her with black-bagged eyes, slumped back in his cloak against the bald rock, looking suddenly like a petulant poorly child on a picnic. She cleared stones and debris as slowly as she thought she might get away with. With every boulder a little more of the view of the watery ridge was revealed, the slippery way became clearer.

If help was coming it needed to come soon.

'X marks the spot,' Dark said. 'The East Side prayer house.'

'Let's hope the Creator's still got an ear going begging,' Fitz said. 'If we're going to find anyone in there we'll need all the help we can get.'

The cab pulled up outside a vast structure unlike any kind of church Anji had seen before. It began with the weird mushroom stalk base of so many buildings here but then branched up into spires and stanchions supporting huge stone turrets like buds, each piling up one upon the other, reaching up for the fading stars and darkness as dawn crept in about them.

Dark paid the driver. 'Keep the change.'

'And spend it quickly,' Fitz added.

They'd left Vettul looking after Braga at Dark's place. She hadn't put up much of a protest at being left behind, accepting the sense of it. With all the girl had been through on her first trip to the city, Anji wasn't really surprised she should wish to stay. Besides, if - when - the mooncalves had something to report, someone had to be there to receive it.

'I'll tell you their news when you come back,' Vettul had said, her smile radiant. Positive that they'd return.

Anji had tried willing herself to feel as certain all the long way over here. Now, staring up at the enormity of this weird building in all its shadowy splendour, she felt less confident than ever.

'How're you feeling?' asked Fitz.

'Sick,' said Anji frankly.

'Cheer up.' He gestured to the improbable spires and obelisks poking up at the sky. 'Finding Hox hiding somewhere in all this lot is going to make finding a bit of self-confidence seem like a doddle. Right?'

Anji had lost track of his logic somewhere there, but it didn't matter, there was no time for thinking now. Dark was leading them inside.

'How long do you think until the police get here?' asked Fitz nervously.

'I think we have to assume we're on our own for now,' Anji advised.

'Armed only with bread knives,' Fitz sighed, looking wryly down at the blade in his hand. 'We're definitely one loaf short of a baker's dozen.'

The heavy oak door gave creakily on to nothing but blackness. Fitz produced a lighter from his pocket and the flame sputtered, as if intimidated by the shadows. Dark groped in a basket in the doorway for candles, lit them, and soon they each had a puny peanut of yellow illuminating their way.

'It doesn't make sense that he should come here,' whispered Fitz as they pressed forward, ears straining for the slightest noise. 'There's no one to blow up.'

'Maybe it's a symbolic thing,' said Nathaniel.

'Symbollocks,' Fitz muttered.

Soon they came to a divergence in the stone passageway - there was a flight of steps leading right and left, stretching up into the stanchions, and facing them was a set of double doors that reminded Fitz of those in the old TARDIS control room.

'Split up?' Fitz said the words with a doomy inevitability.

She nodded. 'Whoever finds him first...'

'... sneaks back and tells the others at no personal risk to themselves,' finished Fitz.

Dark and Anji both agreed. While she took the left stairway and he the right, Fitz softly opened the double doors.

The way the steps spiralled meant that Anji could see no further than a couple of feet in front of her. Her heels echoed softly on step after step. The higher she rose into the dark tower the more the glow of her candle seemed to seep into the stonework. She could imagine the walls were closing in on her.

Then she froze. She'd heard something. Coming up the stairs.

Behind her.

Etty made a great show of pulling away another stone, but Cauchemar clearly couldn't tolerate any further delay.

'All right, that will do,' he said. 'Fetch the infant and get through the gap.'

She bundled the baby up into her aching arms and was about to step over the remaining rocks when he came up behind her, grazing the gun against her ear.

'Slowly,' he said, 'and where I can see you.'

She took a deep breath and wriggled through the passage. The baby's gurgles echoed eerily as they passed under the stone arch.

On the other side, she stopped still, taking in the incredible landscape. The grassy promontory led down towards the open sea – and now, for the first time, she could see the beginnings of the winding ribbon of rock that bridged the ocean to the first great mountainous peak, and then on to the next, and the next, a flat trail the width of a country lane stretching away into the hazy distance. It was as if a mountain range had been chiselled down to a towering stack of rock, with only occasional points left prominent. But no dam could stem the flow of the Creator's water as it rose from the abyss and splashed and swirled in a thousand vortices about the stony surface.

The baby started to struggle and kick feebly in her arms.

'Forward,' Cauchemar ordered.

'No...' Etty felt suddenly dizzy. As she approached the track leading out to the first spire, the whirling water covering its surface seemed to blur before her.

'You're feeling the first tickles of the Creator's fingers in your mind?' Cauchemar asked softly. 'His first warning to keep back.' Then his hacking cough ripped through the trance, jolting her back. 'This is your first and only warning to keep forward,' he said when he'd recovered. She saw him pull a device of some kind from his pocket and scrutinise it.

'You'll kill me,' she whispered.

'I'll save you. Only you.'

'No.'

For a moment she thought she saw actual regret in his eyes as they snapped up to meet her own. 'How could you wish to live without me?' he croaked.

Then she saw sudden movement behind him, coming out of the cover of big scrubby bushes.

It was Myra, her face rapt with concentration, hunched behind Murph in his chair, wheeling him out slowly and stealthily at the top of the rise.

Murph's eyes were closed, and he was hugging himself tightly. Etty realised he was about to become a two-wheeled projectile, flying down the slope to knock into the back of Cauchemar.

Her eyes widened in surprise and alarm, she couldn't help it.

And she knew she'd given them away.

Cauchemar spun round as Myra propelled Murph towards him. With an angry roar he threw himself aside, further up the slope, lashing out at the wheelchair with his foot as it passed.

'Run, Etty!' squeaked Myra. 'Run, run, run!'

But Murph had tumbled from his chair with a shout. Etty laid down the now screaming baby and rushed over to help him. He looked up at her with bright eyes full of dismay, arms flapping, legs dead and useless.

Cauchemar was getting to his feet behind her, gaunt and vampiric in his great cloak. As Etty tried to lift Murph back into his chair, he took an awkward step towards them.

'Flesh of my flesh,' he breathed. 'Diseased and rotten as I am.'

'Keep away from them,' Etty warned him.

'Run, Etty!' Myra shouted again.

'*You* run! Get out of here, Myra!'

Would she go? Cauchemar's billowing cloak, windswept, had blacked out her view. His darkness was closing in on them. Now he smiled, baring his yellow teeth. 'If I am to be cleansed, I must strip away my old impurity.'

Blackness flapped before her like bat wings. 'Myra, go, he'll kill you!'

Murph struggled in Etty's arms as Cauchemar drew closer, aiming the gun.

'I'm going to kill *everyone*.'

Etty shrieked as Cauchemar suddenly flew towards her.

'Actually, I've got something to say about that,' came a familiar voice.

Cauchemar was flying *over* her, propelled by an unseen force. Then he was tumbling down the slope into the scraggy grass at the edge of the watery track. The gun fell from his grasp.

Etty looked up in disbelief to find the Doctor standing above her, crusty blood lining his face, staring coldly at Cauchemar.

* * *

Anji turned on the stair, as the footsteps came closer, squeezing the handle of her knife so tightly she thought it might crack. Should she lie in wait or keep climbing up to the tower? The walls seemed to press in on her as she struggled to make a decision.

'Anji?'

She almost wept with relief. The hoarse whisper belonged to Fitz.

As his long, stubbly face bobbed up nervously into the candlelight, she didn't know whether to be angry at him for scaring her or pleased...

Someone was behind him, forcing him up the steps.

*Hox, a trick, she'd been tricked.*

'Anji, are you all right?'

It was only Nathaniel following behind, earnest and concerned as ever.

'I am now,' Anji said, feeling foolish. 'What's going on?'

'I think I've found him,' whispered Fitz.

They trooped silently back down the steps. On the one hand, Anji was barely able to believe their luck in finding him so quickly. On the other, there was no sign of police sirens, no backup for them of any kind. And still, at any moment, the bombs could be set off and the City set on fire.

Fitz nudged open one of the big doors.

'The prayer hall,' Dark muttered as they stole inside as quiet as mice. 'Where the Diviners make their proclamations.'

All Anji really got from the place in the near-total darkness was a sense of increased scale; their footfalls and scufflings were made breathier with enormous echo.

Fitz pointed to a candle glow in the middle of a long pew, a few rows ahead. 'There.'

Anji squinted into the gloom, held her breath. There was definitely a figure hunched there, the candle flickering by his side.

Dark mimed turning on a light, pointed to his eyes and closed them, warning Fitz and Anji to be ready.

They looked nervously at each other, crept closer to the figure in the pew. Dark should see their own candles, the twin lights converging on the single one they had spotted. Fitz had his bread knife drawn and ready.

'Don't move!'

Nathaniel's shout echoed insanely as the hall flooded with burning light. Anji kept blinking, blinking, trying to see, catching impressions of the great room. Huge candelabra studded with electric lights swung above them. The rough wooden pews could've been hewn from Viking longboats: they stretched on and on. There was an ornate wooden balcony reaching from wall to wall above them in front of a heavy-looking curtain of red velvet. And Dark's footsteps were ringing on dusty flagstones as he rushed to join them.

Anji blinked again. Fitz was holding his bread knife to Hox's throat.

'D-don't hurt me.'

But it wasn't Hox. It was a terrified-looking old man, eyes scrunched up tight with fear behind his glasses, lower lip quivering as if he were about to start crying.

Fitz looked at Anji helplessly, then down at the bread knife as if he couldn't quite bring himself to take it away, to accept it was true. That they had the wrong man, just some poor sleepless soul who'd come here to pray, to be alone and feel closer to his god.

Anji was about to tell him how sorry they were when the shot rang out.

The old man's head smacked back against Fitz's chest in a spray of blood as the awful echoes piled up in the room, dizzying Anji's head. Fitz shouted and jumped back in alarm as the old man's body slumped down in the pew.

Anji stared in horror.

*How sorry we are.*

'There!' Dark yelled.

Up on the balcony, clutching a grey case in one hand and a revolver in the other, was Hox.

'Down!' shouted Anji as Hox fired again. Splinters of wood from a shattering pew brushed her cheek as she fell to the hard, stone floor. She managed to hold on to her candle, but the knife slipped from her grasp and skittered noisily across the floor.

'Found him,' said Fitz weakly.

'He's found us,' Dark hissed.

Anji nodded, staring frightened and wide-eyed at Fitz as Hox fired again. 'And now he's going to pick us off, one by one, or blow this whole place sky-high.'

# Chapter Thirty-four

'Doctor,' spat Cauchemar, lying in a heap half-buried by his cloak.

'You sound cross.' He waggled his foot. 'But I know you got a big kick out of seeing me here.'

'You dared to follow me?'

'Actually, no, it's just a coincidence. Isn't this a pretty spot?' The Doctor lifted Murph back into his chair and turned to Etty, his voice low. 'Sorry I couldn't get here sooner. Myra's right, you must run. Run, and take the baby with you.'

'Murph, too!' Murph was clutching on to her leg, hiding his face in her long skirt.

'Yes, and Murph, too.' The Doctor grinned, and saw Myra scurrying towards them. 'Well done, Murph, Myra. Now quickly, off you go.'

Etty stooped to pick up the crying baby.

And suddenly the Doctor was shouting. 'Cauchemar, no!'

Cauchemar had got back to his feet, and the gun was back in his hand, pointing at Etty. 'Stop, or I'll kill her.'

The Doctor snatched the baby up from the ground and waved it threateningly over the edge of the precipice. 'Kill her,' he said, 'and I'll kill any hope you had of finding your perfect death.'

Cauchemar's voice was weary. 'You would not kill an innocent in cold blood. You *could* not. Bring the baby to me.'

'No.'

'Bring the infant!' Cauchemar roared, waving his gun arm dangerously in Etty's direction. 'I'll kill the cripple too, and that little freak beside him.'

Myra cowered behind Murph's wheelchair.

'Oh, yes, I know,' the Doctor said angrily. 'You're going to kill everyone, everywhere. The culmination of your life's work. What a proud, proud moment for science!'

'Bring the infant to me, then.' His whole body seemed suddenly to sag. 'Let me end this.'

'My ship is nearby, I have equipment, I'm sure I can –'

Cauchemar fired the gun. Etty shouted in anger as the bullet sparked off the wheel of Murph's wheelchair, sending Myra scuttling away and Murph into a frightened fit.

'To me, Doctor!' called Cauchemar. 'Or with the next shot I kill him.'

The Doctor took another step closer, peering worriedly at the ground in front of him and sidestepping some invisible obstacle. Etty saw he was trying to move round in front of the mooncalves to block Cauchemar's aim. But, with each step the Doctor took, Etty felt the strange tickling in her head grow stronger.

She turned woozily to Myra.

'Take Murph,' she said. 'Quickly. Before the man can hurt you again.'

'But, Etty -'

'*Go*, Myra!'

Etty felt disassociated, as if she were viewing the scene - Myra straining wearily to shift Murph's chair, the Doctor still advancing on Cauchemar - from a distance. An energy was crackling through her, sending random memories sparking along her spine, long-forgotten moments, building up like echoes, vibrations, shuddering through her. She followed after him, strangely drawn to the water.

*Sunlight playing in the park with Treena cat dying kissing a boy an envelope falling on a mat*

'Doctor,' she cried out, clutching her head.

'She's feeling it,' Cauchemar breathed, backing away, still covering Etty with the gun. 'The infant is more powerful than I dared hope... The Creator is feeling its force even here, at the periphery of His power... That's right, Jasmine, come to me, closer, *closer*...'

*Told off in school on a stage singing there's a present on the floor big box going into the earth for ever*

Etty felt she was sinking into the ground, that her mind was being teased out of her body like a mussel from a shell. And yet she was still walking. There were other people living in this body with her, moving her now.

The Doctor had stopped still. But Etty found herself approaching closer just as Jasmine was.

'My time approaches, Doctor,' howled Cauchemar, splashing

further along the ridge out to sea, firing the gun again.

*Don't tell a soul in bed hear you breathe dancing for mother one more time will you always love me*

Etty saw the bullet splash into the water at the Doctor's feet, and her eyes went down with it, they were swirling in the water, spiralling and sinking there, two pale-blue eggs washed over the rocks, and inside them... inside...

Anji placed her candle to one side and wriggled forward on her front under the pew until she could reach the old man's dead body. She gingerly tugged off each of his shoes. She wanted to try something.

Fitz stared at her as if she was mad. Anji threw the shoe as far away from them as she could. It clattered noisily against old wood.

Hox fired his gun again, in the direction of the sound. Fitz grinned, gave her a thumbs-up.

Yeah, brilliant. What should she do for an encore?

*Encore!*

The idea was stupid but it was the only one she had. She tossed the shoe across to Fitz, then turned to Dark, who was lying flat on his front in the pew behind, and indicated he should take his own shoes off, and throw them in the same way. He nodded, puzzled.

Then Anji wriggled forward like an uncertain snake, sliding under the rows of pews. She moved slowly, trying to keep as quiet as possible in the awful hushed silence of the hall, until the racket of another crash-landing shoe and its corresponding gunshot afforded her enough cover to shift faster along the flagstones.

'I see you.'

Anji froze as Hox's imperious tones echoed around her. Then her eyes narrowed. That was an old one, surely, even in outer space. She wriggled forward a few feet more, her breath held, but the only repercussions were from another shoe clattering against the stone floor, far behind her.

The big curtain loomed up wide and crimson. That and the anticipatory hush in the hall put Anji in mind of her last trip to the theatre with Dave, back in London. She wished she had longer to wait before this particular show got started.

The balcony was directly above her now. She looked back to see if she could catch any sign of Fitz or Nathaniel but there was no movement at all in the hall.

'It doesn't matter, you know,' Hox shouted. 'You can't stop us. *No one* can stop us.'

He was probably right, thought Anji as she padded across to where the curtains joined in the middle. But right now, there was no harm in trying.

First she peeked quickly behind the curtains: it was an auditorium of some kind, as big again as the prayer hall. The curtain must be here to separate prayer from performance. Probably choirs and stuff. A fun night out.

Testing the heavy fabric to see if it could take her weight, Anji took huge bunches of it in her fist and began to scale the curtain, her feet clamped together round its velvet edge. The higher she got the more dangerously it swung, but she refused to look down. She kept climbing, ignoring the burning cramps in her arms, the voice in her head telling her she was out of her head and that any moment now she was going to fall on it. Well, at least it wasn't a mountainside this time.

The balcony got closer. Yanking herself up ever further till she was alongside it, Anji could see it was lined not with royal boxes but with pulpit-like affairs. It figured: as a symbolic gesture, setting off the bomb in the very spot where the Diviners proclaimed who was going to the Creator and who was not had a certain sick flair to it.

She was high enough now to see a mechanism of some kind built into the wall above her. They must open up the curtains from here when it was show time...

She held her breath.

It *was* show-time.

Hox was hunched behind the balcony rail less than twenty feet away, the gun still smoking in his hand. Behind him was a grey case that could only contain the explosives, with a length of wire leading to the detonator, and the communicator he'd been carrying at the hospital.

Anji swung her legs over the rail, landing crafty as a cat on the plush carpet lining the balcony. He hadn't heard her. If only she still had the knife... She looked around for a weapon, found a piece of splintered wood, a part of the balustrade that had come away. She could come up behind him, bring the club down...

She'd get only one chance.

With a quick check over the balcony rail that there were no more bodies visible in the prayer hall, that Fitz and Dark were still hidden from sight, Anji turned to Hox, still crouched with his back to her.

Stealthily, she advanced, letting her mind linger on all he'd done to hurt Etty, to hurt Fitz, all of them, summoning up the hate inside her to give her the strength to do this. To save the City... To bring this club smashing down on his sick, fuzzy-haired skull...

There was a sudden, insistent beeping from Hox's communicator.

Anji's eyes widened with fear. She rushed to close the gap.

Too late. Hox turned, saw her.

She froze.

He pointed the gun at her chest.

The Doctor turned in alarm as Etty collapsed on her back into the rushing weir water.

'So, who are you going to threaten now, Cauchemar?' he enquired acidly. 'Why not save yourself some time - point the gun at yourself?'

Cauchemar splashed back towards the mainland, to Etty. He stroked her pale wet face, cradled her head in his arm while keeping the Doctor covered with the gun. 'I can feel it, Jasmine,' he said hoarsely, jubilant. 'Is your soul so crass, Doctor, you feel nothing? Nothing at all?'

'You must *stop*, Cauchemar,' the Doctor implored him, stamping a foot in the water. 'Stop before it's too late.'

A stone shifted beneath his foot and he slipped, landed painfully on his back, feeling the cold water soak through his clothes, freezing his skin, stinging the cuts on his face. As Cauchemar laughed mockingly, the Doctor held the struggling baby above him, safe from harm.

It stared around, sightless and wretched. Gently, the Doctor laid it on its back in the shallow water.

Cauchemar had pulled out his communicator. 'Hox,' he said, the name barely comprehensible through his giggles. 'Hox, do you hear me? Answer me, man.'

The Doctor's fingers closed around a rock in the water, and he threw it as hard as he could at Cauchemar's head.

The projectile struck the chuckling maniac in one blackened eye. He gasped and dropped the communicator in the water - then, with an angry shout, scrabbled about for it, unseeing, seemingly oblivious to all else.

Seemingly.

As the Doctor threw himself towards Cauchemar, the gun came up blindly from the madman's side.

As Cauchemar pulled the trigger, the Doctor desperately twisted aside. He heard the blast as he splashed down beside Etty, shut his own eyes.

Behind him, the screams of the baby stopped.

Cauchemar froze for a moment, his lip curling. Then a terrible cry wrenched itself out of him.

The Doctor grabbed hold of Cauchemar's wrist, trying to wrestle the weapon away.

'You fool!' Cauchemar wailed, struggling. 'You interfering fool. What do you care about the fate of these miserable crossbreeds?'

'They're people,' gasped the Doctor, unable to make Cauchemar let go of the gun. 'Ordinary people, whatever their origin. Maybe all this started out as some experiment, or punishment, whatever - I don't know. Maybe the forces that created all this are still at large, watching, or maybe they lost interest and are long gone. But these people were given the tools to build a colony, to build lives and traditions for themselves, and they've done so. This is *their* world now.'

'The Holiest dictate what their lives will be.' Cauchemar tried to strike the Doctor with his free hand, but the blow was parried.

'No, I've spoken with them myself, and that's not true.' The Doctor gritted his teeth, pinning Cauchemar's arms down in the water. 'These people aren't puppets - they think for themselves, they act for themselves, their lives are real, as random and rapid and rare as anyone else's. Maybe God is a given here, but it makes no difference, don't you see? The people still need faith. They have to believe His heaven is worth getting to. Just as you do. But it's not yours to take, Cauchemar.'

'Why not?' Cauchemar hissed. 'I brought this world into being. Is it right that my specimens, my *cultures*, should go on eternally in paradise while I perish in pain?'

Cauchemar was wriggling one arm free. The Doctor, his fingers numbed by the icy water, fought to keep his grip. 'You have no dominion over these people.'

'I don't need to - I have mastery over their Creator. I shaped this world's life, and I will share in its death.'

The Doctor gritted his teeth. 'But you can't!'

'Ever the optimist, Doctor.'

'Not at all.' The Doctor dug his thumb into Cauchemar's wrist, trying to make him release the gun. 'Looking at your glass, Cauchemar, I'd say it was a good deal less than half-empty.'

Then his thumb broke through Cauchemar's thin skin as though it was rotten fruit, and slid stickily inside.

Cauchemar screamed in pain, pulled his other fist free and smashed it against the Doctor's cut face.

The Doctor fell back with a shout, dazed for a moment. Suddenly Cauchemar was back on his feet, kicking him in the chest. The Doctor rolled backwards, took another kick to his stomach, tried to crawl away. Cauchemar stamped down on the back of his head, ground his stinging face into the silty rock beneath the swirling waters.

'Never mind the girl, what about us?'

Hox spun around at Fitz's shout. Fitz had suddenly appeared in the middle of the gangway.

Hox aimed and fired in a single second, but Nathaniel hurled himself at Fitz a fraction faster.

Anji's heart leapt as Fitz was brought down by Dark's rugby tackle and the bullet missed its mark. As Hox whipped the gun back round to cover her she kicked his wrist. The gun went flying from his grip, landing in an explosion of echoes far below.

'Noisier than a shoe,' Anji commented.

Then she brought her makeshift club down hard on Hox's head.

He collapsed heavily back against the balustrade, and his eyes closed. Anji kept watching, but they didn't open again.

The gun's noisy landing was like a starter's pistol beginning Fitz's and Nathaniel's race to join her up on the balcony, each of them dashing up one of the ornate stairways on either side, rushing to meet her in the middle.

'I don't believe it!' Fitz shouted joyfully.

'Neither do I,' Anji replied, looking at him in bafflement. '"Noisier than a shoe"?'

She let the piece of wood slip from her hands.

Fitz hugged her, and she gripped him back, trembling. 'Why waste a good quip on a bad shot?' he murmured in her ear.

'Now *that* one... that was quite good,' Anji laughed, accepting a joyful hug from Nathaniel, too.

'Right,' Dark said, stooping for the little black device, still beeping. 'Now we just get Hox's communicator -'

'*Look out!*'

Anji turned at Fitz's shout to find Hox on all fours scurrying behind her, face twisted in hate, reaching for the detonator device.

Dark swept the bomb out of his reach.

Fitz shoved Anji aside and kicked Hox in the ribs with all his strength, yelling out with pain as he did so.

The balustrade cracked and splintered.

Then it gave way.

Hox stared wildly in terror, arms windmilling for a moment as he tried to keep his balance. But the section of balcony was falling now, and he followed it, screaming his master's name all the way down to the flagstones below.

Fitz held himself against Anji and buried his head against her shoulder, not wanting to see.

'Is he dead now?' he murmured.

Anji found herself compelled to look, that feeling you get in nightmares when you're powerless to resist making the really stupid move.

Hox was spread-eagled on the flagstones, blood pooling around his brown-suited body, sightless eyes looking up at them in disbelief. Anji half-expected him to get back up, shake his fist and chase up the stairs after them. But he stayed there, quite still, as the echoes of his fall gradually died away.

Anji let a tear roll down her cheek, but she wasn't sure exactly who it was for.

Then the sound of sirens came quietly through the thin dawn air.

'Timing,' muttered Fitz, still with his head nuzzling Anji's neck.

'Look,' said Dark.

Anji nudged Fitz, pulled away from him, pointed.

Three cowled figures had appeared at the back of the prayer hall, gliding across the flagstones towards Hox's body. One of the figures stopped, then looked up at them.

Dark turned away.

'Give me the communicator,' said Anji.

The Doctor heard the communicator squawking speech beneath the water, and Cauchemar must have too, for the pressure on his head fell away.

He pushed himself back out of the water, choking and spluttering. Cauchemar had located the communicator, was shaking it with his bloodied hand.

'Cauchemar?' the voice crackled. 'Are you there, Cauchemar?'

'Who is this?' hissed Cauchemar.

'That's Anji,' the Doctor said triumphantly, wiping the wet curls of his fringe from his eyes.

'Hox is dead, Cauchemar.' Anji's voice sounded harsh and high over the communicator's speaker. 'There's no one to give the final signal. Your bombs aren't going off today.'

'It's over,' the Doctor said, getting warily to his feet.

'I don't believe you,' Cauchemar shouted at the communicator, holding it suspiciously at arm's length now, as if it might bite him.

'Would Hox give away your only means of reaching him?' the Doctor pointed out. 'You've blown it, Cauchemar. Or rather you haven't. Now it stops, right here.'

Cauchemar hurled the communicator away and fell to his knees in the water, curling up as if cowering from the world around him. He tried to shake Etty awake. 'Jasmine... She can still come with me... I've weakened the Creator so badly already, her presence alone might...' He stroked her hair with his gory hand. 'It might trigger -'

'No, Cauchemar,' stormed the Doctor, splashing over to Etty and knocking his hands away from her. 'You're not hurting anyone else, ever again.'

Cauchemar sat slumped, beaten, broken in the water as the Doctor carried Etty to the higher ground. He stared at the twisted corpse of the infant, still leaking its blood into the fast current of the water. Its tiny pink body was nudged and buffeted by the vortices, picked at by a cloud of tiny flies, pushed closer and closer to the edge of the ridge.

Then, slowly, so slowly, the infant's corpse slithered over the precipice, and was lost.

When Cauchemar looked up again the Doctor was extending his hand to him. Offering him help, even after all this.

Cauchemar took the proffered hand, used it to help haul himself up.

And then grabbed for the Doctor's throat with the last of his strength, his limbs like heavy wax, cold and unresponsive. The Doctor struggled, fell back under the assault, caught unawares. Cauchemar pressed fingers and thumbs hard against the Doctor's neck. Writhing and bucking to be free, the Doctor was edging closer and closer to the watery precipice. Soon his head was hanging back over the edge of the ridge. Cauchemar looked down, the water whirling and splashing up at him, dizzying him. The sun broke through scattered clouds, bright in his eyes, but his skin still felt so cold.

The Doctor gasped, choked, and Cauchemar pressed down harder. Harder.

Then he was staring in disbelief as his thumbs snapped, as the water lapped at them and corroded them like acid, took his fingertips away while washing the Doctor's bruised skin clean.

'Enzymes... catalysts...' the Doctor gasped. 'All in the waters here.' He shook his head, dark curls spraying water. 'Don't you see? These waters are part of the Creator. They may even be the medium it stores itself in, who knows?'

As Cauchemar looked down he saw a thick black slime sloshing into the water from his legs. He felt for his ankles and brought away a big scoop of flesh in each melting hand.

'Whatever... your body's too weak... too weak to resist.'

'No,' Cauchemar hissed, staring out wildly at the great rocky spires of the water mountains. 'You can't see me,' he shouted to the Creator, 'you can't *see* me!'

His hand broke off at the wrist where the Doctor had punctured the skin, and flopped into the water. The sun's yellow eye seemed fixed on him, melting him away.

The Doctor was looking at him too, sorrow in his grey eyes.

'I could've helped you.'

'Help me now.' Cauchemar collapsed on top of the Doctor, gripped him round the neck. 'Show me where to go, when I die.'

Cauchemar launched himself forward, dragging the Doctor off the edge of the precipice with him. Intertwined, they fell into the long burning drop.

When Etty opened her eyes, the sun was high in the sky and the waters calm. She was quite serene; she knew that something must have happened to her. Something she couldn't quite grasp. The images and memories and guilt that had screamed to her in the waters were just murmurs and whispers deep behind her eyes, sinking into blackness now. As they died away she became aware of the usual niggling aches and sensations that told her she was alive.

Alive.

It felt so good, so sweet, she wanted to laugh out loud.

But then Myra and Murph came into view, staring at her in consternation.

Etty took a deep breath. 'What happened?'

They both shook their heads.

She sniffed. 'Well, where's the Doctor? Where's... where's the other man?'

Myra looked at Murph and they both shrugged.

'Gone, Etty,' Myra said. 'Left us and gone away.'

# Chapter Thirty-five

'You think he's dead, don't you?' asked Vettul.

Fitz didn't answer, just let her get on with rubbing the herbal ointment on to his wounded leg in the cool of Etty's kitchen. His long-suffering limb was actually a lot better now, but the sticky cream and her cool fingers felt good against his skin so he wasn't about to argue. Besides, Etty would have him on mucking-out duty in seconds if she thought he could get about all right.

'Don't you?'

'It's been three days,' was all he could say.

'I know.' Vettul rubbed her hands on a towel. 'Finished.'

'Oh?' Fitz was disappointed.

'So...' She looked at him, shaking her long hair out of her face. 'If the Doctor is dead, will you be staying here?'

Fitz looked down awkwardly. 'I'm not really thinking that far ahead, Vettul.'

'It's been three days,' Vettul repeated.

'Yeah, well... Don't give up on him yet. The Doctor always likes to make a grand entrance.'

Vettul crossed to the sink and washed her hands. 'I ask if you will stay and you believe he's alive again. Why?'

Fitz took a long while to answer. 'I guess you could call it faith.'

Anji and Etty came back from their usual morning search with nothing to report.

After a quiet lunch, Fitz asked Anji to go on a walk with him to the TARDIS and back, to exercise his mending leg. Etty, Braga and the mooncalves were busy catching up on their farming duties. There was a hell of a lot to do.

They walked past the grave they'd dug for Two, on the edge of the farmland.

'Wonder who he was before they got to him,' said Fitz.

'He had nice eyes,' Anji said distantly.

'Can't say I noticed.'

'I suppose the Holiest will account for him in the end. Just as they accounted for all the others.'

'Hey, does that make that bunch like the mooncalves now?'

She nodded. 'Except the Holiest seem more interested in caring than killing now.'

'Well, the Doctor did say –' Fitz broke off, bit his lip. 'Well, they panicked, didn't they, back when they killed whatsherface...?'

'Annetta.'

'Sure... It doesn't seem fair, does it? That the likes of Vettul helped save the Creator when he doesn't even know they exist.'

'D'you think that's why God or whatever doesn't always answer prayers on Earth?' Anji supposed. 'That we were once a closed-off population, and then blokes from outer space like the Doctor came along and started turning the place upside down, breaking all the connections?'

Fitz considered. 'No, Anji, I think you're talking bollocks.'

He was relieved when she laughed, and they carried on walking.

The police box was dark against the pale blue of sky. Fitz felt a pang of homesickness when he saw it standing there alone, a sentinel on the cliff edge.

'Bet you she's looking out for him, too,' he muttered.

Anji gave him a look, and he shut up. They both trudged on in a moody silence until they reached the TARDIS.

'Makes you think about the future, doesn't it?' Fitz said.

Anji was looking out to sea, her black hair gently ruffled by the wind and sea spray. 'Do you think this population really will wind down to no one at all in the end?'

'Well, there'll always be the mooncalves, won't there? Not part of the Creator's Design, or whatever. The meek *shall* inherit the earth, just as the man said.'

'You think the Holiest will let those poor people breed? Even assuming they could... They'd be endangering the whole thing. The whole *point* of this place.'

Fitz felt sad to hear her sound so pessimistic. 'Yeah, well... I actually was talking about *our* future. Together, here.'

'Don't try it on, Fitz,' Anji said warningly.

'No, I mean, no Doctor, no TARDIS... We're staying put.'

'Vettul will be pleased.'

'Don't start.'

He joined her, staring out into the clear blue sky.

'Can you imagine what God would say to you and me if we had a switch like this lot?' Fitz murmured. 'Trying to make sense of all we've been through?'

Anji smiled faintly, closing her eyes, warming her skin.

'Although I wish I'd known... It would've been nice to know how my mum figured in the big scheme of things. I mean all of her life, not just the way it ended... messily.' He sighed. 'She always was a God-botherer. I'd like to think she ended up in some kind of eternal paradise or whatever.'

'I've caught myself thinking the same thing about Dave a few times,' Anji admitted. 'And he wasn't religious at all. I found myself wishing I believed in reincarnation, in the thought that he could come back to live again somehow.'

'And how do you feel after finding out about this place?'

'It makes no difference. Even if Dave did get reborn or whatever, he wouldn't know me, I wouldn't know him. He wouldn't know he was carrying on. We couldn't be together.'

'Yeah,' said Fitz, a little bluntly, 'but the reincarnation deal's meant to be for his benefit, isn't it?'

Anji shrugged. 'All we can be sure about is what's down here. The stuff we see. I don't reckon it really matters what your God thinks, or mine, or what the rest of the world thinks about the people I love. It doesn't make it hurt any less when they're taken away from us, and we're left behind.'

Fitz sighed, not sure what to say, feeling a little out of his depth. 'This is the sort of conversation best had over a large glass of red wine and some herbal cigarettes.'

They stood together in silence for some time, the roar of the sea like deep snoring breaths in and out, comforting them with its company in the afternoon sunlight.

Fitz idly followed the flight of a gull from its nest on the cliff side down to the sea, down to –

Down to what was that?

'There!' Fitz cried, pointing to the dark shape floating in on the shallow tide to the ragged strip of beach.

'Driftwood?' Anji suggested, trying to keep her voice calm and level, but gripping his arm in excitement.

'Carved into the shape of a Doctor,' Fitz yelled. 'It's him!'

'He'll have drowned,' said Anji anxiously, hand over her mouth.

'He switches himself off,' said Fitz. She looked at him oddly. 'He does, I'm not joking! Like when you tried to give him CPR on New Jupiter? He was just coming out of it.' He started peering for a path down to the beach to see. 'Well, come on, we've got to go and see!'

'Mind yourself,' Anji moaned as Fitz leapt awkwardly down on to a narrow ledge.

'I was a mountain goat in a former life.'

'You'll slip and fall.'

'No, I won't.'

'You *will,* you idiot.' Anji shook her head wearily, but he saw she was trying not to smile. 'You showing off your mountaineering skills is how this whole thing started...'

The Doctor's eyes opened, and Fitz and Anji were crouched over him.

'I'm cold,' he said.

'You're alive!' Fitz yelled, and he and Anji hugged each other.

'Welcome back to the real world,' said Anji. 'It's still here, thanks to you.'

'Thanks to you,' the Doctor insisted, flexing his fingers and wriggling his toes.

'And to Nathaniel.'

'He's well?'

'Well...' Fitz shrugged. 'I guess so. He's still clearing things up, in the City.'

'What happened to Cauchemar?' Anji asked. 'Etty didn't see.'

'She's all right?'

'Right back to her old self.'

'Her old self?' The Doctor let his head fall back to the wet sand. 'That's a relief.' The sun was still shining down, just as when he'd last seen the sky.

'So - Cauchemar?'

'I don't know where he is,' the Doctor confessed. 'But he's gone.'

'Dead?' Fitz looked anxiously at him.

'Yes,' said the Doctor firmly, and Fitz relaxed. 'Yes, he's dead all right.'

He reached out his hands. Fitz took one, and Anji took the other.

'The real world, you say?'

His friends grinned at him.

The Doctor smiled back. 'I can show you so many more.'

Vettul watched as the three of them came back over the cliff edge, and as they danced happily around the big blue box Fitz had told her they'd all arrived in. Etty had told her such a thing wasn't possible, but Vettul knew for sure that Etty wasn't always right about everything.

She'd stayed hidden for hours, waiting for them, tension and fear all balled up in her stomach. Now she watched Fitz playing around, his gangly form silhouetted against the setting sun.

She nodded to herself when he went inside the box after Anji and the Doctor. She felt suddenly calm to know for sure he was going after these last uncertain days.

She closed her eyes and imagined him kissing her goodbye.

A strange noise started up, a fierce rushing and whistling as if the air was grating against something invisible. The box started to fade away. She thought she might catch one last glimpse of Fitz standing inside it. But as the box vanished there was nothing to see save for blue sky.

Vettul stayed sitting in the long grass for a while, then headed back to the farmhouse, cradling her hands over her belly as she walked.

# Epilogue

Lanna opened the door and smiled to see him. 'I knew it was you.'

Dark looked at her with mild scepticism. 'Even after all these years?'

'Even after all these years.' She looked at him almost shyly. 'Won't you come in, Holy –'

She bit her lip, but he smiled, shook his head to say it didn't matter.

'If I'm not intruding.'

She shook her head, and showed him in, fixed them both a drink. She saw him take in the furnishings, the empty mug on the table, the silence in the house.

'You're still alone? Not married?'

She clicked her tongue in mock disapproval. 'I was married when you knew me before, Nathaniel.'

He didn't know where to look, embarrassed, and she laughed. 'But anyway, yes, I am alone now.'

'And you're happy?'

'It suits.'

She smiled to see he could still be so flustered. When they looked into each other's eyes, it was just as it had been between them in those last, mad days. He'd really not changed that much at all since leaving the City. She pictured him then, when he'd called round that one final time to explain what had happened, how he'd left his Diviner's calling for good, and why he was going away. He was a bit chunkier now, thicker-set with greying hair, and his skin was more weathered, tanned from long hours out in the sun. The Holy Man had become the Family Man, farming the fringes of the godlands with his precious Etty. But Lanna had changed too of course: lost some weight, dyed her hair. She wondered what Dark thought of her now he was back. She'd always known he'd be back, one day.

'Has it really been so long since the Doctor came?' Dark marvelled. 'I suppose it must be.'

'And you and Etty…?'

'Are friends, still. Good friends. Braga's moved out now, has a place of his own on the southern coastlands. But the farmhouse is still very busy.'

'We have a lot to catch up on,' Lanna suggested.

'We do.'

She decided to be the one to break the silence that followed. 'Why did you come back here?'

'It seemed right to tell you the end of the story, the way I told you the first of it.'

She looked at him, an intrigued smile on her face. 'The end?'

'It's my time to go,' Dark said.

Lanna's smile fell. 'You're dying?'

He nodded. 'Something wrong with my heart.'

'And you've felt the Creator's blessing?'

He grinned, suffused with joy. 'I have.'

'But I thought… You turned your back on him. On… all that.'

He nodded. 'I did.'

She found herself smiling just because he was, although she felt her stomach twist to think that soon he would be…

'The meaning?' she asked him shakily.

He paused, savouring the telling of it to her. 'To bring the people from beyond closer, so that all may be known to the Creator. Vettul. Murph. Myra. All of them, even those whose minds Cauchemar took from them.'

She stared at him. 'But how can that be?'

His grin grew still wider. 'There's no more blind spot.'

'Vettul, though, and the others, you said they didn't have the…' She racked her brain for the right word.

'No godswitch.'

'Godswitch, that's right.'

'I know.'

'So how…?'

'I *don't* know.' Then he looked at her, probing her eyes with his own. 'I can only call it a leap of faith.'

'But that's ridiculous,' Lanna laughed. 'How can a god have a leap of faith?'

'If the Doctor were here, can you imagine what he'd say?' said Dark fondly. '"Poor Nathaniel. Even when you're given absolutes, you can't believe in them." But I do, Lanna. I *do*.' He took her hand in his own. 'I believe, all over again.'

They sat together, holding each other, talking until the sun slipped away from the darkening sky.

# About the Author

**Stephen Cole's** special subject is biting off more than he can chew and then grumbling a lot. Recent projects include writing tie-in books for *Walking With Dinosaurs*, *Guinness World Records* and the *Charlie's Angels* movie, adapting children's books for Usborne publishing, and co-writing another *Doctor Who* book published this month.

## BBC DOCTOR WHO BOOKS FEATURING THE EIGHTH DOCTOR

DOCTOR WHO: THE NOVEL OF THE FILM by Gary Russell
ISBN 0 563 38000 4
THE EIGHT DOCTORS by Terrance Dicks ISBN 0 563 40563 5
VAMPIRE SCIENCE by Jonathan Blum and Kate Orman
ISBN 0 563 40566 X
THE BODYSNATCHERS by Mark Morris ISBN 0 563 40568 6
GENOCIDE by Paul Leonard ISBN 0 563 40572 4
WAR OF THE DALEKS by John Peel ISBN 0 563 40573 2
ALIEN BODIES by Lawrence Miles ISBN 0 563 40577 5
KURSAAL by Peter Anghelides ISBN 0 563 40578 3
OPTION LOCK by Justin Richards ISBN 0 563 40583 X
LONGEST DAY by Michael Collier ISBN 0 563 40581 3
LEGACY OF THE DALEKS by John Peel ISBN 0 563 40574 0
DREAMSTONE MOON by Paul Leonard ISBN 0 563 40585 6
SEEING I by Jonathan Blum and Kate Orman ISBN 0 563 40586 4
PLACEBO EFFECT by Gary Russell ISBN 0 563 40587 2
VANDERDEKEN'S CHILDREN by Christopher Bulis
ISBN 0 563 40590 2
THE SCARLET EMPRESS by Paul Magrs ISBN 0 563 40595 3
THE JANUS CONJUNCTION by Trevor Baxendale
ISBN 0 563 40599 6
BELTEMPEST by Jim Mortimore ISBN 0 563 40593 7
THE FACE EATER by Simon Messingham ISBN 0 563 55569 6
THE TAINT by Michael Collier ISBN 0 563 55568 8
DEMONTAGE by Justin Richards ISBN 0 563 55572 6
REVOLUTION MAN by Paul Leonard ISBN 0 563 55570 X
DOMINION by Nick Walters ISBN 0 563 55574 2
UNNATURAL HISTORY by Jonathan Blum and Kate Orman
ISBN 0 563 55576 9
AUTUMN MIST by David A. McIntee ISBN 0 563 55583 1
INTERFERENCE: BOOK ONE by Lawrence Miles ISBN 0 563 55580 7
INTERFERENCE: BOOK TWO by Lawrence Miles
ISBN 0 563 55582 3
THE BLUE ANGEL by Paul Magrs and Jeremy Hoad
ISBN 0 563 55581 5
THE TAKING OF PLANET 5 by Simon Bucher-Jones and
Mark Clapham ISBN 0 563 55585 8

FRONTIER WORLDS by Peter Anghelides ISBN 0 563 55589 0
PARALLEL 59 by Natalie Dallaire and Stephen Cole
ISBN 0 563 555904
THE SHADOWS OF AVALON by Paul Cornell ISBN 0 563 555882
THE FALL OF YQUATINE by Nick Walters ISBN 0 563 55594 7
COLDHEART by Trevor Baxendale ISBN 0 563 55595 5
THE SPACE AGE by Steve Lyons ISBN 0 563 53800 7
THE BANQUO LEGACY by Andy Lane and Justin Richards
ISBN 0 563 53808 2
THE ANCESTOR CELL by Peter Anghelides and Stephen Cole
ISBN 0 563 53809 0
THE BURNING by Justin Richards ISBN 0 563 53812 0
CASUALTIES OF WAR by Steve Emmerson ISBN 0 563 53805 8
THE TURING TEST by Paul Leonard ISBN 0 563 53806 6
ENDGAME by Terrance Dicks ISBN 0 563 53802 3
FATHER TIME by Lance Parkin ISBN 0 563 53810 4
ESCAPE VELOCITY by Colin Brake ISBN 0 563 53825 2
EARTHWORLD by Jacqueline Rayner ISBN 0 563 53827 9

COMING SOON:

EATER OF WASPS by Trevor Baxendale ISBN 0 563 53832 5 (May '01)
THE YEAR OF INTELLIGENT TIGERS by Kate Orman
ISBN 0 563 53831 7 (June '01)
THE SLOW EMPIRE by Dave Stone ISBN 0 563 53835 X (July '01)
DARK PROGENY by Steve Emmerson ISBN 0 563 53837 6 (Aug '01)
THE CITY OF THE DEAD by Lloyd Rose ISBN 0 563 53839 2 (Sept '01)
GRIMM REALITY by Simon Bucher-Jones and Kelly Hale
ISBN 0 563 53841 4 (Oct '01)